DATE DUE

OC 23 '00			
2 3 08			

DEMCO 38-296

BURMA

Burma

The Challenge of Change in a Divided Society

Edited by

Peter Carey
Laithwaite Fellow and Tutor in Modern History
Trinity College
Oxford

Foreword by Aung San Suu Kyi

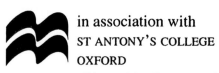

in association with
ST ANTONY'S COLLEGE
OXFORD

21 6XS and London
it the world

Series
General Editor: Alex Pravda
Series ISBN 0–333–71109–2 outside the United States

A catalogue record for this book is available from the British Library.

ISBN 0–333–59572–6

First published in the United States of America 1997 by

ST. MARTIN'S PRESS, INC.,
Scholarly and Reference Division,
175 Fifth Avenue, New York, N.Y. 10010

ISBN 0–312–17422–5

Library of Congress Cataloging-in-Publication Data
Burma : the challenge of change in a divided society / edited by Peter
Carey ; foreword by Aung San Suu Kyi.
p.   cm. — (St. Antony's series)
Includes bibliographical references (p.   ) and index.
ISBN 0–312–17422–5 (cloth)
1. Burma—Politics and government—1948–   2. Burma—Foreign
relations—1948–   3. Burma—Ethnic relations.   4. Burma—Economic
conditions—1948–   I. Carey, P. B. R.   II. Series.
DS530.4.B867 1997
320.9591—dc21   96–46502
                                                        CIP

This book is printed on paper suitable for recycling and made from fully managed and sustained forest sources.

10 9   8   7   6   5   4   3
06 05 04 03 02 01 99 98

Printed and bound in Great Britain by Antony Rowe Ltd, Chippenham, Wiltshire

'The struggle against power is the struggle of memory against forgetting'. –

Milan Kundera

———————

This book is dedicated to all those in Burma for whom the power of memory has proven stronger than the power of forgetting.

Contents

PART III   VIEWS FROM THE PERIPHERY

PART IV   THE CHALLENGES OF DEVELOPMENT

Foreword
Aung San Suu Kyi

Burma is now at a crucial turning-point in her development as a nation. At the beginning of 1948, the country regained the independence which was lost to the British in the nineteenth century. The immediate period prior to independence saw four traumatic years (1942–5) during which Burma was fought over by contending armies. These were followed by another two years of tough negotiations between Burmese nationalist leaders and the British government. Then, on the eve of independence, my father and six other members of the Governor's Executive Council, men who had been chosen by the people to lead the sovereign independent Union of Burma, were assassinated. It was not an auspicious start for the new nation.

During its forty-eight years of independence Burma has never known genuine peace. The government, largely dominated by ethnic Burmans, has faced armed insurgencies from all the other major ethnic groups in these intervening years. The State Law and Order Restoration Council, which assumed power in 1988, has succeeded in negotiating ceasefire agreements with all but one of these ethnic rebel forces. But such ceasefires have yet to be transformed into lasting peace based on mutually acceptable settlement of political differences. To this day the country remains deeply unstable and volatile.

The quarter century of the Burmese Way to Socialism (1962–88) stifled individual enterprise and freedom of thought, turning the country into one of the world's Least Developed Nations. In the late 1950s, Burma and the Philippines were often singled out as the two most promising countries of Southeast Asia: economically and politically they seemed to have the greatest potential. In both countries, however, dictatorial governments killed that early promise, putting a blight on future prosperity. Since it came to power, the SLORC has tried to reverse this process of decay by adopting a 'free market economy'. But it has failed to underpin its economic reforms with a suitable political framework without which there can be no meaningful popular participation in national development.

While Burma is still enmeshed in its political and economic problems, the world around it is moving ahead at breakneck speed. If we miss this historic opportunity to become an integral part of the dawning Asia–Pacific century, we will be condemned to remain on the margins of the developed world indefinitely. Now is the time for the country to bind itself to the region and to its global destiny.

We are today embarked on a struggle as critical as that which led to our independence nearly half a century ago, a struggle which has still to realise the aspirations of those who dedicated their lives to the cause of freedom and justice. The ideal of those leaders was of a Burma which could hold its head high in the community of nations, strong in the sense of its own destiny and the power of a fulfilled people. Today, almost fifty years on, we have a unique opportunity to make that ideal a reality by adopting a vision that will transcend immediate difficulties.

The greatest obstacle in the way of peace and progress for Burma is a lack of trust: trust between the government and the people, between different ethnic groups, between the military and civilian forces. Trust is a precious commodity that is easily lost, but hard indeed to take root. The way forward can only be through a mature political process that will reconcile widely differing points of view and achieve an effective consensus on the challenges that confront our nation and our people. *Burma: The Challenge of Change in a Divided Society* confronts this issue by acknowledging the validity of contrasting and even conflicting opinions. The very fact of this acknowledgement is a vital first step in the effective resolution of deep-seated conflicts, conflicts which are disrupting the harmony of our nation and paralysing the progress of our gifted people.

Rangoon   AUNG SAN SUU KYI
19 June 1996

Preface

Like the quest for democracy in Burma, this book has had a long and painful gestation. It originated nearly five years ago in a conference held at St Antony's College, Oxford, entitled, 'Burma (Myanmar): Challenges and Opportunities for the 1990's' (14–15 December 1991). This took place in the euphoria which followed the award of the 1991 Nobel Peace Prize to Daw Aung San Suu Kyi when it seemed that the cause of democracy in Burma, so remarkably evident in the May 1990 election and the landslide victory of Daw Suu's National League for Democracy, had, at last, achieved the international recognition it deserved.

The third in a series on Southeast Asia sponsored by the Foreign and Commonwealth Office in conjunction with the St Antony's College Asian Studies Centre,[1] the conference brought together some twenty-five leading experts on contemporary Burmese affairs who were asked to discuss four main areas: politics and constitution-making; the economy and the role of foreign aid; the minorities; and foreign policy, in particular Burma's post-independence relations with China. The quality of the papers was high and the meeting generally acclaimed as one of the most valuable on Burma in recent years; the presence of representatives from the key UN agencies (UNICEF and UNDP), currently operating in Burma, being deemed especially useful. When Macmillan expressed an interest in publishing the proceedings in a volume of the St Antony's Series, the prospect of getting the papers into print seemed both timely and straightforward.

If the volume had depended solely on the diligence and enthusiasm of its various contributors, and of the editorial staff at Macmillan, it would have appeared long since. That it has taken so long is a reflection both of life's unpredictability and of the special difficulties working on contemporary Burma. One graphic illustration of this last was the fate of the volume's first editor, Dr Khin (Kelvin) Zaw Win, a dentist by training, who was attached as a researcher to the UNICEF office and whose co-operation had been secured through the good offices of the then UNICEF Representative in Rangoon, Rolf Carriere, a contributor to the present volume (see Chapter 8). Shortly after completing his preliminary editorial work, Kelvin was arrested (4 July 1994) and jailed by the SLORC for fifteen years on charges of 'causing or intending to spread false news', 'membership or contact with an illegal organisation (in this case the opposition National Coalition Government of the Union of

Burma)', and 'possession or control of secret information (presumably papers relating to the political situation in Burma which he was taking back to the University of Singapore where he was enrolled for a Masters' degree in Public Policy [1993–4])'. Now an Amnesty International 'Prisoner of Conscience', he appears to have been punished for his academic research into Burmese politics and his well-known contact with foreigners, including the UN's Special Rapporteur to Myanmar (Burma), to whom he was alleged to have sent 'fabricated news' about human rights abuses in 1992.[2]

The fate of this courageous young man underscores the dangers attendant on research on the current political situation in Burma, which, for Burmese, can exact a huge personal price. If all this did not make it hard enough to prepare the volume for publication, the sudden deterioration of the health of the present editor's youngest son and his need for two major open-heart procedures, prevented the close editorial attention which the papers deserved for nearly two years. Twin metaphors for the travail of both the present volume and the country it chronicles, prison and cardiac surgery now seemed to conspire to prevent the book from ever seeing the light of day.[3]

When, at last, I was able to return to the work, it was already 1995 and the situation in Burma had changed a great deal. The SLORC, whose long-term prospects had looked decidedly problematic in late 1991, had now entrenched itself in power: significant successes had been achieved against the ethnic insurgencies, most of which had signed 'standfast' (ceasefire) agreements with Rangoon, and the military junta's isolation had been breached by closer ties with its regional neighbours, in particular, China and the ASEAN states (which it is set to join perhaps as early as July 1997). The once ailing Burmese economy too seemed to be picking up: Burma's 'Least Developed Country' (LDC) status, accorded in December 1987, was now being metamorphosed by predictions of 'tiger cub' potential in the early twenty-first century. Base metals into gold indeed – what next, one wondered, for the Golden Land?

Although it soon became apparent that the transformations of the early 1990s were not as substantial as the SLORC and its foreign supporters had made out, it was obvious that the papers presented to the December 1991 Oxford Conference would have to be completely revised and updated. This process was embarked on in March 1995 and continued through two periods of research and writing in the extraordinary beauty of the Tibetan Retreat Centre at Dzogchen Beara in West Cork (Republic of Ireland) with its views over the rugged coastline of the Beara peninsula and the wide expanse of Bantry Bay. Working in this environment, one could imagine that even the most intractable situations might one day find a happy resolution. So the editorial task, once seemingly so Sisyphean, became an increasingly pleasurable undertaking. Here the confidence of the contributors that the volume was worth persevering with was crucial: as one especially long-suffering scholar remarked: 'I have remained committed because there is so little that is good on Burma, and you had a lot of good people [at Oxford].' Certainly, the relative dearth of good contemporary studies on Burma, and the increasing public interest in the country, an interest quickened both by the SLORC's own attempts to transform their country's tourist industry in this 'Visit Myanmar Year' (1996–7) and enhanced international scrutiny of the country's human rights record, meant that the issues addressed at the conference retained their topicality. Even so, every effort was made to revise each paper in the light of recent developments and to bring them up-to-date as of the end of March 1996.

Events in Burma are, however, continuing to gather pace. Just as this preface is being written, reports are coming in that over 300 NLD supporters have been arrested to prevent a congress to mark the sixth anniversary of the party's triumph at the polls in the May 1990 election, and there are fears that the military clampdown will result in the re-arrest of those democracy leaders released last year. The effectiveness of such a clampdown will, however, be hostage to greater diplomatic pressure on Burma, even from those Asian countries, such as Japan (currently reported to be engaged in delicate negotiations between the SLORC and the NLD) and South Korea, which have hitherto been prepared to give the SLORC the benefit of the doubt in terms of trade and economic assistance. It is suggested that these pressures, coupled with concern for the enhanced international profile of the democratic opposition, are fuelling an internal debate within the Burmese military regarding the best way of handling the current crisis, with hardliners arguing for a crackdown and moderates pointing out the international costs of such a course. Any split within the *Tatmadaw* would certainly have serious repercussions for the cohesion and longevity of the SLORC, so, it is possible, that political change may be in the offing as some of the chapters in the present volume have foreseen. Only time will tell, however, whether the forces of democracy will prevail in Burma, a country which has been ruled by the military for over two-thirds of its post-independence history, but whose people have shown quite remarkable courage and perseverance in the face of adversity. If self-sacrifice alone could secure democracy, Burma would have long since been free. As for this small volume, it will be for others to judge its worth. Even if it plays but a small part in generating a more informed discussion of the prospects for Burma and its remarkable people then it will have fulfilled its purpose.

Trinity College   PETER CAREY
Oxford
27 May 1996

Postscript

Since writing this preface I returned to Burma for the first time in forty years (I had left it as a six-year-old in 1955) and was able to visit the house where I grew up in Rangoon and to meet with Daw Suu and celebrate her 51st birthday on 19 June 1996. Although I had not seen her since her return to Burma in March 1988 at the start of the 'democracy summer' and so much had happened in the intervening period, it was as though the years had fallen away and we were back together in her house in Park Town, Oxford, discussing family and friends. It was then that I was able to show her the manuscript of this book and tell her how it had originated at the time of her December 1991 Nobel Peace Prize, as well as eliciting her foreword, which she wrote in my presence, amidst her many other duties on that festive day. One could not but admire her fortitude: this was a time when many of her staunchest NLD colleagues and party workers, arrested at the time of the NLD Congress in late May, remained in jail and when one of her closest friends, James Leander Nichols ('Uncle Leo'), a businessman and former honorary consul for various Scandinavian countries, was succumbing to ill-treatment in Rangoon's notorious Insein jail. But what struck me most of all was the sheer human warmth and delight in the company of good friends which emanated from her to all those present. Here was an example of courage which confirmed the truth of what the British historian Godfrey Eric Harvey (1885–1965) had written over seventy years ago when he spoke of the honour paid by the Burmese to women of outstanding quality:

> When other races bound the feet or veiled the faces of their women, or doubted whether she had a soul, the Burmese held her free and enthroned her as a chieftainess or queen.[4]

I came away inspired by what I had seen, yet full of foreboding about the future. The lack of dialogue between the SLORC and the NLD is deeply worrying. Instead, the crudest forms of propaganda and personal vilification abound: two weeks before my arrival red-and-white billboards had begun to appear across the country (one of the first was close to Daw Suu's house in University Avenue) denouncing foreign intervention and calling for opposition to anyone trying to destabilise the country – 'Oppose those relying on external elements, acting as stooges, holding negative views' they exhorted, stating that this was 'the people's desire'. Yet people in the street would have none of it: 'What do they mean it's the people's desire?' said one, 'it's the SLORC's desire!' Indeed, such a pitch of propaganda speaks more of fear than political confidence. Perhaps, when it comes to popularly enthroned chieftainnesses and self-imposed military juntas, the Burmese have already made up their minds?

Notes

1. The others had been on 'Agrarian Reform in the Philippines' (April 1990) and 'East Timor: Fifteen Years On' (December 1990), proceedings of which were both subsequently published: see, J. Putzel, A. Quisumbing, F. Lara and N.W. Armstrong, *Agrarian Reform and Official Development Assistance in the Philippines*, Occasional Paper no. 13 (Canterbury: Centre for Southeast Asian Studies [University of Kent], 1990); and Peter Carey and G. Carter Bentley (eds), *East Timor at the Crossroads: The Forging of a Nation* (London: Cassell, 1995).
2. See Martin Smith, *Fatal Silence? Freedom of Expression and the Right to Health in Burma* (London: Article 19, July 1996), p. 48. A recent Amnesty International report indicates that he, together with other political prisoners, have been subjected to prolonged ill-treatment (ie being placed in tiny cells meant to house military dogs; forced to sleep on cold concrete floors with no bedding; and forbidden family visits), as a reprisal against sending a joint letter (signed by twenty-seven Insein inmates) about prison conditions in Burma to the UN: see Amnesty International, *Myanmar: Renewed Repression* (London: Amnesty International, 10 July 1986), p. 17.
3. Even as the volume was in its very final stages of copy-editing in December 1996, the ill-luck which had dogged it from the beginning continued, when the entire manuscript was stolen from the copy editor's car, and the whole process of preparing the volume for publication had to begin again! (23 December 1996).
4. G.E. Harvey, *History of Burma* (London: Longman, 1925), p. xx.

Acknowledgements

I would hereby like to express my thanks to David Colvin, previously Head of the Southeast Asian Department of the Foreign and Commonwealth Office, for his help in securing the original FCO grant for the Oxford Conference in December 1991; to Queen Elizabeth House for giving me an Oppenheimer grant to visit Burma in June 1996; to Michael Aris and Martin Smith for their comments on my introduction, and the former for extensive copy-editing; to David Winder of the Ford Foundation for his initial reading of the volume and his recommendation of it for publication in the St Antony's Series; to Rosemary Thorp and Alex Pravda of St Antony's for their support as general editors of this same series; to Tim Farmiloe, Felicity Noble, Aruna Vasudevan of Macmillan for the care they have taken in seeing this book through the publishing process; to Keith Povey and Eileen Ashcroft for copy-editing the typescript and overseeing the production process; and to Rolf Carriere for having arranged the preliminary editorial assistance of Dr Khin (Kelvin) Zaw Win at the UNICEF office in Rangoon in 1992. Finally, and perhaps most important, I must acknowledge my deep appreciation of the cooperation of my co-contributors, who have shown immense understanding and patience over five long years. Let us hope that the waiting has been worth while!

Abbreviations and Acronyms

ADB	Asian Development Bank
ABSDF	All Burma Students' Democratic Front
AFPFL	Anti-Fascist People's Freedom League
AMDSC	Anti-Military Dictatorship Solidarity Committee
ASEAN	Association of South East Asian Nations
BADP	Border Areas' Development Programme
BCP	Burma Communist Party (*see below* 'CPB')
BSPP	Burma Socialist Programme Party
CCP	Chinese Communist Party
CEDC	Children in Especially Difficult Circumstances
CPB	Communist Party of Burma
CRDB	Committee for the Restoration of Democracy in Burma
DAB	Democratic Alliance of Burma
DFB	Democratic Front for Burma
DKBA	Democratic Karen Buddhist Army
DKBO	Democratic Karen Buddhist Organisation
EIU	Economist Intelligence Unit (London)
FBIS	Foreign Broadcasts Information Service
FEER	*Far Eastern Economic Review* (Hong Kong)
IMF	International Monetary Fund
INGO	International Non-Governmental Organisation
ICRC	International Committee of the Red Cross (Geneva)
IMF	International Monetary Fund
KIA	Kachin Independence Army
KIO	Kachin Independence Organisation
KRC	Karen Refugee Committee
Kt	*kyat* (Burmese currency)
KNPP	Karenni National Progressive Party
LDC	Least Developed Country
MOI	Ministry of the Interior (Thailand)
MTA	Mong Tai Army
NAM	Non-Aligned Movement
NCGUB	National Coalition Government of the Union of Burma
NDF	National Democratic Front
NGO	Non-Governmental Organisation
NLD	National League for Democracy

NMSP	New Mon State Party
NSC	National Security Council (Bangkok)
NUP	National Unity Party
ODA	Overseas Development Assistance
OECD	Organisation for Economic Co-operation and Development
PDP	Parliamentary Democracy Party
PPP	People's Patriotic Party
PRC	People's Republic of China
Rmb	*renminbi* (Chinese currency)
SEATO	South-East Asia Treaty Organisation
SLORC	State Law and Order Restoration Council
SNLD	Shan National League for Democracy
SSIA	Shan State Independence Army
SSPP	Shan State Progress Party
SWB	BBC, *Summary of World Broadcasts*
UDHR	Universal Declaration of Human Rights
UNCHR	United Nations Commission on Human Rights (Geneva)
UNDCP	United Nations International Drug Control Programme
UNDP	United Nations Development Programme
UNESCO	United Nations Educational, Scientific and Cultural Organization
UNHCR	United Nations High Commissioner for Refugees
UNICEF	United Nations International Children's Emergency Fund
USDA	Union Solidarity and Development Association
UWSA	United Wa State Army
UWSP	United Wa State Party
WHO	World Health Organization

A Note on the Use of the Names Burma/Myanmar and Rangoon/Yangon

Readers will note that, although the name of the country was officially changed from the Union of Burma to the Union of Myanmar (sometimes also spelt Myanma, or *Myanma[r] Naing Ngan* and *Myanma[r] Naing-ngandaw*) by the SLORC on 18 June 1989, several authors in this volume have continued to use the old name, even when dealing with post-June 1989 events. They argue that the new name is unduly exclusive to the dominant Burman (Bamar) ethnic group and does not take account of the Union's high ethnic diversity. For them, 'Burma' continues to be the preferred term, with the world 'Burman' referring to the majority ethnic groups in the Burma heartland of the Irrawaddy River valley and the delta area, and the epithet 'Burmese' being used to denote all the peoples – Burman and ethnic minority – who inhabit the present-day Union of Burma. Other contributors have eschewed these distinctions and have used the term 'Myanmar' or 'Myanma' throughout, both when referring to the country and its people, and when dealing with pre-1989 and post-June 1989 events. Since these choices often reflect the deeply held views on the part of the various contributors regarding contemporary developments in Burma/Myanmar, the present editor has not thought fit to impose any arbitrary uniformity on the way in which the terms have been employed, although it would now be technically correct in any scholarly publication to refer to 'Burma' when dealing with events prior to June 1989, and 'Myanmar [or Myanma]' thereafter.

A somewhat similar divide separates those contributors who have used the term 'Yangon', the more accurate transliteration of the Burmese/Myanmar name of the capital, which was made official by the SLORC on 18 June 1989, and the older epithet 'Rangoon', which Burma inherited from the British colonial period (1826–1948). Again, since the choice of the use of these terms often reflects personal predilections on the part of the various contributors, the present editor has not thought appropriate to interfere with them. Future readers of this volume will be able to draw their own conclusions as to individual attitudes towards the present military regime. One day, Burma/Myanmar, like post-April 1989

Kampuchea/Cambodia, may revert back to its original name, and then the choices of term used at the present time may have a certain historiographical significance.

Note: The terms *naing* and *ngan* mean 'state'.

Notes on the Contributors

Peter Carey is Laithwaite Fellow and Tutor in Modern History at Trinity College, Oxford, where he specialises on the modern history of Southeast Asia. He is the author and editor of several books on Indonesia and East Timor, most recently *The British in Java, 1811–16: A Javanese Account* (London: Oxford University Press for the British Academy, 1992) and *East Timor at the Crossroads: The Forging of a Nation* (London: Cassell, 1995).

Rolf C. Carriere served for four years as UNICEF representative in Burma (1989–92) and is currently (1992–the present) UNICEF representative in Bangladesh.

Paul Cook is a Senior Lecturer in Economics at the Institute for Development, Policy and Management, University of Manchester. He is the author of several articles on the Burmese economy, the most recent being his chapter, 'Privatisation in Myanmar', in P. Cook and F. Nixson (eds), *The Move to the Market* (London: Macmillan, 1995).

Janelle Diller is currently Adjunct Professor of Law at the University of Virginia School of Law at Charlottesville and at Georgetown University Law Center in Washington DC. She was Legal Director of the International Human Rights Law Group in Washington DC (1990–4) and has researched and published widely on human rights and international law and policy. She is the author of *In Search of Asylum: Vietnamese Refugees in Hong Kong* (Washington DC: Indochina Resource Action Center, 1988).

Chi-shad Liang is a former Professor of Political Science at Winston-Salem State University in the United States, Nanyang University in Singapore and National Chengchi University in Taiwan. He is the author of *Burma's Foreign Relations: Neutralism in Theory and Practice* (New York: Praeger, 1990), as well as several articles on Southeast Asian politics. His new book (in Chinese) on the international situation in Europe since 1945 is due out in late 1996.

Martin Minogue is Director of the Development Studies Programme in the Faculty of Economics and Social Studies at the University of

Manchester. He is the author of several books and articles on development policy and practice, including (with P.F. Leeson), *Perspectives on Development: Cross Disciplinary Themes in Development Studies* (Manchester University Press, 1988). He has also co-authored articles on Burma in *World Development* and *Round Table*.

Josef Silverstein is Professor Emeritus of Political Science at Rutgers University. He is the author and editor of several books on Burma, including *The Political Legacy of Aung San* (Cornell University Southeast Asia Program monograph, 1972; rev. edn 1993); *Burma: Military Rule and the Politics of Stagnation* (Cornell University Press, 1977), and *Burmese Politics: The Dilemma of National Unity* (New Jersey: Rutgers University Press, 1980). He was Fulbright Lecturer at Mandalay University in 1961–2, and Director of the Institute for Southeast Asian Studies, Singapore, 1970–2.

Martin Smith is a writer and journalist specialising in Burmese affairs. He is author of *Burma: Insurgency and the Politics of Ethnicity* (London and New Jersey: Zed Books, 1991), *State of Fear: Censorship in Burma* (London: Article 19, 1991), *Ethnic Groups in Burma: Development, Democracy and Human Rights* (London: Anti-Slavery International, 1994), and *Fatal Silence? Freedom of Expression and the Right to Health in Burma* (London: Article 19, July 1996). His television work on Burma includes the documentaries, *Dying for Democracy* (UK Channel Four, 1989) and *Forty Million Hostages* (BBC 2, 1991).

David I. Steinberg is Representative of the Asia Foundation in Korea. He has been Distinguished Professor of Korea Studies at Georgetown University, and was previously the President of the Mansfield Center for Pacific Affairs. A former member of the Senior Foreign Service of the Department of State, Agency for International Development, he is the author of numerous books, monographs and articles on Korea, Burma, and Asian development. His latest volume is *The Future of Burma: Crisis and Choice in Myanmar* (Washington DC and New York: University Press of America and The Asia Society, 1990. Asian Agenda no. 14).

Robert H. Taylor is Vice-Chancellor of the University of Buckingham. He was previously Professor of Politics and Pro-Director of the School of Oriental and African Studies, University of London. His publications include *Marxism and Resistance in Burma* (Athens, Ohio: Ohio University Press, 1984) and *The State in Burma* (London: Hurst, 1987).

Introduction

'Solitudinem faciunt pacem appellant'
They make a wilderness and call it peace.
(Tacitus, *Agricola*, 30)

INTRODUCTION

Few countries of Burma's size – at 47 million it is now one of the twenty-five most populous nations in the world – are so little known. Yet few have aroused such deeply held passions. Renowned in the pre-colonial (that is, pre-1886) era as the 'hermit' kingdom of Southeast Asia, it has remained, until recently, a recluse in a region of dynamic change. During the more than quarter century of General Ne Win's 'Burmese Road to Socialism' (1962–88), the country, once the world's largest rice exporter, experienced steep economic decline, which left it one of the ten 'Least Developed Countries' (LDCs), with a per caput income of less than US$250, on a par with impoverished states in sub-Saharan Africa like Mali and Chad. Previously at the forefront of regional and international politics – it had been one of the founders of the Non-Aligned Movement in the mid-1950s – it became, under Ne Win, the great non-joiner, an introverted state dominated by a xenophobic military and a dictator swayed more by necromancy than normality.

During the past eight years, however, since the State Law and Order Restoration (SLORC) came to power in a military *coup* (18 September 1988), which brought to an end nearly six months of unprecedented pro-democracy demonstrations, Burma (or 'Myanmar' as its new military rulers have styled it) has begun to open to the outside world. New laws governing foreign investment (November 1988) and state-owned economic enterprises (March 1989) have created the possibility of a more dynamic economy. At the same time, Burma's recent admittance to 'observer status' within ASEAN (Association of South-East Asian Nations) in July 1996, seems to have paved the way for its return to the Southeast Asian region and perhaps even the wider international community.

Such a metamorphosis is still, however, hostage to domestic political developments. Like a salamander, the SLORC is constantly consumed by Burma's own inner conflagrations. The systematic destruction of nearly all the independent institutions of the state (for example, the monarchy, royal

1

administration, governance of the Buddhist *sangha*, indigenous landowning and entrepreneurial elites) following the British conquest of Upper Burma in the late 1880s, the introduction of large numbers of non-Burmese (principally Indians and Chinese) into the economy, the division of the colony into Burman ('Ministerial Burma') and non-Burman ('Frontier Burma') areas, and rule from India (until 1937), all tended to disempower the Burman majority, bequeathing a form of government which lacked popular legitimacy and support. Burma became the classic case of a 'weak state, strong society', the latter underpinned, as Steinberg points out, by a fragmented economy based on village-level self-sufficiency.

THE EMERGENCE OF THE BURMESE ARMY AS A POLITICAL FORCE

The upheaval of the Japanese occupation (1942–5), when Burma was twice fought over by contending armies, the problems of post-war reconstruction (not least the assassination in July 1947 of the country's designated leader, U Aung San), and the instability of the civilian governments of the post-independence period (1948–62), all deepened the crisis of the Burmese state. Mocked as the 'Six-Mile Rangoon Government' in the late 1940s, so beset was the young Union of Burma by the multifarious ethnic and Communist insurgencies which followed independence, the state's survival increasingly rested on the Burmese Army (*Tatmadaw*) and the uncompromising new army chief-of-staff, General Ne Win.[1]

The emergence of the army as the predominant force in Burmese political life, hailed as the glue which would hold the country together, was already presaged in May 1945, after the fall of Rangoon, when the then Colonel Ne Win had declared that the *Tatmadaw* 'is not only the hope of the country, but its very life and soul'.[2] Such an elevated view of the military as Burma's only hope had been qualified before his untimely death by General Aung San, who had warned that the *Tatmadaw* should never become separate from the people, but should be their refuge and protector. A true people's army, it should be an institution which ordinary Burmese could 'revere and depend on'.[3] His assassination and the weakness of the civilian government of Prime Minister U Nu (in office, 1948–56, 1957–8, 1960–2), however, opened the way for those, like General Ne Win, who harboured their own political ambitions under the cloak of military professionalism.

This perversion of the army's original mandate is, in no way, unique to post-war Burma. Both Indonesia and Thailand (up to General Suchinda's ouster in May 1992) have experienced somewhat similar developments, with the army encroaching on the power of elected civilian politicians in response to challenges to the integrity of the state. Such encroachments, however, have not compromised economic development: during the past twenty-five years, both Indonesia and Thailand, buoyed by massive foreign aid and investment flows, have experienced remarkable rates of growth, growth which has changed the face of their respective societies. Yet Burma remains caught in a political impasse, the army and the people seemingly pitted against each other, and the nation locked in a cycle of impoverishment. Why?

This is the question which the present volume seeks to answer, while, at the same time, indicating ways in which the impasse might be transcended. Instead of a salamander condemned to live perpetually in the fires, might Burma one day rise like a phoenix from the ashes? Could it once again become the 'golden land' of colonial repute, a land at peace with itself and its political inheritance? Even to glance at this book's table of contents is to realise the range of different views regarding the country's possibilities, the very choice of the terms 'Myanmar' and 'Burma' an unerring guide to present perceptions. *Nomen est omen* indeed!

At the risk of gross oversimplification, what then are the different perceptions of these authors? What divides those who accept (more or less) the current realities of military rule, and those who feel that Burma's future should be a civilian and democratic one? Clearly the different views of the historical processes which have shaped contemporary Burma are vital here and it is to these that we must first turn in order to understand the ground that separates Robert Taylor from Martin Smith, or Paul Cook and Martin Minogue from Josef Silverstein.

THE AUTHORITARIAN MODEL

In broad terms, those who conclude that the *Tatmadaw* will remain the arbiter of Burma's future tend to stress the fundamentally authoritarian nature of the traditional Burmese state. In Steinberg's view, the current, highly personalised, concepts of power and the role of central authority stem back to the Indic roots of Burma's royal past, which bequeathed a system of semi-divine rule pivoted on the monarch's court, the magical centre of temporal power. Although the colonial period had destroyed this monarchical tradition in Burma, the centralising processes of the late Burman monarchy were carried on under the British (1826–1948), with the enhanced efficiency bestowed by superior firepower, modern systems of communication, law and order, and rational government. At the same time, the weakening of the great quasi-autonomous institutions of the pre-colonial order (for example, the *sangha*) meant that the state could intervene as never before in the lives of its subjects.

Since independence in January 1948, the pattern has continued, with state power in the rebellious countryside being represented increasingly by the army. According to Taylor, Burma has 'a long tradition of an army with entrenched political power', which, in his view, stretches back to the pre-colonial state (for example, the *ahmú-dàns* system of military service),[4] the various militia (*tat*) raised by pre-war Burman politicians, like 'Galon' U Saw (1900–48), and the private armies of post-war strongmen (*Bo*) in the delta. Even the university-educated student leaders and young radicals of the *Thakin* movement were drawn into military affairs, although for very different reasons from the bully-boy U Saw: one thinks here of the 'Thirty Comrades', in particular U Aung San (Bo Te Za), who later received military training from the Japanese and went on to found the Burma Independence Army (December 1941), the precursor of the modern *Tatmadaw*.[5] Given the reliance of the civilian politicians on the Burmese army in the late 1940s and 1950s, is it any wonder, analysts of the authoritarian line argue, that the army has assumed such a central role in the political life of the country since the early 1960s? As Steinberg has observed, the *Tatmadaw*'s commitment to its three 'sacred causes' – the integrity of the Union, national unity, and the preservation of Burma's sovereignty – is deeply felt. The army alone, as the SLORC never tires of telling the Burmese people, can hold the state together and protect the country from its many internal and external enemies.

There are interesting parallels here with the post-independence (1945) Indonesian army (*Angkatan Bersenjata Republik Indonesia*, ABRI), which also came to see itself as the one institution which could ensure the country's survival, and, like the Burmese army, achieved political power in the 1960s through a military-dominated regime. It is thus no coincidence, according to Steinberg, that the *Tatmadaw* is seeking to emulate ABRI's political role in Suharto's 'New Order' (1965 to present) by ensuring that its influence is entrenched in the new constitution currently being drawn up by the National Convention, a process which is described in detail by Diller.[6]

Why then has the international community treated Indonesia's New Order and Burma's SLORC so differently? As Taylor rightly stresses, the post-1965 Indonesian regime was 'massively repressive and authoritarian'. Indeed, when one considers the intensity of the anti-communist purges in 1965–6 Indonesia, when perhaps as many as a million civilians were killed and a further 1.5 million were imprisoned, the repression which followed the SLORC's seizure of power on 18 September 1988 (more than 3000 killed, 4000–5000 jailed, and 8000–10 000 forced to flee to the border from the towns and cities of central Burma), seems almost small-scale. Yet New Order Indonesia received unstinting international aid, while SLORC-ruled Burma has been cut off (since 1988) from Western development funds and humanitarian assistance, creating what Carriere has movingly described as a 'silent emergency'. Why?

The answer, in Taylor's view, must be sought in 'intellectual trends' in Western political science – what Steinberg has dismissed as 'fadism' – which, in turn, have influenced the policies of governments and multilateral agencies like the World Bank. Whereas, in the mid-1960s, when Suharto's New Order was establishing itself, the Cold War was at its peak and anti-Communist military regimes were deemed worthy of generous Western support, by the late 1980s, human rights, 'good governance' – and its supposed twin, democracy – held pride of place. SLORC-ruled Burma flew in the face of the new orthodoxy, especially when it refused to recognise the results of the May 1990 elections, which saw a landslide victory for Daw Aung San Suu Kyi's democratic opposition party, the National League for Democracy (NLD). Yet, even here, according to Cook and Minogue, there was a large measure of hypocrisy on the part of the West. How else to explain the West's continued dealings with China, a state every bit as undemocratic and repressive as Burma? How else to understand Japan's willingness, in the light of the so-called 'Kaifu Doctrine' on human rights, to carry on its lending programme to Indonesia in the aftermath of the notorious 12 November 1991 Santa Cruz massacre in East Timor when perhaps as many as 270 Timorese civilians were killed, most gunned down by the Indonesian army in full view of Western journalists?

Clearly the bottom line here, the proponents of the authoritarian model would argue, is not human rights or good governance, but the West's economic interests. Since Burma is poor, it can be kicked around. Richer countries like China and Indonesia, with their lucrative markets and investment opportunities, can get away with murder (although preferably not in front of Western TV cameras). Yet how can Burma develop if it is not given a chance? To expect the military to return to barracks and allow the civilian politicians to take over is not only unrealistic, but flies in the face of Burma's historical experience. As Singapore's Senior Minister Lee Kuan Yew recently put it: 'If I were Aung San Suu Kyi, I think I'd rather be behind a fence and be a symbol than be found impotent to lead the country ... I have visited [Myanmar] and I know that there is only one instrument of government, and that is the army'.[7]

Those advocating the *dirigiste* path – and it must be stressed that their attitudes towards the current military regime vary greatly – present different analyses of the way forward. Both Cook and Minogue, and Taylor, for example, stress the importance of political stability, highlighting the fact that, in Asia at least, democratisation has always followed, not preceded economic change. They give South Korea, Taiwan, Singapore, and Thailand as examples of this, pointing out that India, a relatively stable democracy throughout most of its post-independence history, has had a much less impressive economic record. Indeed, Cook and Minogue cite with approval what has been termed, in the case of pre-Tiananmen China, the 'new authoritarianism'; namely, limited political change (the 'deinstitutionalisation' of the state) and the introduction of market-based reforms. In the case of Burma this would entail, in their view, the separation of the military from the administration, a reduction of military power in relation to state enterprises, limited economic liberalisation, and strictly controlled political liberalisation. This might be followed, eventually, by a transition to full democracy (such as occurred in Korea in 1987 and Taiwan in 1992) and the complete opening, what Cook and Minogue term 'marketisation', of the economy.

Other Asian states besides China have taken this 'new authoritarian' road. New Order Indonesia, for example, has substantially reduced the number of serving officers in the administration (there were some 25 000 at the start of the New Order in 1965, and only about 7000 today), cut the quota of military reserved seats in the 500-member People's Representative Council (from 100 to 75), changed the military–civilian balance in the cabinet (from thirteen out of thirty-two portfolios in 1983 to ten out of forty-one in 1993) and lessened armed forces control of state enterprises (a development hastened by the US$10 billion bankruptcy of the state oil company, Pertamina, in 1975). Economic liberalisation has also preceded apace since the early 1980s, even accompanied, briefly (1990–June 1994), by a measure of political liberalisation or 'openness' (*keterbukaan*) – an opening which reflected the view that military men could 'no longer be the best artillerymen in town, as well as the best politicians', as the Indonesian think-tank chief Jusuf Wanandi put it. In Cook and Minogue's view, all this is immediately relevant to Burma in terms of the SLORC's future options, especially as regards the long-term economic and political role of the Burmese army.

Steinberg, although acknowledging the relevance of the authoritarian or *dirigiste* model for Burma, is much less sanguine about the implementation of meaningful economic reforms in the current political climate. True, he says, states like South Korea did have a highly interventionist record during the years of rapid economic expansion in the late 1960s and 1970s, but then they also had administrations prepared to listen to their economic advisers and implement reforms (many of which struck at vested interests), with the full backing of the political leadership and a professional bureaucracy recruited on merit. Even New Order Indonesia, with its much less reliable civil service, was prepared to heed the warnings of its economists (the so-called 'Berkeley mafia') in the mid-1960s, and carry through, often painful, macroeconomic policies, policies which enabled the Suharto government to extricate itself from the inflationary disasters of the late Sukarno period, and set the country on the road to economic prosperity in the post-1973 'oil boom' era.

Burma under the SLORC, in Steinberg's view, lacks all these necessary elements. It neither has the political will nor the administrative capacity, not to speak of macroeconomic instruments (such as a politically independent central bank), to emulate these examples. This lack of political will is grounded on the SLORC's perception that effective economic restructuring will have serious negative effects on those segments of society (civil servants, military personnel, employees of State Economic Enterprises, vested interest groups) on which it currently relies for its political survival. It is very conscious of the way in which the disastrous currency reform of 5 September 1987 (which wiped out 60–80 per cent of the value of money in circulation) lit the powder trail to the democracy uprising of March–September 1988, an uprising in which a high proportion of civil servants either took part or were openly sympathetic (15 000 were subsequently fired after the SLORC *coup*, and a further 4500 dismissed or disciplined for opposition to government policies in 1991).[8] Economic restructuring is indeed a high risk strategy for any government, how much more so for a deeply unpopular regime like the SLORC, many of whose members would be the first to feel the effects of successful macroeconomic reform. The free float of the grossly overvalued Burmese currency (*kyat*), for example, where official exchange rates are at least 2000 per cent higher than the open market,[9] would immediately destroy the privileges of the favoured few, whose access to foreign exchange currently gives them a huge free gift at the expense of the majority of the population, who are forced to live in a highly skewed and inflationary economy.[10]

As long as stark military repression remains the regime's ultimate tactic, there can be no answer, Steinberg argues, to the pressing problems of the Burmese economy. The fact that 50–60 per cent of the government budget goes on defence spending,[11] and Burma, even using the SLORC's own statistics, has the greatest imbalance of military expenditure against

health and education of any state in Southeast Asia (155 per cent, against
Indonesia's 5.1 per cent, for example, and this in a country with a population four times smaller than that of Indonesia, and with no external
enemies),[12] means that political reform must precede economic restructuring. The SLORC, in this analysis, is as much a part of the problem, as it
may eventually be a part of the solution. Here Steinberg cites the example
of post-Franco Spain, where, in making the transition from a militarised
dictatorship to a democracy after 1975, Madrid decided to give priority
to political reforms over economic restructuring in its move to a fully
marketised system. These reforms were implemented in a socially sensitive fashion: the pain of redundancies caused by the break-up of state-run
enterprises and bloated civil service being eased by the establishment of
economic and social safety nets paid for by increasing short-term debt,
something which Spain could do given its healthy balance of payments
position at that time. Burma is not yet in a position to attempt this path,
Steinberg observes, because of its refusal to implement necessary reforms,
the most pressing of which are political. The US veto, mandatory in the
case of states like Burma which have been decertified as 'narcotics co-
operating countries', also means that it will not be in line for structural
adjustment loans from any of the key multilateral agencies (IMF, World
Bank, and the Asian Development Bank), its principal option for short-
term finance, in the foreseeable future.[13]

What then are these political reforms which Burma should undertake in
order to make economic initiatives possible, inititiatives which all the contributors to this volume agree are essential? If, as Mao Zedong, once said,
'politics are in command', what should these politics be in the case of
Burma in the late 1990s? For this, we need to hear the voices of those who
advocate a democratic model for Burma's future, one which stresses the
importance of representative and civilian institutions over the imperious
demands of the military.

THE DEMOCRATIC MODEL

If authoritarianism forms one strand of the historical heritage of modern
Burma, another is surely that of resistance to central authority through
intellectual dissent, oppositional politics and outright rebellion.
Monarchical Burma may have been heir to a rich Indian-influenced tradition of statecraft and semi-divine kingship, as Steinberg has noted, but it
was also a turbulent and sanguinary place. In the words of the colonial
historian of Burma, George Eric Harvey:

The people were constantly rebelling, not because they were a bad people – they were a good people – but because they were in a sort of slavery, and every now and then they would rise against it and sell their lives dearly; hence the land was ever in turmoil, and government, instead of being stable, was a prey to the strong ... The court was the most stupid and conceited imaginable, and did not contain a single man of common understanding; or, if there were such, he was afraid to show it, for the government was a sanguinary despotism ... People were taxed, but they were not governed ... for it was difficult for the kings to govern when so much of their attention was spent on maintaining themselves in power against endemic rebellion.[14]

This endemic rebellion was evidenced in the colonial period by the difficulties the British encountered in 'pacifying' Upper Burma following their conquest of Mandalay (December 1885), and the periodic uprisings against their rule in other parts of the country, that of Saya San being the best known (1930–1). The nationalist struggle against the British was also marked by bold acts of civil resistance: one thinks here of the celebrated 1920 Rangoon University strike, which ushered in the national school movement, and the events surrounding the 1938 oil-field workers' strike, which heralded the 'year of revolution' and sparked important student and peasant solidarity actions. Nor were democratic procedures unknown to the Burmese. Although democratically elected governments fared badly in the turbulent years following independence, the Burmese people have participated, as Cook and Minogue point out, in no less than five free elections between 1935 and 1942 (under the very restricted 'Ministerial Burma' franchise), and four in the post-war period up to the military *coup* of March 1962. Even under the SLORC, despite massive government control of the electoral process, a high proportion of the population turned out to vote in the May 1990 poll, most casting their ballots for the National League for Democracy (which won 82 per cent of the constituencies) and other opposition parties, totally eclipsing the government-sponsored National Unity Party, which retained only ten seats. All this is proof enough, advocates of the non-authoritarian model would argue, that democracy is still a living force in Burma and one which cannot be manipulated out of existence through the machinations of the current National Convention or a military-dominated constitution with its spurious multi-party system which Diller has analysed so trenchantly.

Nowhere is this issue of democracy more pressing, according to Smith and Silverstein, than in the context of Burma's ethnic minorities. Comprising at least a third of the country's population, many of these groups have been in conflict with Rangoon ever since independence in 1948. Despite the sixteen 'standfast' (ceasefire) agreements negotiated by the SLORC with the insurgent leaders since April 1989, agreements which have focused on economic and military matters, none of the fundamental political and constitutional issues (regional autonomy, centre–periphery relations, fiscal authority, border development/finance, structure of local government) have been addressed. According to the SLORC, all these will be sorted out by the National Convention in consultation with representatives of the ethnic minorities and the principal political parties (though not, since 28 November 1995, the NLD). Now in its fourth year, the Convention is engaged in drawing up a new constitution, Burma's third since independence, which will define, the SLORC insists, the structures and institutions of the state in ways which are more sensitive to the needs of all the major groups in Burma's complex ethnic mosaic.

Current *Tatmadaw* thinking on the minority issue, in Smith's view, however, does not inspire confidence. To dismiss the term 'ethnic minority' as 'no longer conveying a profound meaning', as a SLORC spokesman did in an August 1991 broadcast, is to profoundly misjudge the political realities on the ground in the minority areas. Just how wrong that view is, proponents of the non-authoritarian approach would argue, can be seen from the arguments analysed in Taylor's chapter. Here, cogently propounded by a senior army officer, is the idea that the current problem of the periphery is one of 'highly varied and particularised set[s] of issues based on specific localised situations' rather than an issue involving distinct 'ethnic political or cultural communities'. Minority problems, first addressed in the post-war period by U Aung San on the eve of Burma's independence at the February 1947 Panglong Conference in the Shan States, seemed now to being relegated to the category of 'local' or 'regional' concerns.[15]

This *Tatmadaw* view of the ethnic minorities is clearly based on an interpretation of history which places the army's role as the preserver of national unity in the foreground and accepts a 'common origins' understanding of Burmese society, along the lines of that proposed by the Burmese historian, Daw Mya Sein, whom Taylor quotes in his chapter. Writing in the mid-1940s, she asserted that despite the 'animosities between the three principal sub-families [that is, ethno-linguistic groups] in Burma – the Mon-Khmer, the Tibeto-Burman and the Shan – ... the assimilation and transformation of these races into a united nation has been steadily progressing for generations'.[16] Such a view is rejected outright by Smith, who states that 'post-colonial Burma has yet to find a cohesive national and political identity, which will both bring lasting peace and allow the country to take its proper place ... in the international community of nations'.

This failure to find a national identity based on shared political interests has, according to Smith, spawned an unending cycle of misery in Burma, misery which, like a malignant tide, is now seeping over Burma's borders and undermining the welfare of neighbouring states. Armed conflict along the Thai–Burma border, the refugee crisis (50 000 Burmese Muslims [Rohingyas] still in Bangladesh; 90 000 Karens, Karennis and Mons in Thailand, with perhaps as many as 350 000 illegal immigrants in that country), the narcotics trade (Burma is now the world's principal exporter of heroin),[17] a burgeoning AIDS epidemic (an estimated 500 000 HIV-positive sufferers in 1996), and a growing environmental emergency, precipitated by indiscriminate logging along the Burma's borders with China and Thailand, have all combined, in Smith's view, to create a crisis of regional proportions.

Silverstein, while acknowledging the scale of the crisis, advances the thesis that a 'new politics' has come into being in the minority-held areas since the formation of the Democratic Alliance of Burma (DAB) in November 1988, and that this will one day move centre-stage to play a key role in the national life of the country. By 'new politics', he is referring first and foremost to the coming together of Burmans and members of the ethnic minorities on the basis of genuine equality. The upheavals of the short-lived 'democracy summer' of 1988, and the flight of perhaps as many as 10 000 Burman students and other professionals from the cities of central Burma to the border areas following the September 1988 military crackdown was, in Silverstein's view, crucial here. For the first time since independence, large numbers of educated Burmans had the chance to get to know their fellow countrymen and women through direct personal contact, not through the distorting lens of government propaganda, which, since the military takeover in 1962 at least, had portrayed them as hostile and disloyal subjects of the Union. Here Silverstein echoes Harvey when he speaks of the minorities, although poor, living 'peacefully under their own leaders, enjoying religious freedoms, and the sustenance of viable economies based on trade, agriculture and resource extraction.'[18]

Although many misunderstandings later arose between the Burman students and the minority militias, the connections made at this time, in Silverstein's view, continued to inform political relationships on the border, leading to new initiatives for unification amongst the minorities and their Burman allies. These involved first the DAB, and then the National Coalition Government of the Union of Burma (NCGUB), which came into being after the arrival of Daw Aung San Suu Kyi's cousin, Dr Sein Win, and a group of fellow National League for Democracy MPs at Manerplaw in mid-December 1990. This last pledged itself to restoring national prestige, achieving democratic human rights and self-determination, ending the civil war, restoring peace, and building a true federal union.

It was this last issue of federalism, according to Silverstein, which remains the key to any enduring political settlement in Burma. In the past, he argues, equality between Burmans and the minorities had been guaranteed on paper (for example, in the 1947 and 1974 constitutions), but never carried out in practice, a situation skewed even more in favour of the Burman majority after the military took power in the early 1960s. Now, through intensive discussions between Burman and minority leaders, a federal system was devised in the context of a new draft constitution, which allowed for a central government and national states, the latter encompassing autonomous regions and special national territories. Unlike the 1947 constitution, the right of secession, a provision accorded the Shans and Karenni, and which had given rise to endless misunderstandings, was abandoned. But special clauses were included to safeguard the principle of civilian supremacy and federal control of the defence forces, as well as political and human rights, so that all parties would have an incentive to remain within the legal framework of the constitution, without having to employ threats to leave the Union if they could not have their way.

The two years of deliberations (1988–90) which led to the constitutional draft were, according to Silverstein, a prime example of this 'new politics' in action, a politics predicated on equality, full participation, democratic procedure, and sensitivity to special interests. No one group was allowed to stand above the others and dictate their views. The fact that most of the participants in the subsequent NCGUB were elected MPs, having won seats in the May 1990 election, meant, Silverstein stresses, that they were able to speak for their constituents, something which is very far from the case in the current National Convention, where, up to November 1995, as Diller has pointed out, only about 15 per cent of the delegates were representatives elected in 1990, a proportion which fell steeply after the 28 November 1995 NLD walk-out, when less than 3 per cent of the remaining 590 members were chosen by the people (see Chapter 1, n. 12).

Silverstein's positive account of developments at Manerplaw in these years may seem rather too sanguine in the light of subsequent events: the Thai closure of the border to NCGUB representatives in 1993 and their *de facto* exile in the United States, the fall of Manerplaw in January 1995 to a joint *Tatmadaw* and breakaway Karen (DKBO) group, and the ongoing process of 'standfast' (ceasefire) arrangements with Rangoon, which have been entered into by most of the original DAB members.[19] Widespread human rights violations have also resulted from *Tatmadaw* operations in the border areas: in particular, the continued conscription of civilians by the Burmese army for forced labour and porterage duties (duties which affect some two million inhabitants in central Burma and the border regions), the haemorrhage of refugees due to the fighting in the border zones, especially in the Karen and Karenni areas, and massive internal displacements (for example, in Tenasserim Division [Tavoy District] where a French oil company, Total, is involved in a US$1.2 billion natural gas pipeline project).[20] Yet, it is clear that if there is to be long-term peace in Burma, the issues raised in Silverstein's chapter, particularly the question of political and constitutional guarantees for Burma's ethnic minorities, will have to be addressed, whatever government resides in Rangoon.

What then of Burma's recent admittance to 'observer status' within ASEAN, and the possibility of its full membership of the regional organisation by the end of the decade? Will this have any bearing on the SLORC's capacity to gain wider international acceptance? Can burgeoning economic relationships, even the so-called 'constructive engagement', with other Southeast Asian states, strengthen the junta's hold on power sufficiently for it to avoid addressing the fundamental political, economic and social problems which Smith and Silverstein have so skilfully identified?

BURMA AND ASEAN: AN HONOURABLE ASSOCIATION?

This is a country where there is no rule of law, there's no justice, there's no stability. How can such a country be a credit to the region? I think the [ASEAN states] should care about how far the government is capable of achieving peace and stability, because, unless the government is able to achieve [this], it cannot do the region any good at all.[21]

Thus spoke Daw Aung San Suu Kyi, on the eve of the ASEAN Ministerial Meeting in Jakarta (20–23 July 1996), where Burma's preliminary integration into the regional organisation was to be endorsed. Her words encapsulated the democratic opposition concerns about ASEAN's so-called 'constructive engagement' with the SLORC. Whereas in July 1992, at the height of the refugee crisis in the Arakan (Rakhine State), when upwards of 260 000 Burmese Muslims (Rohingyas) had poured into Bangladesh, the Malaysian Foreign Minister, Abdullah Badawi, had stated emphatically that Kuala Lumpur would oppose any move to accord Burma observer status or full ASEAN membership until the generals running the country 'introduced democratic reform, and improved their record on human rights',[22] by July 1996 Rangoon was being welcomed into the ASEAN fold, or at least its ante-chamber. What had changed in the intervening four years? Had there been such dramatic improvements in human rights? Had democratic reforms been introduced? Hardly. What had changed was money: US$230 million to be precise in Malaysia's case, the sum invested in Burma since 1992 by leading Malaysian entrepreneurs, like Robert Kuok, whose Sino-Burmese partner, Steven Law (U Htun Myint Naing), the managing director of Asia World, is estimated to have a US$200 million stake in the Burmese construction industry.[23]

The fact that Law just happened to be the son of the notorious drug baron, Lo Hsing-han (Law Sit Han), known as the 'King of the Golden Triangle' until his arrest at US behest in Thailand in 1973, was hardly coincidental. Narcotics and business go hand-in-hand in Burma, as the US State Department recently (early September 1996) recognised when they denied the younger Law a visa to visit America on the basis of a US law barring entry to people suspected of involvement in the drugs' trade.[24] In Smith's words:

> Simply too much money is being made, and not just by corrupt officials and armed opposition groups ... which control much of the poppy-growing region and opium trade. It is one of the most open secrets in Burma today that much of the large profit made through narcotics is laundered through official trade, and other new business projects currently under way in Rangoon, Mandalay and the other main conurbations.[25]

Ironically Singapore, with its draconian drug laws, is now thought to be playing host to some of Burma's most notorious dealers: both Lo Hsing-han and ex-Chinese Red Guard and CPB militia commander Lin Mingxian (U Sai Lin), son-in-law of the elder Law's erstwhile rival Pheung Kya-shin, have supposedly set up companies in Singapore and are thought to be regular visitors to the island state.[26] Both have maintained their close involvement with northeastern Burma, in particular Shan State and the Wa and Kokang substates, where opium has long been the principle export crop and source of foreign exchange.[27] With a potential output of 2500 tons of raw opium (or 195 tons of no. 4 grade heroin), Burma, as Smith has described, is currently by far the largest drugs producer in Southeast Asia, forming the base of an international narcotics business which stretches through the heroin refining laboratories along the Burma–Thai border to the streets of New York and other cities in the developed world, where an estimated 60 per cent of heroin sold is of Burmese provenance.[28] Quite apart from the devastating effects of this trade on the populations of the border regions (a recent survey by local health workers of AIDS and narcotics abuse amongst the Kachin and Shan uncovered an addiction rate of 40 per cent in some villages)[29], it is evident that drugs money currently plays a critical role in the wider national economy. The SLORC's treatment of the notorious drug dealer Khun Sa and his Mong Tai Army in January 1996, allowing him immunity from prosecution in return for the surrender of his heroin refineries and drugs-trafficking centres, confirmed what had long been suspected in terms of *Tatmadaw* links to the drugs' trade.[30] Nor were many surprised to see the elder Law, who had been amnestied by Ne Win in 1980, emerge in March–April 1989 on the *Tatmadaw's* side to broker a deal between the SLORC and the ex-CPB Kokang and Wa militias, who control the majority of the opium fields in northeastern Burma.[31]

While profits from the narcotics trade have soared, Singapore has become the largest regional stake holder in Burma, with over US$600 million committed to thirty-eight different projects (mainly hotels, property development and tourism), and two-way trade set to top US$1.5 billion this year (1996).[32] Judging by recent trends, the island state will soon outstrip the UK as the largest foreign investor in Burma.[33] Alongside trade has come increasing military and cultural involvement with Burma, the first evidenced by Singapore's substantial arms supplies to the SLORC since the earliest days of the regime, and the involvement of the Singapore Armed Forces in training *Tatmadaw* special units;[34] the second by the large number of glossy monthly magazines, many directed at the new rich youth in the cities, now published in Singapore for the Burmese market, and the cultural style of the Singapore-based Sedona chain of hotels, now with properties in both Rangoon and Mandalay, whose advertising boasts that it 'aims to export "Singaporeana" through Sedona … with the aim of *creating a Singapore within its hotels* [emphasis added]'.[35]

There is no doubt that ASEAN membership, which may come as soon as July 1997, will speed Rangoon's diplomatic, political, and even cultural, integration into the region, but is involvement with what is fast becoming a narco-dictatorship really an asset to ASEAN? With so much profit being generated by the drugs' trade, and few alternatives in sight until the gas-fields in the Andaman Sea come on line at the end of the decade,[36] will there be any incentive for the SLORC to address the root causes of Burma's domestic crisis, the only remedy for which, Smith argues, is political: namely, the peaceful restoration of the economic, social, cultural and political rights of the ethnic minorities, along the lines envisaged by U Aung San in 1947? Indeed, as Daw Aung San Suu Kyi stresses, until a peaceful settlement is found for the armed conflict in the countryside and a dialogue opened with the democratic opposition in the cities, Burma will have precious little to contribute to ASEAN.[37]

It could even be a destabilising influence, as can be seen from its close relationship with China, a relationship chronicled in detail by Chi-shad Liang in Chapter 3. Whereas other ASEAN countries, especially Indonesia, have become increasingly alarmed over China's claims in the South China Sea,[38] Burma has been deepening its economic and strategic dependence on its great northern neighbour. Nearly US$2 billion of Chinese arms have been acquired by the SLORC since 1988, and the value of cross-border trade is now in excess of US$3 billion, with, every year, substantial numbers (25 000–30 000) of Chinese (mainly Yunnanese) businessmen and settlers moving into Mandalay and other Upper Burmese cities, whose drab new quarters now have the grey concrete aspect of dusty Sino-Burman border towns like Shweli and Muse. While ethnic Burman resentment of the Chinese is on the rise, Chinese military influence in Burma has grown apace, an influence seen most tangibly in the establishment of Chinese supplied radar and naval installations at Bassein and offshore islands in the Gulf of Martaban, whence Indian Ocean shipping and naval movements can be monitored in a wide arc from the Bay of Bengal to the Straits of Malaka. Given all this, Indonesian Foreign Minister Ali Alatas's declaration in July 1996 that ASEAN needed to maintain its 'constructive engagement' with Burma in order to prevent it falling under China's influence rings rather hollow.[39]

Even if ASEAN countries steadfastly ignore these inconvenient aspects of Rangoon's current regional relationships, can Burma really be presented as an attractive prospect for Southeast Asian businesses, particularly manufacturers whose rate of return on capital is usually much slower than in the real estate, hotels and tourism sectors which have dominated non-oil investments hitherto? A recent *Far Eastern Economic Review* headline said it all: 'Business in Burma: More Pain than Gain'. Stressing the country's huge infrastructural problems (clogged ports, bad roads, insufficient electrical power), lack of human investment (particularly in education, see Carriere, Chapter 8 below), government dominance of international trade (the state sector accounts for more than half of Burma's exports, and more than a third of its imports, having a virtual monopoly over trade in rice, teak and minerals), and lack of foreign exchange, the *Review* report concluded that 'there must be serious doubts about whether Burma ... is on its way to becoming an Asian tiger'.[40] At the same time, a US Embassy survey released in August 1996 warned that the country's economic growth (according to government statistics GDP is currently growing at an average of six percent per annum[41]) is 'unsustainable in the medium to long terms' unless investment in infra-structure and education rises.[42]

CONCLUSIONS

What conclusions can be drawn from all this? That the people of Burma suffer, there is no doubt. The appalling statistics presented by Carriere in his chapter on Burma's 'silent emergency' are evidence of the depth of that suffering, suffering which one Western oil company engineer working in central Burma in 1991 spoke of as worse 'than [anything] I had ever come across ... even in Africa'.[43] Yet Burma is not sub-Saharan Africa. It is, as Carriere points out, a country richly endowed with natural, human and cultural resources. Before the war, not only was it the world's largest rice exporter, but it was also a major producer of oil, teak, lead, tea, tin, tungsten and zinc, and, until recently, could claim one of the highest national literacy rates (78.6 per cent) in the developing world,[44] partly a result of its rich tradition of vernacular education based on the Theravadin Buddhist monasteries and temples. Furthermore, until 1962–3, its domes-tic economy boasted over 12 000 private enterprises, and Burma was men-tioned in the same breath as the Philippines, as one of the two most promising states in Southeast Asia in terms of economic prospects. This was a time when Burma's per caput income exceeded that of South Korea, Taiwan, and Thailand. What went wrong? The answer in a word is poli-tics: the failure of successive governments in Rangoon to construct a polit-ical system and constitutional framework in which all the peoples of Burma could find an honoured home.

As Count Ciano once said, victory has a hundred fathers, but defeat is an orphan. In the case of Burma, many are those who are prepared to apportion blame for the country's plight, few indeed will own responsibil-ity for it. The list of those who can be said to have failed Burma is endless, starting with the last Konbaung monarch and ending with the SLORC, but such an exercise is pointless in the present context. What is required is a route map to the future. This is the task of the present volume.

What contours, then, can we discern amidst the rich detail of the indi-vidual contributions? First, that the current crisis in Burma cannot be solved by palliative measures: neither short-term investment by Burma's Southeast Asian neighbours, nor the respites afforded by the numerous 'standfast' agreements with the minorities, nor even Rangoon's burgeon-ing regional relationships with ASEAN, will lead to lasting political solu-tions. Second, that such solutions can only come from meaningful dialogue between all the principal political parties, and the development of a climate of trust. Third, that the different models proposed by the various contributors are really no more than an accurate reflection of the fundamental unresolved polarities in Burma today, polarities which have brought the country to its knees. While these can be addressed outside the country in academic conferences and publications, like the present volume, the intensity of political repression under the SLORC[45] means they cannot be debated openly where it matters most – in Burma itself (outside the very restricted weekly 'democratic fora' at the gate of Daw Aung San Suu Kyi's house at University Avenue). Unless a real discussion of fundamental political issues is allowed, solutions to Burma's problems will always remain elusive.

On 20 September 1994, ten months before Daw Aung San Suu Kyi's release from six-years' house arrest, two of the most powerful SLORC leaders, Senior General Than Shwe (SLORC chairman) and Lieutenant-General Khin Nyunt (SLORC Secretary-One), met with the opposition leader, to discuss what are still undisclosed matters relating to the junta's strategic, political and economic objectives.[46] Although this meeting was followed up by another the following month (28 October), in which Khin Nyunt also participated, they were to have no sequel. Why? Some pointed to the hard-line advice given by Chinese premier Li Peng during his three-day official visit in late December 1994; others looked to internal SLORC politics and the fear that, once engaged on the path of dialogue, the junta thought they might be on a slippery slope towards official recognition of the democratic opposition; still others that pressure had been put on Khin Nyunt himself for fear that ongoing dialogue with the NLD leader might strengthen his own position within the ruling Council.

Whatever happened, the process was cut short. The result has been continuing political stasis – deadlock not dialogue. In such a situation the only thing that can flourish is fear, a fear born of incomprehension and insecurity. It is perhaps no coincidence here that when Raul Manglapus, then Philippine Foreign Minister, visited Rangoon early in 1992, the SLORC leadership constantly referred to the 1945–6 Nuremberg War Crimes Tribunal, as though a similar fate might lie in store for them should they relax their grip on power.[47] The replacement of fear by trust is a painstaking task, one which requires quite unusual reserves of patience and humanity. This is recognised by the NLD leadership, in particular by Daw Aung San Suu Kyi, who has shown exemplary forbearance and civil courage in the pursuit of meaningful dialogue with the military. In this context, Senior Minister Lee Kuan Yew's remarks about the opposition leader being found 'impotent to lead the country' seem wide of the mark.[48]

The willingness to seek consensus and agreement rather than confrontation is the hallmark of a mature politician, one who has the concerns of the wider national community, rather than mere personal survival, at heart. Moreover, the results of the May 1990 election must weigh heavy here. How many Southeast Asian leaders would get a similar vote of confidence today were they to put themselves to the test of a genuinely popular ballot? How many would be in line for the Nobel Peace Prize for showing outstanding civic courage? It is this, too, which sets Daw Aung San Suu Kyi apart from Megawati Sukarnoputri, a still relatively untested figure in Indonesian politics. Here lies the rub. With relatively few exceptions – Thailand and the Philippines perhaps – current Southeast Asian regimes find the idea of popular democracy deeply unsettling. The lengths to which President Suharto has recently gone in his battle against Megawati's leadership of the far from threatening Indonesian Democracy Party (PDI) shows just how inimical he is to the prospect of open contest for presidential office. All sorts of explanations have been advanced, many not so different from the SLORC's 'three sacred causes',[49] in rejecting the suitability of such democratic forms in Indonesia. This suggests that, while present-day SLORC-ruled Burma may be an uncomfortable presence in ASEAN, a democratic Burma based on the May 1990 election results might be altogether more challenging.

Now, it may be that the winds of change will sweep through Indonesia and effect a transformation in the character of the political regime there. It may be too that pressures from an increasingly articulate and politically demanding middle class, following the example of their peers in South Korea and Taiwan, will secure a more responsive system of government both in Indonesia and other parts of Southeast Asia (one thinks particularly of the Indochinese states). But the odds on this happening in the immediate future are not good. So, the likelihood of meaningful pressure being placed on the SLORC by its ASEAN partners to open a dialogue with Daw Aung San Suu Kyi is slight. Such pressure can only come from the wider international community, Japan being especially critical here. Steinberg's appraisal of the latter's potential role in facilitating a political opening between the SLORC and the NLD is certainly relevant. So too is his insistence on the need for political reforms to take place before major economic restructuring. Any attempt to reform the Burmese economy in the present situation – however dire the suffering of the Burmese people – would only strengthen the current military regime, as the then US Permanent Representative to the UN, Madeleine Albright, observed after her visit to Burma in September 1995 when asked how one can help people living under despotism, without helping the despots themselves.[50]

This classic dilemma has been confronted elsewhere, notably in pre-1990 South Africa, where the apartheid regime was ultimately forced into a political dialogue with Nelson Mandela and the ANC through the effect of international economic sanctions. Such sanctions will not work in the same way in Burma, where – apart from Japan – the West's economic leverage is much smaller (and where consumer/shareholder boycotts of the key oil companies have yet to produce results). At the same time, there is no figure of F.W. de Klerk's stature in the ruling junta to reach out to the opposition (although Khin Nyunt might well have become such if the September–October 1994 meetings with Daw Aung San Suu Kyi had been allowed to continue – which is precisely why they were probably aborted by the other SLORC members). Yet pressure on the regime both from within and without is still the only way forward. One must be prepared for the long haul.

In this struggle for justice and peace in Burma, the power of the spirit will ultimately weigh more than than the power of the sword. Threats may instil temporary obedience, but lasting authority can only come from respect. Fearlessness, courage and leadership are key elements here, as Daw Aung San Suu Kyi herself has shown.[51] When the forces of repression are in the ascendant, courage must be renewed from day to day. In such a situation, it is easy to give way to despair, but even the smallest dawn will eventually transform the longest night.

Notes

1. Martin Smith, *Burma: Insurgency and the Politics of Ethnicity* (London: Zed Books, 1991), pp. 118–21.
2. Ibid., p. 121.
3. Aung San Suu Kyi, *Freedom from Fear and Other Writings* (Harmondsworth: Penguin, 2nd edn., 1995) p. 188, pp. 194–5.
4. See Victor B. Lieberman, *Burmese Administrative Cycles: Anarchy and Conquest, c. 1580–1760* (Princeton: Princeton UP, 1984), index under: '*ahmú-dàns*' and 'service system'.
5. Robert Taylor, personal communication, 26 May 1996.
6. See further John McBeth and Bertil Lintner, 'Model State: Burma's Generals Want Indonesian-style Politics', *FEER*, 17 August 1995, p. 27.
7. Reported in *Irrawaddy*, 4.12 (30 June 1996), p. 17.
8. Bertil Lintner, *Outrage: Burma's Struggle for Democracy* (Bangkok: White Lotus, 1990), pp. 67–8. On the dismissal of administrative personnel, see below Chapter 6, p. 169.
9. The official exchange rate is currently (September 1996), Kt5.6: US$1.00, whereas the black market rate is Kt125: US$1.00, and has gone as low as Kt172: US$1.00 in July 1996 due to the poor rice harvest (about a third is estimated to have been destroyed by an insect plague) and rumours that the

junta was planning to fund a 60 per cent pay rise for civil servants on 1 August 1996 by printing more money, see *FEER*, 4 July 1996, p. 12; *FEER*, 25 July 1996, p. 12; and *FEER*, 15 August 1996, p. 64. *Burma Debate*, 3.3 (May–June 1996), p. 39, gives a Kt200: US$1.00 exchange rate for June 1996.

10. Although the government only admits to a year on inflation rate of 20–30 per cent (based on the official consumer price index), real rates of inflation are currently 35–45 per cent, the highest in Southeast Asia, see EIU, 'Country Report: Myanmar (Burma)', 1st Quarter 1996, pp. 3, pp. 17–18; US Embassy (Rangoon), 'Foreign Economic Trends Report: Burma', p. 137; and below, Chapter 8, n. 3.

11. Burma's defence expenditure has been recently estimated at 48 per cent of the total government budget, not counting capital expenditure for the purchase of Chinese-supplied weaponry and so on, see US Embassy (Rangoon), 'Foreign Economic Trends Report', quoted in Deborah Charles, 'US Says Burma Economy Unstable under Forced Rule', Reuters, 6 August 1996. See also Martin Smith, *Fatal Silence? Freedom of Expression and the Right to Health in Burma* (London: Article 19, July 1996), p. 34.

12. *Burma Debate*, 3.3 (May–June 1996), p. 29; Smith, *Fatal Silence?*, p. 34 cites the slightly lower figure of 152 per cent for 1992, but warns that projections indicate it could climb to 200 per cent by 1996.

13. Statement of Kent Wiedemann (Deputy Assistant Secretary of State, Bureau of East Asian and Pacific Affairs [presently US Chargé d'Affaires in Myanmar]), *Burma Debate*, 3.3 (May–June 1996), p. 37.

14. G.E. Harvey, *History of Burma* (London: Longman, 1925), pp. 360–1.

15. There is an interesting parallel here with New Order Indonesia, where, confronted by Western critics of its July 1976 annexation of the former Portuguese colony of East Timor, government spokesmen in Jakarta had taken to referring to the problem as a 'regional question' (*unsur kedaerahan*), rather than one of national self-determination; see Carey and Carter Bentley (eds), *East Timor at the Crossroads*, p. 2.

16. See Chapter 2, n. 6.

17. See *Burma Debate*, 3.2 (March–April 1996), p. 29; and Smith, *Fatal Silence?*, ch. 7.

18. Compare Harvey, *Burma*, p. 361, who spoke of, 'the remote areas, perhaps the greater part of the country, escap[ing] the king's attention; here men breathed more freely, the good qualities of the people asserted themselves, the administration of the local magnates was reasonable, and the peasantry were probably more comfortable...'

19. See Smith, *Fatal Silence?*, p. 60, p. 80 n. 10, who states that, as of May 1996, seventeen of the twenty largest armed opposition groups in Burma, with over 50 000 men under arms, have ceasefires with the SLORC. Those yet to agree such an arrangement include the KNU, Nationalist Socialist Council of Nagaland and Rohingya Solidarity Alliance. As of January 1996, the ceasefire agreed between the SLORC and the Karenni National Progressive Party (KNPP) on 21 March 1995 had also broken down due to clashes over the use of civilians for forced labour and porterage, and access to teak forest and other resources.

20. Karen National Union, *Report the Facts. The Yadana Gas Pipeline Construction in Tavoy District. Tenasserim Division* (Mergui/Tavoy: KNU, 1996). See also below, Chapter 4, n. 46.

21. Nussara Sawatsang and Saritdet Marukatat, 'Unstable Burma is Worthless to ASEAN Says Suu Kyi', *Bangkok Post*, 11 July 1996.

22. S. Jayasankaran, 'Seeing Red: Lobby Groups Protest over Burmese Visit', *FEER*, 29 August 1996, p. 18.

23. Gordon Fairclough, 'Good Connections: Firms Linked to Junta Draw Lion's Share of Business', *FEER*, 15 August 1996, p. 67.

24. *FEER*, 5 September 1996, p. 12.

25. Smith, *Fatal Silence?*, p. 95.

26. 'A Strange Kind of Non-Interference', *Irrawaddy*, 4.12 (30 June 1996), p. 18, quoting *The Nation* (Bangkok).

27. See Smith, *Fatal Silence?*, pp. 92–8; Ta Saw Lu, *The Bondage of Opium: The Agony of the Wa People* (United Wa State Party, Foreign Affairs Department, 1993); and Benjamin Min, 'The Bondage of Opium: The Agony of the Wa People. A Proposal and a Plea', *Burma Debate*, 2.1 (February–March 1995), pp. 14–17.

28. See *Burma Debate*, 3.2 (March–April 1996), p. 29; and, 3.3 (May–June 1996), p. 36.

29. Smith, *Fatal Silence?*, p. 98.

30. (Ibid.), pp. 97–8; EIU, 'Country Report: Myanmar (Burma)', 1st Quarter 1996, p. 10; Chao-Tzang Yawnghwe, 'Shan Opium Politics: The Khun Sa Factor', *Burma Debate*, 2.1 (February–March 1995), pp. 22–8; and Adrian Cowell, 'Silver Jubilee of the "War on Drugs"', *Burma Debate*, 3.2 (March–April 1996), pp. 12–20.

31. Smith, *Burma*, pp. 315, 376.

32. EIU, 'Country Report: Myanmar (Burma)', 2nd Quarter 1996, p. 19; *The Irrawaddy*, 4.12 (June 1996), p. 18, quoting *The Nation* (Bangkok).

33. According to recently released government data, out of US\$895 million in new foreign direct investment (FDI) approved in the first five months of 1996, Singapore was the largest investor with US\$293 million, followed by the UK (US\$211 million) and Malaysia (US\$193 million), see *Malaysian Business Times*, 14 August 1996. It should be noted that most of what is listed in Burma as 'UK investment' is mostly offshore (that is, the Bahamas, Cayman Isles, Isle of Man, Channel Islands) and does not originate in the UK at all.

34. See Andrew Selth, 'The Myanmar Army Since 1988: Acquisitions and Adjustments', *Contemporary Southeast Asia*, 17.3 (December 1995), pp. 248, 250–1; Bertil Lintner, *Outrage*, p. 140; and ibid, 'Consolidating Power', *FEER* (5 October 1989), p. 23.

35. I am grateful to Dr Anna J. Allott, Emeritus Reader in Burmese at the School of Oriental and African Studies, London, for this quote. On the popularity of monthly magazines, see her *Inked Over, Ripped Out: Burmese Storytellers and the Censors* (New York: PEN American Center, 1993), pp. 18–19.

36. See *Burma Debate*, 3.3 (May–June 1996), p. 32, citing Unocal President, John F. Imle's, Testimony to the US Senate Committee on Banking, Housing and Urban Affairs (Hearing on Burma), 22 May 1996, in which he

reported that 'no significant income is expected to be generated [from the natural gas fields] until the year 2000, and it will be another three years ... before the partners [Total, Unocal, Myanmar Oil and Gas Enterprise, and the Petroleum Authority of Thailand Exploration and Production] expect to recover their original investments'. According to the KNU (*Report the Facts*, p. 20), the Burmese government stands to gain US$400 million in annual revenue from concession and right-of-way fees, share of sales revenues etc, a sum which is disputed by a recent *FEER* report (15 August 1996, p. 66), which gives the much lower figure of US$100 million.

37. See above, n. 21.
38. In August 1996, a top Indonesian stategist warned that Southeast Asian countries may have to prepare themselves for 'a possible military confrontation with China' over seabed resources; see, Rizal Sukma, 'Indonesia Toughens China Stance', *FEER*, 5 September 1996, p. 28. On ASEAN's concerns regarding China's moves in May 1996 to extend its maritime boundaries to include the Paracel Islands, see *FEER*, 1 August 1996, p. 15.
39. Barry Wain, 'ASEAN Diplomatic Values', *Asian Wall Street Journal*, 20–1 July 1996, quoted in *Irrawaddy*, 4.13 (31 July 1996), p. 2.
40. Gordon Fairclough, 'Enter at Own Risk', *FEER*, 15 August 1996, pp. 62–5.
41. EIU, 'Country Report: Myanmar (Burma)', 2nd Quarter 1996, p. 16.
42. *FEER*, 15 August 1996, p. 63; and see above n. 11.
43. Yan Ko Naing, 'Tough Going for Oilmen in Burma', *The Nation* (Bangkok), Business Section, 2 October 1991.
44. Smith, *Fatal Silence?*, p. 34.
45. Recent legislation has made open political discussion even harder: on 7 June 1996, the SLORC issued Law no. 5/96, which threatens a twenty-year prison sentence to anyone expressing their views publicly, see Amnesty International, *Myanmar: Renewed Repression* (London: Amnesty International, 10 July 1996), p. 1.
46. Bertil Lintner, 'Lip Service: Generals Open Dialogue with Aung San Suu Kyi', *FEER*, 6 October 1994, pp. 21–4.
47. Kavi Chongkittavorn, 'Asean's Links with Burma May Strain Ties with West', *The Nation*, 28 July 1992; Aung San Suu Kyi, 'Towards a True Refuge', Eighth Joyce Pearce Memorial Lecture (Oxford: Refugee Studies Programme with the Perpetua Press, 1993), p. 32.
48. Senior Minister Lee Kuan Yew seems to have a penchant for passing snap judgements on situations and countries where subsequent political developments have turned out very differently from his predictions: one recalls here his views about the Khmer Rouge in Cambodia, where he reportedly asserted that they would win 15 per cent of the vote in the general elections of May 1993 and would have to be brought into the government. In fact, they boycotted the elections, have since split apart (July 1996), and are now a rapidly declining force in the political life of the country.
49. See below, Chapter 6, n. 14.
50. Madeleine Albright, 'Burmese Daze', *New Republic*, 4 December 1995, quoted in Smith, *Fatal Silence?*, p. 115.
51. Aung San Suu Kyi, 'Freedom from Fear', in her *Freedom from Fear and Other Writings*, pp. 180–5.

Part I
Politics and
Constitution-making

1 The National Convention: an Impediment to the Restoration of Democracy[1]

Janelle M. Diller

DEVELOPMENTS LEADING TO THE NATIONAL CONVENTION

Nearly six years after the 1990 elections, Burma's military rulers continue to refuse to seat the People's Assembly elected in 1990. A constitution-drafting exercise, known as the National Convention, stands as the response of the military junta, called the State Law and Order Restoration Council (SLORC), to the 1990 landslide election victory of the National League for Democracy (NLD). The National Convention, now in its fourth year, was conceived by the SLORC as a mechanism to draft a new constitution for the country in accordance with military wishes.

Two months after the May 1990 elections for a parliamentary assembly (*Pyithu Hluttaw*),[2] the SLORC unilaterally decided not to convene the assembly immediately but rather to require the writing of a new constitution as a pre-condition to a transfer of power to an elected government.[3] In its Declaration 1/90, the SLORC stated that 'the representatives elected by the people are responsible for drafting a constitution for the future democratic state.'[4]

Fifteen months later, despite earlier promises that the new parliament would be 'independent' and 'unrestricted· in writing a constitution',[5] the SLORC announced that it would call a National Convention to be attended by 702 delegates, including elected representatives.[6] Based upon the Convention's consensus, the elected representatives would draft a new constitution with 'all necessary assistance' and 'suggestions' from the SLORC,[7] in a process which could take five to ten years.[8]

In 1994, two years after the National Convention began, a SLORC minister announced that the junta planned to propose a new constitution that would be adopted by referendum and then hold a general election in accordance with the new charter.[9] None the less, some observers have speculated that the risk of losing a referendum may turn the SLORC to yet another strategy: submittal of the new charter for ratification by a constituent assembly elected under restrictive rules now provided by the National Convention 'guidelines' which, for example, require candidates to have military experience. Under either scenario, yet another election to form a governing assembly would ensue before the SLORC would transfer power, at least in name, and the 1990 elected body would apparently never be convened.

THE NATIONAL CONVENTION

As set forth below, the SLORC has muffled the very political representatives whose active contribution is essential to the process of legitimate constitution making. Political leaders are marginalised into a permanent minority within the National Convention. In addition, the SLORC has imposed severe restrictions on Convention delegates to prevent free discussion and informed decision-making. In response to pleas for a genuine political dialogue, the SLORC has proffered the Convention as the only forum for dialogue. The Convention has also served as a stalling device to continue the government's methodical attempt to dismantle independent political organisation and activity. As the Convention enters its third year, a crackdown on political dissent is increasing in the aftermath of the NLD's 86-delegate expulsion from the Convention on 30 November 1995. At the same time, SLORC-controlled decisions within the Convention embed a constitutionally-entrenched permanent role for the military and its supporters in the government of the nation.

Supplanting the Will of the People Expressed by Electoral Mandate

Permanent Minority Role for Elected Representatives
Through the vehicle of the Convention, the SLORC has attempted to side-step the mandate of the 1990 elections in which the people expressed their will for a civilian democratic government. It has repeatedly rejected requests by the NLD to convene the elected People's Assembly (*Pyithu Hluttaw*), the most recent of which was made on 25 March 1996.[10] Instead, the SLORC created the constitution-drafting National Convention with elected representatives permanently in the minority.

At the start of the Convention in 1993, only about 15 per cent of all delegates were representatives elected in 1990, in marked contrast to the NLD's win of 82 per cent of the seats in the People's Assembly.[11] In the 1990 elections, the National League for Democracy (NLD) won 392 of

485 contested parliamentary seats. Other pro-democracy parties took many of the remaining seats, including the Shan Nationalities League for Democracy (SNLD) with twenty-three seats, while the military-backed party, the National Unity Party (NUP), won only ten seats. At the National Convention, however, the People's Assembly elected representatives serve on only two out of the eight groups at the Convention: the 'Members of Parliament [MPs]-Elect' group and the 'Political Parties' group. Other delegates, hand-picked by the SLORC, form the other six groups at the Convention: national races, peasants, workers, intelligentsia and technocrats, public service personnel, and other invitees.

On 30 November 1995, the SLORC expelled the eighty-six NLD delegates who had boycotted the Convention for two days following the SLORC's summary denial of an NLD request to review the Convention's working procedures. The expulsion has highlighted the lack of any meaningful representation at the Convention. The MPs elected in 1990 now constitute less than 3 per cent of the total current delegates to the Convention.[12] The expulsion followed the NLD's written request to speak to the 'views of the Working Committee of the National Convention' as an organisation 'in favour of the successful implementation of the National Convention'.[13] When the SLORC refused, the NLD announced its intention not to continue attendance at the Convention. The SLORC's Work Committee then revoked the delegacy of the NLD delegates because they had failed to request permission for their two-day absence from the Convention, as required by the Convention Rules.[14] It is a matter of speculation whether the remaining elected delegates from the SNLD and other ethnically-based parties are acting in co-ordination with the NLD, or whether they believe they can wrest some meaningful concession at the Convention.

The NLD's rationale for its bold move was signalled in an earlier press conference in which NLD General Secretary Daw Aung San Suu Kyi expressed the party's concern that the National Convention had not realised the leading role of political parties in constitution drafting that had been outlined in SLORC's Declaration 1/90 that followed the election.[15] Other concerns included the permanent minority role of political parties and the imposition of SLORC's objectives and working procedures for the Convention.[16] Following the walk-out, NLD leaders announced that the boycott of the National Convention will last 'until such time as a dialogue is held on national reconciliation, the genuine multi-party democracy system, and the drafting of a constitution which is supported and trusted by the people'.[17] Daw Aung San Suu Kyi reiterated that 'at the moment the NLD has only said that they will not be attending the

Convention until such time as a proper dialogue has been successfully achieved ... It would be regrettable and sad, indeed, if elections had been held in 1990 to hoodwink the people of Burma and the world'.[18]

The SLORC's expulsion and harsh public response to the NLD's boycott demonstrates the military leaders' inability to accept that, as elected representatives, the party's actions are based on its authority mandated by the people. The leading government newspaper, *New Light of Myanmar*, characterised the NLD's request to reply to the Convention's Work Committee as actions that 'were made with intent to mar the successes achieved so far by the National Convention ... their National League for Democracy would replace [the NC] with a Convention they would be able to dominate as they like, giving priority to promotion of the interests of their party'.[19] The government media promised that the armed forces would 'resolutely take action against and annihilate those who mar or disturb the interest of the entire nation.'[20] Post-boycott attempts to vilify Daw Aung San Suu Kyi in the government press included an article casting the political leader as Maung Ba Than, a reviled nineteenth-century traitor who helped British forces conquer Burma in 1885–6.[21]

Restrictions on Freedoms of Convention Delegates
Along with a minority role for elected representatives, the SLORC created a working atmosphere for the Convention that punishes free thought and discussion and rejects independent decision-making. Six months before the opening of the National Convention, the SLORC held preparatory meetings to establish the operating rules of the meeting.[22] As in the Convention itself, the NLD representatives who attended the preparatory meetings were under-represented among political party delegates and delegates at large.[23] The decisions imposed were telling: there would be no immunity from prosecution for statements made at the Convention, only those with 'a positive stand' would be welcome and no instigating of unrest would be allowed.[24]

The National Convention delegates live and work in an environment that suppresses debate and prevents delegates from taking papers from the meeting room to their lodging areas.[25] At the opening of the Convention, the SLORC distributed Convention regulations to all delegates requiring that all speeches for debate be pre-cleared by the chairmen of the groups concerned. The rules forbid walk-outs, individually or in groups, and any other shows of protest, and also prohibit delegates from distributing leaflets, wearing badges, bringing in papers which are not approved by the

SLORC Oversight Committee, and lobbying or influencing other representatives.[26] Prior review of all speeches made was required.[27]

The SLORC has not hesitated to use the criminal arm of state justice to enforce the Convention's strict rules. In 1994, one NLD delegate, U Aung Khin Sint, was sentenced to twenty years in prison for allegedly publishing leaflets critical of the junta's role in the National Convention.[28]

No signs of relaxation of the restrictions are in sight. As if to excuse its actions, the SLORC stated in late November 1995 that, with

> ten political parties and many indigenous groups returning to the legal fold ... it has become necessary ... to develop principles and procedures to avoid extremes in flexibility in order to ensure the development of the genuine multiparty system we aspire to. No one disputes or dislikes our goal – the emergence of a democratic nation. We may have a common goal, but *we must avoid the mistake of being too earnest about reaching our goal* [emphasis added].[29]

Obstructing Genuine Dialogue

The government has roundly rebuffed any calls for negotiations among the SLORC, the NLD and its leader Daw Aung San Suu Kyi and representatives of ethnic nationalities, even from highly respected elders in the country. Daw Aung San Suu Kyi repeatedly expressed a desire for dialogue in the period between her release from house arrest in July 1995 and NLD's expulsion in November 1995. In late November 1995, twenty-three senior Burmese independence leaders and politicians signed a letter urging the SLORC and the NLD, led by Daw Aung San Suu Kyi, to hold a dialogue 'for the sake of the people and the country'.[30] In a meeting with the SLORC and its criminal investigators to which the authors of the letter were summoned, the SLORC threatened the elders and called them 'stooges'.[31] Also in late November 1995, the SNLD made an appeal to Senior General Than Shwe and Daw Aung San Suu Kyi to strive together for national reconciliation.[32]

Pressure on the SLORC to enter into dialogue with pro-democracy activists has come from various foreign states and the UN as well.[33] Both the UN General Assembly and the Human Rights Commission have called on the government to do so. Several months ago, the General Assembly urged the government 'to engage, at the earliest possible date, in a substantive political dialogue with Daw Aung San Suu Kyi and other political leaders, including representatives of ethnic groups, as the best means of promoting national reconciliation and the full and early restoration of democracy'.[34]

To all these pleas, the SLORC's answer has been constant: the National Convention is the only forum for dialogue. The answer leaves unaddressed the fact that Daw Aung San Suu Kyi – and now her party as well – play no role in the National Convention. Yet Daw Aung San Suu Kyi remains convinced that a dialogue is inevitable, and even the SLORC leaves open such a possibility. Following the NLD's expulsion and satire against SLORC at a private New Year's party held at the NLD leader's home,[35] the official media stated:

> If she [Aung San Suu Kyi] had remained ... patient ... the dialogue she desires so much would have already been in progress ... even now she fails to anticipate that the military leadership, well aware of their responsibilities, may yet be contemplating such a dialogue ... and foolishly goes on to antagonize them with her strident demands and invectives.[36]

In an interview before the expulsion, Daw Aung San Suu Kyi reportedly stated that '[d]ialogue is a way of finding a solution that will benefit all sides, that will be acceptable to all sides, and we think that they will see in time that this is what dialogue is about, but we would like them to see it sooner rather than later.'[37] As long as the National Convention continues in its current form, it appears that 'sooner' will become 'later'.

Dismantling Political Structures and Suppressing Independent Activity

Now entering its fourth year of an unspecified time table, the National Convention has helped the SLORC gain time in its efforts to suppress independent political structures and activities. The SLORC's Election Commission officially recognised the results of the election shortly after the vote count but has yet to issue a final report on the 1990 elections.[38]

As detailed below, in the nearly six years since the election, the Election Commission has stripped almost 25 per cent of elected representatives of their elected status, banned half of those from participating in future elections, and de-registered more than 80 per cent of the parties that participated in the 1990 elections. In addition, the government has implemented a policy of retaliation against individual activists, particularly those in the NLD party, taking the form of arrests, detention, denial of education and economic necessities, and violent threats.

Nullification of Elected Candidates' Status

Since the election in 1990, the SLORC has systematically cancelled the elected status of winning candidates and, in more than half the cases, forbidden the candidate from running in future elections, either for ten years or permanently. More than three-quarters of the nullifications were based on the fact that SLORC had charged or convicted the winners of criminal offences. However, in most of those cases, reliable information reveals that the conduct complained of amounted to nothing more than a peaceful exercise of freedom of expression, association and assembly and the criminal charges do not meet internationally recognisable standards.

SLORC's nullification campaign has left vacant at least ninety-four of a total of 485 seats[39] in the membership of the yet-to-be convened parliamentary assembly, and disbarred at least forty-nine MPs from running for another election, half for a ten-year period and the rest permanently.[40] The nullifications were based on a variety of reasons. In the vast majority of cases (seventy-four out of ninety-four identifiable cases), the Election Commission nullified the elected status of winners after they were charged or convicted of criminal offences.[41] The NLD party has suffered the overwhelming majority of arrested and convicted MPs.[42] Indeed, top NLD leader Daw Aung San Suu Kyi was disqualified as a candidate prior to the election, first on the ground of alleged allegiance with a foreign country and, on appeal, because of alleged links to outlawed organisations in armed revolt against the state.[43]

Many of the nullifications imposed after the election were based on charges under two key laws: section 122-1 of the Penal Code and the 1950 Emergency Provisions Act. Twenty-seven MPs were charged with violations under section 122-1 of the Penal Code, which reads: 'Whoever commits High Treason within the Union of Burma shall be punished with death'.[44] The SLORC reportedly commuted death sentences passed by civilian courts.[45] Eighteen other MPs were charged under the 1950 Emergency Provisions Act, of which two commonly used sections read:

> If anything is done intentionally to spread false news knowing it to be false or having reason to believe that it is false, or if any act which is likely to cause the same is done; ... he shall be punished with imprisonment for a term which may extend to 7 years, or with fine or with both.

> He who ... causes or intends to disrupt the morality or the behavior of a group of people or the general public, or to disrupt the security or the

reconstruction of stability of the Union: ... such a person shall be sentenced to seven years in prison, fine or both.[46]

Along with exercising its authority to nullify elected status, the Election Commission also exercised retroactively its authority under Election Law amendments to ban qualification to run in future elections.[47] The Commission imposed a permanent ban on twenty-four MPs from running in future elections[48] and a ten-year ban on standing for election in twenty-five other cases.[49] The SLORC granted the Commission authority to ban the running in future elections more than one year *after* the 1990 elections but applied retroactively to the candidates who won the 1990 elections.[50] Of the other twenty cases of nullification, at least eight occurred due to death of the candidates.[51] One of the MPs, NLD leader U Tin Maung Win, died while held in custody on 18 January 1991.[52]

Deregistration of Political Parties
Since the 1990 election the SLORC has engaged in a similar dismantling of the multi-party structure that developed in the context of the 1990 election. As of the time of writing (March 1996), only ten of the ninety-five political parties which contested the 1990 elections remain as lawfully functioning parties.[53] In order after order, the Election Commission abolished political parties, in many case for reasons apparently not provided by law.[54] In some cases, the reasons for deregistration appeared to come from SLORC's own *ad hoc* philosophies and no prior notice or opportunity to appeal was given to the organisations. For example, in striking nine political parties, including the Union Nationalities League for Democracy (UNLD), a multi-ethnic coalition organisation that won one seat in the election, the SLORC announced:

> In scrutinizing political parties, it has been found that some have been unable to present specific party membership and party branch lists. Some have been unable to specify their party's political aims and objectives, while some of its responsible personnel have been found to be lacking in abiding with [*sic*] existing laws. Others have neglected their organizational activities because they thought their party's standing was based on representatives' being elected... The Commission believes that in implementing a compact and stable democratic system, such political parties should not be allowed to continue to exist.[55]

Even organisations which won seats in the 1990 elections were subject to summary abolition.[56] Other organisations were deregistered because they were 'unable to form at least 10 party organizations' or because they had no one elected in the 1990 election.[57] In contrast, three of the ten remaining political parties failed to win seats but inexplicably were not deregistered. As of March 1996, the ten legally existing political parties were: the NLD, SNLD, NUP, United Karen League, Union Pa-O National Organisation, Shan State Kokang Democratic Party, Mro O Khami Unity Organisation, Kokang Democracy and Unity Party, Lahu National Development Party, and the Wa National Development Party.[58] All but the NLD and the NUP represent the parties of ethnic nationalities.

Political Restrictions on Parties and Activists
Even for the remaining political parties, maintaining independent party life is nearly impossible because of goverment-imposed restrictions. Government surveillance of political parties is intense and reportedly has increased for NLD members since the NLD expulsion from the Convention.[59] Leaders of some political parties are not allowed to travel except with military permission.[60] Organising activities like distribution of party literature to the public, printing or photocopying bulletins and statements, and assembling in groups of five or more are prohibited without government permission.[61] Notable exceptions include the NUP's distribution of literature and holding of meetings, and the weekend gatherings of several thousand people outside the home of Daw Aung San Suu Kyi to hear the NLD leader speak and respond to letters sent.[62] None the less, recent reports indicate that barbed wire barricades are placed along both sides of the road on weekends during the NLD leader's addresses and observers report a feeling of tight military scrutiny; the placement of the wires led to a protest that left three NLD supporters jailed.[63] In a veiled threat, the government-controlled media reported that '[t]his group that blocks the road is ... conspiring to sabotage the success so far achieved at the National Convention'.[64]

Of serious import is the interference with party structures themselves. The NLD's attempt to reinstate Daw Aung San Suu Kyi as their General Secretary, following her forced removal during her six years of house arrest, was reportedly rejected by the SLORC Election Commission.[65] Vacancies in the central executive committees of the parties are reportedly not allowed to be filled;[66] if the committee drops below a certain minimum, the party is abolished.

Along with revoking the status of winners and political parties, the government has implemented a policy of retaliation against individual activists, particularly those in the NLD party. The retaliation has taken various forms, including arrest, detention, denial of educational or economic benefits, and violent threats. Among at least eighty MPs that have suffered arrest, detention and, in some cases, criminal convictions, fifteen remain in detention and nineteen members were arrested in the crackdown in late May at the time of the NLD Convention.[67] Although over 2000 political detainees have been released since April 1992, including Daw Aung San Suu Kyi in July 1995, hundreds, and perhaps thousands, of political prisoners remain detained, serving long sentences.[68] Along with political leaders, political prisoners include Buddhist monks, students, journalists, labourers and people from various classes and professionals.[69]

Since the NLD expulsion from the National Convention, a significant crackdown on NLD supporters has resulted in a written protest by NLD to Senior General Than Shwe.[70] In a recent incident, an NLD activist was denied counsel in his own defence and sentenced to five years for involvement in a minor car accident, while the son of a senior military officer in a car accident that resulted in a death was granted bail and allowed a lawyer to defend him.[71] NLD leader Daw Aung San Suu Kyi reportedly criticised the activist's trial and sentence as 'sheer lawlessness much worse than anarchy'.[72]

Political activists, in particular NLD supporters, and their children suffer discrimination in receiving equal economic and educational access. Reliable sources report that, in many townships, members of the NLD are debarred from taking part in meetings of Parents and Teachers Associations to plan educational projects, reflecting a built-in bias against those who desire to work toward democratisation. In addition, political activists are not eligible for training or receiving contracts from UN agencies and are passed over in favour of township military leaders and persons close to village authorities.

Ensuring Permanent Military Control over Law and Politics

Constitutional Principles that Entrench Military Control
The SLORC has insisted that the National Convention adopt principles that will permanently ensure military control over civilian executive and legislative bodies at all levels of government.[73] To do so, the SLORC has required that all constitutional principles at the Convention conform with a key objective: to provide a leading role for the military in the political life of Burma.[74] Substantial yet unsuccessful resistance by elected representatives and political parties to the notion of a leading military role was reported early in the Convention process. Even as recently as December 1995, a Convention delegate representing the SNLD report-

edly stated that principles should serve as bases for the constitution only when they stand the 'test of the fundamental principle "sovereignty resides in the citizens,"'[75] a position which was not adopted. More recently still (March 1996) thirty delegates from five political parties objected to military appointments and called for all representatives to be popularly elected.[76]

As stated in the government-controlled media, '[t]he *Tatmadaw*'s responsibilities are not over with the writing of a firm constitution. It must take suitable responsibilities.'[77] Rather than leaving the 'suitable responsibilities' for future delineation, the SLORC has ensured that the National Convention's principles are so detailed that little discretion can be left to future drafters. Among those principles are provisions authorising the military to exercise emergency powers during 'states of emergency' broadly defined as situations in which lives, shelter, or property are threatened in a region, state or self-administered area, or where adequate information exists that such threats could occur, or where attempts are made to take sovereign power of state by force, disturbances and violences, or there is a conspiracy to do so.[78]

The guidelines adopted at the National Convention guarantee the military a leading role in government through a series of rules relating to qualifications for office and composition of government bodies.[79] The rules are prescribed for the various units of government, which themselves were set up by the SLORC proposal at the Convention: the central or Union level, state and regional divisions, townships and districts, and self-administered areas created for certain ethnic groups.[80] Despite demands by ethnic nationalities for a federal system granting ethnically diverse areas with greater local autonomy, the SLORC's Convention rules entrench a centrist system of government in which central authorities maintain all residual power and exercise detailed governance over constituent units. Under the SLORC's rules, for example, the country's president will prescribe the number of ministries to be formed at the regional and state level and the national constitution would stipulate the qualifications for region or state chief ministers, ministers, and legislative representatives. In creating the new state structures, the SLORC ruled at the Convention itself on requests by ethnic groups for self-administered areas despite acknowledging the need for updated data; in ruling on the requests of ethnic groups, the SLORC used a formula that resulted in arbitrary denials. For example, along with other denials, no self-administered areas were allowed for Rohingya Muslims in the western Arakan (Rakhine) State of Burma, where local persecution has reportedly been responsible for mass exoduses of refugees in recent years.[81]

The Presidency Despite opposition by elected MPs and political party leaders at the National Convention, the SLORC insisted on a presidential rather than parliamentary system for the country.[82] None the less, even the country's president is to serve at the behest of the military's commander-in-chief. Under principles adopted by the Convention, the president has no authority to reject the selection of, or dismiss from service, the military appointees nominated by the commander-in-chief to serve as ministers of defence, security/home affairs and border affairs.[83]

Qualifications for the country's president have written out Daw Aung San Suu Kyi virtually by name: twenty years continuous residency, political, administrative, military and economic experience, and the president's spouse, children and children's spouses may not be citizens of foreign powers or entitled to rights and privileges as foreign citizens.[84] Despite concerns expressed by the Convention's then elected representatives, election for the country's president is to occur, not directly, but through an electoral college with a strong defence services composition.[85]

Executive bodies in all constituent units across the country are to include military appointees, nominated by the commander-in-chief to undertake responsibilities to defence, security and border administration.[86] At the district and township levels, the defence services role is to be even broader: the commander-in-chief is to assign military personnel to 'participate together with District Administrators in affairs' and not only for 'security' but also for 'enforcement law, regional peace and tranquility'.[87] Like the country's president, the chief ministers of constituent units will be powerless to reject nominations or dismiss military ministers.[88] Restrictive qualifications for ministerial appointments exclude persons who have criminal convictions for any offence, thus barring the many MPs-elect who have been convicted on politically-based charges.[89]

Legislative Power Under the SLORC's Convention 'principles', legislatures at union, region and state levels will have military representatives nominated by the commander-in-chief in ratios preset by the SLORC.[90] In both houses at the union level,[91] military personnel will comprise 33 per cent of the total; at the region and state levels, military nominees will comprise 25 per cent of the total. The SLORC rationale for requiring an unelected legislative power to the country is '[i]n order that the *Tatmadaw* [military] may be able to participate in the national political leadership role of the future state'.[92] The reserved military seats in the legislature were adopted over the objections of five political parties.[93]

The Convention's principles further bar any independent legislative authority over the military and prescribe instead that military matters will be taken up by military legislative representatives in military committees.[94] Restrictive qualifications for union-level representatives are similar to those in the current *Pyithu Hluttaw* Election Law but require, in notable addition, birth to parents who are both Burmese citizens and a clean criminal record.[95] As with the ministerial and presidential posts, MPs-elect who have been the subject of political prosecution will be barred from participation, even if no separate retroactive bar on standing for election has been imposed as we have seen above ('Nullification of Elected Candidates' Status', pp. 33–4). Significantly, defense personnel are not excluded from qualifying for election, unlike the current *Pyithu Hluttaw* Election Law.[96]

Judicial Power In designing the judicial power, the National Convention principles provide that '[t]he Tatmadaw has the right to independently administer all affairs concerning the forces', which presumably excludes ordinary judicial jurisdiction even over common crimes committed by military personnel.[97] The SLORC's plan for judicial power requires that judges not be members of political parties.[98]

Individual Rights and Responsibilities Under the SLORC's prescription, individual rights are seriously limited by being available only 'according to law'. SLORC-sponsored principles emphasise those limitations in such statements as 'necessary laws shall be enacted to ensure the freedom, rights, benefits, responsibilities of and restrictions on citizens' and 'all citizens shall have equal rights [to] freedom of opinion and worship – if they are not against law and order, public morals, public health and other [constitutional] provisions'.[99] Even those rights that will be recognised appear to be granted only to citizens, not all persons within Burma. A limitation based on citizenship is particularly onerous to many ethnic and linguistic minorities living in Burma who have been denied citizenship, either as a matter of law or due to the arbitrary denials of government officials.[100] Notably, one of the duties of 'every citizen' will be to 'learn military science'.[101]

Development of a Nationwide Patronage System for Political Support
In the same year that the National Convention started, the SLORC created (September 1993) a countrywide political association, the Union Solidarity and Development Association (USDA), to serve as a patronage system to buy or force popular allegiance to the SLORC. As of December 1995, the membership of the USDA was reported at two million people, mainly students and other young people.[102] According to corroborated

reports, government employees and students are forced to enroll in the USDA on threat of losing their jobs or opportunities to sit for examination. In other cases, special privileges are given exclusively to USDA members, such as obtaining a passport or buying air tickets easily, and getting preferential consideration for jobs in the public sector.[103]

Although the SLORC called the USDA a 'private association' in its public report to the UN,[104] that image is negated by the praise which SLORC has given the association as 'a national force who [which] will serve the national interests hand in hand with the Defense Services'.[105] Indeed, the SLORC has bluntly stated that the USDA was formed to prevent similar events to those of 1988, when more than 3000 pro-democracy demonstrators were gunned down *en masse.*[106]

In recent months, and especially after expulsion of the NLD from the Convention, the USDA has sponsored forced attendance at mass rallies to support the work of the National Convention and the SLORC has pointedly cited the rallies in support of the proposition that 'the National Convention is meant for the country'.[107] Traders allegedly reported that people are woken early in the morning and put on private vehicles whose owners are press-ganged into transporting others to rallies, and many must spend the whole day without food in a distant location attesting allegiance to the National Convention.[108] Other reports indicate that those who refuse to show for the rallies are subject to Kt50 to Kt500 fines.[109] The SLORC has reported that, in recent rallies, motions have been passed 'to express support for the success of the National Convention' and 'to crush those who are sabotaging the National Convention',[110] and 'oppose and ostracise' them.[111]

CONCLUSIONS OF LAW

Rather than moving Burma toward democracy, the National Convention is impeding the democratisation process by failing to create structures of accountability and transparency and by obstructing processes for growth of independent political life.[112] According to the UN Secretary-General, a durable democratisation process requires, among other elements, the 'establishment of armed forces respectful of the rule of law, the training of police forces that safeguard public freedoms and the setting up of human rights institutions'.[113] If democracy is to function effectively, it requires dialogue – in the Secretary-General's words, 'a political culture of participation and consultation'.[114]

As a participating member of the international community at the World Conference on Human Rights in 1993, Burma committed itself to 'support the strengthening and promoting of democracy, development and respect of human rights and fundamental freedoms in the entire world', including within its own borders.[115] Indeed, as a treaty party to the UN Charter, Burma is bound to promote 'universal respect for, and observance of human rights and fundamental freedoms for all without distinction as to race, sex, language, or religion.'[116] The Universal Declaration of Human Rights (1948) provides an authoritative statement on the rights recognised by the Charter, certain of which have reached the status of customary international law binding on all states, including Burma.[117]

The National Convention and the SLORC's repression of political freedoms and genuine political dialogue violate Burma's UN Charter obligations, illuminated by the Universal Declaration, and its recent affirmations made at the World Conference on Human Rights. The facts detailed above reveal gross violations of political, civil, economic, social and cultural rights.[118] Several are discussed below.

Obstruction of Political and Associational Rights
Among many breaches, the pattern of systematic repression documented above demonstrates the SLORC's deliberate obstruction of the realisation of fundamental political and associational rights. The foundation of fundamental political rights is recognised in article 21(3) of the Universal Declaration, which declares that 'the will of the people shall be the basis of the authority of government [and] shall be expressed in ... genuine elections'. The will of the people for civilian controlled, democratic government was expressed in the landslide win of the NLD and other pro-democracy parties in the 1990 *Pyithu Hluttaw* elections which the SLORC is actively obstructing, as detailed above. The SLORC's compulsory association, the USDA, and its forced mass rallies, grossly violate the related associational right that stipulates that '[n]o one may be compelled to belong to an association'.[119]

The SLORC's practices further breach established norms of non-discrimination with regard to the exercise of political rights. The Convention on the Political Rights of Women, which Burma has signed but not yet ratified,[120] provides that 'women shall be eligible for election to all publicly elected bodies [and entitled to hold public office and exercise all public functions], established by national law, on equal terms with men, without any discrimination'.[121] The General Assembly recently stressed its conviction that equal opportunity for all citizens to become candidates was required in an electoral process to determine the will of the people.[122] The extent to which women are prevented by prejudice, in practice if not by law,[123] from having equal access to government service in elected and appointed posts is unknown given the requirements of various experience, including military service, for the presidency, other elected posts, and all reserved military posts in the legislatures and executive bodies at all government levels.

Violations of Economic and Social Rights

The facts presented also demonstrate violations of the most basic human rights to non-discrimination and equality in economic and social life. The customary norm of non-discrimination is recognised in, among other documents, the UN Charter, the Universal Declaration, and the 1989 Convention on the Rights of the Child, a treaty to which Burma is a party.[124] In the economic sphere, the threat of loss of one's job on the basis of political opinion, and required participation in the USDA and its rallies upon threat of losing one's job, breaches those non-discrimination provisions as well as the right to equal work opportunities recognised in article 23 of the Universal Declaration. The barring of NLD parents from Parent and Teacher Association meetings and compulsory participation in the USDA on threat of refusing opportunities to sit for examinations grossly violates the right of equal access to education, both for children themselves, and for parents in choosing the kind of education to be given their children.[125]

Conclusions

The current National Convention and the social environment surrounding political life in Burma impedes the restoration of democracy and violates Burma's obligations as a member of the international community to promote human rights and fundamental freedoms. If one looks to the future and to a Burma in which the results of the May 1990 elections are honoured and a multi-party democracy restored, then certain steps will need to be taken. Amongst the most important are: the immediate rescission of the SLORC-led National Convention, and its replacement by a *Pyithu Hluttaw* (People's Assembly), in which those MPs and parties elected in May 1990 are represented. Given the need for a new constitution, this assembly could act as Burma's Constituante (Constitutional Convention) until such time as a new constitution has been framed and fresh elections held. In order to achieve this last, the following will have to be undertaken immediately:

1. the release and unconditional pardon of all political prisoners and expungement of all criminal records based on political convictions;

2. the reinstatement of all deregistered parties and recognition of the status of all elected MPs from the May 1990 poll, especially those who have been arbitrarily stripped of their position by the SLORC;

3. the commencement of a substantial political dialogue among the NLD, ethnic representatives and the SLORC to include, among other elements, discussion of the seating of the 1990 *Pyithu Hluttaw*; and, finally,

4. the acceptance of international cooperation and joint action in solving problems respecting human rights and fundamental freedoms, including full co-operation with the UN Secretary-General, UN High Commissioner for Human Rights, UN Special Rapporteur on Myanmar, and the International Committee of the Red Cross.

These may seem bold and ambitious steps in the context of the present political impasse in Burma, but they hold out the only prospect for a future in which the Burmese people themselves will be able to enjoy the true inheritance of their potentially rich country and justify the sacrifices of the generation which won Burma's independence from the British nearly half a century ago and of their successors who keep that promise alive today.

Notes

1. A fuller version of this chapter was published with four appendices under the same title: *The National Convention: An Impediment to the Restoration of Democracy* (henceforth: *National Convention*), by the International Centre for Human Rights and Democratic Development (Montreal, Canada), and by the International League for Human Rights in New York, USA, with the support of the Associates to Develop a Democratic Burma (Shawville, Canada), on 2 April 1996.

2. *Pyithu Hluttaw* Election Law, 31 May 1989, SLORC Law no. 14/89; for full text, see Diller, *National Convention*, Annex I.

3. 'Full Text' of SLORC Announcement' 1/90, July 27, 1990 (henceforth: 'Declaration 1/90'), *FBIS-EAS-90-146*, para. 18. The SLORC unilaterally announced in the same declaration that 'the wish of the majority of political parties that contested in the multi-party democratic general elections is to draw up a new constitution.' Several years later, the SLORC explained that '[t]he 1947 and 1974 constitutions emerged in accordance with the times. They cannot be applied any more because of the changing and developing situations over the years', see 'Myo Nyunt Speaks at National Convention', Radio Rangoon, 2 September 1994, reported in *FBIS-EAS-94-173*, 7 September 1994.

4. Declaration 1/90, para. 18. The decision to have the elected representatives draft a new constitution was inconsistent with the terms of the Election Law, see n. 1 above, in which SLORC stated that the assembly being

elected was the *Pyithu Hluttaw*, a population-based parliamentary assembly that had existed as a state governing structure since independence.

5. Agence France Presse (henceforth: 'AFP'), 28 May 1990 (report of statement of U Kyaw San, SLORC Information Committee and quoting Colonel Ye Htut, SLORC Information Committee, saying, 'If we offer ideas, we'll be imposing our will on them [the elected representatives]').

6. Address by Foreign Minister U Ohn Gyaw to the UN General Assembly, 4 October 1991 (copy on file with the International League for Human Rights).

7. Ibid.

8. *South China Morning Post*, 11 September 1991.

9. 'Myanmar's Junta Plans Referendum on Constitution', 4 December 1994, Kyodo News International (Asian Political News), Tokyo (henceforth: 'Kyodo'), reporting statement of National Planning and Economic Development Minister Brigadier-General David Abel, 2 December 1994, Yangon, to twenty-four Japanese businessmen.

10. See U Aung Shwe (NLD Chairman) to Senior General Than Shwe (SLORC Chairman), 25 March 1996 (henceforth: 'NLD Request'), cited in full in Diller, *National Convention*, Annex II.

11. See, for example, 'Report on the Situation of Human Rights in Myanmar, prepared by Mr Yozo Yokota, Special Rapporteur of the Commission on Human Rights, in accordance with Commission Resolution 1995/72, UN Doc. no. E/CN.4/1996/65 (5 February 1996)' (henceforth: 'UNCHR 1996 Report'), para. 177 (one in seven National Convention delegates is an elected MP); and United Press International (henceforth: UPI), 'Suu Kyi Blasts Junta's Constitution', 22 November 1995, reported on *BurmaNet*, 23 November 1995.

12. As of January 1996, the number of delegates remaining at the Convention after the NLD expulsion was 590, see 'National Convention Plenary Session Continues', Radio Rangoon, 29 November 1995, reported in *FBIS-EAS-95-229*, 19 November 1995; 'Plenary Session Continues 9 January', TV Myanmar, 9 January 1996, reported in *FBIS-EAS-96-012*, 9 January 1996; and 'Reports on Judiciary Chapter of Constitution Presented at National Convention', Radio Rangoon, 17 January 1996, reported in BBC, *Summary of World Broadcasts* (henceforth: '*SWB*'), 19 January 1996. Since the expelled NLD delegates numbered eighty-six, the total number of delegates before the expulsion was 676 (590 + 86), reflecting a 26-member attrition from the starting figure of 702. Before the expulsion, the number of elected delegates constituted 15.24 per cent of the total (ie 103 out of 676), see Deborah Charles, 'Burma Opposition Pulls out of Constitutional Talks', Reuters News Service (henceforth: 'Reuters'), 29 November 1995; 'Suu Kyi Blasts Junta's Constitution', UPI, 22 November 1995 (quoting figure given by Daw Aung San Suu Kyi). Following the expulsion, only seventeen elected delegates remained at the Convention, including representatives from the NUP, the military party. The composition of the 1996 Convention thus bears a ratio of all delegates (590) to elected delegates (17) of 34.7 to 1, or 2.88 per cent elected delegates. As of the time of writing [March 1996], the total number of eligible delegates appears to have decreased to 586. It is not

clear whether the four newly dismissed delegates were elected MPs, see, 'National Convention Delegates Hear Proposals on Judiciary', TV Myanmar, 30 March 1996, reported in *SWB*, 1 April 1996.

13. Letter from U Aung Shwe (NLD Chairman) to U Aung Toe (National Convention Chairman), 27 November 1995 (copy available at the International League for Human Rights).
14. 'Burma: Committee Expels 86 Opposition Delegates from National Convention', Radio Myanmar, Rangoon, 30 November 1995, reported in *SWB*, 2 December 1995.
15. See above, n. 3.
16. See Aung San Suu Kyi, 'The Observations of the National League for Democracy on the National Convention', press conference statement, 22 November 1995 reported in 'NLD's Suu Kyi Issues Statement on Convention', *BurmaNet News*, 23 November 1995, reported in *FBIS-EAS-95-227*, 23 November 1995.
17. Marcia Phu, 'More Reportage on NLD Boycott of Convention – NLD Leaders Explain Boycott', BBC Burmese Service, reported in *FBIS-EAS-95-230*, 30 November 1995 (words of U Aung Shwe).
18. Ibid. (words of Daw Aung San Suu Kyi).
19. *New Light of Myanmar*, 29 November 1995.
20. Deborah Charles, 'Burma Generals Spurn Suu Kyi's Concerns', 6 December 1995, reported by Reuters, 7 December 1995. For a discussion of the crackdown on NLD activists and supporters generally, see the discussion in Section C below.
21. 'Burma: Burmese [sic] Military Issues Warning to Suu Kyi', Reuters, 5 December 1995, reporting articles in *New Light of Myanmar* and *Mirror Daily*.
22. See discussion in Janelle Diller, 'Constitutional Reform in a Repressive State: The Case of Burma', *Asian Survey*, 33.4 (April 1993), pp. 393–407.
23. Diller, 'Constitutional Reform', p. 401, n. 19.
24. Ibid. p. 400, n. 18.
25. 'Report on the Situation of Human Rights in Myanmar, prepared by the Special Rapporteur, Mr Yozo Yokota, in accordance with Commission Resolution 1994/85, UN Doc. no. E/CN.4/1995/65 (12 January 1995)' (henceforth: 'UNCHR 1995 Report'), paras 137–40.
26. See 'SLORC Restrictions on Delegates to the National Convention', excerpts (unofficial translation on file with the International League for Human Rights) (henceforth: 'Convention Restrictions'). See also Janelle Diller, 'The National Convention: Lessons from the Past and Steps to the Future', *Burma Debate*, 1.2 (October–November 1994), p. 6.
27. 'Convention Restrictions', sec. 29(b).
28. *New Light of Myanmar*, 5 August 1993 (on charges against U Aung Khin Sint); Associated Press (henceforth: 'AP'), 'UN Investigator Visits Leading Burmese Political Prisoner', 14 November 1993 (on sentencing).
29. 'Minister Addresses National Convention Opening', TV Myanmar, 28 November 1995, reported in *FBIS-EAS-95-229*, 29 November 1995.
30. 'Senior Politicians Urge Rangoon-Suu Kyi Talks', *BurmaNet News*, 29 December 1995, reprinted in *FBIS-EAS-96-001*, 2 January 1996.

31. 'Politicians Threatened Over Dialogue Letter', *BurmaNet News*, 20 January 1996, reprinted in *FBIS-EAS-96-018*, 26 January 1996 (reporting on a meeting with the twenty-three held on 26 November 1995).

32. SNLD, 'An Appeal for National Reconciliation', signed by Khun Tun Oo (SNLD Chairman) to Senior-General Than Shwe (SLORC Chairman) and Daw Aung San Suu Kyi (NLD General Secretary), 26 November 1995 (unofficial translation) (copy on file with the International League for Human Rights).

33. 'Burmese Junta Making Progress', Kyodo, 8 November 1995, reported in *FBIS-EAS-95-216*, 8 November 1995 (Japanese Foreign Minister Yasuo Fukuda urging dialogue and stating renewal of aid on a case by case basis).

34. UN Doc. no. A/C.3/50/L.52 (5 December 1995), para. 6; compare UN Commission on Human Rights, Res. 1995/72, UN Doc. no. E/CN.4/1995/L.11/Add.5 (9 March 1995), para. 5 (urging the government to open a substantial political dialogue with Daw Aung San Suu Kyi and with other political leaders, including representatives of ethnic groups, as the best means to arrive at national reconciliation and the complete and rapid installation of democracy).

35. The satire resulted in the arrest, charging, and conviction of four NLD activists – two comedians and two NLD organizers, see, 'Court Jails Four for Disrespect to Junta', Radio Australia, 20 March 1996, reported in *SWB*, 21 March 1996. See also the discussion below, under 'Dismantling Political Structures and Suppressing Independent Activity'.

36. 'Eight NLD Members said Held for Lampooning Burma Junta', AFP, 10 January 1996.

37. 'Suu Kyi: Arrest of 3 Party Members "Injustice"– Increases Public Criticism', interview with Evan Williams, Radio Australia (Melbourne), 9 November 1995.

38. 'NLD Request', Annex II, paras 6–11 (citing Election Commission Notification nos 896 (1 July 1990) and 1014 (24 March 1992), unspecified Election Commission notifications entitled 'Notifying the Names of Elected Representatives' pursuant to *Pyithu Hluttaw* Election Law, sec. 41(d), and publication of names of elected representatives in unspecified editions of *Burma [Government] Gazette*). See also, 'Myanmar Election Commission to Take Action Against Parliamentary Candidates', Xinhua News Agency (henceforth: 'Xinhua'), 25 March 1992 (report on 2201 of 2296 candidates issued by Election Commission). By law, the Election Commission is obligated to submit a final report after reviewing all expense reports of candidates and other technical matters, see, *Pyithu Hluttaw* Election Rules, Election Commission Rules no. 1/89, ch. XIII (procedure for reporting and reviewing of expenses of candidates declared to be elected); 'Myanmar SLORC Vice-Chairman on Transfer of Power', Xinhua, 8 March 1991 (General Than Shwe speech); 'Election Commission Explains Work on Final Report', Radio Rangoon (on Announcement no. 966 of the Election Commission), 16 September 1991, reported in *SWB*, 24 September 1991.

39. Of the 485 total, 479 winners came from twenty-seven parties respectively; six other winners ran as independents, see 'Official Election Statistics', Burma Broadcasting System, 30 June 1990, reported in *SWB*, 2 July 1990 (on SLORC-announced results).

40. More MPs may lose their seats if irregularities are found in the expense accounts of another 85 NLD MPs, see further above n. 38; and David Brunnstrom, 'Burma Junta Jails Dissidents, Moves on Opposition', Reuters, 14 October 1992.

41. The Commission's authority to nullify elected status is found in Section 11 of the *Pyithu Hluttaw* Election Law, which governed the 1990 elections, as amended by the Law Amending the *Pyithu Hluttaw* Election Law, SLORC Law no. 10/91 (10 July 1991), published in *Working People's Daily*, 28.192 (11 July 1991), p. 1. For a discussion of the nullification of elected status, see 'Status of Five NLD MPs Revoked for Rebel Links', Radio Rangoon, 21 April 1992, reported in *FBIS-EAS-92-080*, 24 April 1992; 'Four More NLD MPs' Status Revoked by Regime', Radio Rangoon, 11 April 1992, reported in *FBIS-EAS-92-017*, 13 April 1992; 'Commission Revokes Status of Four NLD MP's', Radio Rangoon, 9 April 1992, reported in *FBIS-EAS-92-070*; 'Status of NLD MP from Magwe Revoked', Radio Rangoon, 19 February 1992, reported in *SWB*, 21 February 1992; 'More Removals Announced', Radio Rangoon, 9 January 1992, reported in *FBIS-EAS-92-007*, 10 January 1992; 'Commission Revokes Status of More NLD MPs', Radio Rangoon, 6 January 1992, reported in *FBIS-EAS-92-004*, 7 January 1992; 'Commission Revokes Status of More NLD MPs', Radio Rangoon, 2 January 1992, reported in *FBIS-EAS-92-003*, 6 January 1992; 'Status of 5 Elected MPs Revoked by Commission', Radio Rangoon, 27 December 1991, reported in *FBIS-EAS-91-251*, 31 December 1991; 'Commission Revokes Status of More Elected MPs', Radio Rangoon, 30 December 1991, reported in *FBIS-EAS-92-251*, 31 December 1991; 'Elected Opposition Members of Parliament Have Status Revoked', 23 December 1991, reported in *SWB*, 30 December 1991; 'National League for Democracy MPs' Status Revoked by Government Commission', Radio Rangoon, 18 December 1991, reported in *SWB*, 23 December 1991; 'Commission Revokes Status of Five NLD Officials', Radio Rangoon, 18 December 1991, reported in *FBIS-EAS-91-244*, 19 December 1991; 'National League for Democracy MP's Status Annulled', Radio Rangoon, 12 December 1991, reported in *SWB*, 16 December 1991; 'Five NLD Assembly Representatives Suspended', Radio Rangoon, 10 December 1991, reported in *SWB*, 12 December 1991; 'Commission Revokes Status of Three NLD Members', Radio Rangoon, 25 November 1991, reported in *FBIS-EAS-91-228*, 26 November 1991; 'Two NLD Representatives Disqualified', Radio Rangoon, 14 August 1991, reported in *SWB*, 21 August 1991; '"Parallel Government" Members Stripped of People's Assembly Member Status', Radio Rangoon, 30 April 1991, reported in *SWB*, 2 May, 1991; 'Commission Cancels Status of Five Representatives', Radio Rangoon, 22 February 1991, reported in *SWB*, 22 February 1991; 'People's Assembly Status of Parallel Government Members Annulled', Radio Rangoon, 26 December 1990, reported in *SWB*, 28 December 1990.

42. See above, n. 41.

43. 'Aung San Suu Kyi Barred from Burmese Election', *Reuters Library Report*, 17 January 1990.

44. *The Burma Code*, 8, ch. 6, sec. 122(1).

45. Amnesty International, 'Myanmar: Human Rights after Seven Years of Military Rule', October 1995 (henceforth: AI, 'Seven Years'), p. 17.
46. Emergency Provisions Act of 1950, sec. 5(e) as quoted in Inter-Parliamentary Union, Resolution adopted without a vote by the Inter-Parliamentary Council at its 157th session (Bucharest, 14 October 1995), and sec. 5(j), as quoted in AI, 'Seven Years', p. 12.
47. Law Amending the *Pyithu Hluttaw* Election Law, SLORC Law no. 10/91 (10 July 1991), sections 80-A to 80-D; for full text, see Diller, *National Convention*, Annex III.
48. The permanent ban on running in future elections was based on section 80-A of the *Pyithu Hluttaw* Election Law amended in 1991, see Diller, *National Convention*, Annex III.
49. The ten-year ban was based on section 80-B of the *Pyithu Hluttaw* Election Law as amended in 1991, see Diller, *National Convention*, Annex III.
50. See above, n. 47.
51. SLORC announced the eight deaths about eighteen months after the election, see '82 Parliament Representatives Declared as Disqualified in Myanmar', Xinhua, 14 January 1992.
52. 'NLD Representative Dies: Struck Off Elected Members List', Radio Rangoon, 31 January 1991, reported in *SWB*, 2 February 1991 (announcing death of U Tin Maung Win). See also the *Independent* (London), 6 August 1996 reporting the death of NLD MP U Hla Than, after suspected torture.
53. See 'Election Commission Notes Candidature Situation', Radio Rangoon, 23 February 1990, reported in *FBIS-EAS-90-038*, 26 February 1990 (ninety-three parties); 'Chairman Addresses Opening Session of National Convention', TV Myanmar, 28 November 1995, reported in *SWB*, 30 November 1995.
54. The Political Party Registration Law issued by the SLORC in 1988 provides only five reasons for the Commission to revoke the registration of a political party. Deregistration is authorized if a political party is: (1) illegal under domestic laws; (2) engages in violent conflict against the state; (3) gets assistance from a foreign entity; (4) makes use of religion for political gain; (5) has amongst its membership, personnel, including members of the Defence Services, who earn salaries from state funds, see, 'Political Party Registration Law Enacted', Radio Rangoon, 27 September 1988, reprinted in *FBIS-EAS-88-188*, paras 6 and 3(A)–(F). The reference to illegality under domestic law appears vague and susceptible to abuse of discretion in application.
55. 'SLORC Abolishes Nine More Political Parties', Radio Rangoon, 11 March 1992, reported in *FBIS-EAS-92-050*, 13 March 1992.
56. Ibid.
57. 'SLORC Issues Order Abolishing 17 Minor Parties', Radio Rangoon, 2 February 1992, reported in *FBIS-EAS-92-025*, 6 February 1992 (on SLORC Order 4/92 deregistering those parties unable to form at least ten local party organisations); 'Government Abolishes Nine Minor Parties', Radio Rangoon, 22 January 1992, reported in *FBIS-EAS-92-015*, 23 January 1992 (on SLORC Order 2/92 deregistering parties because no members had been elected and for 'not presenting organisational standing'). See also, 'Patriotic Youth Organisation De-registered', Radio Rangoon, 17 March 1992, reported in *SWB*, 20 March 1992 (on Election Commission announce-

ment 926 deregistering the party because 'student members wished to return to school').
58. See, 'UNCHR 1995 Report' para. 136; 'Party Leaders' Proposals for Composition of National Convention', Radio Rangoon, 30 June 1992, reported in *SWB*, 4 July 1992. Indeed, the three parties which won no seats in the election even have representatives in the National Convention, see UNCHR 1996 Report, para. 148.
59. UNCHR 1996 Report, paras 128, 133.
60. Ibid. para. 130.
61. Ibid. paras 128, 131.
62. Ibid. paras 61, 129.
63. 'Three Jailed After Protest at Suu Kyi's House', Radio Australia (Melbourne), 23 November 1995, reported in *FBIS-EAS-95-226*, 24 November 1995. See further n. 70 below on 'NLD Protest'.
64. 'Opposition Gathering at Suu Kyi Home Denounced', Radio Rangoon, 11 December 1995, reported in *FBIS-EAS-95-237*, 11 December 1995.
65. See, 'Aung San Suu Kyi Rejects Convention Set-Up', AFP (Hong Kong), 22 November 1995, reported in *FBIS-EAS-95-225*, 22 November 1995, 'Myanmar – The Sound of Silence', *Asiaweek* (Hong Kong), 27 October 1995 ('Election Commission reportedly rejected the NLD's new line-up'); 'SLORC Rules Party Leadership Role for Suu Kyi is Illegal', AP, reported in *The Nation* (Bangkok), 24 October 1995.
66. Statement by U Daniel Aung, Presidium Member Representing Political Parties Bloc at the National Convention, 26 May 1994 (copy on file with the International League for Human Rights) (henceforth: 'U Daniel Aung Statement').
67. See 'UNCHR 1996 Report'; Inter-Parliamentary Union, Committee on the Human Rights of Parliamentarians, Myanmar, decision adopted at its 72nd session (Geneva, 22–25 January 1996). See AI, *Myanmar Renewed Repression* (London: AI, July 1996), reporting that 19 NLD members arrested in the May 1996 crackdown were still in prison.
68. UNCHR 1996 Report, paras 93–4 ('hundreds' of political prisoners); AI, 'Seven Years', Summary, p. 1 ('thousands' of political prisoners).
69. See discussion in AI, 'Seven Years', pp. 11–16; Amnesty International, Union of Myanmar (Burma), 'Arrests and Trials of Political Prisoners', January–July 1991, December 1991.
70. The NLD's 'Protest Against Lawless Proceedings' documents four incidents in which thirty-seven NLD activists and supporters have been unfairly charged and/or sentenced, almost all without defence lawyers allowed and some *in absentia*, see 'Protest Against Lawless Proceedings', letter by U Aung Shwe, NLD Chairman, to Senior General Than Shwe, SLORC Chairman, dated 28 March 1996, cited in full in Diller, *National Convention*, Annex IV (henceforth: 'NLD Protest'). See also, UNCHR 1996 Report, paras 93–105; 'Court Jails Four for Disrespect to Junta', Radio Australia, 20 March 1996, reported in *SWB*, 21 March 1996 (arrest and sentencing of NLD entertainers for criticism of SLORC).
71. 'NLD Protest', p. 1; 'Burmese Activist Jailed for 5 Years for Dangerous Driving', Deutsche Presse-Agentur (henceforth: 'DPA'), 1 April 1996; 'Suu Kyi "No Justice in Burma"', UPI, 1 April 1996.

72. 'Burmese Activist Jailed for 5 Years', DPA, 1 April 1996.
73. See below, in this section, for a discussion of the principles presented in the opening speech given by Convention Chairman U Aung Toe to Convention delegates in 1993, with those adopted by the Convention and recorded in the report presented by Chairman U Aung Toe to the Convention delegates in 1994.
74. The objective of a 'leading role for the military' is one of six fundamental Convention objectives, among them the promotion of a genuine multi-party democratic system, and of universal principles of justice, liberty and equality, see, Radio Rangoon, 13 September 1993 reported in *SWB*, 21 September 1993 (giving text of speech by Convention Chairman U Aung Toe at the plenary session of National Convention in which the Chairman summarized thirty-three sets of principles 'prescribed by the National Convention Co-ordinating Work Committee as the basic principles on which fundamental principles of state should be based') (henceforth: 'Aung Toe Speech'), Sections II(4)–(6). On the corollary principle, which prescribed that the defence services have the main responsibility to ensure the non-disintegration of the union, the non-disintegration of national unity and the perpetuation of national sovereignty as well as to defend and safeguard the state responsibility – the 'three [sacred] causes' of the *Tatmadaw* – see, Sections X(5)–(6); and Chapter 6 n.12 below.
75. 'SNLD Report at National Convention Noted', *New Light of Myanmar*, 23 December 1995 (henceforth: 'SNLD Report').
76. 'SLORC Tries to Bar Suu Kyi from Office', *Bangkok Post*, 30 March 1996 (reporting approval of appointed seats for military in parliament) (henceforth: 'SLORC Bar'); and see EIU, 'Country Report: Myanmar (Burma)', 2nd Quarter 1996, p. 10, on the objection to military appointments by the minority parties.
77. Philip Shenon, 'Army Wants Permanent Role in Burma Rule', *International Herald Tribune*, 17 July 1995, quoting 'Destiny of the Nation', *New Light of Myanmar*, 22 July 1995.
78. 'Aung Toe Speech', Secs XXIX(2)–(3).
79. 'SLORC Bar', *Bangkok Post*, 30 March 1996; 'Burma's Democracy Party Seeks House Session', Reuters, 29 March 1996 ('Burma's Democracy Party') (reports of adoption of Convention guidelines on the form of the executive, legislature and judiciary).
80. 'U Aung Toe Report to National Convention, Part IV', Radio Rangoon, 2–5 September 1994, reported in *SWB*, 23 September 1994 (henceforth: 'Aung Toe Report IV'). A December 1995 SNLD proposal revisited earlier issues, requesting, for example, that the central legislature be vested with legislative power over common affairs, and region and state legislative bodies be vested with all remaining legislative power, see 'SNLD Report'.
81. The formula prescribes self-administered areas for ethnic nationalities other than those which already have state status (either as a region or state) and if they have the appropriate population and have existed as a united group in two contiguous territories. See Aung Toe Speech, Principle IV(5) and 'U Aung Toe's Report to National Convention, Part I', Radio Burma (Rangoon), 2–5 September 1994, reported in *SWB*, 19 September 1994 (henceforth: 'Aung Toe Report I') (announcing SLORC decisions on

denials at opening speech of plenary session of National Convention on 2 September 1994 based on unspecified data gathered by the Immigration and Manpower Dept. dated 15 August 1994). See also Diller, 'National Convention: Lessons', pp. 8–9; and below, Chapter 4, n. 34.

82. See Diller, 'National Convention: Lessons', p. 8 (discussing, among other responses, SNLD concern over the chief executive becoming a dictator). As recently as December 1995, the Lahu National Development Party representative, U Kya Shi, voiced his party's opinion that, '[t]he President of the State, although being the Head of State, the highest organ of the sovereign powers in the nation is the Pyidaungsu Hluttaw [which should have the right to criticise and discuss the President's nomination of an Attorney General]', see 'Delegate Groups Submit Proposal Papers on "The Executive"', *New Light of Myanmar*, 12 December 1995, p. 3. According to a reliable source, even the National Unity Party (NUP), which received backing from the SLORC in the 1990 elections, opposed the presidential system.

83. 'U Aung Toe's Report to National Convention, Part III', Radio Burma, Rangoon, 2–5 September 1994 reported in *SWB*, 22 September 1994, para. 7 (henceforth: 'Aung Toe Report III').

84. 'Special Supplement; Burma National Convention', TV Myanmar, 18 January 1994, reported in *SWB*, 24 January 1994, paras 26–31. See also 'SLORC Bar'.

85. The electoral college consists of three groups: (1) MPs from the House of Equal Representation; (2) MPs from the House based on population; and (3) defence service members nominated by the commander-in-chief to the two chambers of parliament, see 'Aung Toe Speech', 13 September 1993, sec. V(2); and discussion in Diller, 'National Convention: Lessons', p. 8.

86. See 'Aung Toe Speech', 13 September 1993, sec. VIII(3); and 'Aung Toe Report III', 2–5 September 1994.

87. 'U Aung Toe's Report to the National Convention, Part V', Radio Rangoon, 2–5 September 1994, reported in *SWB*, 24 September 1994 (henceforth: 'Aung Toe Report V'), sec. I. Even at the Yangon City Council, the Union President is to appoint military personnel nominated by the commander-in-chief to 'integrate and coordinate security responsibilities', 'Aung Toe Report IV', 2–5 September 1995, para. 21.

88. 'Aung Toe Report III', 2–5 September 1994, para. 7.

89. See n. 41 above.

90. See 'SLORC Bar'; 'Burma's Democracy Party'.

91. The SLORC Convention maintained the central legislature, known as *Pyidaungsu Hluttaw*, as a bicameral assembly composed of a body based on population, the *Pyithu Hluttaw*, and a traditionally weaker body based on equal representation, the *Amyotha Hluttaw*, see 'U Aung Toe's Report to National Convention, Part II', Radio Rangoon, 2–5 September 1994, reported in *SWB*, 21 September 1994 (henceforth: 'Aung Toe Report II').

92. 'Aung Toe Report II', para. 12. See also 'Aung Toe's Speech', sec. VII(4).

93. 'SLORC Bar'. In an innovative, but unsuccessful, suggestion in December 1995, the SNLD proposed that military nominees by the commander-in-chief have the right to stand election in the constituencies of the union, region and state *hluttaws* (people's assemblies). Under the SNLD proposal, if the serviceman is elected, he can participate as a *hluttaw* representative;

if not, he can return to military ranks, see 'SNLD Report', 23 December 1995.

94. 'Aung Toe Report II', para. 12.
95. Compare 'Aung Toe Report II' with *Pyithu Hluttaw* Election Law, ch. 5.
96. See *Pyithu Hluttaw* Election Law, ch. 5, sec. 9(1).
97. 'Aung Toe Report V', para. 6.
98. Ibid.
99. 'Aung Toe Speech', secs XI(9) and XXIV(7).
100. See 'UNCHR 1996 Report', para. 163.
101. Ibid., sec. XI(6).
102. 'Government Supporters Hold Anti-opposition Rallies', Radio Australia (Melbourne), 10 December 1995.
103. Bertil Lintner, '"The Generals' New Clothes": Junta Sets up New Civilian front Organization', *FEER*, 25 November 1993, p. 30 (likening the USDA to Indonesia's ruling Golkar party).
104. Statement of U Tin Kyaw Hlaing, Ambassador and Permanent Representative of Myanmar to the United Nations, at the 50th session of the Commission on Human Rights, Geneva, 7 March 1994.
105. 'Than Shwe links SLORC's Goals with USDA Objectives', Rangoon Radio, 29 August 1994, reported in *FBIS-EAS-94-169*, 29 August 1994 (speech of SLORC Chairman, Senior General Than Shwe, to USDA executives' management course, referring to trainees as the 'hard core forces of the Association').
106. TV Myanmar, 7 March 1994, quoted in Amnesty International, 'Myanmar: Human Rights Still Denied', November 1994.
107. 'Myo Nyunt Speech', Rangoon Radio, 6 December 1995, reported in *FBIS-EAS-95-235*. The SLORC had earlier recorded that four million people participated in public rallies held in twenty-six major towns in January 1994, see 'Minister Addresses National Convention Opening', TV Myanmar, 28 November 1995, reported in *FBIS-EAS-95-229*, 29 November 1995 (speech of Lieutenant-General Myo Nyunt at opening Convention session). After the NLD expulsion from the Convention, SLORC reported eleven rallies nationwide supporting the exercise with attendance ranging from about 10 000 to 16 000, see 'Rallies Supporting National Convention Reported', reported in *FBIS-EAS-95-247*, 26 December 1995.
108. 'Thousands Forced to Attend Junta's Rallies', Reuters, reported in *Bangkok Post*, 29 January 1994 (compare, 'U Daniel Aung Statement', 26 May 1994).
109. 'NLD in "Liberated Area" Denounces Rallies', *FBIS-EAS-95-238*, 6 December 1995, reported on *BurmaNet News*, 12 December 1995.
110. 'Nationwide Rallies Support [for] National Convention', *New Light of Myanmar*, 10 December 1995 (reporting on 120 000-strong rally on 9 December 1995 in Rangoon and five other separate rallies totalling 134 000 in Taunggyi, Bago, Katha, Pyapon and Thayet).
111. 'Burmese Government-sponsored Rallies Condemn Aung San Suu Kyi', AFP, 26 February 1996, quoting *New Light of Myanmar* regarding mass rally in southwestern Arakan State.
112. According to the UN Secretary General, a democratization process is a process by which 'an authoritarian society becomes increasingly participa-

tory through such mechanisms as periodic elections to representative bodies, the accountability of public officials, a transparent public administration, an independent judiciary and a free press'. A pre-condition to such process includes the 'ability ... to associate freely and form political parties or movements, thus allowing a multiparty system or coalitions of parties and movements to develop; and ... to enjoy full access to information', Report of the Secretary-General, 'Support by the United Nations System of the Efforts of Governments to Promote and Consolidate New or Restored Democracies', UN Doc. no. A/50/332 (7 August 1995), paras 6 and 12.

113. Ibid., para. 125.

114. Ibid., para. 13.

115. Vienna Declaration and Programme of Action, UN Doc. no. A/CONF/157/23, sec. I(8), September 1993. In the same paragraph, Burma agreed that '[d]emocracy is based on the freely expressed will of the people to determine their own political, economic, social and cultural systems and their full participation in all aspects of their lives. In the context of the above, the promotion and protection of human rights and fundamental freedoms at the national and international levels should be universal and conducted without conditions attached.'

116. UN Charter, 26 June 1945, 59 Stat.1031, T.S. no. 993, art. 55(c) (see also, art. 1[3]).

117. Ian Brownlie, *Principles of Public International Law* (Oxford: Clarendon Press, 4th edn 1990), pp. 570–1 and n. 76. Customary legal norms are binding on all states that fail to persistently object to the norms during their development (Brownlie, p. 10). The customary norms reflected in the Declaration include, for example, the right to freedom from torture and a systematic pattern of other gross violations, see, American Law Institute, *Restatement Third of Foreign Relations Law*, sec. 702. Far from objecting to these norms, Burma continues to deny that violations of the norms are taking place.

118. Among other violations, Part II of this report documents violations of the right to enjoy human rights free from discrimination (UDHR, art. 2), the right to life and freedom from torture or cruel, inhuman or degrading treatment or punishment (UDHR, arts 3, 4), the right to equal protection of the law (UDHR, art. 7), the right to be free from arbitrary arrest and detention (UDHR, art. 9), the right in full equality to a fair and public hearing by an independent and impartial tribunal (UDHR, art. 10), the right to freedom from retroactive penalties (UDHR, art. 11), the right to freedom of movement (UDHR, art. 13), the right to freedom of thought, opinion and expression (UDHR, arts 18 and 19), the right to peaceful assembly and association (UDHR, art. 20[1]), the right to an adequate standard of living, including social security (UDHR arts 22 and 25), the right to work for just remuneration and to free choice of employment (UDHR, art. 23), and the right to participate freely in the cultural life of the community (UDHR, art. 27). Other rights violated follow in the text discussion.

119. UDHR, art. 20(3).

120. The Convention on the Political Rights of Women, UN Doc. no. A/RES/640(vii), 20 December 1952. As a signatory, Burma has a good faith obligation to respect the terms of that treaty. Burma is not a party to the

human rights treaties prohibiting discrimination on the basis of race and gender.

121. Convention on the Political Rights of Women, arts 2 and 3.

122. GA Res. 43/157, 8 December 1988, discussed in United Nations Action in the Field of Human Rights, UN Doc. ST/HR/2/Rev.4, Sales no. E.94.XIV.11 (1994), para. 1117.

123. The *de facto* exclusion of women from political posts in Burma is apparent in the composition of the National Convention. Although there is no known bar of women from the National Convention, no source known to this author cites information revealing the presence of women delegates at the Convention.

124. UN Charter, arts 1(3) and 55; UDHR, art. 2; Convention on the Rights of the Child (henceforth: 'Children's Convention'), UN Doc. no. A/RES/44/25, 20 November 1989, art. 2. See further Chapter 8 below, under 'Social Programmes for Children'.

125. Children's Convention, art. 28 and UDHR, arts 2 and 26. Under Article 28 of the Children's Convention, Burma 'recognize[d] the right of the child to education, and ... to achieving this right progressively and on the basis of equal opportunity'.

2 The Constitutional Future of Myanmar in Comparative Perspective
Robert H. Taylor

INTRODUCTION

Since July 1988, when, in the midst of unprecedented political unrest, U Ne Win opened the subject of the constitutional future of Burma at an extraordinary congress of the now defunct Burma Socialist Programme Party (BSPP), every prominent public figure, with the immediate exception of the majority of the congress members, has indicated a desire to see Myanmar/Burma[1] develop in the direction of a multi-party democracy. But what multi-party democracy means, how it is to be achieved, and which individuals, interests and groups are to have significant power and influence after any transition from the current military rule takes place, remain issues of serious political conflict, not to say bitterness and frustration, on all sides.

The interests and groups which predominate in drafting the principles and structures contained within the independent state's third constitution will largely establish the framework of any new order. If it is to be more successful than the constitutions of 1947 and 1974, neither of which survived more than fourteen years, the constitution will have to define the structures and institutions of the state more acceptably for all the major actors and social forces in the country's complex and divided society, including the majority and minority communities and civilian and military interests. Experience suggests this will not be easy, especially given the profound disagreements which divide the current military government from its dwindling number of armed and, now more significant, unarmed opponents.

THE MAY 1990 ELECTIONS AND THE PROBLEMS OF CONSTITUTIONAL TRANSITION

Students and other pro-democracy demonstrators, before and after 1988, have been unwilling to accept the conditional promises of successive governments, including the current State Law and Order Restoration Council (SLORC), to organise and manage a programme of constitutional transition to a form of elected government. The rejection by the BSPP Congress of U Ne Win's proposal for a national referendum on whether the one-party system should be abandoned was interpreted by the growing band of sceptics as proof of the insincerity of his proposal. Dr Maung Maung's subsequent attempts during his brief month (18 August–18 September 1988) as president to advance a programme of reforms, first by abandoning the idea of a referendum for a process of public consultation and then offering elections in three months, was also rejected by the leaders of the emerging anti-army movements on the grounds that any elections managed by the existing authorities would of necessity be unfair. The SLORC then came to power in a military *coup* on 18 September 1988, curtailing these initial promises of a constitutional transition.

Central to the demands of the majority of political parties which eventually emerged in the wake of the fall of the one-party order was the establishment of an interim government under the original 1947 parliamentary-style constitution, with self-appointed civilian leadership from the parties, to preside over a transition to a new order. The army officer corps rejected this demand on two grounds, both seen as specious by its critics. The first was that the old constitution was flawed by its colonial origins: in particular, they opposed the grant of the right of secession after ten years to the Shan State and the Kayah State, along with the fact that the constitution was drafted while the country was still under colonial rule and was not approved by the public via a referendum. The second was that the army claimed that there were no obvious and experienced individuals to whom they could hand power on an interim basis. The subsequent inability of the National League for Democracy (NLD), the landslide victor in the May 1990 national elections, to be allowed to form a government, or meet as a body under an earlier constitution in order to draw up a new one, heightened passions in the debate in and out of Myanmar on the constitutional future of the country.

At the end of 1991, the SLORC made it clear that there would be no movement toward a transition to a new constitutional order until certain preliminary steps were carried out. First, the Election Commission had to finalise the results of the 1990 election, including the accounts and appeals of all candidates. That this process had taken over a year and a half without clear resolution allowed critics to claim that the government was merely stalling and demonstrated that there had never been any intention of transferring power to an elected government. Second, the SLORC indicated that a consultative assembly representing all the political parties which fielded candidates in the election, plus representatives of 135 ethnic groups and other individuals, would have to meet together to draw up guidelines for the drafting of a constitution.

In May 1992, the government announced that a preliminary group to organise a constitution drafting body – the National Convention – would convene on 23 June and that a larger body to draft guidelines for a new constitution would meet within six months. By the end of 1995 no complete set of draft guidelines had been produced. The Convention had met on several occasions since its first meeting on 9 January 1993 and had drawn up guidelines on the nature of the presidency, the outline constitution and its sections, and certain basic principles. Of the latter, the most controversial was that which provided for a continuing role for the military in the future government of the country. The SLORC has indicated that, after a constitution is agreed, new elections will be necessary in order to form a legislature from which a government might be formed, presumably at the same time as newly elected institutions of local government. Whatever else, and however this process may be further lengthened, the SLORC has made it clear that it will not hand over power to other than a 'strong and firm government' under a new constitution. A transitional process has begun and, in one way or another, a new constitutional order will emerge under SLORC auspices unless some major event throws the regime off course. This seems unlikely, though the unconditional release of Daw Aung San Suu Kyi from nearly six years' house arrest on 10 July 1995 created a new factor in the political context of drafting the constitution, one which was underscored by the 28 November 1995 walk-out (and subsequent SLORC expulsion) of the eighty-six NLD delegates from the Convention.

CONSTITUTIONAL REVISION: A BURMA ARMY VIEW

What SLORC initially thought might be the nature of an 'appropriate constitution' for the polity was outlined in an article by a senior army officer published in the government's *Lou'tha: Pyithu Nei.zin* on 6 and 7 August 1991.[2] The officially led discussions in the National Convention since then have basically followed the ideas outlined in these articles. Pointing up the senior officer corps' perceptions of the major issues facing the country's constitutional future, the article began with a discussion of the terminology to be used in conceptualising the ethnic diversity of Myanmar. The original Burmese version is rather more precise and less open to misconstruction than is the English translation. In particular, the translation relies on the old-fashioned terminology of 'national races' inherited from the colonial era.

The author, as translated, argues that the concepts 'ethnic group' and 'minority' (both *lu-myou:-ne* in the Burmese original), are out of favour and that 'national race', (*lu-myou:* in Burmese), is to be used. In referring to the minority communities or groups living in the border areas of the country, the phrase often used is *taing:-yin:-tha: lu-myou:mya:*, but this terminology is not used in this text as the discussion refers to the majority as well as minority groups. In the nineteenth century, *lu-myou:*, literally 'kind of person', was coined to encapsulate the Social Darwinian concept of race. While usage in English has changed since that time, the term in translation in Burmese has remained unchanged.

With this semantic discussion, the author was attempting to make a political point. In earlier colonial and post-colonial constitutional orders, Burma was divided into six to eight 'big race' (*lu-myou:-kyi:*) zones which were reflected in the administrative and political organisation of the country. These were what the British used to call 'Burma proper', largely populated by one 'big race', the Burmans (or Bamar or, in some usages, Myanmar), administratively divided into the seven 'divisions' of the 1974 constitution. The remainder of the country, the great horseshoe of territory around the Irrawaddy Valley and its related lowland areas, is occupied by five to seven composite ethnic communities, also 'big races', being the Karen (or Kayin), Karenni (or Kayah), Shan, Kachin (or Jinghpaw), Chin, Mon, and Rahkine (or Arakanese).[3] These, of course, are the ethnic designations of the seven 'states' of the 1974 constitution. The 'big race theory' of ethnicity and politics in Myanmar, which gave the semblance of legitimacy to this organisational concept, is now dying out, he argues. In doing so the author poses a rhetorical question: if it is *not* now dying out, why are there Pa-O, Palaung, Wa, and Lahu insurgents in the Shan State? Furthermore, he argues, the 'big race theory' is increasingly irrelevant because if it were not, there would only be Kachin insurgents in the Kachin State and the Naga would have to consider themselves Chin.

The constitutional guidelines on ethnicity and political authority drawn up by the National Convention have taken these ideas forward as administrative principles. While maintaining the existing seven divisions and seven ethnically-designated states, and re-establishing the old district level of administration between them and the townships, the guidelines have also established six 'self-administered zones'. Three townships in Sagaing Division have been designated as a Naga self-administered zone. Similarly, in the Shan State contiguous townships have been grouped together to create self-administered zones for the Danu, Pa-O, Palaung, Kokang, and Wa groups. These areas were not previously under close government administration, as they had been dominated by the old Communist and ethnic insurgents with whom the SLORC had been able to negotiate political agreements during the period following the collapse of the CPB in March–April 1989 (see further Chapter 3). The promise of these autonomous administrative zones fits with the military's willingness to allow former opponents to enter into the 'legal fold' while remaining armed in exchange for government assistance in developing their regions. With enhanced trade and communications between these regions and the remainder of the country, they will, it is expected, become more politically integrated with the centre.

While one cannot be certain, it seems probable that it is the officer corps' experiences in confronting the various insurgent groups and attempting to govern the border areas for the past forty years which encourage them to perceive the problem of politicised ethnicity as a highly varied and particularised set of issues based on specific localised situations, rather than in terms of numerically larger ethnic, political or cultural communities.[4] While ethnographers would possibly agree with the underlying assumptions and empirical observations of this perspective,[5] advocates for the causes of the Kachin Independence Army (KIA), the Karen National Union (KNU), and the Shan insurgent groups would doubtless argue that the army is proposing a strategy of 'divide and rule', just as Burmese nationalists argued in the pre-independence era that they attacked the division of Burma proper from the border areas by the British on the basis of ethnic and cultural differentiation. The success of the military government in negotiating ceasefires with sixteen insurgent groups since 1989 suggests that this new perspective has created a policy which has proven successful from the perspective of Yangon.

Despite the differing views of various groups in Myanmar over these constitutional issues, there has been remarkable agreement between the government of Burma since 1948 and their minority opponents with regard to the lack of ethnic assimilation and integration in the country's history and therefore the need to use 'big' or 'little' concepts of ethnicity in legitimising political movements and constitutional structures. The translated version of the article on the future form of the state, reflecting current international expectations, refers to Myanmar as a 'multi-racial society'. The insurgent leaders demand political power on the basis that the ethnic group they stand for possesses a status equivalent to a nationality which, in this age of nationalism, requires political recognition. It is, therefore, somewhat ironic to read the text of Daw Mya Sein, written nearly half a century ago, about the basically common origins and assimilationist trends of Burma's social structure. Were this to be written today, the author might well be accused of distorting the country's 'true' history:

> On the whole one can perhaps say that the races of Burma – with the exception of the few Selungs or sea-gypsies, living on the islands of the Mergui Archipelago – are all from the same original stock. They came from the same countryside and are more or less distantly related and connected; the animosities between the three sub-families – the Mon-Khmers, the Tibeto-Burmans and the Shans – have been bitter at times, but *the assimilation and transformation of these races into a united nation has been steadily progressing for centuries* [emphasis added].[6]

Casting anew the political and constitutional implications of the 'big race theory' is seen by our *Tatmadaw* officer-author as essential for ending insurgency in Myanmar. If the state were to be organised 'on the basis of the concept of "self-administration of all the national races"', this would be accomplished, he argues. This concept is turned into a slogan in the form of 'Unity within Unity within Unity', suggesting a pyramidal construction of administrative units from the smallest ethnic groups and communities through to the central administration in Yangon. The translation then proceeds to say that:

> All the national races are to establish self-administrative entities depending on the race and area, then to go one step higher forming self-governing districts [township zones] and then the self-governing districts are to form the State governing body. Only this kind of formation will enable the nation to overcome the problem of having to decide whether the Unity Principle or the Federal Principle is suitable for the state.

The nominally decentralised 'federalist' concepts of the 1947 constitution would thus be combined with the unitary 'democratic centralist' concepts of the 1974 constitution.

Within the local level self-administrative units 'every national race will be able to fulfil its desires by exercising the legislative, executive and judiciary powers in the areas where it is in the majority'. At the central level, the legislative powers will be performed by an elected legislature with a supreme court conducting judicial powers and a head of state delegating executive powers to a government appointed by the head of state but formed from a joint meeting of the two houses of the legislature. The differing natures of the two halves of the legislature were not specified. The text merely states that 'the racial problems and the legislative problems of the township self-administrative regions can be supervised and guided by having two houses of the *Pyithu Hluttaw* [People's Assembly] established at the central level.' It was thus tenuously implied that one house might be elected on a basis similar to the 1947 lower house and the 1974 single house: that is, universal suffrage and the principle of 'one person-one vote'; whereas, the other might be formed on the basis of minority or ethnic representation, as in principle was the nature of the second house, the Chamber of Nationalities, under the 1947 constitution.

In the anonymous officer's article, the head of state was to have been directly elected by the people and would, therefore, incorporate the concept of unity in the state. The position was described as analogous to that of the King of Thailand or the President of Pakistan. In the National Convention conclusions, however, a different means of determining the president was established. The president will now be chosen by three groups: the proposed two houses of the national legislature, a 440-member *Pyithu Hluttaw* (House of Representatives) and a 224-member *Amyotha Hluttaw* (House of Nationalities) or National Assembly, plus the 110 army members appointed to the *Pyithu Hluttaw* and the 56 army-appointed members of the *Amyotha Hluttaw* meeting as an electoral college. Not only does this system give the 166 army members of the two bodies two votes, but it also provides them with the ability to determine the presidency. Each of the three bodies will nominate a candidate, one of whom will be the president and the other two vice-presidents. The agreed guidelines for eligibility to be chosen president exclude Daw Aung San Suu Kyi because of the rules that the head of state should have been resident in Myanmar for at least the previous twenty years and should not be married to a foreigner.[7]

The Head of State will have the power to dissolve the legislature and appoint and revoke the appointments of ministers. Given the elective position of the president, the state, it was suggested, should be renamed the 'Republic of Myanmar' rather than the present 'Union'. Unlike the 1947 constitution, where the presidency was a nominal position, or the 1974 constitution, where the presidency was subordinate to the chairman of the ruling single-party, the BSPP (when they were not the same person, as was the case in 1974–80 when U Ne Win was both President of the Union of Burma and Chairman of the BSPP), the present proposed constitutional order will create presidential powers and authority similar to that in the current Indonesian constitutional system.

It is intended that local administrative and legislative bodies will be elected by the people of their respective areas. Above the village administrative unit there will be formed a second, township, level of self-administrative government. Noting that the intention of the 1974 constitution to avoid an overly bureaucratic form of administration had failed because of the nature of the one-party system, the author suggests that experience had shown that there were too many townships for the previous state and divisional level governments to manage effectively. Therefore, townships should be grouped together into 'township zones/district administrative bodies' similar to the districts of the British colonial period, which were only finally abolished in the early 1970s. In order to avoid weakening the self-administrative principle in regard to the potentially numerous minorities and the majority group communities within an existing state or division, the state/divisional level of administration should be abolished, he argued, and the district bodies would relate directly to the central government.

The restored district/township zone level of administration would have legislative, executive and judicial powers 'to a certain extent depending upon the local conditions'. State/divisional judicial officers would continue to handle existing legal cases through the new district/township zone administrations but they, along would other government personnel now working at that level, would eventually be transferred to the new units. His suggestion that, where a particular minority lives in two to six townships, such as the Wa and Pa-O, these could form a township zone, a self-administrative unit, which has been enshrined in the constitutional guidelines. His text states, 'the desires and wishes of the people of the townships concerned can be ascertained and the population figures of the national races in the townships are to be taken into account in designating a region as a township zone self-administrative district.' Supporters of the federal principle in the organisation of the state will doubtless perceive these proposals as a scheme to undermine the potential autonomy of the existing ethnically designated states *vis-à-vis* the centre. It would allow the government to come to particular arrangements with specific community leaders, thus undermining the organisational cohesion of the various supra-community or multi-ethnic anti-Yangon groups previously at arms in the border areas.

THE CONSTITUTIONAL PRECEDENTS OF 1947 AND 1974

In addition to outlining the form of administrative and political order the army officer corps would find acceptable, the constitutional suggestions also called for the inclusion of a declarative section such as the second chapters of both the 1947 and 1974 constitutions. The author does not, however, suggest the content of the basic principles which should guide the government, but notes that the 1947 constitution is in keeping with current public calls for equality while the 1974 constitution sets forth important goals for the state to maintain.

Of particular interest in Chapter II of the 1947 constitution are the sections on citizenship, equal rights, civil rights, religious rights, cultural and educational rights, economics, criminal law rights, and rights to constitutional remedies. In light of the federalism versus centralism arguments which divide the government from the minority insurgents, it may be noted that citizenship was granted as a Union, or central right, under the 1947 constitution.

The second chapter of the 1974 constitution is similar in intent to Chapters II, III, and IV of the 1947 version. It contains twenty-four articles spelling out basic rights and freedom as noted above, plus statements of principle such as the goal of a socialist society, the establishment of socialist democracy, and the ideals to be followed in managing the state's affairs. The importance of the chapter seems to be derived from the last article, number 27, which notes that, 'these basic principles constitute the guidelines for interpreting the provisions of this Constitution and of other laws.'[8] The army author of the article argues that any section on citizenship, rights, and declaratory principles should also include a stipulation in regard to the 'qualifications and abilities' that members of the central government institutions should possess. This is discussed in the context of Myanmar's position between China and India and the need to ensure that the country does not 'fall under the influence and sway of aliens'.

This schematic set of constitutional suggestions left many issues undiscussed, such as the nature of the powers of the executive (beyond the basic tasks of forming and dismissing governments), and the division of legislative, judicial and executive powers among the three levels of government proposed. Similarly, while it is clear that elections are to be the means of choosing the members of the various government bodies, the role of political parties is not noted, nor is it made clear to what extent, if any, the judiciary is to be independent of the other arms of government or the electorate. Other issues, which are also fundamental to the political future of the country, include the political and administrative roles of the military, the structures of economic and fiscal decision making, and the relationship of the state to the economy.

MYANMAR'S POLITICAL FUTURE: THE RELEVANCE OF REGIONAL MODELS

Various models have been held out as examples of the direction Myanmar might go in the future now that it is clear that one-party rule has been abandoned and the principle of a market-orientated economy has been accepted by the military and all the major political parties. Other than simply transferring the forms of Western-style constitutional government to Myanmar, the most common regional models mentioned are those of Thailand and Indonesia. Both of these countries, though for different reasons growing out of their own modern historical experiences, have gone through long periods of military dominance. Both have been remarkably successful in developing their economies along capitalist lines in recent years. Now both are facing internal and external pressures to democratise their political systems and persuade the army to retire from the centre of political and administrative affairs.

The parallels between Myanmar and Indonesia or Thailand are not precise, however. When Indonesia abandoned Sukarnoist autarky and joined the West as regards its economic and political orientations in 1965–6, the Cold War in Asia was at its peak. Thus, despite the massively repressive and authoritarian nature of the military government, it received widespread support from the United States and other Western governments because of its staunch anti-Communist policies. The anti-Communist card no longer works in world politics today, and human rights are now held to be the centrepiece of most developed countries' foreign policies. Similarly, when the military rose to dominance in Thailand, most completely after the installation of the Sarit government in 1958, the country's strategic relationship to China and Vietnam encouraged Western governments to ignore the human rights issues and democratic principles which underlay the rhetoric of Thai army policy. The Thai and Indonesian army governments, therefore, when faced with the difficult task of realigning their economic policies in a market-orientated direction, and loosening state control of the economy, received support from foreign powers. Even the dominant voices in Western political science hailed military government as an essential stage in the construction of democracy in Third World conditions.

Those days are now over. Intellectual trends, as well as governments and multilateral agencies such as the World Bank, advocate policies of 'good government' and its assumed correlate, democracy, as the solution to the economic and political problems of countries like Myanmar. Here, of course, political science faces a dilemma. In Indonesia and Thailand, it is widely debated, democracy is/will emerge because of the growth of the economy and the rise of new urban-based middle classes. These consumer and business elites demand not only good government in the sense of properly executed laws and the constraint of corrupt practices, but also the right to have a say in who rules them and how. Events like the 23 February 1991 *coup* in Bangkok or the bloodshed following the May 1992 elections, or the overthrow of the Indonesian Democracy Party leader, Megawati Sukarnoputri, in Jakarta in July 1996 are not seen to be obstacles to these inevitable trends. What is needed is more time and more economic growth, and any stoppage to trade, aid and investment which halts economic expansion would be a setback to the commercial forces pushing for democratisation and good government.

In contrast, however, for countries such as Myanmar and Vietnam, democracy is seen by the majority of Western institutions and individuals as a prerequisite to economic growth. One-party or military-dominated regimes are seen as incapable of carrying out the economic successes of their anti-socialist military dominated neighbours. The reason for this is said to be the politicised nature of their bureaucracies and their restrictions on free policy debates and the widespread flow of information necessary for the functioning of a market-orientated economy. This may indeed be true. One cannot but question, however, whether in a country where there has been a long tradition of an army with entrenched political power, reform can take place without the participation of the military.

CONCLUSION

The introduction of multi-party democracy in the midst of societies with weak traditions of civil society, low levels of economic development, and patron-clientalist social structures cannot be simple. The consequences of trying to transplant institutions, which work in quite different ways within the Western political tradition, to societies whose modern history and social experience are quite different have also to be considered. So too, in the same context, does the advocacy and application of free market economics.

Ecological issues are now recognised as intertwined with these political and economic challenges. The deforestation of large parts of Southeast Asia was the result, not of authoritarian or democratic politics, but of unregulated economic forces. Strong anti-market economic regulation allowed Burma to maintain most of its forests up to the late 1980s, when logging contracts with Thai and Chinese entrepreneurs led to a rapid depletion of hardwood resources (see Chapter 4). Advocates of radical change who do not also think that there will be ecological and economic consequences contrary to their own values and desires may fail to see the lessons of neighbouring states. Whether a more democratically based multi-party government in Bangkok would have done a better job of saving Thailand's forests and also developing the economy is debatable. But what is clear is that public opinion in Myanmar, and international trends outside the country, make it imperative for some form of more open political processes to emerge in Myanmar in the next decade. Creating a constitutional order which will ensure political stability, human rights, economic development and environmental responsibility, while also recognising the interests and fears of all elements of the society, will not be easy, especially while passions rage.

Notes

1. In accord with official usage since June 1989, the transliterated name 'Myanmar' will be used in this chapter to refer to post-1988 events and conditions, and 'Burma' will be used in references to prior events, and so on. Readers should note that the bulk of this paper was written in 1991.
2. The articles were translated and printed in four parts in the English-language *The Working People's Daily* (Yangon) on 7, 8, 9, 10 August 1991, under the title 'What Should be the Form of State of the Future?' by 'A High-Ranking Tatmadaw Officer'.
3. The 1983 census uses these eight categories, plus two additional 'races', 'Other Indigenous' and 'Foreign Race (including Mixed Burmese and Foreign)'. Disputed by the government's opponents for allegedly undercounting the minority groups, the 1983 census concluded that 69 per cent of the population were Burmese and the other 'big races' were distributed as follows: 8.5 per cent Shan, 6.2 per cent Karen, [5.3 per cent Foreign Race: that is, Chinese, Indian], 4.4 per cent Rakhine, 2.4 per cent Mon, 2.2 per cent Chin, 1.4 per cent Kachin, 0.4 per cent Kayah, [0.1 per cent Other Indigenous] (*Burma 1983 Population Census* [Rangoon: Immigration and Manpower Department, Ministry of Home and Religious Affairs, June 1986], Table A-6, 'Percentage Distribution of Total Population by Race for 1973 and 1983', Figure 3, pp. 1–210). The census notes that the coverage was not complete in as much as, of the 13 756 village tracts in the country, 112 were only partially enumerated and 830 were not included for security reasons. However, it was claimed that 96.6 per cent of the total population was

included. This is based on an estimate that 1 183 005 individuals lived in insecure areas, see *ibid.*, Table A-1, 'Area Covered in 1983 Census by State and Division', pp. 1–12 and text on pp. 1–11. On the basis of BSPP organisational data, I estimated in 1984 that 1 344 210 persons were outside any significant web of relations with the central state, see Robert H. Taylor, *The State in Burma* (London: Hurst, 1987), p. 334.

4. Martin Smith lists thirty-one insurgent groups in existence in March 1989, with support from at least twenty-four different ethnic communities/groups. Of these, at least nine were operating across internal or international borders and twelve were active in the Shan State, see Smith, *Burma: Insurgency and the Politics of Ethnicity* (London and New Jersey: Zed Books, 1991), Chart 1: 'Insurgent Organisations at Time of CPB [Communist Party of Burma] Mutinies, March 1989', p. xii); Smith's map, 'Major Ethnic Groups of Burma' (ibid., p. xvi), though greatly simplifying and schematising the ethnic complexity of the society, provides a graphic scheme revealing the location of eleven groups, three of which are sub-divided into three other categories and one of which indicates an ethnic medley so mixed as to require a two-group category of its own, that is, 'Karen and Burman'. Of the twenty-nine political parties which elected one or more members to the 489-member *Pyithu Hluttaw* (People's Assembly) in 1990, twenty-one had minority ethnic designations, see R.H. Taylor, 'Myanmar 1990: New Era or Old?', *Southeast Asian Affairs 1991* (Singapore: Institute of Southeast Asian Studies, 1991), Table 1, p. 203.

5. 'Table 4, Population and Linguistic Affiliation of Ethnic Groups of Burma', in Peter Kunstadter, 'Burma: Introduction', in Kunstadter (ed.), *Southeast Asian Tribes, Minorities and Nations*, vol. I (Princeton: Princeton University Press, 1967), pp. 87–8, lists twenty major ethnic groups and twenty ethnic sub-groups, several of the latter further subdivided. For a brief, but cogent, discussion of some of the issues involved in understanding ethnicity within Burma, see F.K. Lehman, 'Ethnic Categories in Burma and the Theory of Social Systems', in ibid., pp. 93–124.

6. Mya Sein, *Burma* (London: Oxford University Press, 1944), pp. 9–10.

7. Daw Aung San Suu Kyi is married to a Briton and, until her return to her country in March 1988, was resident in the UK.

8. 'The Constitution of the Socialist Republic of the Union of Burma' (1974) is reprinted in translation in Albert D. Moscotti, *Burma's Constitution and Elections of 1974* (Singapore: Institute of Southeast Asian Studies, Research Notes and Discussions no. 5, September 1977), pp. 73–130. The 1947 constitution, with amendments, are reprinted as Appendices VII, VII, and IX of Maung Maung, *Burma's Constitution* (The Hague: Martinus Nijhoff, 2nd edn, 1996), pp. 258–312.

Part II
Foreign Policy

3 Burma's Relations with the People's Republic of China: from Delicate Friendship to Genuine Co-operation
Chi-shad Liang

Relations between Burma (officially known as the Union of Myanmar since June 1989) and the People's Republic of China (PRC) may be divided into two periods. Prior to the latest period of military rule in Burma beginning in September 1988, this relationship was based on delicate friendship; since then it has been marked by genuine co-operation. This chapter will look first at the historical background of Sino-Burmese relations from the time of Burma's independence in January 1948 up to the military *coup* of 18 September 1988, when the State Law and Order Restoration Council (SLORC) assumed power, and second at developments which have taken place between September 1988 and March 1996.

RELATIONS OF DELICATE FRIENDSHIP, 1948–88

Sino-Burmese relations in the period 1948–88 were largely defined by the existence of the Communist Party of Burma (the CPB). Characterised by a form of delicate friendship, they remained the norm until the remarkable transformations of the post-September 1988 period.

Three months after Burma obtained independence from Britain in January 1948, the CPB joined the regional insurrections and launched a military campaign against the Rangoon government. The Party soon established close contacts with the Chinese Communist Party (CCP), then in the last phase of its successful struggle against the Nationalist government of Chiang Kai-shek. After October 1949, the newly established PRC vowed to assist the armed struggle of the Communist parties in other parts of non-Western world, most of which were still under colonial rule or had only recently been decolonised.[1] Fear of possible PRC support for the CPB and anxiety to please Beijing, were undoubtedly the principle reasons why Burma was the first non-Communist Asian country to recognise the new Chinese Government. Two weeks before Burma's action on 17 December 1949, Burma's Foreign Minister, U Kyaw Nein, stated in London, 'We shall have to recognize the new government of China soon ... it is not that we want to link each other as friends ... We have, of course, reason to be nervous of the spread of Communism in China across our borders.'[2]

For the first two years after independence, Rangoon had looked to London and Washington for assistance in stabilising and developing the young Union of Burma. Following the outbreak of the Korean War in June 1950, however, Burma adopted a neutralist stand in foreign policy. In so doing, it was attempting to steer clear of superpower conflicts and avoid giving offence to either Beijing or Washington. Rangoon's policy towards the PRC at this time was focused on courting the friendship of its giant neighbour in order to deflect possible Chinese intervention in its internal affairs.

Despite this much bruited non-aligned policy, Burma was unable to win over the Chinese, who adopted a particularly hostile stance in the early 1950s, even labelling the Burmese Prime Minister, U Nu, an 'imperialist stooge'. But, the imperatives of the Cold War also meant that China needed Burmese support for its anti-imperialist struggle: it thus sought to use the threat of the CPB as a lever to influence Burma's foreign policy. This strategy was quite successful and ensured that relations between Beijing and Rangoon remained guardedly friendly until the transformation of Sino-Burmese ties in the post-September 1988 period.

Burma's Policy Towards the PRC

The CPB problem remained Burma's principal concern in its bilateral relations with the PRC throughout the whole period from 1948 to the late 1980s. When the Chinese Prime Minister, Zhou Enlai, paid his first goodwill visit to Rangoon in 1954, the U Nu government complained that Burmese Communist cadres were being given sanctuary and political and military training across the Chinese border. The fact that this border was long and only partially demarcated exacerbated the problem for the Burmese leadership, who were concerned not to provoke China by sending troops into its territory, but still wanted to get China to agree to end all cross-border facilities for the CPB. They knew this task would require diplomacy of a high order.

Their first move was to send substantiating documentation to Zhou on his return to Beijing,[3] and they subsequently encouraged Prime Minister Nu to raise the matter again when he visited China in December 1954. In a speech at his farewell banquet on 10 December, Nu touched on the issue in a manner designed not to upset his Chinese hosts, referring to the matter as though it was now a thing of the past: 'Since our first meeting in Rangoon and in the course of our subsequent meetings, I mentioned to Prime Minister Zhou how *we had at one time* [emphasis added] entertained grave apprehensions about the possibility of the People's Republic of China interfering in our internal [political] affairs.'[4]

Although the situation improved with the signing of the Sino-Burmese border agreement of 4 January 1961, relations underwent a rapid deterioration when the Cultural Revolution (1966–9) in China spilled over into Burma, causing anti-Chinese riots in Rangoon in June 1967, which left at least fifty Chinese dead. Following the subsequent diplomatic rift between Beijing and Rangoon (1967–71), General Ne Win, the new head of the Burmese military government, sent out feelers to the Chinese in February 1969 urging them to let bygones be bygones and indicating his readiness to normalise diplomatic ties in return for the Chinese government stopping its support of the Burmese Communists.[5] The assassination of the CPB leader, Thakin Than Tun (1911–68), in September 1968 seemed to highlight tensions within the CPB leadership, and U Ne Win may have felt the time was propitious for a new diplomatic initiative. This was certainly his line at the Fourth Seminar of the Burma Socialist Programme Party (BSPP) in November 1969, when he reiterated his desire to improve relations with China and admitted that, since 1967, fighting had been taking place on the Sino-Burmese border, leaving 113 Burmese dead and a further 250 wounded.

Two years later, in August 1971, his six-day state visit to China provided the opportunity for the resumption of full diplomatic contacts, the Chinese ambassador returning to Rangoon in mid-March the following year after a five-year absence; but the question of China's continuing support for the CPB remained unresolved. U Ne Win brought the matter up again during a second state visit on 11–15 November 1975, when he asked his Chinese hosts to clarify their relations with Rangoon and asked for guarantees with regard to the CPB. Although the visit resulted in the signature of a Sino-Burmese non-aggression pact, CPB military activities continued to escalate, with the Rangoon government coming under pressure during the 1977 dry season (January–June) campaign when weather conditions permitted offensive operations. A hurried visit to China in September 1977, the second that year, clearly underscored U Ne Win's concern that Beijing was stepping up its support for the CPB. But even the general's sacking of two pro-Soviet ministers on the eve of his visit as a goodwill gesture did nothing to placate the Chinese.[6]

When Deng Xiaoping visited Burma in January the following year, China–CPB relations were again top of the agenda. The Chinese leader's statement in Kuala Lumpur just prior to his arrival in Rangoon that 'government–government relations were different from party–party relations', had started alarm bells ringing in Rangoon, for it seemed to imply that Beijing would continue to support the CPB and other Communist-led rebellions in neighbouring countries whatever the state of bilateral relations between sovereign governments.[7] The matter only began to be resolved satisfactorily from the Burmese point of view the following year, when U Ne Win paid yet another visit to Beijing (October 1980), an event which will be considered in more detail below.

Throughout this whole period from the early 1950s to the early 1980s, Burma tried its utmost to side with China's position on international issues. Even if it could not always take Beijing's side, Rangoon went out of its way not to antagonise China, cleaving throughout to a neutralist policy. Thus, it voted against the 1951 UN General Assembly resolution which branded the PRC as the aggressor party in Korea, and later abstained on another vote on the embargo of strategic items to North Korea and the PRC, even though, as a founder member of the Non-Aligned Movement, it was adamantly opposed to the use of force as a means of resolving international disputes. Burma's persistent campaign for a UN seat for China was no doubt partly a public relations exercise, but Rangoon also felt that a PRC presence in the United Nations would safeguard Burma's national security by bringing Beijing's diplomatic activities within the confines of the world organisation. Burma likewise sought to placate China by announcing its withdrawal from the Non-Aligned Movement at the Havana Summit in 1979 in protest against the domination of the Movement by the Soviet bloc and the criticisms levelled against Beijing by the Cuban leader, Fidel Castro, for its February 1979 incursion into Vietnam. A year later, at the October 1980 UN General Assembly meeting, the Burmese Foreign Minister, U Lay Maung, again took China's side, joining in its strong condemnation of the Vietnamese and the Soviets for their respective invasions of Cambodia and Afghanistan.

The PRC's Policy Towards Burma

As we have seen, the PRC used the CPB as a lever to keep the Burmese government on friendly terms, employing a classic policy of reward and punishment, which involved China increasing its support for the CPB at times of strained relations, and reducing it when relations improved. When

U Nu visited China in late 1954, following Zhou Enlai's previous June visit to Burma, the Chinese leadership promised that they would uphold their commitment to non-interference. This was reiterated in April 1963 when the CCP Chairman, Liu Shaoqi, visited Burma and obtained a Burmese understanding on the recent Sino-Indian border conflict. Only a few months later, Beijing supported Rangoon's offer for amnesty talks with the insurgents and arranged for thirty exiled CPB leaders residing in Beijing to be sent to Rangoon to take part in the negotiations.[8]

The outbreak of the Chinese Cultural Revolution in late 1966, however, led to a marked radicalisation of Chinese foreign policy: dominated by so-called 'Red Guard' diplomacy, the aggressive export of Mao Zedong's thought and the encouragement of world revolution were now its top priorities. Burma became a target of this Red Guard diplomacy in the summer of 1967, leading to violent Sino-Burmese riots in Rangoon and a sudden deterioration of bilateral relations. In response, the CCP announced its open support for the Burmese Communist armed struggle against 'the counter-revolutionary, fascist and reactionary' Ne Win government, and large-scale fighting was soon reported along the China–Burma border, with many Communist guerrillas crossing into the People's Republic, thus publicly linking insurgent activity with external Chinese support.[9]

Shortly before Ne Win's August 1971 visit to Beijing, photographs appeared in the Chinese press of Premier Zhou Enlai in the company of two Beijing-based CPB leaders, Party Chairman U Ba Thein Tin and Central Committee member U Pe Tint. The same intimidatory tactics were used six years later in February 1977 at the time of the visit to Rangoon by Madame Deng Yingchao, widow of the recently deceased Zhou Enlai, and the Vice-Chairman of the Standing Committee of the National People's Congress, when the CPB launched a savage attack on government forces in the Delta region. Similarly, battles erupted on 1 February 1978, only one day before Deng Xiaoping, then Chinese Deputy Premier, left Rangoon. These incidents were by no means coincidental; rather, they were orchestrated by the Chinese as reminders to the embattled Rangoon government of the strength of their relations with the CPB.

After the Vietnamese invasion of Cambodia on 25 December 1978, the PRC needed Burma's friendship and co-operation to prevent further Vietnamese and Soviet expansion in Southeast Asia. It therefore temporarily downgraded its relations with the CPB, greatly reducing, and even, for a time, stopping, all military and financial support for the Burmese Communists. Under pressure from the Chinese, the CPB opened peace talks with the Rangoon government in Beijing in September 1980. At the same time, the Chinese decision to invite U Ne Win to Beijing in October of that year in his capacity as Chairman of the Burma Socialist Programme Party indicated official Chinese recognition of the Burmese ruling party, an important step forward in bilateral relations given the importance attached by the CCP leadership to party-to-party links.

PRC–Burma Boundary Agreements and Non-Aggression Treaties

Capitalising on Burmese concern for its support for the CPB, the PRC had been relatively successful in bringing Burma into line with its foreign policy objectives. But it was not just the threat of Beijing's links with the CPB, skilful personal diplomacy also played a key role here. Nowhere was this more evident than at the time of Premier Zhou Enlai's first visit to Rangoon in 1954, when he established a good working relationship with U Nu, and reached agreement with him on the Five Principles of Peaceful Co-existence; (1) mutual respect for each other's territorial integrity and sovereignty; (2) non-aggression; (3) non-interference in each other's internal affairs; (4) equality and mutual benefits; and (5) peaceful co-existence, as the guidelines for the relationship between China and Burma.[10]

From Rangoon's perspective, this declaration went some way towards allaying its fears about the CPB threat, while, for China, it successfully prevented Burma from joining the recently established South-East Asia Treaty Organisation (SEATO) thus ensuring that Burma remained one of the 'friendly' countries arrayed against US encirclement. The major purpose of Zhou's diplomacy had thus been achieved. Beijing followed this up with an invitation to General Ne Win, then head of the eighteen-month military Caretaker Government (1958–60), to visit Beijing to discuss the Sino-Burmese border question, a visit which eventually resulted in an important border agreement (see further Chapter 4, n. 2 below). Burma had long sought such an outcome, and China later used it as an emulative model for the solution of the increasingly serious Sino-Indian border dispute which China wanted settled peacefully. *Jen-min jih-pao*, an official Chinese organ, specifically mentioned this Sino-Burmese border agreement in an editorial on 1 February 1960 stating that: 'The [China–Burma] Boundary Agreements provide an excellent example of Asian countries seeking reasonable settlement of their boundary disputes.'[11]

While in Beijing, General Ne Win also signed a Treaty of Friendship and Non-aggression with China which provided, *inter alia*, that 'each Contracting Party undertakes not to carry out acts of aggression against the other Contracting Party and not to take part in any military alliance directed against the other Contracting Party.'[12] While Burma felt happy to be guaranteed 'friendship and non-agression' by its powerful neighbour, the main interest for China was that the treaty would prevent the United States from using Burma as a base from which to launch an attack on its territory, thus removing a serious threat to its security. Fifteen years later, in November 1975, at the end of U Ne Win's four-day state visit to China, a joint communiqué issued by the Burmese head of state and the Chinese leadership stated that both China and Burma pledged not to join military alliances directed against each other nor to carry out aggressive actions against each other.[13] In this way, just as in 1954, China had obtained assurances that Burma would not provide military facilities for the US, so now it had guarantees that Burma would not join any Soviet alliance against China.

RELATIONS OF GENUINE CO-OPERATION, 1988–THE PRESENT

The military, led by General Saw Maung, Defence Minister in the 'civilian' Government of Dr Maung Maung (in office 18 August–18 September 1988), staged a *coup* in Rangoon on 18 September 1988. This was aimed at reasserting army control over the country by the faction loyal to the recently retired U Ne Win, following nearly six months of mass demonstrations and strikes which had demanded a return to democracy after twenty-six years of authoritarian one-party rule. So violent had these protests been and so widespread that the embattled BSPP leadership had been forced on the defensive, with repeated government changes leading to the virtual paralysis of the administration. Following the 18 September crackdown, the new military junta, known as the State Law and Order Restoration Council (SLORC), committed itself to four main tasks: restoring law and order; facilitating transport and communications; alleviating food, clothing and housing shortages; and holding genuine multi-party elections.

To accomplish the first and second tasks, the SLORC strengthened the armed forces, which rose from some 185 000 on the eve of the September 1988 crackdown, to 230 000 in 1990, and 320 000 in 1994 (the projected target for the year 2000 is 500 000), many of the new recruits being teenage boys (that is, aged sixteen and over).[14] Some elite units, for example the 22nd Light Infantry Division, a division considered most loyal to U Ne Win and the former BSPP leadership, were equipped with new weapons, many of them acquired from the Chinese. To resolve the food, clothing and housing shortages, the SLORC liberalised the economic system in October and November 1988, opening up trade for the co-operative and private sectors, accepting foreign-owned enterprises and joint ventures, and promulgating a new foreign investment law which purported to give foreign investors tax relief, the right to remit hard currency, and guarantees against nationalisation.

Nationwide multi-party elections were held on 27 May 1990 in fulfilment of the SLORC's fourth declared task. To the consternation of the junta, the main opposition party, the National League for Democracy (NLD), led by Daw Aung San Suu Kyi, won a landslide victory at the polls, taking over 80 per cent of the contested seats. In the face of this electoral disaster, the SLORC played for time, announcing that it would not transfer power until a new constitution had been drafted and adopted, and a new government formed (see further above, Chapter 2). Its commitment to accomplishing its 'four main tasks' remained intact, the SLORC declared, but, before a multi-party political system could be instituted, a new state constitution had to be agreed by representatives of the political parties, the national races (that is, the ethnic minorities), peasants, workers, technocrats and the intelligentsia, civil servants and other 'special invitees' at a specially convoked National Convention.

While these portentous events were taking place in Rangoon, the rank and file of the CPB army, mainly made up of Wa tribesmen and Kokang Chinese (with some Shans and Kachins), mutinied and ousted the party's ageing Maoist Burman leaders, forcing them into ignominious exile in China on 17 April 1989. The CPB then split into four different regional armies based on ethnic lines, all of which discarded the former Party's Communist ideology. Between April and November 1989, negotiations with the SLORC succeeded in bringing these armies into 'standfast' agreements (that is, ceasefires with retention of weapons and recognition of the authority of the Rangoon government) in return for unprecedented access to border trade, the main source of contention between the CPB leadership and Rangoon, especially in drugs (raw opium and heroin being the principal exports of the Wa and Kokang regions), and the promise of generous development aid.[15]

Between March 1989 and March 1996, the SLORC succeeded in entering into similar standfast agreements with most of the ethnic insurgent groups – as of the time of writing (March 1996) only the National Socialist Council of Nagaland, the Rohingya Solidarity Alliance, the Chin National Front, the National Unity Front of Arakan, the Karenni National Progressive Party (KNPP), the Karen National Union (KNU) and the scattered units of the All-Burma Students' Democratic Front (ABSDF) army the KNU helped train on the border after September 1988 are still fighting. While these agreements were being negotiated, however, the SLORC had to try to maintain control over the civilian population in the crucial central Burman heartland. As Lintner has pointed out:

> [The] general political situation in the country was extremely serious from the [Rangoon] government's point of view: eager to fight the SLORC, thousands of dissidents were at precisely [this] time [that is, 1989] desperately looking for a source of arms and military training. It was of the utmost importance to the SLORC to neutralise as many of the border insurgencies, *no matter [what] the consequences* [emphasis added].[16]

In the immediate aftermath of the September crackdown, various opposition groups came into existence. The most important of these was the Democratic Alliance of Burma (DAB), a front set up on 19 November 1988 and comprising 23 ethnic resistance armies, underground student groups and other Burmese anti-government organisations, which vowed to wage an armed struggle against the SLORC regime. Two years later, on 18 December 1990, a parallel government, the National Coalition Government of the Union of Burma (NCGUB), was established at Manerplaw under the aegis of the Karen National Union, the strongest of the ethnic groups fighting the Rangoon government. Led by Dr Sein Win, a successful NLD candidate in the May 1990 elections and a first cousin of Daw Aung San Suu Kyi,[17] the NCGUB immediately allied itself with the Democratic Alliance. At the same time, Rangoon was forced on the defensive by a new Chin insurgency along the border with India – Delhi, at this time, taking a firm stand in favour of Burma's pro-democracy movement.

The open-door policy, including the sale to foreign interests of the rights to exploit Burma's natural resources, increased Rangoon's foreign-exchange reserves (minus gold) from less than US$10 million in September 1988 to US$550 million in September 1990, enough to cover four months' imports.[18] But efforts to improve the people's living conditions met with only limited success, with the majority of the people still suffering from high commodity prices and runaway inflation. The SLORC recognised that a resolution of these problems was crucial for its survival. A sound economy and a strong army were two sides of the same coin in their view. But, given the suspension of aid and the imposition of an unofficial embargo which cut off the supply of arms from traditional Western sources (Germany, the USA, Yugoslavia and Israel being the most prominent here),[19] it was forced to turn to neighbouring countries. One of the first of these neighbours to recognise the SLORC was the PRC, which soon became one of Burma's most significant trade partners and its main arms supplier. The combination of the SLORC's need to consolidate its grip on the country, the collapse of the BCP (which eliminated the element previously used by China to manipulate Burmese–Chinese relations), Beijing's modernisation drive, and the end of the Cold War, all meant that Burma and the PRC could now embark on a much closer relationship, one marked for the first time by genuine co-operation.

Political and Diplomatic Co-operation

Ever since its seizure of power in September 1988, the SLORC has received strong political and diplomatic support from the PRC. Not only was it one of the first countries to accord the SLORC diplomatic recognition, but its ambassador in Rangoon also maintained particularly close contacts with junta leaders, helping to co-ordinate the disintegration of the Communist Party of Burma after the CPB army mutinies of March–April 1989. Following the arrival CPB Chairman U Ba Thein Tin and other Central Committee members in China on 17 April 1989, Beijing refused to allow them to establish a political base, and played a key behind-the-scenes role in the negotiations which led to the standfast agreements with the splintered BCP army remnants between April and November. At the same time, by allowing a continuous flow of consumer goods and weapons across the border, the PRC was critical in enabling the SLORC to consolidate its hold on power.

The SLORC's reliance on Chinese assistance in the aftermath of the September 1988 *coup* turned Burma into one of the PRC's closest allies, a situation which continues up to the present – as evidenced by the remark made in December 1995 by the SLORC chairman, Senior General Than Shwe, to the visiting Chairman of the Chinese Peoples' Political Consultative Conference, Li Ruihan, when he stated that China was 'the Myanmar [Burmese] people's most trusted friend'.[20]

In the wake of the June 1989 Tiananmen crackdown on pro-democracy protests in Beijing, SLORC Secretary-1 Brigadier-General (now Lieutenant-General) Khin Nyunt met with the Chinese Ambassador to Burma, Cheng Rushing, and, on behalf of General Saw Maung, expressed Burma's understanding and sympathy for the Chinese government's stand on the counterrevolutionary rebellion. He said that the Burmese government supported the Chinese government's opposition to external interference and expressed the hope for a further development in Sino-Burmese relations.[21]

On the diplomatic front, China and Burma also co-operated closely in international fora. At the Third Committee of the 1990 UN General Assembly in New York, a draft resolution introduced by Sweden censuring Burma for contempt of its citizens' basic rights had to be withdrawn due to fierce opposition by China and other Asian countries, which considered it rank interference in Burma's internal affairs.[22] A similar draft resolution was re-introduced at the Third Committee of the 1991 UN General Assembly, but this time it was unanimously approved without a vote, China dropping its opposition after Sweden had agreed to delete a sentence expressing concern at 'the continued deprivation of liberty of a number of democratically elected political leaders'. Intense international pressure following the award of the 1991 Nobel Peace Prize to Daw Aung San Suu Kyi, leader of Burma's main opposition party, and the fact that India, a major Asian country and an opponent of the 1990 draft resolution, had agreed to co-sponsor the 1991 draft resolution, were both critical in determining China's decision.[23] On human rights issues, Burma has always sided with China, making similar arguments about the need to take account of a country's specific historical, social, economic, and cultural conditions, and asserting that there should be no outside interference in the domestic affairs of a sovereign state.

Economic and Technical Co-operation

Economic and technical co-operation between China and Burma have been greatly enhanced since the advent of military rule in September 1988. In that year, Chinese engineers helped Burma repair and reconstruct bridges which had been damaged or destroyed by pro-democracy protesters. At the same time, the construction of a number of TV relay stations for the state broadcasting corporation, Myanmar Television, was carried out with technical assistance from China. A year later, in November 1989, no less than six Sino-Burmese trade and economic agreements were signed with the SLORC by the visiting Yunnan Governor, He Zhigiang, including co-operation in geological surveys and the development of coal and tin mining operations.[24] Similar agreements on economic and technical co-operation were initialled during the December 1989 visit to Burma of a Chinese delegation headed by Wang Wendong, Assistant Minister at the Ministry of Foreign Economic Relations and Trade. Under the terms of this agreement, the Chinese government undertook to give the Burmese government an interest-free loan of Rmb 50 million (US$15 million) to supplement the Rangoon–Thanhyin rail and road bridge construction project.[25] A further Rmb 50 million interest-free loan was extended following General Saw Maung's visit to China in August 1991, earmarked for the construction of a TV station and other unspecified projects, which will be discussed further below.[26]

As early as 5 August 1988, at the height of the democracy protests in Rangoon, Burma and China signed their first official border trade agreement during the visit to Rangoon of Xin Weinong, deputy general manager of the Yunnan Province Import and Export Corporation. Under the terms of this agreement, which came into effect in October 1988, Burma agreed to sell 1500 tons of maize, valued at US$180 000, in exchange for Chinese milk powder, soap and toothpaste. In December 1989, another Yunnan delegation arrived in Rangoon to sign a memorandum of understanding with Burma's Ministry of Trade on bilateral commerce, which involved agreements between Burma and the Yunnan provincial authorities to open department stores to market each other's goods, to promote tourism and to form joint ventures to mine tin and market coal in Shan and Kachin states respectively.[27]

Since the August 1988 opening of the border, trade between Burma and China has taken three main forms:

1. trade agreements between the Chinese provincial government and the local SLORC authorities (such as the one negotiated in Rangoon in December 1989);
2. small-scale border-trade between commercial companies in towns on both sides of the border involving no written contracts, but being agreed through face-to-face negotiations);
3. free trade on both sides of the border.[28]

As regards this last, it was reported in 1989 that more than 2000 Chinese items were being sold in Burmese markets, the cross-border trade providing China with a wide variety of raw materials and Burma with badly needed consumer goods (see further Chapter 4).

The rapid growth of cross-border trade between Burma and Yunnan can be seen from Table 3.1 below. This shows that the total value of the official Yunnan–Burma import–export trade grew from 37.88 million *yuan* (US$16.25 m.) in 1984, and to 1066.978 million *yuan* (US$222.65 m.) in 1990, a year in which the *New York Times* reported Yunnan's cross-border trade at US$200 m., 90 per cent of it with Burma and the remainder split between Laos and Vietnam.[29] If one tries to take account of unofficial trade as well, this figure would almost certainly go higher: in 1987, a Chinese report estimated the value of the trade at US$1 bn, a sum that had doubled two years later after the SLORC *coup* and the collapse of the CPB.[30]

When one turns to the broader picture, the growth of Sino-Burmese trade can be graphically illustrated from the statistics published in the annual *Almanac of China's Foreign Economic Relations and Trade*. This shows

Table 3.1   Trade Between Yunnan Province of the PRC and Burma 1984–90

Year	Value of imports and exports (yuan m.)	Increase (%)
1984	37.88	
1985	109.72	189
1986	172.39	57
1987	396.60	130
1988	789.52	99.89
1989	965.00	26
1990	1066.978	11

Source: Beijing Review, 19–25 August 1991, p. 38

Table 3.2   Burma's Trade with the PRC 1958–95

Year	Exports to China (US$ m.)	Imports from China (US$ m.)	Total
1958–67	134.1	215.6	349.7
1968–77	23.455[a]	113.003	136.458
1978–87	50.95	173.85	224.8
1988	1.81	7.7	9.51
1989	24.60	51.43	76.03
1990	26.13	102.51	128.64
1991	96	315	411
1992	119	285	404
1993	150	357	507
1994	142	368	510
1995	202[b]	480[b]	682[b]

[a] Statistics for exports to China in 1968 and 1969 are left blank in the yearbooks of these two years.
[b] estimated
Source: International Monetary Fund, Direction of Trade Annals and Direction of Trade Statistics Yearbook (New York: IMF, 1958–94); Economist Intelligence Unit, 'Country Report: Myanmar', 4th Quarter 1995, p. 49; 1st Quarter 1996, p. 31.

that in 1987 the value of Sino-Burmese trade was US$150.65 m., with China's exports worth US$64.42 m. and imports worth US$86.23 m.; by 1988 this had risen to US$255.62 m. (exports US$140.83 m. and imports

US$117.79 m.), and had increased again to US$392 m. by 1991 (exports US$286 m. and imports US$106 m.).[31] Further corroboration of this remarkable growth emerges from data from the International Monetary Fund and the Economist Intelligence Unit's 'Country Report' on Burma given in Table 3.2 above. These indicate a striking rise after 1988, when Burma's official export trade with China stood at a paltry US$1.81 m. (a time when the lucrative smuggling trade across the border was still in the hands of the ethnic insurgents), to US$24.6 m. in 1989, US$150 m. in 1993, and an estimated US$202 m. in 1995. By then, China's exports, consisting largely of light industrial goods (which made up the bulk of the border trade and accounted for 70 per cent of all Sino-Burmese commerce by 1995), capital equipment and raw material for the construction of power stations, roads and bridges, and telecommunications facilities had reached an estimated all time high of US$480 million.[32]

Military Co-operation

Alongside the burgeoning trading links which bound the military regime in Rangoon to the Chinese after 1988, was another, more sinister, connection: arms. Deprived of its traditional sources of supply and desperate to expand and reequip its armed forces lest the combination of popular uprisings in the Burman heartland and minority insurgencies on the non-Burman periphery overwhelm its authority, the SLORC turned to the PRC to modernise its armed forces. In August 1990, just a year after the pro-democracy protests in Rangoon, a massive US$1.2 billion deal was signed with Beijing for the provision of 60 medium-size tanks, 25 multi-barrelled anti-aircraft guns, several batteries of 120-mm and 105-mm howitzers, six 30-knot Hainan-class fast patrol boats (a further four were delivered in 1993), a squadron (twelve planes) each of F-7 jet fighters and F-6 attack fighters capable of air-to-ground combat (that is, highly suitable for counter-insurgency operations), a number of shoulder-fired Hongying HN-5 (and HTM5-A) missiles, nine armoured personnel carriers, and a range of other military hardware.[33] Special payment terms were arranged with the cash-strapped Rangoon regime: only 30 per cent (US$400 million) being demanded in hard currency (a sum which was paid from the sale of timber and other natural resources), the rest being divided between 10 per cent in grants and soft loans, and 60 per cent in short and long-term barter trade.[34] In order to facilitate these purchases, the secretive Chinese government arms agency, the Poly Technologies, set up an office in Rangoon.

The arms agreement also included a training programme for some 400–600 Burmese personnel at army bases and military colleges in nearby

Yunnan. In 1989, even before the agreement was signed, several groups of army officers from four armoured and artillery units had received training in China. Under the provisions of the August 1990 deal, this training was now greatly expanded, with 180 field-grade army officers (mostly lieutenants and captains), as well as airforce and naval personnel (400–600 in all), embarking on specialised courses, with the latter receiving instruction in how to operate the new Chinese fighters and naval craft.[35] For the first time since the immediate post-independence period, foreign military personnel were based in Burma, with five instructors from the Chinese Air Force (a lieutenant, three sergeants and a warrant officer) arriving at Myitkyina air base in early September 1990. They were followed later by seventy Chinese naval personnel – half of them middle-rank officers – sent to train local crews and maintain newly installed radar equipment, some of it destined for new bases at Hainggyi in the Irrawaddy River estuary near Bassein, Ramree island south of Sittwe (Rakhine [Arakan] State), Zadetkyi Kyun (St Matthew's Island) off the Tennasserim coast in the southeast, and Coco Island, 300 kilometres south of the Burmese mainland in the Andaman Sea.[36]

Despite the size of the 1990 deal, the SLORC felt the need to conclude a further US$400 m. arms purchase from China in November 1994. This involved the purchase of twenty helicopters, fifty heavy artillery pieces, a further sixty armoured personnel carriers, six more Hainan-class patrol boats and a number of smaller gunboats (both acquired to guard Burma's newly-developed offshore oil and gas fields, and fisheries, in the Andaman Sea), air-to-surface missiles, AK-47 assault rifles and 800 parachutes.[37] By then, the completion of a large new bridge over the Shweli River, near the Burma–China border, in October 1992, had greatly expedited the delivery of arms by land (the initial August 1990 equipment having been brought to Rangoon by sea), and by the end of 1993, arms were said to be flowing into Burma from China 'at a faster pace than at any time since ... August 1990'.[38] Such massive reliance on Chinese supplies had its problems, however: despite all the training provided, the Burmese military found much of the new equipment unfamiliar and difficult to handle, with artillery pieces frequently misfiring, armoured vehicles breaking down, and the Chinese army trucks not nearly as reliable as the previous, Japanese-supplied, Hino and Nissan vehicles.[39] It was partly for this reason that, since 1988, other suppliers have been sought in Singapore (Chartered Industries), Pakistan, Portugal, Israel, South Africa, North and South Korea, and the Czech Republic.[40] In late October 1995, overtures were even made to the Russians, when Lieutenant-General Tin Oo, the army commander-in-chief, visited Moscow and signed a deal for Russian-made helicopter gunships, the first two of which were delivered to Rangoon by air in November 1995.[41]

Official Visits and the Strengthening of Bilateral Co-operation

Frequent exchanges of high-ranking officials and political leaders have been the principal way in which Sino-Burmese bilateral cooperation has been strengthened in the SLORC period. Since September 1988, more than ten Burmese delegations have gone to Beijing, while no less than fifteen Chinese delegations have come to Rangoon. Amongst these, the visits of Generals Than Shwe and Saw Maung to China, as well as Premier Li Peng's to Burma, have been particularly significant.

During the period 18–27 October 1989 Lieutenant-General (now Senior General) Than Shwe, then army commander-in-chief (now SLORC Chairman), led a 24-member Burmese delegation to Beijing where they were welcomed by General Xu Xin, Deputy Chief of the General Staff of the Chinese People's Liberation Army, who enthused that 'the visit of [the] Myanmar goodwill delegation will further strengthen Sino-Myanmar friendship and the mutual contacts between our defense forces. ... We are very happy to learn about the desire of the Myanmar side to boost economic and trade relations and the contacts between our two defence forces'. General Than Shwe, in turn, spoke of the need to further strengthen Sino-Burmese friendship and the promotion of greater exchanges between the two defence services, adding 'since Myanmar is now practicing an open-door policy, many opportunities have emerged to expand economic and trading relations between the two countries.'[42]

The twin concerns of military co-operation and border trade thus loomed large during the visit, and these concerns were returned to when the SLORC Chairman, Senior General Saw Maung (in office, 1988–92), accompanied by senior Burmese officers and his Trade Minister, Brigadier-General David Abel, paid his first goodwill visit to China on 20–5 August 1991. Both the delegation's hosts – PRC Chairman, Yang Shangkun, and the CCP General Secretary, Jiang Zemin – stressed the importance of strengthening friendship between Burma and China through adherence to the Five Principles of Peaceful Co-Existence, which had first been agreed by Zhou Enlai and U Nu back in June 1954, and, in reply, General Saw Maung pointed out that no matter what changes had taken place in the international order (a reference to the recent collapse of the Soviet Union and the end of the Cold War), friendly relations would continue to grow.[43] In the presence of the Chinese premier, Li Peng, who had given an account of China's economic reforms, the general then set forth Burma's domestic and foreign policies, emphasising that his country attached great importance to developing friendly relations with its neighbours.[44]

While these exchanges were taking place, the main work of the visit was being done by the Burmese Trade Minister David Abel and his Chinese counterpart Li Langing, Minister of Foreign Economic Relations and Trade, who signed an economic co-operation agreement in a ceremony witnessed by Yang Shangkun and General Saw Maung. At the same time, Brigadier-General Myo Thant, Director of Signals of the Burmese Defence Ministry, signed a further agreement regarding Myanmar Television Station's Channel 5 project with the Vice-President of the Chinese Sitit Company, Wang Zhong.[45] In this fashion, Chinese assistance in the telecommunications field, already extended in 1988 for the construction of TV transmission and relay stations was carried a step further, the dissemination of government propaganda being deemed crucial to the survival of the SLORC regime.

On their way back to Burma, the SLORC Chairman and his party stopped in the Yunnanese capital, Kunming, to visit the Kunming Electrical Machinery and Electric Cable plants, which were both heavily involved in exports of power generation equipment to Burma.[46] The Burmese leader also held talks with the Governor of Yunnan Province on matters concerning border trade and economic and technical cooperation, particularly the construction of all-weather cross-border roads vital for the transport of heavy goods between Burma and Yunnan.[47]

In December 1994, Premier Li Peng finally visited Rangoon, the first visit by a Chinese head of government since the SLORC seized power six years earlier. He stiffened the SLORC leadership's resolve not to make any deals with the NLD leader, Daw Aung San Suu Kyi, then languishing in her sixth year of house arrest, with an eye to ending the Western trade and investment embargo, stressing instead that 'China is willing to promote trade and economic cooperation with Myanmar on the basis of equality and mutual benefit.' During a formal reception by the SLORC Chairman, Than Shwe, he praised 'the time-tested traditional good neighbourly relationship between China and Myanmar [which] is developing steadily and has broad prospects', eliciting a panegyric from Than Shwe who spoke of the historical significance of Li Peng's visit and the way in which frequent exchanges of visits between the leaders of the two countries would promote 'the continuing development of friendly relations'.[48]

CONCLUSION

As we have seen, two distinct phases can be discerned in Sino-Burmese relations, with a clear change taking place in mid-1988. In the 1949–88 period, fear of the potential or real support of China for the Communist Party of Burma, at this time the country's most powerful insurgent group, dominated Rangoon's thinking towards the PRC. Burma's decision to recognise China in December 1949, the first non-Communist country to take this step, must be seen in this context. So too must its leaning towards the PRC during the Cold War, despite its avowed neutralist foreign policy. Both were done to avoid offending the PRC and to court its friendship. On its part the PRC, after taking a hostile attitude toward Burma in the early years, decided to use the CPB as a weapon to turn Burma into a political follower in the era of the Cold War. The visit of Zhou Enlai to Rangoon in June 1954 marked a turning point in the relations between the two countries, ushering in a period of 'delicate friendship' which lasted, but for the five-year interruption (1967–71) caused by Chinese Red Guard diplomacy, until the present period of military rule in September 1988.

Since then relations between Burma and the PRC have shifted rapidly towards genuine co-operation, a shift dictated largely by changes in the internal politics of the two countries and the end of the Cold War. Following the trade and military agreements of 1988–90, Burma looked to the PRC for consumer goods to ease popular grievances and for weapons to fight the ethnic rebels and the 'destructive [democratic] elements' within the country. The PRC, for its part, focused principally on the economic dimensions of its relations with its Southeast Asian ally. Certainly, Burma's foremost concern in its dealings with its giant neighbour, ever since the Communists came to power in October 1949, has always been the survival of the Rangoon government, a concern which has, if anything, intensified now that it is clear there will be no swift end to the informal Western investment and arms blockade following Daw Aung San Suu Kyi's release from house arrest on 10 July 1995.

The real challenge Burma faces in the late 1990s, however, lies not in the survival of a government but in the future of the nation. At no time since independence in January 1948 has Burma experienced such a grave crisis. For three and a half decades the Burmese people have remained under authoritarian rule deprived of political freedom. Popular hatred of the present regime has increased following its arbitrary decision not to transfer power after the May 1990 elections. Despite the standfast agreements, ethnic insurgency is still a threat in many rural areas, and national disunity has been deepened by the anti-government sentiments of the civilian population and the establishment of a parallel government. Military expenditure, direct and indirect, is estimated at more than 60 per cent of the national budget. The combination of Ne Win's disastrous 'Burmese Way to Socialism' (1962–88) and thirty-five years of military rule have transformed a once prosperous nation into a 'least-developed country', with a per caput income of less than US$250, on a par with Bangladesh and Mali. Current economic policies are at best only *ad hoc* measures to raise money for present needs. All major aid donors, with the partial exception of Japan which has recently (February 1996) allowed Rangoon some modest debt-relief, have suspended aid until democratic government is installed. At the same time, US pressure is ensuring that Rangoon is deprived of the multilateral aid which it so desperately needs to restructure its economy and float its currency.

Despite ASEAN's 'constructive engagement' – Burma is due to become a member of the regional organisation perhaps as early as July 1997 provided its key sponsors (Malaysia, Singapore and Indonesia) have their way – and the support of China, Burma is still diplomatically isolated. The crisis presents a serious challenge to Rangoon. The SLORC, acting allegedly as a transitional government, has committed itself to move from a single-party system to a multi-party system. It has also pledged to hand over political power to a duly elected government after the approval of a new constitution. But no time has been set for the transitional period and there are grave doubts as to whether the present government will ever consent to relinquish power.

Given the right leadership and vision, Burma has the chance of one day becoming a unified and prosperous country. The Burmese people are not demanding much: they could easily be satisfied with basic political freedoms and material needs. If the long years of inept and brutal military government has taught them anything it is to be content with little. But that little must include some essentials which are not negotiable: a new constitutional guarantee of minority rights, for example, which could bring the ethnic rebels into the legal fold; a law code which ensures basic civil and human rights; an end to corruption and the abuse of office; and the abolition of censorship. In brief, a government answerable to the people, not to a narrow military clique.

With substantial reserves of oil, timber and other natural resources, the economy has great growth potential. Provided the right political leadership is in place, there is no reason why Burma should not prosper. True, there is a shortage of indigenous development experts and technicians due to the frequent closures of higher educational institutions, a result of the political turmoil of the past few years, but development experts, as well as capital and technology, can be drawn in the short term from foreign countries by offering favourable conditions. Furthermore, with the Cold War over, Burma need not follow traditional neutralism any more but can instead pursue an active foreign policy and freely seek co-operation with all countries in the service of its national interests. The opportunities to develop a unified and prosperous Burma will be lost, however, if the Burmese government is not a duly elected one and fails to command the support of the Burmese people and the confidence of the international community.

Given Burma's continuing political impasse, Rangoon and Beijing will doubtless strengthen their relations of genuine cooperation. But this is dependent on the present governments of the two countries remaining in power, and current policies not being challenged by popular protest: in Burma there are already many voices being heard, some at senior military levels, questioning the wisdom of such close economic ties with Beijing, ties whose benefits seem to be largely for the benefit of China and the large number of Chinese (mostly Yunnanese) economic migrants. Indeed, some of these criticisms are being taken up by Burma's closest ASEAN neighbours: Thailand, in particular, is increasingly concerned that China may one day use Burma as a springboard for increased political and economic influence in Southeast Asia. The establishment of a democratically elected civilian government in Rangoon would not immediately resolve these worries – Burma would still have to maintain close ties with any future Chinese government in the interests of her economy and security – but it would certainly be able to balance these with other international relationships which might go a long way towards ensuring the type of support which Burma and its long-suffering people so desperately need.

Notes

1. See the statement by Liu Shaoqi, a leading figure and later PRC's Chairman, at the Australasian Trade Union Conference in Beijing in November 1949. *New China News Agency* (Beijing), 23 November 1949.
2. John W. Henderson *et al.*, *Area Handbook for Burma* (Washington, DC: The American University Foreign Area Studies, 1971), p. 189.
3. George McTurnan Kahin, *The Asian-African Conference, Bandung, Indonesia, April 1955* (Ithaca, New York: Cornell University Press, 1956), p. 7.
4. Harold Hinton, *China's Relations with Burma and Vietnam. A Brief Survey* (New York: Institute of Pacific Relations, 1958), p. 37.
5. *FEER*, 20 February 1969, p. 311.
6. *Asian Recorder* (New Delhi), 22–8 October 1977, p. 13990; 12–18 November 1977, p. 14021.

7. David I. Steinberg, 'Burma Under the Military: Towards a Chronology', *Contemporary Southeast Asia*, 3.3 (December 1981), p. 279.

8. John H. Badgley, 'The Communist Parties of Burma', in Robert A. Scalapino (ed.), *The Communist Revolution in Asia: Tactics, Goals, and Achievements*, 2d edn (New Jersey: Englewood Cliffs, 1969), p. 325; Maung Maung Gyi, 'Foreign Policy of Burma Since 1962: Negative Neutralism for Group Survival', in F.K. Lehman (ed.), *Military Rule in Burma Since 1962* (Singapore: Maruzen Asia, 1981), p. 17.

9. *New York Times*, 20 March 1968; Steinberg, 'Burma Under Military Rule', p. 262.

10. Burma Socialist Programme Party Central Organization Committee, *Foreign Policy of Revolutionary Government of the Union of Burma* (Rangoon: Government Printing Office, 1968), Appendix (A), p. 127.

11. *Jen-min jib-pao* (Beijing), 1 February 1960. In 1985, another joint Burma–China border survey was instituted, see further Chapter 4, n. 2.

12. *Beijing Review*, 2 February 1960, p. 13.

13. *Economic Review* (London), no. 1 (January 1976), p. 12.

14. FEER, 18 October 1989, p. 23; *Jane's Defence Weekly*, 15 June 1991, p. 1053; FEER, *Asia 1991 Yearbook* (Hong Kong: FEER, 1990), p. 87; Martin Smith, *Ethnic Groups in Burma: Development, Democracy and Human Rights* (London: Anti-Slavery International, 1994), p. 118 (on recruitment of teenagers); and Bertil Lintner, 'Ethnic Insurgents and Narcotics', *Burma Debate* (Washington), 2.1 (February–March 1995), p. 19 (for the 1994 figure of 320 000).

15. *FBIS-EAS-Daily Report*, 22 May 1989, p. 33; *Jane's Defence Weekly*, 8 July 1989, p. 25; *FEER*, 24 August 1989, p. 28, 23 May 1991, p. 12; Lintner, 'Ethnic Insurgents and Narcotics', pp. 18–21; and Smith, *Ethnic Groups*, pp. 125–9. The Rangoon government promised Kt 70 m. (US$11.6 m. at the official exchange rate of Kt 6 to the US dollar) for a 'Border Areas Development Programme' to build roads, bridges, schools and hospitals. Little of this money ever reached the region, which is still one of the least developed in Burma, see further Benjamin Min, 'The Bondage of Opium: The Agony of the Wa People. A Proposal and a Plea', *Burma Debate* (Washington), 2.1 (February–March 1995), pp. 14–17.

16. Lintner, 'Ethnic Insurgents and Narcotics', p. 20.

17. *FEER*, 3 January 1991, pp. 10–11; *Asiaweek* (Hong Kong), 4 January 1991, pp. 16–17.

18. *FEER*, 21 December 1989, p. 22; 8 August 1991, p. 57. The figure is now US$561.1 m., slightly down from the August 1995 peak of US$663.1 m., but still sufficient to cover 3.8 months of import cover at the 1994/5 level of imports, see further EIU, 'Country Report: Myanmar', 1st Quarter 1996 (London: EIU), p. 29.

19. *FEER*, 5 October 1989, p. 18.

20. EIU, 'Country Report: Myanmar', 1st Quarter 1996, p. 12.

21. *FBIS-CHI-Daily Report*, 19 June 1989, p. 10.

22. *New York Times*, 25 November 1990.

23. Ibid., 30 November 1991.

24. *FBIS-EAS-Daily Report*, 15 August 1991, p. 36.

25.   Ibid., 29 December 1989, p. 27; *SWB-FE-Daily Report*, 3 January 1990, p. A3/1.

26.   *FEER*, 3 October 1991, p. 24.

27.   Ibid., 23 February 1989, p. 13; *FBIS-EAS-Daily Report*, 7 December 1989, p. 35; *Keesing's Record of World Events*, February 1991, p. 37285.

28.   *Beijing Review*, 19–25 August 1991, p. 38.

29.   Ibid.; Nicholas D. Kristof, 'China Province Forges Regional Trade Links', *New York Times*, 7 April 1991.

30.   Martin Smith, *Burma: Insurgency and the Politics of Ethnicity* (London: Zed Books, 1991), p. 361; *FEER*, 8 June 1989, p. 105 (which estimated legal and illegal trade between the two countries at US$1.5 bn in the late 1980s); and Michael Vatikiotis, 'Catching the Wave', *FEER*, 16 February 1995, p. 50 (who estimated the value of cross-border trade with China at US$800 m., or 40 per cent of Burma's total trade, in 1994).

31.   *Almanac of China's Foreign Economic Relations and Trade* (Hong Kong: China Resource's Advertising Company, 1988), p. 454; (1989–90), p. 366; (1992–3), pp. 398, 428.

32.   EIU, 'Country Report: Myanmar', 1st Quarter 1996, p. 12.

33.   *FBIS-EAS-Daily Report*, 28 November 1990, p. 32. In 1991, Bertil Lintner reported cumulative arms deals with China worth US$1.4 bn, making Burma one of China's important customers for military hardware in the 1988–91 period, see *FEER*, 3 October 1991, p. 24; and *FEER*, 16 December 1993, p. 26. For a more detailed listing of the arms and military training obtained from China in the period 1988–95, see Andrew Selth, 'The Myanmar Army Since 1988: Acquisitions and Adjustments', *Contemporary Southeast Asia*, 17.3 (December 1995), pp. 249–50.

34.   *FEER*, 6 June 1991, p. 12.

35.   Ibid., 13 September 1990, p. 28; 6 December 1990, p. 28; 6 June 1991, p. 12; and Selth, 'Myanmar Army', p. 250, (reporting on the training provision for 400–600 officers in China).

36.   *Jane's Defence Weekly*, 15 June 1991, p. 1053; *FEER*, 16 December 1993, p. 26; *FEER*, 4 August 1994, p. 12. See further Chapter 4, n. 50. According to Selth, 'Myanmar Army', pp. 250–1, some of the seventy-five Chinese instructors working in Burma at this time (1992–3) were also involved in advising Burmese troops in the field: Karen insurgents, for example, claimed to have seen Chinese officers at artillery bases near Manerplaw in 1992 (Selth, p. 262, n. 90). There have also been unconfirmed reports that in 1991 Pakistan sent a number of instructors to Burma to help the Burmese Army become more familiar with those types of Chinese equipment, also used in Pakistan, and to provide special forces training, including airborne training, at the Armed Forces' Airborne School at Hmawbi just to the north of Rangoon (Selth, pp. 250–1).

37.   *Jane's Defence Weekly*, 3 December 1994, p. 1.

38.   Selth, 'Myanmar Army', p. 250, quoting Lintner, 'Arms for Eyes', *FEER*, 16 December 1993.

39.   Ibid., p. 255, quoting Lintner, 'Myanmar's Chinese Connection', *International Defense Review*, 27.11 (November 1994), p. 26.

40.   Selth, 'Myanmar Army', pp. 248–9.

41.   *FEER*, 21 December 1995, p. 14.

42. *FBIS-EAS-Daily Report*, 31 October 1989, p. 37.
43. *SWB-FE-Daily Report*, 22 August 1991, p. A3/2; 27 August 1991, p. A3/1.
44. Ibid., 23 August 1991, p. A3/3.
45. Ibid., 27 August 1991, p. A3/1; 28 August 1991, p. A3/5.
46. On the construction of new power plants, see EIU, 'Country Report: Myanmar', 1st Quarter 1996, pp. 12, 26. Currently two new power stations are under construction: a 200-megawatt facility near Rangoon, and a 65-megawatt plant in Kanbauk in Mon State.
47. *SWB-FE-Daily Report*, 27 August 1991, p. A3/1.
48. *FBIS-CHI-Daily Report*, 28 December 1994, p. 18.

Part III
Views from the Periphery

4 Burma's Ethnic Minorities: a Central or Peripheral Problem in the Regional Context?
Martin Smith

> The convenient thesis that Burma is a happy little country, geographically self-contained and psychologically uninterested in its neighbours, does not correspond with the facts of history.[1]

INTRODUCTION

In the three decades since Dorothy Woodman wrote the words above, Burma's international reputation of isolation as the 'Albania of Asia' has largely continued. Published in 1962 in the shadow of General Ne Win's second military *coup* of 2 March, Woodman's study, *The Making of Burma*, is the only detailed investigation into how the present geo-political shape of Burma came to be drawn. Burma currently shares a 1357-mile border with China (including a small part of Tibet), a 1304-mile border with Thailand, an 857-mile border with India, a 156-mile border with Laos, and a 152-mile border with Bangladesh. But while nobody can seriously expect any substantial redefinition of Burma's external borders today,[2] it is essential in the present political crisis to put the clock back and re-address some of the fundamental points that Woodman raised, if a lasting peace is ever to be found for this deeply troubled land.

This re-examination of nationality and regional relationships is necessary not only for Burma's neighbours, the ruling State Law and Order Restoration Council (SLORC), which assumed power in September 1988, and other parties and international agencies at the present political centre in Rangoon. Equally important during any process of reflection is the need to reassess – through consultation – the pivotal importance of Burma's ethnic minority peoples who inhabit all these vast borderland areas. They

97

are, after all, in the front-line of regional change. History has repeatedly shown that they are not simply a peripheral problem, as has often been characterised by governments in Rangoon, but have become one of the most central issues facing the country today. 'Today the term "ethnic minority" no longer conveys a profound meaning', a SLORC spokesman claimed in 1991 (see further above, Chapter 2).[3] In fact, as the constant political and ethnic violence of the last forty years so tragically demonstrates, nothing could be further from the truth.

Since the short-lived 'democracy summer' of 1988, hopes have continued to be raised of a fundamental change in Burma's political climate in what has now become the country's third critical period of political transition since independence in 1948. Inside Burma the need for reform has been reflected by all the key actors, including the military regime, which has offered ceasefires to the country's armed ethnic opposition groups, the ethnic insurgent forces themselves, which have accepted such military truces in increasing numbers, and also by the National League for Democracy (NLD) which won – although it has since been denied – victory in the May 1990 election. Indeed, perhaps the most poignant description of the present period of upheavals has come from the NLD's leader, Daw Aung San Suu Kyi, who has called the task now facing the country 'Burma's second struggle for independence'.[4]

Outside Burma, too, international interest has begun to gain momentum, with both Asian and Western governments struggling to redefine long-standing policies in a bid to keep up with – or influence – events inside the country. In such a changing environment, various agencies of the United Nations have also become increasingly involved, as Rolf Carriere's chapter in this volume shows (see Chapter 8).

However, despite such universal recognition of the need for reform, the fact remains that for many Burmese citizens post-colonial Burma has yet to find a cohesive national and political identity, which will both bring lasting peace and allow the country to take its proper place, with defined and equitable relationships, in the international community of nations. For this to be achieved, Burma's long-standing minority problems must first be solved as a substantive part of any process of lasting reform.

HISTORICAL OVERVIEW

A number of historians and political scientists, notably Michael Aung-Thwin, Robert Taylor and Daw Ni Ni Myint (the wife of General Ne Win), have investigated or tried to prove the long traditions of a national Burmese – or Myanmar – state, largely dominated by the Burman majority in the central Irrawaddy plains.[5] However, in ethnic terms, Burma's frontiers and divisions have always been loosely defined. Situated between modern-day Bangladesh, India, China, Laos and Thailand, ethnic minority peoples, such as the Zos or Chins (Mizos/Zomis), Nagas, Kachins, Shans (Tais), Lahus and Karens live in substantial numbers on both sides of the current borders, and in many areas constitute the majority. Even today, other than the military and government bureaucracy, ethnic Burman influence is minimal in most border regions. Indeed in the case of the Shan and Kachin states, the first Burman-majority towns lie several hundred miles away from the present international frontiers.

Across the centuries, territory has frequently been annexed or exchanged by different rulers, invaders and monarchs. The Tavoy–Mergui districts of the Tenasserim Division, for example, were under Siamese control as recently as 1792, while the Shan substates of Mong Pan and Kengtung were handed over by Imperial Japan to the Thai government during the Second World War. Even today the Thai *baht* predominates over the Burmese *kyat* in several areas Thailand (pre-1932, Siam) formerly controlled, which suggests that for many local inhabitants, the natural trade routes still lie in directions away from the Burmese interior.[6]

At the beginning of the Second World War, the Japanese also considered transferring vast areas of Upper Burma to the Nationalist government of Chiang Kai-shek. This analysis appeared to support a 77 000 square mile territorial claim by the Kuomintang (KMT), which was briefly pursued by the post-1949 Communist government of China during the 1950s, and, according to some local maps, at least, may still be pursued by the Nationalist government in Taiwan. It is perhaps no coincidence then that, until the 1989 mutinies that led to its demise, the insurgent Communist Party of Burma (CPB), which Communist China had backed for many years, was most deeply entrenched in some of the very areas in northeast Burma that China had historically claimed.[7]

Similar confusion and transfers of territory or authority have occurred along the borders of what have become modern India and Bangladesh. For example, Manipur and Assam, which were seized by the British in the 1820s at the same time as Arakan, are presently included within the borders of India, despite strong nationalist or secessionist movements in both confederal states. Meanwhile, both Buddhist and Muslim ethnic insurgent groups have remained active in Burma's Arakan or Rakhine State adjoining the Bangladesh border. Further east, ethnic Zo (Chin/Mizo) and Naga groups have also continued to wage armed struggle against governments in both New Delhi and Rangoon, sometimes operating on both sides of the border in tandem.

Ethnic nationalist leaders thus contend that these frequent shifts in historical alignments and territory, which have gradually brought Burma's minorities within the political orbit of Rangoon, do little to alter the basic justice of the minority cause in their struggle for self-government and distinctive political and cultural rights. 'There is undoubtedly no community of language, culture or interests between the Shans and the Burmans save religion, nor is there any sentiment of unity which is the index of a common national mind', claimed the Shan State Independence Army (SSIA) in 1959 at the beginning of the Shan insurrection.[8]

Nevertheless, Burma's ethnic minorities have not remained untouched by the political changes around them. Although a relatively free movement of traders and migrants has continued, the final delimitation of Burma's borders by the British in the late nineteenth century (along the approximate lines of Konbaung dynastic frontiers) has had lasting implications for all the region's minority peoples. In particular, it ossified an uneven pattern of development, which has continued well into the late twentieth century, much to the detriment of the borderland communities.

In deciding borders, the British priorities were straightforward: security and profit, with clear lines to prevent conflicts with France, China, Siam and other rival interests. However, the convenient river or mountain watershed boundaries, which the British preferred, has left the debilitating legacy of the – often quite arbitrary – separation of many minority peoples and communities. Mountain passes or rivers, such as the Salween, Mekong and Moei, should not be viewed as security barriers to isolate Burma from the outside world. They are, in fact, the natural thoroughfares of the region, as modern economists in the 'Golden Quadrangle' region of Thailand, Laos, the Shan State and China's Yunnan province increasingly recognise. Neighbouring Tai (Shan), Lahu and Akha communities, for example, have been divided between Burma, China, Laos and Thailand, and, until the 1990s, into four very different political and economic systems. The Zos (Chins), too, were completely dissected between Burma and India by what the Zo historian Vumson describes as an 'imaginary line' drawn by British administrators across the hills from the source of the Namsailung river.[9]

From the minority perspective, the British divisions of territory were then further compounded by a second, internal separation of many ethnic groups within colonial Burma between 'Ministerial Burma', where the monarchy was abolished in 1886 and a form of Western-style democracy eventually introduced in the 1930s, and the ethnic minority 'Frontier

Areas' which, in the main, were left under their traditional headmen or rulers.[10] Again, such divisions ensured different speeds of political and economic development. The Karens, for example, were divided into five different political regions of Burma, despite growing calls for the right of national self-determination. The Shans (Tais), too, who constitute a distinctive branch of one of the largest ethnic families in Southeast Asia, were similarly spread across Burma's political map in a manner which ultimately disempowered the ability of all minority peoples from taking an effective part in broader national affairs.

These were by no means the only distortions which the British imposed on regional or ethnic relationships, distortions whose lasting effects are still felt today. For example, as soon as it became clear that no easy trade route could be found into China, the original focus of British commercial interests in East Asia, British attention remained with India, the jewel in the late colonial crown. Indeed, until 1937, Burma was administered as a province of the British Indian Empire.

One side result was the massive immigration of labour from India. By 1931, the Indian population (from several ethnic and religious groups) had already passed the one million mark out of a total population of 14.6 millions. This soon proved to be a catalyst behind the fast-spreading Burmese national liberation movement of the inter-war years. Violent anti-Indian riots, in which hundreds died, broke out several times in the 1930s.[11] Eventually, during the Second World War, an estimated 500 000 Indians were chased out of the country by elements of the Thakin movement and young nationalists of the Burma Independence Army. Unknown numbers were killed at this time. Subsequently, another 300 000 Indians left Burma following Ne Win's mass nationalisation programmes of the 1960s, and until the present day, little attempt is made to disguise a strongly anti-Indian feeling in the government-controlled media. Inhabitants considered to be of Indian ethnic origin, especially Muslims in the Rakhine State, remain one of the most discriminated against groups in Burmese society, a situation which reached new heights during the post-1988 period (see below, n. 29).

Similar tension was felt over the large number of migrants from China. Small populations of ethnic Chinese have traditionally lived in several parts of northeast Burma, especially in the Kokang sub-state, and many families have long since intermarried into the community. General Ne Win himself enjoys a Chinese–Burman ancestry. However the rapid growth in the Chinese population under British rule provoked a similar resentment to that of Indian immigration, especially over their predominance in business. Stirred up by agitators, this later proved a key contributory factor behind the outbreak of anti-Chinese riots in Burma in 1967 and the immediate break-off in all relations between Beijing and Rangoon which took five years to restore (1967–71). This, in turn, was the cue for China's full military backing for the CPB and a dramatic escalation in fighting in northeast Burma, which only subsided with the CPB's internal collapse after the SLORC came to power in 1988. The role of the Chinese minority in Burma thus remains, like that of the Indian or Muslim communities, one of the most contentious ethnic issues facing the country today, and it has been heightened by the large influx of Chinese migrants and entrepreneurs from Yunnan following the SLORC's post-1988 military and trade deals with the PRC (see further Chapter 3 above).

None the less, if British rule did set the stage for a future generation of ethnic problems, it also brought about an increasing integration of the local economies of remote minority areas with that of central Burma, albeit at the expense of commercial relationships with traditional economic partners. The northern Shan States, for example, which had previously traded largely with China, now began to move more produce westwards into Ministerial Burma. Equally important, while the British quickly pushed ahead with a massive expansion of rice agriculture, petroleum production and light industries on the plains of Ministerial Burma, the era of British rule in the Frontier Areas was characterised by a deep neglect. With timber and other raw materials paying most of the costs of local administration, little money was ever invested in infrastructural or economic development and only a handful of new industries were introduced. These included the world's largest wolfram mines at Mawchi in the Karenni State, the sugar mill at Sahmaw in the Kachin hills and the lead/silver mines at Bawdin and Namtu, and the tea factory at Namhsam, both in the (then) Shan States.

Despite the proud rhetoric of successive governments in Rangoon, this basic structure of economic, social and political development remained little changed in the decades following Burma's independence in 1948, that is until the announcement of the SLORC's controversial Border Areas Development Programme in May 1989. Indeed, in many minority areas the quality of life seriously regressed and several historic trade routes, such as the Ledo Road to the Indian border, fell into disrepair. The long-running ethnic and communist insurgencies, which broke out at independence in 1948, are no doubt a major cause, but many ethnic minority leaders instead put the blame on Burman leaders in Rangoon who, they claim, have systematically torn up the guarantees in the 1947 Constitution and have ridden roughshod over minority aspirations.

Many of these accusations first surfaced in the parliamentary era of 1948–62, when, amid the chaos of the early insurrections, ethnic minority leaders were successively squeezed out of any key role in national political life. But it is, above all, General Ne Win and his creation, the modern Burmese army or *Tatmadaw*, whom most hold responsible after his disastrous 26-year experiment with the 'Burmese Way To Socialism'. Indeed, there are many ethnic minority citizens who deny that the 'Burmese Way to Socialism' was any political philosophy at all, and instead claim that Ne Win had simply reverted to the tactics of military conquest, following in the footsteps of Anawrahta (r. 1044–77), Alaungpaya (r. 1752–60), and other powerful Burman rulers of the past, in order to impose a new coercive form of central authority in the hills. The one-party system of the Burma Socialist Programme Party (BSPP) was, they claim, merely a cover for military rule. According to the historian and former Shan insurgent leader, Chao Tzang Yawnghwe, whose father, Sao Shwe Thaike, was Burma's first President at independence:

> Ancient Burma was not a modern national state. It was a premodern 'mini-empire', a political system based on personalised tributary relations in which war between various rulers was a perpetual feature ... Bo Shumaung [Ne Win] chose to rebuild a Burman mini-empire, and to achieve this, he had first to enslave and impoverish the Burman. Only by doing so, was he able, from 1962 onward, to wage an imperial war against the non-Burman.[12]

Seen from this perspective, it is easy to understand the frustration of many non-Burmans with the failure of central government to re-establish normal relations with their neighbours after the British departure. How could any local ethnic minority party set up a proper political and economic exchange with cross-border authorities when the political centre in Rangoon, which demands the right to control policy, has been subject to such periodic swings in character and mood? No sustained and coherent foreign or economic policy has ever been allowed to develop. Indeed, in 1979 Burma became so isolated from world affairs that Ne Win even left the Non-Aligned Movement, which his country had helped to found in the mid-1950s.

Thus, rather than formulating an equitable basis for the maintenance of Burman majority–ethnic minority relations, successive governments in Rangoon, including the Anti-Fascist People's Freedom League (AFPFL) of the 1950s, have simply tried to impose control by the cynical 'divide-and-rule' methods of the British. For far too long, this has necessarily meant determining policy on an *ad hoc* basis as circumstances dictate and only talking to people whom you know will agree with you. Many of the worst mistakes of the British have, as a result, been repeated.[13]

Since assuming power, the SLORC has announced an 'open-door' economic policy and begun a ceasefire movement in many borderland areas, but military rule in Burma still continues. There is still clearly a very long way to go if this dysfunctional historical legacy, which has kept most minority regions in a state of crisis and isolation from the world, is ever to be successfully settled.

THE PRESENT CRISIS

Despite Ne Win's attempt to impose a totalitarian, one-party system, Burma remains a country of extraordinary ethnic diversity and depth. Over one hundred different languages or ethnic sub-groups are still clearly recognisable today, including such distinctive cultures as the Nung-Rawang crossbow hunters in the snow-capped mountains of Burma's far north and the 'giraffe-necked' Kayans (Padaungs) in the Shan/Kayah State borderlands. The critical importance of such ethnic diversity, however, has rarely been obvious to most international visitors, who have, for the most part, been compelled to enter the country through the tightly-controlled corridors emanating from Rangoon. As a result, until the BSPP's collapse in July 1988, Ne Win's belief in a unique and unifying 'Burmese' culture, shared by all the country's peoples, stood largely unchallenged.

When considering political reform, the examples of China, where autonomous regions have been created, or India, where confederal states have been formed, present interesting models of alternative development for minority peoples, such as the Kachins or Nagas, who live along both sides of the Burma–India and Burma–China borders. But in general in Burma, in common with other post-colonial countries in the region (for example, Vietnam, Laos and Indonesia), there has been a tendency by most political or diplomatic analysis to relegate ethnic minority questions to a peripheral – or secondary – security issue. As a result, there has been consistently little discussion of the central importance of ethnic political reform.

Given the scale of insurgencies in the region over the past forty years, this is partly understandable. However, in Burma's case it is wrong – and on two major counts. First, as the fighting which broke out between the *Tatmadaw* and the Karen National Union (KNU) in the Irrawaddy Delta in October 1991 dramatically proved, whatever the demarcations of the political map under the 1974 constitution, few areas of Burma can be described as ethnically exclusive. In Burma's complex ethnic mosaic, many parts of the country have gone through periods of considerable social flux. In such an ever-changing political environment, regional loyalties have often superseded ethnic loyalties, and a complex process of change and assimilation has constantly been taking place.[14] Indeed, the main body of ethnic Burman migration into Lower Burma only occurred in the second half of the nineteenth century when the Delta 'frontier region' began to be cleared for rice cultivation by the British.

In addition, as previously mentioned, an estimated 1.5 million ethnic Indian and Chinese inhabitants still remain closely intermingled into many communities across the country today, where their business role remains as vital as ever. This is a role that both groups have been quick to accelerate following the economic reforms introduced by the SLORC, with social consequences which are yet to be foreseen. Indeed, until the upheavals of the Second World War, Rangoon itself was a highly cosmopolitan city with Indian, Chinese, Anglo-Burmese, Karen and other ethnic communities predominating over the ethnic Burman minority.

Secondly, since much of Burma has officially remained off-limits to outside visitors (a situation which may now change given the SLORC's more liberal tourist policies) there has been a temptation to scale down the size of the ethnic minority problem. From the Rangoon perspective, it has all too often been portrayed as a remote issue, lost somewhere in the mountains on Burma's most distant borders. Until the SLORC's recent ceasefire policy, face-to-face discussions between different political and ethnic leaders of the very real problems of political rights and representation have been few and far between; moreover, when, in March 1962, the legally elected representatives of the Shans, Kachins and Karennis tried, with other ethnic minorities, to proceed with the 'Federal Seminar' to give these issues a proper hearing, Ne Win's response was to seize power in a military *coup*.[15]

This does not mean that political life has come to an end in these regions – in fact quite the reverse. Occupying half the land area and making up at least one-third of Burma's current 47 million population, local ethnic, communist and other armed opposition forces have continued, since independence, to run much of the local economy and administration in outlying rural areas. Several, such as the KNU and Kachin Independence Organisation (KIO), have maintained substantial infrastructures and governmental organisations of their own.

Despite a lack of official diplomatic recognition, their strength has not been lost on Burma's neighbours, which, recognising their apparent authority, have often received different insurgent delegations from across the border for military and political talks (see further Chapter 5 below). Concerns for the local economy has always been a prime factor. By the early 1980s, despite the exigencies of Ne Win's 'Burmese Way to

Socialism', the 'illegal' trade by some armed opposition forces with their neighbours had grown to massive proportions, more than demonstrating the ability of minority groups to develop and manage their own economies. The most lucrative forms of trade were those involving jade, timber, opium, luxury and other black market goods, but over the years antiques, cattle and other agricultural produce have also been illegally exported in huge quantities abroad.

Even after the SLORC assumed power, armed opposition 'liberated zones' along the border have often been more prosperous than the *Tatmadaw*-controlled territories nearby. Few reliable figures are recently available, but in 1983 the KNU Finance Minister, Pu Ler Wah, estimated the income of the KNU zone alone at Kt 500 m. (US$75 m. at the official exchange rate), an astonishing figure in an otherwise impoverished provincial backwater.[16] Faced with this reality, local villagers, traders and even the local Thai authorities across the border have, not surprisingly, preferred to trade with armed opposition forces rather than with the Rangoon government. As a result, for many years vital arms' purchases were extremely easy to arrange – providing that they could be paid for in barter or hard currency.[17]

It was much the same story on the Burma–China as well as parts of the Burma–India and Burma–Bangladesh borders. Indeed some ethnic forces, notably the 15 000-strong United Wa State Party (UWSP), which defected from the CPB in 1989, have prospered even further after the agreement of ceasefires with the SLORC. The fact remains that for much of the last forty years the land borders of Burma's seven ethnic minority states – the Chin, Kachin, Karen, Kayah (Karenni), Mon, Shan and Rakhine (Arakan) – as well as many border crossings in the Tenasserim and Sagaing Divisions, have been under the control of forces in armed opposition to the central government. Government-controlled border towns, such as Myawaddy in the Karen State and Tachilek in the Shan State, have been few and far between.[18] With the first priority of the Burmese army to protect territory in a defensive ring around the central plains, it has, therefore, been the predominantly ethnic Burman *Tatmadaw* columns which have more often been seen as the 'invader' in the ethnic minority hills.

The contrast with the days of the British, when, on the eve of the Second World War, just forty expatriate members of the colonial government were administering the entire Frontier Areas, is remarkable. The British, as we have seen, employed the tactics of 'divide and rule', relying for the most part on the traditional chieftains and rulers. But, at least, their policy did not involve them in perpetual conflict with their own people, as has been the case with the policies pursued by successive governments in

Rangoon until the SLORC's recent ceasefire initiatives. Widespread antipathy and resistance have been the legacy of these policies in the border areas, a legacy tainted by reports of gross human rights' abuses committed by government forces in the course of counter-insurgency operations such as the notorious 'Four Cuts'.[19]

Quite how the new ethnic minority strategy being developed by the SLORC will fare in the long term is still unclear. Although, in an important change of policy, the SLORC has apparently recognised the legitimacy of all 'ethnic minority' armed opposition groups since the ceasefire movement began in 1989, it has so far balked at calling these 'political' agreements; all ceasefires to date have been purely military.[21] Having overturned the result of the 1990 election, in which nineteen ethnic minority parties won seats, the SLORC has instead pressed ahead since January 1993 with its own selected National Convention to draw up the principles for Burma's new constitution, the country's third since independence. The model appears to be inspired by countries like Indonesia or pre-May 1992 Thailand in which, although ostensibly democratic, the military retains *de facto* power (see further Chapters 1 and 2 above).[21]

Ambiguities, however, abound, with some armed ethnic opposition groups now 'legitimised' by the SLORC following their ceasefires, fighting still continuing in other areas, and many important political leaders, including Daw Aung San Suu Kyi, excluded from these discussions. Meanwhile, despite the announcement of the SLORC's Border Areas Development Programme, progress in many areas has been extremely slow. There have also been continuing reports of forced labour, compulsory relocations and other grave human rights' abuses, which have fuelled internal displacement and the flight of refugees in several borderland areas.[22]

After so many years of conflict and bloodshed, all sides are agreed that building a genuine peace will take time. None the less, there are still no indications as to how the various ethnic militia will eventually be brought inside the political process. For the moment, therefore, there are many aspects of the ceasefire treaties which are reminiscent of the discredited Ka Kwe Ye (KKY) 'Home Guard' programmes of the 1960s and 1970s. In allowing insurgent forces to keep their arms, these earlier agreements gave free licence to several opium-producing syndicates and militia units to expand their trade. Significantly, several of the key figures in the initial round of ceasefires with the SLORC, including the Shan leader, Hso Ten, and the Kokang Chinese leaders, Lo Hsing-han and his brother, Lo Hsing-min, are all former KKY commanders.[23] Equally striking, in the Shan State at least, the signing of the recent ceasefires has been used to play one ethnic force against another, notably – until the surrender of Khun Sa (himself a former KKY commander) on 5 January 1996 – the UWSP against the Mong Tai Army (MTA). This led to heavy fighting that has frequently closed off areas along the Thai border.[24]

In all these methods, there are thus disturbing precedents for the piecemeal approach to minority affairs adopted by earlier governments in the 1940s, 1950s and 1960s. Hopefully, this time the warnings should be clear.

BURMA'S NEIGHBOURS AND THE HISTORIC INSURGENCY QUESTION

Although the political situation remains confused in most borderland areas, all of Burma's neighbours have welcomed the SLORC's post-September 1988 free-market 'open-door' economy policy and the greater interest shown by Rangoon government in regional and border development schemes. Self-interest is undoubtedly a major factor: China and Thailand, in particular, were quick to take advantage of some extremely attractive conditions for trade after September 1988, including low prices for timber, fisheries, precious stones and other natural resources.

However, parallel to this desire to resume business is long-standing recognition of the need to normalise political relations with what is widely regarded as a quixotic and unpredictable neighbour. Despite general disapproval of the manner in which the SLORC came to power, the only obvious hesitation in recognising the new Burmese regime came from India, where All India Radio initially came out in outright opposition to the SLORC.[25]

How Burma, during the present period of political crisis and transition, will eventually come to fit into the regional balance of relations is difficult to predict. Burma's neighbours are, nevertheless, well positioned to play a critical role, especially in the borderland areas. Thus, as dialogue with Rangoon increases after years of self-imposed isolation, it is important to emphasise that several of Burma's neighbours have been heavily involved in supporting insurgent movements inside the country at different stages in the past. Indeed, the full restoration of normal diplomatic relations between Rangoon and Beijing in 1989 was only possible after the break-up, due to ethnic mutinies, of the CPB's 15 000-strong People's Army, which China itself had been responsible for building up and arming (see further Chapter 3 above). The speed and vigour with which the local Chinese authorities leapt to this task after the anti-Chinese riots in Rangoon in June 1967 – supplying training and arms, officers, engineers and even two hydro-electricity plants, roads and a radio station across the border – have left an indelible reminder of China's willingness to meddle in Burma's internal affairs. Despite the public protestations of friendship in Beijing, some of this ambiguity continues up to the present. For example, three of the breakaway CPB leaders, who have been negotiating with the SLORC since 1989 – Lin Mingxian (U Sai Lin), Li Ziru (U Liziyu) and Zhang Zhi Ming (U Kyi Myint) – are, in fact, former Red Guard volunteers from China.

Similarly, in the 1950s, Thailand developed a border policy of surrounding itself with anti-communist buffer-states. In the 1950s, the main beneficiaries of this policy were the Kuomintang remnants from China who had fled into the Shan State. But, in the Vietnam War era of the 1960s and 1970s, this policy was discretely expanded to include the KNU, New Mon State Party (NMSP), Karenni National Progressive Party (KNPP), Shan State Progress Party (SSPP) and Khun Sa's (then) Shan United Army. This strategy was still being supported in high military circles in Bangkok when the SLORC came to power in 1988. Furthermore, in the late 1960s, the Thai government even permitted former Prime Minister U Nu (1907–95), Bo Let Ya (also known as Thakin Hla Pe, 1911–78), Bo Yan Naing (also known as Ko Tun Shein, 1918–89), and other heroes of Burma's independence struggle to enter Thailand to launch, with the CIA's tacit backing, the Parliamentary Democracy Party (PDP) movement to try and overthrow Ne Win by force. Even today, despite growing military setbacks since the SLORC came to power, armed ethnic opposition groups remain the *de facto* authorities along much of the Burma–Thai border.

In the fast-changing world of the late 1990s, many of these struggles have an increasingly outdated look in their present form, especially to Burma's neighbours. In the main, however, although both Thailand and China have considerably increased official trading with the SLORC since 1988 (including a US$1.2 bn arms deal by Beijing in August 1990, see further Chapter 3 above), all the region's governments still claim to be merely interested observers in watching the development of Burma's internal political affairs.

The question is how they will use their obvious power and influence in the difficult years to come? In 1963 and 1980, for example, China was instrumental in arranging peace talks between the CPB and Ne Win. More recently, in 1989, Thailand's then armed forces commander, General Chaovalit Yongchaiyut, personally conveyed the offer of peace talks from the Karen leader, General Bo Mya, to the SLORC Chairman, General Saw Maung.[26]

Thus, whatever the government in Rangoon, such historic involvements are indicative of the importance attached by all front-line states to settling Burma's ethnic problems in the borderland areas if a stable political future is to ensue. Past history has also warned that they are prepared to support opposition groups, whenever necessary, to express their dissatisfaction with the political direction of Rangoon. Despite its isolation, Burma's neighbours can most definitely affect political events within the hermit state.[27]

DILEMMAS FOR THE FUTURE

Turning to specific issues, at least six major topics are likely to dominate discussions of Burma's relations with its neighbours during the coming decade. The first is, of course, the ethnic minority question, in particular the ongoing state of armed conflict, which has taken such a terrible toll of human life on both sides of the border. Since 1988 fighting has spilled over all of Burma's frontiers, most obviously in several cross-border attacks on the KNU base at Kawmoorah in which the Thai border town of Wangkha was destroyed by the *Tatmadaw*. The Thai inhabitants demanded, although did not receive, 20 m. *baht* (US$800 000) in compensation.[28]

The second problem for Burma's neighbours is closely connected to the first: the growing refugee crisis. Refugee statistics are contentious, especially as increasing numbers of 'illegal' emigrants have joined the refugee exodus from Burma due to the deteriorating social and economic conditions in many parts of the country. Officially, diplomats have preferred to deal with this as a 'government to government' issue – that is, between Rangoon and Bangkok or, more recently (1992–3), Rangoon and Dacca – but again it is Burma's ethnic minority peoples who have been the most adversely affected. Initially, the United Nations High Commissioner for Refugees (UNHCR), like the International Committee of the Red Cross, took no public part in this issue other than to give UNHCR 'persons of concern' status to some 1600 students (mostly ethnic Burmans) in Bangkok. But, given Thailand's obvious alarm, this proved poor protection: during 1991 alone two UNHCR 'protected' students were killed by local policemen and over forty forcibly repatriated to Burma, when the patience of local Thai authorities began to run out.[29]

Emergency relief for ethnic minority refugees, many of whom have escaped from the devastation of war and sustained human rights' abuses, has thus had to come from a disparate group of foreign non-governmental organisations, many of whom face their own difficulties operating as guest agencies in host countries such as Thailand and China. In the meantime, a heavy burden is placed on local cross-border communities who, despite their poverty, have often been remarkably generous in providing land, food and temporary shelter for the exiles. The fact that they are sometimes – though not always – from the same ethnic group (that is, Kachins, Shans, Karens and so on) does not alleviate the problem.

By November 1991, there were already 55 000 refugees (mostly Karens, Karennis and Mons) in official camps in Thailand, over 40 000 Muslim (also known as Rohingya) refugees in makeshift camps along the Bangladesh border, 8000 refugees in China and an undocumented number of refugees (probably 3000–5000) in India. But these figures are just the tip of the iceberg. There are an estimated 50 000 Kachin refugees displaced along the Chinese border and, according to the ethnic minority National Democratic Front, over 100 000 Karen, Karenni, Kayan, Mon and Pao refugees internally displaced close to the Thai border. All of these, opposition leaders claim, could well cross over into Thailand if fighting escalates or there is no end to the war.[30]

As international attention increasingly comes to focus on this problem, it would be quite wrong, however, to think of the refugee crisis as simply a recent phenomenon. It is true that most of the Karen refugees in official camps in Thailand have only arrived since 1984 when the *Tatmadaw* made its first major breakthrough in the Dawna Range, overrunning the strategic KNU stronghold at Mae Tah Waw. But, since the early 1950s, a steady stream of other ethnic minority refugees have also been fleeing across the mountains to escape the conflict in Burma. Although virtually unrecognised by the outside world, these exiles include Shans, Akhas, Lahus and several thousand Chinese KMT soldiers who had originally escaped into the Shan State from China after Mao Zedong came to power in October 1949.

Many of these refugees have long since settled down, married and brought up their own families. Until the mid-1980s, while the Thai Army continued its policy of using the KMT, KNU and other minority forces as anti-communist bulwarks, their legal status went largely unnoticed. Even in the 1990s, when compared to the Laotian and Cambodian borders, the Burma frontier remains relatively unpoliced. However, since the hijacking by Burmese students in November 1990 of a Thai Airways flight *en route* from Bangkok, the Thai Ministry of Interior has begun an investigation into the real number of refugees from Burma who have settled in Thailand, and mass repatriations are contemplated in the Sangkhlaburi, Kanchanaburi and Mae Sot areas. Realistically, it would appear an impossible task; one Thai Intelligence officer with three decades' experience in monitoring the cross-border traffic privately estimated that the true number of refugees from Burma could total 'at least half a million'.[31]

An equally daunting problem in any mass repatriation scheme is that hitherto most refugees have been free to return to any cross-border location they choose – whether it is controlled by the Rangoon government or armed opposition forces. However, with the *Tatmadaw* now permanently occupying more and more territory along the Thai border as a result of sustained military offensives, complex ethical and political issues are likely to arise over the manner of their repatriation should such large numbers of refugees be forced back. Already, in 1991, to the concern of human rights' organisations such as Amnesty International, hundreds of refugees were forcibly sent back to Burma against their will at the border-crossings of Ranong and Myawaddy. For some this process happened several times.[32]

Ever since independence in 1948, similar confusion has existed along the Arakan border. But it was first highlighted in 1978, when over 200 000 Muslims, sometimes also known as Rohingyas, from the Maungdaw, Buthidaung and Rathedaung regions joined a mass exodus into Bangladesh amidst widespread allegations of rape, murder and robbery during the *Tatmadaw's* heavy-handed *Nagamin* census operation.[33] The effect of this offensive was to bring an end to a lingering *Mujahid* campaign for the secession of the old Mayu Frontier Division into its Islamic neighbour. After a rare intervention by the United Nations, most of the refugees were allowed to return. Subsequently, however, many Muslims complained of continuing harassment under Burma's strict citizenship laws and left Burma again for exile in other countries across the Muslim world where they have been dubbed Asia's 'new Palestinians'.[34] In November 1990, this harassment spilled over into the beginning of another mass exodus when the *Tatmadaw* began a major security operation relocating dozens of Muslim villages in the northwest frontier region. Although, a year later, the SLORC and Bangladesh foreign ministries agreed, in principle, the repatriation of all refugees who flee Burma, the Muslim question is likely to remain a major cause of instability well into the next century.[35]

Although, for the most part, locally contained, Buddhist-Muslim tension is undoubtedly the most volatile communal problem Burma faces today and has not been helped by a series of articles in the government-controlled press, entitled 'We Fear our Race May Become Extinct', which has accused 'Kalas' (Indian foreigners) of taking 'Burmese wives', giving birth to 'impure Burmese nationals' and having a faster birth-rate.[36] As a result, many Muslims fear that the *Tatmadaw* leadership has long had a secret agenda to clear the northern Rakhine State of all its Muslim inhabitants.[37] The intensity of this campaign has also created a backlash, causing problems for Buddhists (mostly ethnic minority Rakhines) who have historically lived on the other side of the Naaf River boundary in Bangladesh. Over the past twenty years many Buddhists have left Bangladesh heading in the opposite direction for Arakan where they have generally been welcomed by the Buddhist majority.

The third and, in the eyes of many observers, most disturbing long-term cause of concern for Burma's neighbours is the country's intractable narcotics problem. Since the late 1980s, this has become closely interwined with a fourth major crisis: Asia's spreading AIDS' epidemic. Burma today is the source of an estimated 90 per cent of the raw opium cultivated in Southeast Asia's Golden Triangle region and is the main refining centre for illicit heroin and morphine. As poverty worsens for many Burmese inhabitants, so opium production continues to soar. By some estimates, output has more than doubled since 1988 to a current peak of over 2000 tons per annum making Burma, along with Pakistan and Afghanistan, the world's largest producer of illicit heroin. This is causing increasing problems for all of Burma's neighbours, especially Thailand and China, which lie on the drug traffickers' main routes.[38]

Most veteran observers are agreed that the twin problems of narcotics and insurgency are inseparable. But, with the failure of international drug agencies to halt the traffic, there has long been a tendency to blame local ethnic nationality forces or impoverished hill-tribe farmers. These last, however, see little of the money made from the trade. The real profits are made elsewhere. In the 1980s, for example, a *joi* (1.6 kg.) of raw opium, which sold for as little as US$20, the farmer's price, in the Shan State, could fetch as much as US$200 000 on the streets of New York after refining into pure (no. 4-quality) heroin.[39]

The simple fact is that the drug trade spawns a long trail of corruption, inextricably linked in a complex web of intrigue from the hills of northeast Burma to the streets of Bangkok, Hong Kong, Amsterdam or New York. Tragically, for Burma's minorities, most of the opprobrium attached to the trade comes to settle on the most vulnerable link in the chain – the poor farmers who plant and harvest the poppies. No amount of co-ordinated interdiction – whether in Thailand, Yunnan, India or Hong Kong – is going to work, however, if there is no political settlement at the root of the problem in Burma. International intelligence and drug enforcement agencies have long known that far more money is made out of the drugs trade by Chinese syndicates or in influential official circles among some of Burma's neigbours than is ever made by ethnic minorities in the Shan and

Kachin States. Political expediency, however, has meant that eyes have all too frequently been turned elsewhere. Inside Burma too, battle-lines in the war on narcotics have become ever more complex after the SLORC made ceasefires in 1989 with armed ethnic forces in the Wa and Kokang sub-states, where most of the prize poppy fields are located.

By contrast, there are already indications that the burgeoning AIDS crisis, which is being spread rapidly across international borders through prostitution and intravenous drug use, is forcing long overdue policy changes. In China's Yunnan province the authorities have recently begun the public execution of alleged drug traffickers, including several from Burma, as an apparent deterrent. However, as long as the present political chaos continues, such draconian measures are unlikely to have much effect. Health workers in Thailand believe that any preventive measures introduced at this stage may already be a case of too little, too late for millions of citizens across the region.

After denying there was any AIDS problem in Burma – cartoons in the country's only newspaper, the *Working People's Daily*, depicted it as a 'foreigner's' disease – a gradual change occurred in 1990. It was then that the Burmese health authorities first began to announce low rates of HIV infection, causing their neighbours in Thailand to complain of Burma's inadequate response. Indeed, when seventeen out of nineteen Shan teenage prostitutes from Burma, none of whom had any knowledge of AIDS, tested HIV-positive in April 1991 after a raid on a brothel in Chieng Rai in Northern Thailand, the Thai Minister in the Prime Minister's Office in Bangkok responsible for health-related issues, Mechai Viravaidya, alleged, 'Our neighbours are coming over the border and taking the virus back. This is not just a health issue, it's a social issue. We are fighting a lot of ignorance and vested interests.'[40]

By initial estimates, Burma, one of the world's poorest countries and one with little AIDS/HIV expertise, had over 100 000 people carrying the HIV-virus in 1992, including soldiers in the Burmese army, a figure which has now (March 1996) quadrupled.[41] All health experts are agreed that only concerted international action will be able to cope with this new threat. Again it is Burma's ethnic minorities who are in the front-line of regional concern (see further Chapter 8 below).

The fifth inextricable problem for Burma's ethnic minorities is the growing environmental crisis which, like the refugee, narcotics and AIDS' issues, cannot be looked at in isolation. As a result of the changes introduced by the SLORC under its 'free-market' economic policy, several of Burma's once abundant natural resources are now under serious threat. For example, fish stocks have already been so seriously depleted by the mass invasion of Thai ocean-going trawlers into the Andaman Sea that many local fishermen (predominantly Mons, Burmans and Tavoyans) allege that they have been put out of business. Local community leaders insist that they were not consulted, nor do the licenses sold by the SLORC to foreign concessionaries bring any compensation to those inhabitants whose lives have been disrupted. These are lucrative business transactions made over their heads between Rangoon and Bangkok. Indeed, after fighting broke out in the area, a number of refugees from the Kanbauk area arrived at the Thai border in late 1990 claiming that their boats had been destroyed on the orders of local *Tatmadaw* officers to prevent them getting in the way of this trade with their new Thai partners.[42]

Perhaps the greatest cause for concern – in the early years of the SLORC regime at least – was Rangoon's massive new timber trade with its neighbours. During 1989–91, logging continued at an alarming rate in ethnic minority regions along the Chinese border with the Shan and Kachin states. This went largely unreported to the outside world, however. It was rather Burma's new timber trade with Thailand which attracted world headlines – although even they were few and far between.

In an increasingly interdependent world, it would be foolhardy in the extreme to think that any environmental problem can be simply contained within international boundaries. The history of the timber trade between Burma and Thailand, however, tells a tragic tale with many warnings over the manner in which future economic change must not be allowed to proceed. In January 1989, the Thai government was forced to declare a countrywide logging ban after a series of natural disasters in the south of the country in which over 350 people died. However, having brought their own country to the edge of ecological disaster by years of indiscriminate over-felling, more than thirty Thai logging companies now rushed to take advantage of the bargain-basement prices for concessions offered by the SLORC. They thus began exporting Thailand's environmental problems to Burma.

It would be hard to find any situation in the world which parallels the cynicism with which the forests in southeast Burma were felled in 1989–91. The almost complete disregard for the interests of the indigenous inhabitants, whose livelihood depended on them, was shocking even in the history of Burma's long civil war. Many of these logging operations were located in minority areas which have never been under the effective control of any central government in Rangoon – be it British, Japanese or Burman. To deal with this problem the SLORC developed a simple two-fold strategy, which has since been widely reported – the *Tatmadaw* clears the way, the Thai loggers then move in. The *Far Eastern*

Economic Review's headline of 22 February 1990 summed it up –
'Partners in Plunder'.[43]

In December 1989, for example, a team from Britain's Channel Four
TV filmed a *Tatmadaw* unit looting the Karen village at Sitkaya, which
they had attacked without warning the previous day. At least seven villagers were killed, twenty captured and over 200 escaped, including
several wounded women and children, by swimming across the Moei river
into Thailand. The sanctuary offered by the local Thai authorities availed
the survivors little, however: within a week Thai loggers had moved in to
set up operation, and the homes and fields, which the Karen villagers had
so recently been forced to abandon, were destroyed.

Given the dangers in reporting the situation (Thai journalists who have
tried to file stories about the issue have been threatened and attacked[44]),
much of the evidence of the logging trade remains necessarily anecdotal.
But some of the worst clear-felling is known to have happened in the
mountains north and south of Myawaddy. Hastened by the SLORC's
capture of a string of KNU bases along the border, prime forest reserves,
some of them planted in the days of the British colonial forestry service,
simply disappeared within months. In one forest reserve west of Wale, for
example, over 100 000 trees (mostly teak) were cut down in 1989 alone.
The effects of this drastic overfelling were soon felt. In the 1991 monsoon
season, heavy flooding occurred – local villagers say for the first time ever
– in the valleys to the west of Wale near Kyainsekkyi in which, according
to incomplete reports, over sixty people were killed.

This incident was mirrored by a similar disaster close to the China
border in the Kachin State, where heavy felling had taken place in the
watershed of the Baknoi river around the Kambaiti pass in 1989–90. The
area is controlled by the New Democratic Army, one of the ex-CPB forces
which declared a ceasefire with the SLORC in 1989. Tragedy struck in
June 1991 when at least eighty-three people were killed in flash floods
which washed away twenty-two villages and a field hospital. Local trav-
ellers again blamed the disaster on indiscriminate over-felling.

In three short years, areas on both sides of the Burma–Thailand border
have become potential environmental disaster zones. By some estimates,
within ten years Burma's teak forests, once Asia's largest, will be gone,
unless there are substantial changes in logging practices. Such destruction
would undoubtedly have the most serious economic and environmental
consequences throughout the region. For the moment, in these ethnic
minority borderland areas of Burma at least, there appear to be no long-
term reforestation plans – and certainly none which involve the local population. Indeed, many community leaders allege that the origin of

SLORC's attack on the forests had a calculated double purpose – namely, to raise revenue and to act as a counter-insurgency measure by undermining the financial viability of armed opposition in the ethnic minority regions. The cruel irony is that until these new timber deals were struck in late 1988, many forest reserves, most of them long established, were still being relatively well preserved in the midst of conflict.[45]

With the logging trade as a model, similar concern is now being felt in many ethnic minority communities over several other joint-projects currently being proposed between Rangoon and Bangkok. Notable here are various hydro-electric schemes involving the building of dams along the Moei and Salween rivers. These will inevitably cause extensive flooding in areas long at the heart of the Karen insurgency. Another project, which has come in for criticism, is now being realised: namely, the construction of a gas pipeline from the Yetagun and Yadana offshore fields in the Andaman Sea through Mon and Karen territory in southeast Burma to Thailand. Already, thousands of villagers are being threatened both with forced labour and permanent relocation. Quite how any of these projects can be completed without the support of the local people or while the political turbulence continues remains to be seen.[46]

This raises the final issue between Burma and its neighbours: the question of cross-border economic development. Given the brief life of many of these proposals and the perennial lack of reliable statistics and information, it is often difficult to make generalisations. Along the borders, however, there have been several immediate and distinguishable changes in the pattern of trading under the SLORC. Since the free trade in many items was banned under the BSPP (1962–88), previously much of the cross-border traffic in basic commodities and luxury goods went through areas held by insurgent forces, who controlled much of Burma's once-thriving black market. By one unofficial World Bank estimate, in 1988 as much as US$3 bn, or 40 per cent of Burma's GNP, annually changed hands through these channels.[47] Clearly, much of this trade now goes through government-held territory. Hastened by a flood of Chinese capital and migrants back into the country since 1988–9, it has mushroomed, especially between Mandalay and China's Yunnan province (see further Tables 3.1 and 3.2 above).

Regional trade is, therefore, likely to accelerate. However, there are already many of the same warning signs of the dangers of the central government trying to bypass the local people in the vital borderland areas. Two examples – one from the China border and one from Thailand – illustrate the piecemeal way in which the SLORC has so far tried to control the natural course of cross-border trade.

Beginning in the mid-1980s, the Chinese government had, in fact, already targeted Yunnan province for a major expansion of legal trading across the 1357-mile border with Burma. In 1987, the Frontier Trade Division of the Yunnan Province Export Corporation drew up a list of 2000 items for trade, mainly agricultural, mineral and forestry produce for exchange with manufactured goods, such as bicycles and household goods, from China. In 1987, the value of this trade was estimated at US$1 billion, but it was only after the SLORC *coup* and the 1989 collapse of the CPB that the trade really took off, reaching some US$2 bn that year.[48]

We have seen from Chapter 3, how, following the CPB break-up, as an apparent part of the SLORC's Border Areas Development Programme, several 'open border trade regions' were agreed with the Chinese government with legal trading permitted on three different bases (trade agreements, small-scale border-trade, and free trade). From the Burmese side, few figures have been released, but according to Chinese authorities, on the 503.8 km border of the Dehong Dai and Jingpo Nationalities Autonomous Prefecture, this new trade rapidly expanded, showing a 29 per cent increase in the first five months of 1991, to 530 million *yuan* (US$110 m.) over the same period of 1990. Most of this trade was reported to fit into the second category of business.[49] It was, however, hardly a trade of equals and has had immediate and disturbing repercussions on local communities along the Burmese side of the border.

First, with a *kyat* (Kt)–*renminbi* (Rmb) exchange rate that has increased in China's favour from some Kt100 = Rmb10 in 1989 to the present Kt100 = Rmb5.8–6.2, Chinese traders promptly began purchasing anything that was locally available, from rice, maize and pulses to gems, timber and metals. Secondly, the new trading contracts were not available to all would-be entrepreneurs, but only to local traders favoured by the SLORC, especially Kokangese traders sold licences by Pheung Kya-shin, the former insurgent commander who had led the first defections from the CPB in March 1989. Pheung Kya-shin's traders, too, immediately began buying up all the maize they could lay their hands on at high prices with which no local could compete. The cumulative effect of these measures was skyrocketing inflation and the emptying of traditional markets by sweeping wholesale purchases. In particular, eggs and chickens became prohibitively expensive and virtually disappeared from sale due to the shortage of feed.

Finally, on 25 October 1991, the SLORC's Ministry of Trade issued a notification prohibiting the export of some thirty items in the cross-border trade, including rice, maize, teak and gems. However, whether officially or unofficially, a thriving cross-border trade still continued in both these items as well as in an ever-expanding array of other goods, all evidence of Rangoon's inability to institute reforms capable of developing the border economy for the benefit of the local Burmese peoples. This has led to a joke by local traders, who describe themselves as the 'economic underdogs': 'What we provide the Chinese with is precious and lasting [gems, timber and metals], but what we get from them is only transformed into urine [beer] and smoke [cigarettes].'[50]

An even more remarkable situation developed at the Myawaddy border-crossing with Thailand in late November 1990, when the local *Tatmadaw* garrison closed down the border after a bomb exploded, wounding eight civilians. The SLORC put the blame on the KNU and demanded that Thailand take stern action. However, after the KNU issued an uncharacteristically firm denial and customs and immigration posts on the Burma side remained closed, Thai traders became suspicious. Rumours began to circulate that it was, in fact, a bomb planted by SLORC's Military Intelligence Service, in order, temporarily, to deny Thai traders access to Burma.

Thus, in retaliation, one week later the Thai authorities also shut down their side of the border. Day after day army officers from both sides of the border argued, but only when the crossing finally reopened after an expensive interval of one month did a possible reason for the closure emerge. Angry Thai traders, who estimated the value of the cross-border trade at *baht* 30–40 m. (US$1.2–1.6 m.) a day prior to the shut-down, alleged that the SLORC had used the closure to tighten restrictions on the import of luxury goods apparently to appease Korean and Singaporean firms which had signed expensive contracts for the export of goods by sea to Rangoon.[51] Whatever the real reasons, local Thai traders, who, in 1988, had originally welcomed SLORC's new 'open-door' approach, were now agreed it was an extraordinary way to do business.[52]

SUMMARY

While no one can expect that the answers to Burma's many and deep-seated political problems will be easy, the evidence from all these grave issues sends one simple message: namely, that no real progress will be made until a peaceful settlement is brought both to the current state of armed conflict in the countryside and the political deadlock in the cities. For the ethnic minorities this means the full restoration of the economic, social, cultural and political rights which were promised them by U Aung San in 1947, and the chance to reassert control over their own destiny. For Burma's neighbours this will mean the normalisation of relations with the border peoples, relations which have suffered over a century of upheavals and disruption. It is in the interest of every ethnic group and party to solve this issue soon. Failure to do so now, at this historic time of transition, could well condemn the Burmese peoples to another forty years of fruitless conflict.

Postscript

Since this paper was first written in 1991, the political and ethnic deadlock in Burma has largely continued. The key issues facing Burma, its diverse ethnic minority peoples, and all the country's regional neighbours remain the same. Indeed, in many respects, they have become more poignant, as international concern over the deep social and political problems of Burma has continued to heighten.

Two important areas, however, stand out where events have begun to accelerate in new directions and therefore need highlighting. The first is the ever more rapid spread of the ceasefire process. As of March 1996, sixteen armed ethnic opposition groups had agreed military truces, including such important groups as the Mon along the Thai border and the Kachin along the Chinese border. The increasing success of this movement can be dated back to the replacement of the SLORC chairman, General Saw Maung, by General Than Shwe in April 1992, and the announcement (28 April) of a unilateral ceasefire against armed ethnic forces 'in the name of national unity'.

It should be stressed, however, that all the underlying problems still remain, and, although further ceasefires are predicted, fighting has been continuing in several other areas, especially where Karen, Karenni, Shan, Naga, Chin and Rohingya Muslim forces are active. Until the ceasefires translate into real political agreements, the situation is likely to remain unpredictable.

The second important development is the speed with which all of Burma's neighbours, despite continuing border problems, have become involved with the SLORC. As competition escalates over trade and political influence, this has triggered a debate over which economic and political region of Asia Burma most naturally fits into. Although there has been an increasing acceptance of Burma as a Southeast Asian country, this is at best a geographical designation. It has only loosely clarified just where Burma belongs in terms of wider regional groupings, whether as an integral part of Southeast Asia (hence its supposed destiny within the Association of South East Asian Nations [ASEAN]), or as the eastern flank of the wider Indian sub-continent (South Asia), or as an adjunct of China.

In particular, ASEAN members have developed a much publicised policy of 'constructive engagement' with the SLORC, which stands in obvious contrast to the policy of isolation and 'human rights' pressure employed by the West. Despite concerns by Malaysia and Indonesia over the plight of Muslim refugees in Bangladesh from 1992 onwards, the SLORC was invited to attend sessions of the annual ASEAN foreign ministers' meetings in Bangkok in July 1994 and in Brunei in July 1995. It has also has been allowed to sign the regional grouping's Treaty of Amity and Co-operation (27 July 1995), strongly suggesting that Burma will become a full member of ASEAN, probably in July 1997 when ASEAN celebrates its thirtieth anniversary. Although there are doubts that Burma can meet the economic requirements for membership by that date, the prospect of ever closer ties with its Southeast Asian neighbours obviously has long-term implications for all of Burma's peoples.

Already, Burma's recognition by ASEAN has been backed up by closer individual relations: in March 1994, Singapore's Prime Minister, Goh Chok Tong, visited Rangoon, while the SLORC Chairman, Senior General Than Shwe, himself visited Laos in 1994 (his first foreign visit) and Vietnam, Singapore and Indonesia in the first half of 1995. One of the results of these closer relations has been the inauguration of new direct air links within the region: with Laos and Japan in December 1995, and with the Indian state carrier, Indian Airlines, in early 1996.

Of all Burma's immediate neighbours, however, it remains China which has achieved the most obvious cross-border influence (see further Chapter 3 above). These closening ties were apparently cemented by the December 1994 visit of the Chinese premier, Li Peng, the first by a Chinese leader since Premier Deng Xiaoping (then Deputy Premier) came to Rangoon in the late 1970s. Chinese trade now predominates across much of northeast Burma, and it was this apparent burgeoning of trade with China which prompted India to improve diplomatic and economic relations with the SLORC after 1993. Bangladesh, too, where a border war appeared possible in early 1992, has also drawn closer to the SLORC.

Burma, after eight years under SLORC rule, is thus taking its first tentative steps back into the world of normal international relations. But in a voraciously developing region, it remains very much the hermit country of Asia, with many acute problems still to be resolved, as other chapters in this volume explain so graphically.

Notes

1. Dorothy Woodman, *The Making of Burma* (London: Cresset Press, 1962), p. 11.
2. There have been several minor adjustments to Burma's borders with its neighbours since independence in 1948. The most notable was the 1960

Boundary Agreement, signed by U Ne Win and Zhou Enlai, under which three Kachin villages commanding the Hpimaw Pass and the Panhung-Panlao region of the Wa substate were 'returned' to China in exchange for the Namwam Assigned Tract, which the British had leased. More recently, in 1985, another joint Burma–China border survey was instituted. Minor adjustments have also been mooted along the Burma–Thailand border, largely to take account of natural changes in the course of rivers. The situation is more complex, although largely uninvestigated, in the far north along the Indian border where China has historically claimed an adjoining part of Arunachal Pradesh.

3. Rangoon Home Service, 6 August 1991, in BBC, *SWB*, 8 August 1991.

4. Martin Smith, *Burma: Insurgency and the Politics of Ethnicity* (London and New Jersey: Zed Books, 1991), pp. 420–1.

5. In keeping with long-standing practice, for the purposes of this paper 'Burman' refers to the majority ethnic group, while 'Burmese' denotes to citizenship or language: that is ethnic nationalities, such as the Karen or Mon, can also be Burmese citizens. Myanmar, rather than Burma, is the international name chosen for such an historic 'Burmese' state by the SLORC in June 1989.

6. For example, during a journey along the Tenasserim River in late 1989, the writer could not find one trader or store-keeper then willing to take Burmese *kyats*.

7. For a more detailed discussion on ethnicity and the demarcation of Burma's borders, see Smith, *Burma*, pp. 27–44, 156–7.

8. Smith, *Burma*, p. 36.

9. Vumson, *Zo History* (Mizoram: Aizawl, 1986), p. 107.

10. Smith, *Burma*, pp. 44–8.

11. Ibid., pp. 43–4.

12. Chao Tzang Yawnghwe, in *Committee of One for Democracy*, 2.1 (November 1991).

13. For example, when the Karen National Union boycotted elections to the Constituent Assembly of 1947, the AFPFL drew up an unrepresentative agreement with sympathetic elements of the far less influential Karen Youth Organisation. The result was that the KNU remained outside the political process and this eventually led to the outbreak of the Karen insurrection in January 1949. Similarly, following Ne Win's seizure of power, a ceasefire treaty was drawn up in 1964 with the much smaller, breakaway Kawthoolei Revolutionary Council faction, led by Saw Hunter Tha Hmwe, causing a widening split in the KNU movement and convincing Karen leaders of BSPP insincerity.

14. For examples, see Smith, *Burma*, pp. 27–39.

15. Ibid., pp. 195–7. The only previous peace talks of any real significance or duration took place in 1949, 1963–64 and 1980–1, and, even then, only with certain ethnic groups.

16. Smith, *Burma*, p. 283.

17. Despite increasing pressure on armed opposition groups since 1993 as part of Thailand's rapprochement with the SLORC, even during 1994–5 the Mong Tai Army of Khun Sa was still able to buy modern weapons, allegedly including SAM-7 surface-to-air missiles, from well-protected

dealers in Thailand – much to the chagrin of SLORC officers (when 12 000 MTA troops surrendered at the end of January 1996, 7000 firearms, including fifteen SAMs were handed in, see EIU, 'Country Report: Myanmar', 1st Quarter 1996, p. 10). In several areas, an unofficial trade in timber, precious stones and other goods was also continuing, a situation which ceasefires are unlikely to change.

18. Even in 1995, despite some recent ceasefires in the areas, both Myawaddy and Tachilek again came under guerrilla attack in fighting witnessed from Thailand.

19. Despite the offer of ceasefires, such operations have since continued in several areas; see Martin Smith, *Ethnic Groups in Burma: Development, Democracy and Human Rights* (London: Anti-Slavery International, 1994), pp. 78–84.

20. This was still the situation in March 1996, by which time sixteen groups had signed ceasefires. The SLORC was also still rejecting peace talks with any Burman-majority groups, notably the All Burma Students' Democratic Front (ABSDF), remnants of which still existed in a few border areas. Its unwillingness to discuss substantive political issues, such as regional autonomy and the powers of state governments under a federal constitution, has also been the reported reason for the lack of progress in recent talks held between the KNU and the SLORC representatives in Moulmein in December 1995 and February 1996, see further Chapter 5, n. 37, below.

21. The SLORC's planned constitution has continued to unfold along these lines after the National Convention belatedly began in January 1993. Burma's future president must have military as well as political experience, and 33 per cent of all seats in both houses of parliament will be reserved for military appointees and a further 25 per cent in the region and state-level assemblies. The existing seven minority states will also be retained. However, in an apparent gesture towards local sentiments, new administrative territories will be created for several previously unrecognised minorities in borderland areas, notably the Was, Nagas, Palaungs, Kokangese and Paos. Their future powers are, for the moment, undefined. See further, Smith, *Ethnic Groups*, pp. 125–9.

22. For an update on all these issues, including the Border Areas Development Programme, see Smith, *Ethnic Groups*, pp. 69–121.

23. Smith, *Burma*, pp. 95–6, 315, 376–80.

24. Fighting continued through much of 1995 with the 15 000-strong MTA facing increasingly serious difficulties as the only remaining force in the Shan State not to have agreed a ceasefire with the SLORC. In July, however, 5000 MTA soldiers mutinied against Khun Sa and a month later formed their own Shan State National Army (SSNA) declaring that they were opposed 'to Chinese businessmen using the Shan national cause to conceal their involvement in the drugs trade' (a clear reference to Khun Sa, who is himself half Chinese and uses ethnic Chinese military advisers). On 22 November Khun Sa announced his resignation as MTA commander and formally surrendered to the SLORC on 5 January 1996, the majority of his MTA troops turning themselves in by the end of the month, see EIU, 'Country Report: Myanmar', 4th Quarter 1995, pp. 38–9; ibid., 1st Quarter 1996, p. 10; and n. 17 above. Since his surrender, the former opium warlord

has apparently been well treated by the SLORC and a deal struck for the peaceful take over of his military headquarters in return for Rangoon's refusal to allow him to be extradited to the USA. Other Shan opposition leaders, however, continue to try and reform the resistance movement.

25. Relations with the SLORC gradually began to improve after the visit of the Indian foreign secretary, J.N. Dixit, to Rangoon in March 1993. In part, this change of policy appeared to be in competition to the growing economic ties between China and Thailand with Rangoon. From October 1994, an 'open border' trade was announced between the two countries to undercut insurgent groups and smugglers. In 1995, too, there was evidence for the first time of co-ordinated military operations against the National Socialist Council of Nagaland (NSCN) which operates on both sides of the border.

26. Smith, *Burma*, pp. 207, 318, 413.

27. Since 1991, all of Burma's neighbours have put increasing pressure on all sides, including the SLORC, to talk peace. The bonus of the SLORC has been in the 'carrot' form of international recognition and trade, while persuasion on the armed ethnic opposition has largely been in the 'stick' form of increasingly tough trade and travel restrictions along the border for groups which hesitate to take part. China took the first steps, but India, Bangladesh and Thailand have all followed suit.

28. Smith, *Burma*, pp. 408–9. Kawmoorah was finally captured in February 1995 after the SLORC broke off its unilateral ceasefire offer following a Buddhist mutiny by Karen soldiers against the KNU's mostly Christian leaders in the Paan area (see further Chapter 5 below). Official numbers are unknown but, in addition to civilians, at least one Bangladeshi, one Chinese and over a dozen Thai border police or other military are also reported to have been killed during cross-border attacks by the Burmese army since 1989.

29. This paper was originally written in late 1991 on the eve of a massive exodus of over 260 000 refugees into Bangladesh, which resulted in both the UNHCR and the ICRC launching appeals for multi-million dollar programmes for relief in Bangladesh. As of March 1996, an estimated 50 000 refugees remained in Bangladesh after a bilateral repatriation under UNHCR auspices. The UNHCR was, however, still not officially involved in refugee problems on Burma's other borders, although it has since given 'persons of concern' status to some fifty Burmese refugees students in India. See further n. 37 below and the sources cited therein. On the killing of the two UNHCR 'protected' students, see Article 19, *State of Fear: Censorship in Burma* (London: Article 19, December 1991), p. 14.

30. By March 1996, in an ever volatile situation, official refugee numbers stood at over 90 000 in Thailand and 50 000 in Bangladesh, while undocumented refugees were believed to have decreased in China but grown to 30 000 in India. Despite the ceasefires with armed opposition groups, hundreds of thousands of Burmese citizens were also still internally displaced or forcibly relocated in the borderland areas.

31. Interview, 19 December 1990. These potentially high numbers have since been confirmed by a number of Thai immigration studies. For example, an investigation by the Social and Population Research Institute in the mid-1990s revealed 334 000 'illegal immigrants' from Burma (*Bangkok*

Post, 22 January 1995). Official refugee numbers in the camps had also risen to around 90 000 by February 1995, but there are still many other refugees who are believed to have gone unrecorded.

32. See, for example, Amnesty International, *Thailand: Concerns about Treatment of Burmese Refugees* (London: Amnesty International, 1991). In 1995, despite the spread of ceasefires, the border situation remained complex and the concerns of human rights' organisations still acute. The agreement of ceasefires with Mon and Karenni opposition groups potentially allowed for an official resettlement programme at some stage in the future. However, following the Buddhist mutiny from the KNU, SLORC-backed militia repeatedly crossed into Thailand in early 1995, burning several refugee settlements and kidnapping or killing unrecorded numbers of inhabitants', apparently to force them to return. Eventually, Thai troops had to be deployed to protect the camps and, after Thai aerial and artillery support was brought into action, a major international incident was only narrowly avoided (see further Chapter 5 below). For examples of how pressures on refugees and borderland communities have continued to mount, see, Human Rights Watch/Asia, *The Mon: Persecuted in Burma, Forced Back From Thailand*, 6.14 (December 1994); Human Rights Watch/Asia, *Burma: Entrenchment or Reform*, 7.10 (July 1995); and Amnesty International, *Myanmar: 'No Place to Hide'* (London: Amnesty International, June 1995).

33. Smith, *Burma*, p. 241.

34. M. Smith, 'Burma's Muslim Borderland', *Inside Asia* (July–August 1986), pp. 5–7. Under a 1982 citizenship law which exempts 'indigenous' races, such as the Shans or Burmans, full citizenship is restricted only to those who can prove ancestors resident in Burma before the first British conquest (that is, the Anglo-Burmese War) of 1824–6, a practically impossible task in north Arakan, where Muslim and Buddhist communities have historically intermixed on both sides of the Naaf river border.

35. See above, n. 29 and n. 37.

36. *Working People's Daily*, 20–7 February 1989.

37. In early 1995, Muslim opposition groups claimed that another plan was unfolding during the mass repatriation scheme then underway. The apparent change of heart, which allowed refugees to return, followed pressure on the SLORC by the UNHCR, criticism from Malaysia, Indonesia and other Muslim neighbours, as well as intercession by China. The refugees, however, were not always being returned to their old towns and villages. A Muslim buffer-zone, interspersed with Buddhist settlements, seemed to be projected in a heavily-controlled security region along the northernmost frontier. For a summary of these concerns, see, Médecins Sans Frontières, *The Rohingyas: Forcibly Repatriated to Burma* (Paris, September 1994); and, *MSF's Concerns on the Repatriation of Rohingya Refugees from Bangladesh to Burma* (Amsterdam/Paris: mimeo, 1 May 1995).

38. See, for example, United States General Accounting Office, *Drug Control: Enforcement Efforts in Burma are not Effective* (Washington: USGAO, 1989); and the articles in the *Burma Debate* (Washington), 2.1 (February–March 1995), esp. Frank Mastersen (pseud.), 'The Burmese Heroin Pipeline: America's Growing Epidemic', pp. 8–11.

39. Smith, *Burma*, pp. 314–5.
40. *Burma Alert*, June 1991.
41. *WorldAIDS*, July 1991 (which gave a figure of 80 000); *Bangkok Post*, 10 October 1992 (which gave a figure of 100 000). The rapid spread of HIV-infection in Burma has since continued at the same alarming rates. By 1995, UN agencies were reporting estimates of 400 000 HIV-carriers in Burma, with tested rates of 90 per cent HIV-infection amongst intravenous drug-users in ethnic minority towns such as Myitkyina in northeast Burma; for the geo-political dimensions, see David Winters, 'Facing the Challenges of AIDS', in *Burma Debate* (Washington), 1.1, July–August 1994, pp. 22–7. The other main route of transmission – the sex trade with Thailand – also involved mostly ethnic minority communities and again demonstrated the importance of regional and crossborder links; see Smith, *Ethnic Groups*, pp. 113–16; and Asia Watch, *A Modern Form of Slavery: Trafficking of Burmese Women and Girls into Brothels in Thailand* (New York: Asia Watch, 1993). See also Martin Smith, *Fatal Silence? Freedom of Expression and the Right to Health in Burma* (London: Article 19, July 1996), p. 85, who cites the 1995 WHO estimates of up to 500 000 HIV-carriers.
42. Interviews, 7 December 1990.
43. *FEER*, 22 February 1990.
44. Article 19, *State of Fear*, p. 13; *FEER*, 22 February 1990.
45. After 1992, there is some evidence that the SLORC, partly under pressure from international opinion, belatedly began to wake up to the scale of the problem, but only after most of the original concession areas had been logged out along the Thai border. In November 1993, Burma's colonial Forest Law was revised for the first time since 1902 and a new directive instructed that all timber exports must leave Burma by sea. Logging still continued in other areas, however, especially along the Chinese border, see Article 19, *Paradise Lost? The Suppression of Environmental Rights and Freedom of Expression in Burma* (London: Article 19, September 1994), pp. 12–16.
46. These questions remained equally poignant in early 1996, by which time construction of the 420-kilometre gas pipeline from the Yadana gas field (with estimated reserves of 6 trillion cubic feet) in the Andaman Sea through Karen and Mon territory to Thailand was well advanced, involving Total (France), Unocal (USA), PTT Exploration and Production of Thailand and the state-owned Myanmar Oil and Gas Enterprise (other Western oil companies. Texaco [USA], Premier [UK] and Nippon Oil [Japan], have a stake in the development of the Yetagun field further south, whereas still others, for example, Atlantic Richfield [USA], are prospecting in other blocs). The strength of popular hostility to the project was tragically illustrated in March 1995 when five members of a Total survey team (all Burmese citizens), working on the pipeline, were killed by Karen insurgents. Another attack occurred in December 1995, reportedly resulting in the death of one member of the security forces guarding the installation, see EIU, 'Country Report: Myanmar', 1st Quarter 1996, p. 24. There are also plans for a second pipeline from the Yetagun field, 200 kilometres offshore from Mergui, to join the Yadana pipeline where it reaches the coast. The use of forced labour (according to some estimates, 30 000 villagers have been

involved) for the construction of a military base at Heinze Island in the Andaman Sea to protect the undersea portion of the pipeline, and the Ye-Tavoy railway, which is to be used to transport materials, equipment and workers to the site, have also been widely reported, see ibid., p. 24; Article 19, *Paradise Lost?*, pp. 19–20; Amnesty International, *Myanmar: Human Rights After Seven Years of Military Rule* (London: Amnesty International, October 1995), pp. 25–6; interview by John Pilger in *New Internationalist*, 'Burma: A Cry for Freedom', no. 280 (June 1996), pp. 12–13; and Karen National Union, *Report the Facts. The Yadana Gas Pipeline Construction in Tavoy District, Tenasserim Division* (Mergui/Tavoy: Karen National Union, 1996).

47. Smith, *Burma*, p. 98.
48. Ibid., p. 361. Compare the figures given by Chi-shad Liang in Chapter 3, Tables 3.1 and 3.2.
49. *Beijing Review*, 19–25 August 1991. See further Chapter 3, Table 3.1.
50. Since the SLORC policy changes of April 1992, many Burmese citizens believe that trade with China has continued on the same unequal footing, with Mandalay, in particular, becoming a Chinese-backed 'boom town' from which many locals now feel excluded. Illegal immigration has also accelerated. In return, Communist China has become Burma's largest trading partner and has continued to supply the SLORC with sophisticated modern weapons, including fighter planes and fast-attack naval vessels, at favourable exchange rate terms (see further Chapter 3 above). At the same time, increasing infrastructural development is also beginning to take place between Kunming and northeast Burma, including the construction of roads, bridges, hydro-electric plants (for example, at Chyng-hkrang in Kachin State) and hotels by Chinese engineers working inside the country. Power stations and radar installations (for example, at Hainggyi naval base near Bassein, St. Matthew's Island [Zadetkyi Kyun] off Victoria Point in Tennasserim Province, and Coco Island in the Indian Ocean, for SLORC navy patrols in the Andaman Sea) are also reportedly being built in Lower Burma through direct assistance from Beijing. Ethnic opposition and ceasefire groups in the border areas have been watching all these developments with keen interest. For a recent Chinese viewpoint, see, 'Sino-Myanmar Relations and its Prospects', in *Burma Debate*, 2.3, June 1995, pp. 22–6.
51. *Bangkok Post*, 8 December 1990; *FEER*, 27 December 1990.
52. With the rapid improvement of Thai–SLORC relations during 1994 (including the SLORC's attendance at the ASEAN foreign ministers' meeting in Bangkok in July), at the end of the year Thailand began constructing a modern 'Friendship Bridge' over the Moei river at Myawaddy. Somewhat remarkably, however, history repeated itself in June 1995 when the SLORC suddenly closed down the border, stopped the construction of the bridge, and began an apparent border boycott of Thai goods. The following month, in apparent retaliation for the murder of three Burmese crew members of a Thai trawler, Rangoon closed down all three border checkpoints with Thailand (Tachilek–Mae Sai, Myawaddy–Mae Sot and Victoria Point–Ranong). Local analysts speculated on a number of reasons, including the Burmese government's desire, once again, to protect trading contacts

through Rangoon – and also displeasure at continued military activities by KNU and MTA forces along the border, which the SLORC wanted Thailand to help prevent. For a recent analysis on economic reform and Burmese society, see, Article 19, *Censorship Prevails: Political Deadlock and Economic Transition in Burma* (London: Article 19, March 1995); and EIU, 'Country Report: Myanmar', 1st Quarter 1996, p. 15, which reported that, following the surrender of Khun Sa on 5 January 1996, the SLORC had indicated its willingness to reopen at least one checkpoint (as of the time of writing [March 1996] Tachilek–Mae Sai has been reopened). In the first ten months of 1995, according to the same source, trade with Thailand fell off by over 50 per cent as a result of the border closures.

5 The Civil War, the Minorities and Burma's New Politics[1]
Josef Silverstein

INTRODUCTION

In the recent history of Burma, two dates stand out: 18 September 1988 and 28 April 1992. On the former, the Burmese army seized power and instituted a military dictatorship, justifying its action by declaring that it was necessary in order to restore order and save the nation from disintegration. On the latter, the military rulers, organised as the State Law and Order Restoration Council (SLORC), ordered a halt to its military operations against the Karens 'to expedite the attainment of amity among all races for national unity with a view to strengthening national solidarity ...'.[2] SLORC's change of tactics was followed a year later by important policy changes in Thailand, which, taken together, had a direct bearing on the civil war. The actions of the two governments were to alter significantly the balance of forces in the civil war and the new politics of Burma.

The civil war began shortly after independence in January 1948 and has seen the number of participant groups and their objectives change over time. Although the fighting since the early 1950s has been largely limited to the border areas, its impact has been felt throughout the nation. To the outside world, much of its history is unknown both because of the isolation of the areas in which the war was fought and the limited information about it, especially in the international media.

It will be argued here that until April 1992 the civil war was unwinnable by either side, and that until November 1993 there were two centres of politics in Burma, one in Rangoon and one at Manerplaw, the Karen National Union (KNU) capital, on the Thai–Burma border. It will also be argued that during this time, the centre of Burmese politics was gradually shifting to the border area capital (that is, Manerplaw), where the KNU and its guests, the Democratic Alliance of Burma (DAB) and the National Coalition

Government of the Union of Burma (NCGUB) had their headquarters. In this process, a new national politics was beginning to emerge which had the potential for reshaping relations between the ethnic minorities and the Burmans on the basis of national unity and peaceful democratic politics.[3]

The second main argument proposed here is that the political changes in Rangoon in 1992, and those in Thailand a year later, led to the exclusion of the NCGUB from Burmese soil, marginalising it in the domestic struggle, isolating the members of the DAB from each other, and breaking up the unity which was in the process of being forged between the opposition groups. This paved the way for the ceasefires or 'standfast' agreements entered into between Rangoon and sixteen of the ethnic groups in revolt. The final argument is that, while this gave the outward appearance to the world that the civil war was being brought to an end, in fact it only effected a temporary reduction in the war against the SLORC, leaving all the other issues to the future, when a new Burmese government and constitution will be forced to address them.

THE WAR AGAINST THE MINORITIES, 1988–92

The Military and Political Balance

Among the SLORC's first actions after taking power on 18 September 1988 was to enlarge its army and strengthen its air and naval forces.[4] In the process SLORC replaced much of its old armoury with new and better weapons, most acquired from China in a series of deals beginning in August 1990 (see further Chapter 3 above). As a result, it not only vastly outnumbered its enemies (between 1990 and 1991 the army had expanded from 190 000 to over 250 000), but it now had superior firepower and the ability to enter Thai terrritory – with or without its neighbour's permission – to launch assaults on its domestic rivals. More important, because of the collapse of its oldest foe, the Communist Party of Burma (CPB), and the disintegration of the Party's armed forces in March–April 1989, the Burma army was able to concentrate against fewer enemies and had less fear of multiple or simultaneous attacks from different quarters.[5]

Much has been written about the military campaigns on the Moei River in 1988 and 1989, where the Burma army was able to seize six trading gates which, until that time, the KNU had used as exchange points in the traffic of illegally traded goods between Thailand and Burma. At least two of these fortified enclaves fell because the Burma army was able to attack from the Thai side of the river. Indeed, until 1989, the Karen defenders believed that

Thailand would never permit the Burma army to use its territory to make war on its own people. Despite the subsequent use of this tactic against the Kawmoorah trading gate, the Karens not only successfully beat off several attacks, but, also, inflicted severe casualties on the Burma forces arrayed against them.[6] If the Karen losses seemed spectacular to the outside world, they only represented territory, not fighting men; therefore, the Karen army remained largely intact and could continue the war in other areas.

In 1990, the Burma army captured Wa Paw Koe, a base on the Moei River about 40 kilometres north of Manerplaw, a loss which the Karens soon reversed, retaking it during the first week of July 1991, thereby demonstrating that the SLORC's army was by no means invulnerable and its hold on Karen territory ephemeral.[7] Without control of the Moei River and its confluence with the Salween, just north of Manerplaw, the Burma army was unable to bring its superior size and equipment to bear on fighting the Karens.

If, in 1989–90, the Karens displayed something of a 'bunker' mentality in their defence of their river enclaves, in 1991, it was evident that they had effected a partial return to guerrilla warfare tactics, regaining strategic sections of territory as well as boosting their confidence in their fight against the SLORC. By late 1991, the Karens were moving with relative ease through their traditional areas, and even striking south and west to Moulmein and the Irrawaddy River. There they had the choice of making hit-and-run attacks or standing and fighting outside their home ground. No longer bottled up on the border, they were able to infiltrate armed special forces into the Irrawaddy delta region in October 1991. Fighting in five townships around Bogale, they drew on voluntary support from local Karen, Burman and Arakanese communities, who used makeshift weapons and brought the fighting to the very outskirts of the nation's capital.[8]

During the first four months of 1992, the Burma army made an all-out effort to defeat the Karens and capture their headquarters. Employing no fewer than four infantry divisions, fighter planes and other new weapons acquired from the Chinese, it announced that Manerplaw would be captured on 27 March, Burma's Armed Forces Day. But, despite its massive superiority in the air and on the ground, its troops remained on the west bank of the Salween, a good 22 kilometres from Manerplaw. When it sought permission from the Thais to cross over into their territory to attack Manerplaw from the east, the Thais refused, thus denying SLORC forces the advantage of opening out a second front against the enemy. As the fighting reached its climax in March, the Karens were suddenly able to purchase badly needed weapons and ammunition, giving them the means to hold the Burma army at bay.

On 28 April 1992, the SLORC announced that it was halting its offensive, declaring that this was part of a new strategy to achieve by politics what could not be gained on the ground by fighting. However, it took care to dig into its advanced positions while the Karens continued their efforts to dislodge them from recently captured outposts.

There was evidence that many of the units facing the Karens had no desire to fight and that their morale was low. Although they had been reported to have been issued with new and better weapons, those captured in the Manerplaw area were found to be old and of limited effectiveness. At the same time, the Burma army was beginning to use some of its new Chinese-supplied artillery (120-mm and 105-mm howitzers) and Hongying shoulder-fired missiles in its long-range attacks on Karen villages and other suspected strong points.[9]

There was now a new military force in the Karen area: the army of the Democratic Alliance of Burma. Numbering some 1400 and recruited from the Burman students who had taken refuge amongst the minorities after the bloody military suppression of the pro-democracy demonstrations in Rangoon and other Burman heartland cities in September 1988, they had been trained under the supervision of Lieutenant-Colonel Aye Myint, a retired Burma army officer, who had left Rangoon at about the same time as the students. U Aye Myint was a 1960 graduate of the 26th Officer Defence Training Course at Maymyo, who, during his service career, had fought first against the Karens, and later, as Operations Officer in the Northeast Command, against the Communists and the Kachin Independence Army (KIA). He strongly believed that SLORC was both the creation and creature of General Ne Win, and that armed struggle was the only way to get rid of both. The Lieutenant-Colonel, together with his Karen trainers, had brought the recruits to fighting readiness and by March 1992 they were involved in a variety of battlefield encounters, some joint operations with the Karens and other minorities, some solo engagements. They had their headquarters at Manerplaw and flew the fighting peacock flag of the All Burma Students' Democratic Front (ABSDF) as their battle standard. Although their military experience was limited, reports spoke well of their fighting spirit, and their presence on the battlefield gave the lie to the SLORC's contention that it was only fighting minority insurgents whose aim was to destroy the union.

Because the northern part of Burma was least accessible to foreign reporters, there was less news about the war in Kachin State than the other areas. There, the Burma army was mainly a static force, concentrating on holding the major towns of Bhamo and Myitkyina, and the road and rail line which joins them. Since mid-1990, it had forced the local population (numbering upwards of 100 000) to leave their homes and villages, and relocate around army strongpoints, both to separate them from the KIA and to act as protective shields against enemy attack.

Early in 1991, there was extensive fighting in the Hukawng Valley, in the western part of the state, as the Burma army tried to wrest control of that important food producing area. There, the Kachin fighters reported facing troops with newer and better arms than they had seen in the past. There was also intensive fighting in the area north and east of Myitkyina, and near Lashio, both along different sectors of the Burma–China border. In April 1992, in the depth of the dry season, heavy fighting broke out in the Kachin Third Brigade area, the territory east of Bhamo stretching up to the China border. By early June, the fighting had spread westwards as the KIA seized control of two towns, Pang Sau and Nam Yung, capturing a number of Burma army officers and soldiers.

During this period, the Kachin forces proved to be more than a match for the Burma army. Their morale was high and their leaders confident that they could prevent a repeat of the disastrous 1987 army attack which had cost them the temporary loss of their political and military headquarters at Pajao. At that time, the Kachins did not believe that their supposedly friendly neighbour, the People's Republic of China, would permit the army to launch an attack from its territory, but this is in fact what happened. Five years later, in 1992, the Kachins believed they could hold their bases while pursuing a guerrilla war elsewhere in Kachin State.

The Kachins did eventually suffer an important loss, but not on the battlefield: approximately 400 soldiers and their leader, Major Mahtu Naw, in the Lashio area decided to accept the SLORC's offer of a 'standfast' agreement (which allowed them to retain their weapons and bases in return for cooperation with the Burma army). Despite the size of the defection in an important area, it did not lead to other Kachin leaders or military units following suit. In fact, the KIA was able to move new forces into the area and close the gap in its defences.[10]

In the war against the Mons in the southeast, the Burma army achieved success in overrunning its headquarters in the Three Pagodas Pass region on the Burma–Thai border. But most of the Mon army was able to escape and reassemble to the north and south of their former base, fighting alongside the Karens.[11] The Karenni area in Kayah State was also overrun in 1989, but the Karenni forces did not surrender; instead, they continued to battle the Burma army on a hit-and-run basis, remaining resolute in their resistance to SLORC rule.

Not all minority groups were united in their wars against the Rangoon regime. Several Shan groups were drawn together by Khun Korn Jerng and the drug baron Khun Sa, and, on 1 April 1984, formed the Tailand Revolutionary Council (TRC) and the Tailand Revolutionary Army (TRA) – later known as the Mong Tai Army (MTA) – to fight for the eventual independence of the Shan State. Financed by profits from the opium trade, in which Khun Sa was a pivotal figure, the movement was located on the Burma–Thai-Lao border in an area known as the Golden Triangle. For years Khun Sa worked alongside Burma army officers in his area, sharing profits from the sale and transport of narcotics, and joining forces with the Burma army in fighting against rival dealers and minority groups who refused to come under his authority. The TRC/MTA never joined the National Democratic Front because its political objectives were different, especially as regards the goal of independence.[12]

The 'Standfast' Agreements between the SLORC and the Minorities, 1989–91

In this period of the late 1980s and early 1990s, the Burma army was unable either to win a clear victory or to reduce the effectiveness of its opponents on the battlefield. Instead, it proved more successful in its nego-tiation efforts with individual commanders and groups, winning agreements to halt the anti-SLORC campaigns, and encouraging them to turn their weapons against rival minorities or former allies. A classic illustration of this was the way in which the Burma army succeeded in making 'standfast' agreements with several different minority groups following the revolt of the ethnic cadres of the BCP – Kokang Chinese, Was, Shans and Kachins – against their ageing Burman leaders, effectively neutralising each group. In exchange for halting their war against the SLORC, the Burma army promised to provide desperately needed rice to the border areas, bring development projects to the region under the aegis of the May 1989 'Border Areas Development Programme' (for which the initial sum of Kt70 million [US$12 million] had supposedly been allotted),[13] allow the minor-ity group armies to retain their weapons and nominal control over their own areas, and be free to engage in trade, which meant drug trafficking, opium and refined heroin being the main exports of the impoverished border economies. The SLORC also extracted a commitment from the Wa and Kokang Chinese to fight against Khun Sa and his Mong Tai Army, as well as against the Kachin Independence Army (KIA).[14] In July 1990, a year after the agreement, which was finalised on 11 November 1989, both the Wa and Kokang Chinese stopped fighting the KIA as they realized they had no real grievance against them.[15] But the Wa continued their campaign against Khun Sa for control of the lucrative opium trade in the northeast.

Under the 1989 and subsequent 'standfast' agreements, continuing up to the present (March 1996), the SLORC sought only to neutralise its enemies, encouraging them to fight each other and leaving all political and constitutional questions to be answered sometime in the unspecified future. Indeed, the terms of these agreements differed radically from those offered by the Rangoon government to opponents in previous insurgencies. In the 1963 negotiations between the representatives of General Ne Win's Revolutionary Council and the BCP, KNU, New Mon State Party (NMSP), Karenni National Revolutionary Progressive Party and the Chin Presidium Council, and again in 1981, in a meeting hosted by the PRC in China (14 May), when talks were held with the CPB leader, U Ba Thein Tin, and later continued in northern Burma with representatives of all the above groups, the Ne Win government demanded that the opposition surrender its weapons, give up all political claims and accept Rangoon's authority. Under the SLORC scheme, political capitulation was not called for, and the promise of food and continuing administrative control of their areas made acceptance much easier for the minorities.[16]

The success of the neutralisation policy in 1989 inspired the SLORC to further efforts during the next two years. In 1990, the unity of the Shan State Progress Party (SSPP) collapsed as key leaders accepted SLORC's terms, while the majority of its fighting units defected to join Khun Sa's Mong Tai Army. Thus, although the SSPP leader, Sai Lek, remained loyal to the goals of the NDF, his forces were so reduced that neither they nor the party they served carried any political weight in the Front, with the result that they were soon dropped from its membership.

In 1991, using carrot-and-stick tactics, the SLORC ordered the Burma army to concentrate its attacks on the followers and military forces of the Palaung State Liberation Party (PSLP) and the Pa-O National Organization (PNO). This soon led both to accept 'standfast' agreements, the loss of these two groups, despite their relatively small size, being a blow to the morale and unity of the other minorities battling the Rangoon government.

At the same time, the Burma army sought to draw the larger minorities, such as the Kachins and the Karens, into 'peace talks'. Talks with the Kachins were initially facilitated by an unofficial indigenous mediating group, the Burma Peace Committee. A meeting between the SLORC and the Kachin Independence Organisation (KIO) was then held near Lashio in October 1990, but the discussions got nowhere because the Kachins demanded that any real negotiations for ending the civil war must be held in public with the DAB leadership. Despite a tentative agreement to hold further talks in April 1991, this second round never took place because the SLORC insisted on negotiating with individual groups and refused to recognise the DAB as the organisation empowered to negotiate on behalf of the minorities and the opposition Burmans.

Human Rights and Control of Natural Resources

The war between the Rangoon government and the minorities is much more than just a struggle between opposing armies. During the long years of civil conflict, the Burma army has acquired one of the most notorious human rights records, using extensive violence against non-combatants and forcing them, in clear breach of the humanitarian principles of the four Geneva Conventions of 1949 (to which Rangoon has been a signatory since August 1993), to act as porters and human minesweepers in the combat zones. Foreign governments and non-governmental organisations have reported in detail the names, dates and places where such actions have taken place. Those actions brought Burma to the attention of the UN Commission on Human Rights (UNCHR) in Geneva in 1989, and the Commission has been seized with the issue ever since, appointing two different special *rapporteurs* (Mrs Sadako Ogata and Professor Yozo Yokota) to investigate and report on the human rights situation in Burma. While the SLORC complied in allowing these representatives to enter the country and talk with its officials. It only permitted them temporary access to a small group of political prisoners in Insein jail in 1993–4, and has since not allowed them to carry out prison visits as the Commission intended. It has recently only permitted special *rapporteurs* to have access to a number of prisoners in Insein jail and then only interviews, not going into the cells. Indeed, despite strong resolutions both by the Commission and the European Union, the SLORC has made no efforts to ameliorate its human rights record, either inside the Burma heartland or in the combat areas on the border. The constant violation of international standards of human rights is apparently of no concern to the SLORC, even though Burma apparently sets much store by its membership of the UN, which it joined immediately after independence in 1948, whose Universal Declaration of Human Rights it voted for and whose highest office, the UN Secretary-Generalship, was held for a decade (1961–71) by one of its most illustrious sons, U Thant.[17]

The war was also a contest for the control of natural resources and trade in the minority areas. During the twenty-six years (1962–88) of General Ne Win's military rule and constitutional dictatorship, illegal cross-border trade was conducted on nearly every frontier. While much of it was in rice, cloth and antiques (for example, Buddhist statuary) smuggled out of the Burman heartland, there was also a lively trade in timber, minerals, gems, opium and other products of the minority areas. Since the 18 September 1988 coup, the SLORC has sought to take over all aspects of the border trade. This has meant sharing the exploitation of resources and trading profits earned by the local minorities, principally through selling timber and fishery concessions to contractors in neighbouring countries (for examples Thailand and the PRC/Yunnan), and entering into partnerships with foreign firms to exercise direct control over trade and commodity production. For the duration of the war, trade and resource exploitation have gone on without regard for the rights of minorities in whose areas the resources are located.

Opium, a major crop in some minority areas, has also been a source of revenue for the SLORC, despite its repeated denials of involvement in the lucrative drugs trade. The 'standfast' agreements entered into with the Wa and other minority groups from 1989 onwards, have allowed these groups to cultivate and trade opium openly, an arrangement which has been widely acknowledged to have brought profits to the SLORC leadership.

Conclusion

The record of the civil war until April 1992 indicated that the Burma army was not winning on the ground. In the areas it controlled, it behaved like a foreign occupation force rather than an army of the people. Without popular support anywhere in Burma, especially in the minority areas, and with its own rank and file suffering from ever declining morale, the army was slowly losing the military struggle. During this same period, the politics of the border areas were becoming ever more important and influential in determining Burma's future.

THE BURMAN STUDENTS AND THE MINORITIES

Until the military *coup* of 18 September 1988 and the flight of over 10 000 Burman students, monks, and others, the war between the Rangoon government and the minorities was never really understood by the average Burman living in the nation's heartland. Few either wanted or were able to visit the border areas, and those who might have been interested were strenuously discouraged by the authorities in Rangoon. Given the military's control of the media, the Burman people were constantly presented with a one-sided view of the minorities as hostile and disloyal subjects of the Union, most of whom had remained loyal to the British during the

Second World War and had fought against the Japanese-sponsored Burma National Army and its predecessors. After the war, according to government propagandists, the minorities had either wanted to remain under British rule or have their own states outside the proposed Union; the subsequent civil war was thus a just struggle by the army to preserve the integrity of the nation against the secessionist demands of the various minorities, who were intent either on seizing land and resources to form their own rival states, or joining with the CPB to overthrow the legitimate government of Burma and impose a Communist regime in its stead.

The flight of students and others from Rangoon and the Burma heartland in the wake of the military crackdown in September 1988, forced them to seek out the help and protection of the very minorities whom they had been taught to distrust and revile. For many, it was their first contact with the non-Burman population, and it was a revelation. While the students were aware that U Aung San (1915–47), the father of Burma's independence, had brought most of the minorities together to form the Union of Burma in 1947, most of them did not know why it failed and how the subsequent civil war was caused.[18]

When the fleeing students and people from the heartland arrived amongst the minorities, they found a situation very different from that painted by the military propagandists. Although most of the minorities were poor and their home regions underdeveloped, they seemed to live peacefully under their own leaders, enjoying religious and other freedoms, and the sustenance of viable economies based on trade, agriculture and resource extraction. The Burman refugees found that most of the minority leaders, and many of their people, were able to speak Burmese, in addition to their native languages, and that they were prepared to share what little they had with their unexpected guests. However, there were also misunderstandings: many of the students believed that the minorities would immediately provide them with arms and include them in their campaigns against the Burma army, little realising that the minority militias were themselves short of weapons and had their own independent battle plans. The students did not anticipate the length of time it would take to train them for guerrilla warfare, nor the health problems they would encounter: most had never lived in the jungle before and, without adequate clothing, shelter and medicine, many fell sick with malaria and other tropical diseases. In brief, they were unprepared for the physical and mental hardships of their new lives: some died, others sought refuge in neighbouring Thailand, while still others drifted back to their erstwhile homes in the Burma heartland, confused about their political future.

New Initiatives for Political Unification amongst the Minorities, 1976–89

The students found that the minorities, although united under the umbrella of the National Democratic Front, were still divided along ethnic lines, and that there was often as much tension and friction as there was unity of purpose in their attempts to co-ordinate their war effort against the SLORC and plan for the future. What unity they found amongst the minorities can be traced back to the efforts of General Bo Mya (born 1927) and the Karen National Union starting in 1976. Before that date, there had been periods when some of the minorities had united for a time either with ex-Prime Minister U Nu (1907–95; in office, 1947–56, 1957–8, 1960–2) in his effort to overthrow General Ne Win in the early 1970s, or with the Burma Communist Party, in order to benefit from their Chinese-supplied arms and military training. But they had no common political objective: some wanted independence outside the Burma Union, while others wanted autonomous states inside a weak federation. The National Democratic Front, which General Bo Mya and the KNU helped to estab-lish in 1976, drew several of the minorities together in a military alliance, allowing each to be responsible for their own areas and the command of their own forces, while, at the same time, being able to call upon the help of their co-NDF members if they were attacked by the Burma army.[19]

The students learnt that in 1984 the NDF had adopted a common politi-cal programme: namely, to remain part of the Union of Burma in a newly constituted federation based on the principles of equality, liberty, auton-omy and self-determination. In the military sphere, it had begun to plan for an integrated army recruited from the minorities, but these plans had never got beyond company level units. At times, there was friction between member groups, and some withdrew from the Front as others joined.

In 1987, just a year before the students arrived, the NDF had held its second congress and had chosen a new leadership. Saw Maw Reh, Chairman of the Karenni National Progressive Party (KNPP), was elected to replace General Bo Mya as chairman, while other new officers included leaders of the Shan State Progress Party (SSPP), Arakanese Liberation Party (ALP), and the New Mon State Party (NMSP). The elections proved to be an important milestone in the maturation of the NDF as a political organisation: the new leaders, drawn from the smaller parties, replaced the older generation of founders with no threats of secession or challenges to the democratic election process being made. Despite the leadership change, the NDF headquarters remained at Manerplaw on account of its superior facilities and location, a striking illustration of the fact that leadership change could occur without violence or organisational break-down. The congress also adopted position papers calling for a peaceful resolution of the civil war, and an appeal to the international community to assist in achieving that end.

Despite advances made at the congress, disputes continued to arise from time to time between NDF members. In 1988, for example, outright war broke out between the Karens and Mons for the control of trade on the Thai–Burma border in areas under their joint control. But the will to remain united eventually led to a peaceful resolution of the conflict, a powerful illustration of the fact that, through trial and error, members could learn to live and work together whatever their differences. The growing sophistication of interrelationships within the NDF now made it possible for them to find political rather than military solutions to their problems.

The arrival of the Burman refugees ended the isolation of the minorities and made it possible for them to unite with their guests and form a new organisation where Burmans and minorities could work together for common goals. This was the Democratic Alliance of Burma (DAB), which was born at the General Conference of Opposition to the Rangoon Military Regime called by the NDF on 19 November 1988. Meeting at Klarday in the Karen State, and comprising representatives of twenty-two organisations, twelve minority parties and ten NDF members, it elected General Bo Mya as Chairman, Maran Brang Seng, the KIO Chairman, as 1st Vice-Chairman, Nai Shwe Kyin, the NMSP Chairman, as 2nd Vice-Chairman, General Thwin of the People's Patriotic Party (PPP) as 3rd Vice-Chairman, and U Tin Maung Win, Chairman of the Committee for the Restoration of Democracy in Burma (CRDB), a prominent émigré group, as General Secretary. The conference then set four objectives for the new organisation: the overthrow of the SLORC regime and the establishment of a democratic form of government, the ending of the civil war, the restoration of internal peace and national reconciliation, and the creation of a genuine federal union which would respect regional autonomy.

The meeting was historic because it was the first at which representatives of all groups in Burma agreed to struggle for common military and political ends. These ends were genuinely Burma-centred rather than Burman or regional, and reflected both the goals sought by the minorities in their fight against the military, and those espoused by the people of the Burman heartland in their failed democratic revolution of August–September 1988. All participating groups were treated equally regardless of size or origin, the principle of mutual trust being evident in the selection of leaders from both minority and non-minority groups.

The conference briefly considered the creation of a rival government to challenge the authority of the SLORC, but speedily put the idea aside as premature. In the meantime, the DAB in no way displaced the NDF: members of the latter remained in control of their own military formations and continued to have responsibility for governing and defending their own areas. In fact, the two groups continued to coexist with relatively little friction between them.

In May 1989, the DAB gained a certain international standing when the civil war became the subject of foreign mediation, with the DAB accepting an offer by the Thai armed forces commander-in-chief, General Chaovalit Yongchaiyut, to broker a ceasefire between the two sides.[20] The initial offer was made because of the way in which the Burma army had made use of Thai territory in trying to attack its enemies, a tactic which had caused serious damage to a number of Thai villages, damage which the Thais did not wish to see repeated. Initially, a Thai military spokesman reported that the SLORC had accepted the offer, but a day later (26 May) Senior General Saw Maung, the SLORC Chairman (in office 1988–92), turned down the proposal saying, 'we shall continue to fight them until they are eliminated.'

Despite the failure of the Thai proposal, the fact that it was made at all is indicative of two things: first, that the civil war was threatening to become internationalised, and, second, that Bangkok recognised the newly formed DAB as the co-ordinator of the anti-SLORC opposition and thus a proper partner in any negotiations for a political settlement.[21] Maran Brang Seng, the DAB 1st Vice-Chairman, thanked the Government of Thailand for its efforts and expressed the hope that it would continue to 'press on' towards finding a peaceful resolution of the civil war.

The May 1990 Elections and their Aftermath

When the SLORC announced that it would permit the peoples of Burma to hold free and fair general elections as a basis for the transfer of power, the DAB was initially sceptical. It decided to adopt a wait-and-see attitude, and, together with the NDF, agreed not to do anything to interfere with the announced electoral process in order to give it every chance to achieve its objective. Three days after the 27 May election, which resulted in a stunning victory for the National League for Democracy (NLD), the DAB called for the immediate transfer of power to the elected representatives and the release of all political prisoners, including the NLD Secretary General, Daw Aung Suu Kyi, the NLD Chairman U Tin U, ex-Premier U Nu, and many others. When it became clear that the

SLORC was stalling and had no intention of transferring power, the DAB called on the National League for Democracy, which had won over 80 per cent of the seats in the National Assembly, to meet with the SLORC and discuss the issue, asking it to report its conversations to the public, convene parliament, end the civil war, and summon a National Convention with representatives of all political parties, ethnic groups and organisations (including the DAB) to draft a new constitution. It also called on members of the armed forces who had voted for the NLD to 'co-operate with the Burmese people and urge the SLORC to immediately transfer power to the NLD'.

By these and other actions, the DAB sought to bridge the gap between the popular leaders in the Burma heartland and itself, thus preparing the way for internal peace in Burma. This, the DAB asserted, 'is the most important issue facing Burma [today]. Whatever government comes to power it cannot achieve advancement or make progress unless it is able to end the civil war. If anyone really wants internal peace then the primary problem, which is [at heart] a political one, must be solved first'.

In two short years, politics amongst the minorities had gone from local issues and regional warfare to interaction with a wide variety of Burman groups, both national and expatriate, in a coalition whose leadership was concerned with national issues such as peace and democracy. Since the military persisted in ignoring the election results, harassing and imprisoning the elected parliamentary representatives, and suppressing all dissent, the centre of Burmese politics moved away from Rangoon and the Burma heartland to Manerplaw, where rival movements challenged the SLORC both in politics and war.

The Formation of the National Coalition Government

In December 1990, politics amongst the minorities and their Burman allies took a new turn, as the DAB watched the SLORC intimidate, arrest and imprison people whose only crime was to have won seats in a free and fair election. Having studied the SLORC's decree no. 1/90, which declared that the army: (1) ruled by martial law; (2) observed no constitution; (3) enjoyed international standing as the Government of Burma; (4) did not need to hold discussions with the political parties; (5) would not allow any group to draw up a constitution and govern by it, the Alliance considered declaring a provisional government and challenging the SLORC's right to rule.[22]

While the DAB was discussing this move and unbeknown to them, those National Assembly electees not under arrest were holding a secret meeting in Mandalay on 28 September 1990. They decided to send thirty of those present to the border area to form an interim government consistent with their election mandate and the Gandhi Hall Declaration drawn up by NLD members at their first party meeting on 28–9 July following the election. The selected members were divided into three groups of ten: two groups to go to the Thai–Burma border, and the third to go to the Burma–India border. Only one of the groups destined for the Thai–Burma border, that led by Dr Sein Win, a cousin of Daw Aung San Suu Kyi, reached Manerplaw.[23]

After its arrival on 4 December, the group immediately began discussions with the DAB leaders. On 14 December, after ten full days of deliberations, the two sides reached agreement and announced a nine-point Memorandum of Understanding,[24] which agreed that they would work jointly for the goals of restoring and raising the national prestige of Burma in the world, achieving democratic human rights and self-determination, ending the civil war, restoring peace, and building a true federal union. To achieve these ends, they agreed to form a National Coalition Government of the Union of Burma (NCGUB), composed exclusively of elected members to the still to be convened National Assembly, for the purposes of:

1. waging war against the military regime;
2. convening a national conference of all elected leaders, DAB representatives, democratic elements and other notable personages;
3. drawing up a constitution of the federal union and
4. forming a true democratic government.

The core of the Memorandum, according to Dr Sein Win, was that 'the minorities invited all elected representatives to avail themselves of the liberated areas to form a democratic government, and accepted the NCGUB as the legal government during the transition period.'[25]

The NCGUB came into existence on 18 December 1990, with Dr Sein Win as prime minister and seven other elected members of the *Pyithu Hluttaw* (People's Assembly) forming his cabinet. The DAB gave its support to the NCGUB as the legitimate government of Burma because it was based on a popular national election and stood in marked contrast to the SLORC, which only ruled by force and intimidation.[26]

The DAB and NCGUB also agreed to the formation of a supreme council of Burma democratic forces as the policy making body *ad interim*. This Council, under the leadership of General Bo Mya, called the Democratic Front of Burma (DFB), was composed of six Burmans and five minority representatives drawn from the two organisations. Two of the DAB representatives were Burmans, thus demonstrating how far ethnic integration had progressed in its organisation.[27] Military affairs were placed under a War Council responsible to the DFB, although the separate armed forces under its aegis continued to be controlled by their own local commanders and operated primarily in their own areas. It was also agreed to establish an NLD 'Liberated Area' Central Organizing Committee under the leadership of U Win Khet, one of the two original founding members of the NLD. Its purpose was to create mass organisations at the local level in the minority areas.

On 22 February 1991, the DFB was renamed the Anti-Military Dictatorship Solidarity Committee (Liberated Zone) (ADNSC) and had fourteen members, half from the DAB and half from the NLD. In addition to its supervisory role, it was given responsibility for developing ways of improving, strengthening and expanding unity between the peoples of the Burma heartland and their counterparts in the minority areas. Through the formation of these new institutions, the DAB and NLD had taken important steps to end the isolation between their two areas of influence and unite the people of Burma as one. The Memorandum of Understanding was in itself a historic document in the sense that it represented only the second time (the first had been the 12 February 1947 Panglong Agreement between U Aung San and the Chin, Kachin and Shan traditional chiefs) when recognised Burman leaders and representatives of the minorities had agreed to work together for common ends in a united Burma.

The coming together of all the political forces of Burma at Manerplaw, the emergence of integrated political institutions, and the establishment of responsible leadership for the affairs of the Burmese people, gave all the peoples of Burma a new model for the politics of the future.

The National Coalition Government and the International Community

The NCGUB quickly made its presence felt on the world stage. Early in 1991, its foreign minister, Peter Limbin, travelled to Geneva to attend the UN Human Rights Commission (UNCHR) meeting on Burma as a guest of a recognised non-governmental organisation. He was also permitted to speak, over the protests of the SLORC representative, and told the world forum about the brutality, illegality and cruelty of the military regime in Burma. Later, he was invited to visit the foreign ministries of several European states, with the full knowledge of the SLORC missions in those countries.

In October 1991, Dr Sein Win went to the United States to lobby for support and recognition from the US Congress in Washington and the UN in New York. At a hearing before a Sub-Committee of the House of Representatives, he asked for help from 'the United States and other freedom loving people to assist in restoring freedom and democracy to Burma and to allow our political process [begun by the May 1990 elections] to be completed'.[28] Although the NCGUB did not receive any official recognition, its international stature as the legal interim government gradually gained ground. Norway, for example, granted quasi-recognition to the NCGUB as a result of a series of SLORC actions, which included their refusal to allow the Norwegian ambassador to Burma to visit Daw Aung San Suu Kyi and inform her of the award of the 1991 Nobel Peace Prize; their unwillingness to permit the UN Commission on Human Rights (UNCHR) special *rapporteur*, Mrs Sadako Ogata, to see her and ascertain her state of health, as well as seeing political prisoners in Insein jail; and their inability to respond positively to the 1991 UN General Assembly resolution which expressed 'concern at the grave human rights situation' in Burma, and called for the SLORC 'to allow all citizens to participate freely in the political process in accordance with the principles of the Universal Declaration of Human Rights'.[29] Following the SLORC's inaction, the UNCHR adopted another strong anti-SLORC resolution at the March 1992 meeting in Geneva, and the new Japanese Foreign Minister, Michio Watanabe, upon taking office on 5 November 1991, was moved to say:

I would like to urge Myanmar's rulers to submit to the results of the [May 1990] election, because they lost the election ... If they refuse to accept these results, I believe they will duly have no alternative but to suffer the sanctions of the international community.[30]

As the SLORC's international standing faced ever growing challenges in the early 1990s, its claim, in its Declaration no. 1/90, that 'it is a government that has been accepted as such by the United Nations and the respective nations of the world', steadily weakened, while that of its rival, the NCGUB, improved.

CONSTITUTION-MAKING AND THE EMERGENCE OF A NEW POLITICS IN BURMA

The creation of the DAB began a process of new politics and thinking in Burma. The coming together of Burmans and minorities on the basis of genuine equality marked a crucial change in their political relationship. In the past, equality between Burmans and the minorities had been stated in constitutional documents but never carried out in practice. Even at the time of independence, the Burmans, organised as the Anti-Fascist People's Freedom League (AFPFL), were instrumental in writing the constitution, and, although they created a federal union, the minorities had very little positive input in its construction.

If the minorities had reason to complain under the 1947 constitution, they had even more reason to criticise its 1974 successor. In it, federalism was retained in name only, the centralising institutions and political process greatly diminishing the standing of the minorities as the military rulers attempted to impose Burman domination on the entire country. The *Tatmadaw* (Burma Army), which ruled the nation with weapons and terror, had little room for minority members. While it retained the original ethnic names of some of its military formations, their members and leadership remained overwhelmingly Burman. Inequality between races, and even amongst the Burmans themselves, was the hallmark of military rule after 1962.

The events and developments at Manerplaw, however, represented a new beginning in Burman–minority relations. In forming the DAB, a new politics was launched, a politics based on equality and mutual respect for the traditions and aspirations of all participants. It began by pledging support for shared ideas which united all groups in the new politics, rejecting those which sought the advantage of one group against another. It agreed to a free market system for Burma and discussed whether or not the nation should join regional development programmes. It also declared its policy to be one of 'active neutrality based on the Five Principles of Peaceful Coexistence' (that is, the mutual respect for each other's territorial integrity and sovereignty; non-aggression; non-interference in each other's internal affairs; equality and mutual benefits; and peaceful coexistence, enunciated by the U Nu government in June 1954, see further Chapter 3, p. 76 above).

These, and other decisions, came about not by one group dictating to the others but by open and forthright discussion. They laid the foundation for considering the sensitive problems which no government in the past had solved satisfactorily: namely, a political system in Burma wherein human rights and civilian supremacy were guaranteed and power was divided between national and state governments. The DAB devoted two years of study to these and other fundamental questions, producing three working drafts for a proposed constitution. In the third draft, the authors sought to correct the post-1962 history of political and human rights abuses under military rule, devoting no less than fifty-five detailed articles to the subject.[31] In addition to enumerating citizen's rights, they also called for the creation of a National Human Rights Commission to hear complaints and resolve them through mediation; at the same time, the Commission was given responsibility for developing information and education programmes 'to promote the understanding of [the] human rights provisions in the constitution.' The authors provided for these rights issues to be heard in civil and criminal courts with power for judges to make rulings against the government.

Another key provision, which grew out of the bitter experience of the recent past for both the Burmans and the minorities, was the establishment of civilian supremacy. In the third draft of the DAB constitution, the federal congress was vested with exclusive power to make rules regulating the conduct of the defence forces. In including this provision, the framers of the DAB constitution were not unmindful of the fact that, although the 1947 constitution had laid down the principle of civilian supremacy, this had been usurped by the military. They were also well aware that the written word alone could not correct the situation were it to arise again. But, by inscribing the principle in the draft document, they hoped it would eventually lead to the re-education of the armed forces and the encouragement of the people to be constantly vigilant against a repetition of the past.

The most important issue facing the framers of the draft constitution was the form and content of the federal system. Since the minority members of the DAB had struggled so long and so hard for such rights as self-determination, autonomous status within the new union, and full equality of states and their residents, the constitutional experts paid careful attention to the drafting of articles pertinent to these issues. The DAB concept of a future federal union, for example, was an attempt to respond to the difficulty of creating a balance between states and sub-units within states, a balance, which, while adequately reflecting the diversity and aspirations of the minorities, endowed the central government with sufficient powers to govern effectively without, at the same time, overwhelming the states. In the third draft of the proposed DAB constitution allowance is made for a central government and national states, with the latter having provision for autonomous regions and special national territories.[32] Clearly, the authors were determined to ensure that the peoples of Burma would be able to protect their local cultures and traditions, and govern themselves in all matters not specifically related to the national government.

The proposed basic law rejected the right of secession. As we have seen, the NDF had decided a decade earlier to commit its members to remain permanently within the Union of Burma and to resolve all questions within the legal framework of the constitution, without employing threats to leave the Union if they could not have their own way. The right of secession had existed in the 1947 constitution for two groups (Karenni and Karens) and had led to endless misunderstandings. The authors of the DAB third draft wanted to avoid a repetition of this problem in the future. The draft constitution thus protects the integrity of the union, national unity and sovereignty, the very three goals which the military insists are its *raison d'être* for holding on to power.[33]

The draft constitution represented the most serious constitutional thinking undertaken in Burma since national independence in 1948. Unlike the work which went into drafting Burma's first constitution, the DAB drafts were the product of a real partnership which had been established between Burmans and minorities, and were the result of open and forthright discussion about the fears and aspirations of both groups.

The unity achieved in the DAB deliberations is an example of the new politics and thinking of the groups gathered at Manerplaw. The new politics meant essentially four things: (1) universality of participation in discussions and decision making at all levels; (2) equality of all participants; (3) concern for the sensitivities and interests of these participants; and (4) the resolution of problems through discussion and democratic procedures. There was no attempt at dictation and no one group was allowed to stand above the others. The participants were all representatives of the people of Burma and their mandate gave them the right to speak for their constituents.

The new politics and the thinking which lay behind it were not easy for everyone to accept. The memories of decades of mistrust and misunderstanding could not be dispelled overnight, despite the best efforts of the leaders to put them aside. People were still unwilling to talk openly on all subjects because of an instinctive culture of fear inculcated by the military during three decades of rule. Also it was difficult for some Burmans to accept the idea of equality with their minority hosts. Disagreements did indeed exist at Manerplaw, and resulted in splits in a few organisations. Change did not come easily, even in the relatively free atmosphere of the KNU headquarters, especially when there had been so little preparation for it. The minorities too had their differences, both between groups and within them. But there were leaders, both amongst the Burmans and the minorities, with the stature to break down the barriers between groups, and to act on the basis of equality and respect, thus setting an example for their own people.

THE SLORC'S APRIL 1992 POLICY CHANGES AND THEIR IMPACT ON THE MINORITIES

The SLORC's sudden suspension of its war against the Karens on 28 April 1992 followed personnel and policy changes in Rangoon. Five days earlier (23 April), General Saw Maung was replaced as SLORC Chairman by General Than Shwe, who was given the rank of Senior General. Declaration no.10/92, issued on 24 April, announced that political prisoners would begin to be released and that, within six months, the process of writing a new constitution would begin with the convening of a National Convention 'to lay down the basic principles for drafting a firm and stable constitution'.[34] A day later, the SLORC declared that Daw Aung San Suu Kyi, who had been under house arrest and kept incommunicado since 20 July 1989, could begin to receive visits from her immediate family.

On the battlefields large-scale operations halted, although smaller skirmishes and fire-fights still continued here and there. With this lull in the fighting, the SLORC quietly intensified its efforts to get those minorities still in revolt to enter into new 'standfast' agreements, thus weakening the burgeoning unity between the minorities and the Burmans: one condition of these agreements being that the signatories had to promise to break off all contact with the DAB and the NDF. Over the next four years (up to March 1996), sixteen groups, including the KIA, entered into agreements with the SLORC, leaving only the KNU and their trained student army, the All Burma Students' Democratic Front (ABSDF), as well as the Karenni National Progressive Party (KNPP) in Kayah State still fighting.[35]

In November 1993, Lieutenant-General Khin Nyunt, SLORC Secretary-1 and head of military intelligence, launched a new 'peace' campaign. Appealing directly to those minority groups still at war and addressing them as 'armed groups' and 'national brethren' rather than 'bandits' and 'terrorists', he called on them to join the 'legal fold' and not miss out on the chance 'to join hands with the government and strive for regional development.'[36] His offer, he said, still applied to the opposition *qua* independent groups, but not to the NDF or DAB of which they were a part. He also called for 'peace' talks to be held inside Burma, and not abroad under a third-party chairman.

The SLORC's new policy found an eager ally in Thailand, which was anxious to see an end to the fighting on their western border. In order to begin to recover some of their lost trade with Burma, the Thais too inaugurated a new policy towards the minorities. This involved closing the border and no longer allowing representatives of the minorities and the NCGUB passing through Thailand on their way to the outside world. Coming as it did at a time when the NCGUB leaders were in New York attending the 1993 UN General Assembly annual meeting, it isolated them from their Manerplaw headquarters and forced them into *de facto* exile in the USA. The Thai authorities then let it be known to the minorities still battling the SLORC that they would not be able to receive any new weapons and ammunition and that any refugees attempting to cross over into Thailand would be immediately pushed back, thus making them open to arrest and physical abuse by the Burma army. To make their new policy more appealing to the minorities, they promised that aid and development project funds would be forthcoming from Bangkok as soon as peace had been achieved.

Although the three groups (Karens, Mons and Karenni/Kayah) then still at war with the SLORC did not take up the military's offer, they began to look for ways of talking with the SLORC as equals by offering terms and conditions. The military, however, refused, believing that they were on the verge of bringing all the fighting to an end, while political discussions could be delayed until the National Convention had completed its work and produced a new constitution which would legalise the military's rule once and for all.

The KNU Split and the Fall of Manerplaw

In December 1994, dissension broke out amongst the Karens at Manerplaw when the Buddhist Karens revolted against their Christian leaders. During the struggle, which lasted through to Christmas, the Burma army was able to move into new areas closer to Manerplaw and strengthen their forward positions. As the year ended, it seemed that the Karens had solved their differences, but, in early January 1995, the dissident Karens formed themselves into their own Democratic Karen Buddhist Organisation (DKBO) and 300 of their soldiers went over to the Burma army to guide them by little known paths on their final assault on Manerplaw. Aided by its new Karen allies, the army now closed in on the KNU headquarters. On 30 January 1995, the KNU leadership ordered their followers to cross the Moei River and take refuge in Thailand. Manerplaw had fallen, but not before an international incident had taken place, when the Burma army fired across the river at the fleeing Karens, causing Bangkok to protest openly at Rangoon's threat to its land and people (see further, Chapter 4 n. 32 above).

The Burma army and the DKBO units allied with it, units now organised into the Democratic Karen Buddhist Army (DKBA), followed up their victory at Manerplaw with an assault on the last KNU stronghold on the Moei River, Kawmoorah. Faced with continuous shelling and with no chance of raising the siege, the KNU ordered the 1400 Karen defenders to abandon their positions, cross the river and take refuge in Thailand. The capture of Manerplaw and Kawmoorah did not end the Karen struggle, however. After a period of recuperation in Thailand, most of the KNU's surviving military forces reassembled back inside Burma to continue fighting a guerrilla war.[37]

The defeat of the Karen army put added pressure on the remaining minority groups to accept 'standfast' agreements in return for the cessation of hostilities. The principle groups involved were the Karennis, Mons, and Shans, all of whom entered into agreements with the SLORC by the beginning of 1996 (the Karenni National Progressive Party [KNPP] on 21 March 1995, the New Mon State Party [NMSP] on 29 June 1995, and Khun Sa's Mong Tai Army [MTA] in January 1996 following their leader's submission to Rangoon on 5 January). But, even with the 'standfast' agreements in place, continued co-operation between the minorities and Rangoon was not guaranteed. Just three months after their 21 March agreement, intense disputes broke out between the Karenni leadership and Rangoon over the control of teak forests in Kayah State, the Karenni homeland. After a failed trip to Rangoon in November aimed at salvaging the March accord, the KNPP renounced the ceasefire and began fighting again in January 1996. By February 1996, there were reports that the KNPP and KNU had agreed to join forces in fighting the SLORC.[38] The whole episode illustrates just how fragile these 'standfast' agreements actually are since they have failed to address the basic economic, political and constitutional questions of concern to the minorities, issues which have divided the minorities and Burmans since the nation recovered its independence in 1948.

Conclusions

Despite these developments, the civil war is not over. The fighting continues, and Burma army pressure on the civilian populations in the war zones on the Thai-Burma border has led to more than 100 000 refugees crossing into Thailand. As long as the various forces which signed the 'standfast' agreements, retain their weapons, administer their own areas and control the bulk of local economic activity, fighting can resume at any time – as the KNPP example has shown. Thus, there is a lull not an end to the war. Until the SLORC addresses the political issues which initially triggered the fighting, there will no true peace.

The actions of the Thai government, coming at a time when the bulk of the NCGUB leaders were abroad, struck a sharp blow to the efforts of the rival government to return to Burma and maintain its claim to legitimacy inside the country. With the aid of foreign friends, it has established a new exile headquarters in Washington DC, where Dr Sein Win and his cabinet members continue their diplomatic efforts, while the Democratic Voice of Burma, the opposition radio station, partly funded by the Government of Norway, which began broadcasting on 19 July 1992, continues its transmissions from the tiny island of Kvitso near Stavanger, keeping the peoples of Burma informed about what the NCGUB is doing and what actions foreign governments are taking with regard to Burma.[39]

The absence of the NCGUB from Burma has clearly weakened its position, while strengthening the SLORC's claim to be the unchallenged government. But, despite recent setbacks, the new politics is still alive. Although the 'standfast' agreements do not approve it, contact between the Wa, Kachins and Karens exist since both are increasingly disenchanted with their agreements with the SLORC. The Wa desperately need rice to feed their people and international help to transform their opium economy into one based on non-narcotic cash crops and local industry. The Kachins entered into their agreement with the SLORC in the hopes of participating in a national peace process and in genuine constitution making which would reflect the ideas and aspirations of the minorities on federalist and human rights issues. But, so far, they have found no willingness on the part of Rangoon to listen and take their views seriously.

Abroad, the NCGUB works closely with most Burmese émigrés, regardless of ethnicity. Its position is national not partisan. Indeed, it is somewhat ironic that both the SLORC and the NCGUB continue to talk about state structures based on national unity, structures in which human rights and democracy will be upheld; yet, the SLORC will not talk to its rival, even though its members were duly elected to a national assembly which has never been convened. At the same time, it will not allow the participants in the long-running National Convention to speak freely with one another about their ideas for the principles of the future constitution. The SLORC has also refused the assistance of the office of the UN Secretary-General, even though the 1994 and 1995 UN General Assembly Resolutions on Burma called on the Secretary-General to assist SLORC's efforts in achieving national reconciliation.[40]

The SLORC appears convinced that it has all but ended the civil war, silenced the opposition in the Burma heartland, and upheld national order with its soldiers and spies. But its power is wielded without genuine popular support, and the soldiers-turned-politicians know that their main political rival, Daw Aung San Suu Kyi, has the backing of both the Burmans and the minorities, even though she remains, despite her 'release' from house arrest in July 1995, severely restricted in her movements. Her party's withdrawal from the National Convention on the very day it reconvened (28 November 1995) in protest against the SLORC's refusal to discuss the Convention's terms of reference and procedures, underscores her determination not to remain silent in the face of the regime's attempts to create a constitutional dictatorship based on spurious popular mandate.

The DAB, NCGUB and Daw Aung San Suu Kyi symbolise the new politics of Burma. They have built on the February 1947 agreement between the Burmans and the minorities which Daw Suu's father, General Aung San, worked out at Panglong in the Shan State, setting the nation on the path to unity under a federal system. They have likewise carried forward the ideas initiated in the mid-February 1962 Federal Seminar which Prime Minister U Nu called and chaired, a seminar whose work was never completed because the military overthrew the constitution (2 March 1962) and began the dictatorship which continues to this day. Finally, they have been true to the demands of the August 1988 uprising when the people launched a peaceful revolution to transform dictatorship into democracy. Today, thanks to their courage and persistence, the new politics for which the older generation strove, and the Burmese people so recently fought and died, are a reality. One day, those politics will return to the centre of Burmese life and Burma will at last come into its true inheritance.

Notes

1. This chapter is based on the author's field research conducted on the Thai-Burma border area between 1987 and 1991, where extensive and repeated interviews were held with minority leaders, Burman students and others involved in the events described and analysed. It is also based on documents given to the author and on published newspaper accounts.
2. *Working People's Daily* (Rangoon), 29 April 1992.
3. Throughout this chapter, the term 'Burman' refers to the majority ethnic groups in the Burma heartland, the Irrawaddy River valley and the delta area. The term 'minority' refers to the several ethnic groups living mainly in the hill areas surrounding the Irrawaddy River valley. It also refers to the minority ethnic groups such as the Mons, Karens and Arakanese who live intermingled in the Burma delta and coastal regions. The term 'Burmese' is used as a political epithet to refer to all the peoples – Burman and ethnic minority – who inhabit the present-day country of Burma. Although the current military rulers arbitrarily changed the nation's name from Burma to

Myanmar after the 18 September 1988 military *coup*, the latter is not used in this paper unless as a quotation or part of a cited document. It is not used because of its Burman emphasis.

4.   See above Chapter 3, 'Relations of Genuine Co-operation, 1988 – the Present'.
5.   For a good account of the collapse of the CPB, see Bertil Lintner, *The Rise and Fall of the Communist Party of Burma (CPB)* (Ithaca: Cornell University Southeast Asia Program Monograph, 1990).
6.   FEER, *Asia 1991 Yearbook* (Hong Kong: FEER, 1990), p. 96.
7.   *The Nation* (Bangkok), 11 July 1991.
8.   'Defense Commander Warns Over Insurgent Links', *FBIS*, 20 November 1991; *FEER*, 14 November 1991.
9.   Material about the fighting between the KNU and the SLORC in the first four months of 1992 is based, in part, on reports written by foreign military observers who were in the area, saw the fighting close to and discussed strategy and tactics with some of the Karen leaders. Because the reports were given to the present author on a confidential basis, they cannot be attributed here. On the provision of Chinese weapons to the SLORC after September 1988, see Chapter 3, 'Relations of Genuine Co-operation, 1988 – the Present'.
10. Most of the material about the fighting between the Kachins and the SLORC comes from extensive interviews by the present author with Kachin leaders. A good précis can also be found in Martin Smith, *Ethnic Groups in Burma: Development, Democracy and Human Rights* (London: Anti-Slavery International, 1994), pp. 38–41. Material reflecting the SLORC's views of the campaign is drawn from various issues of the *Working People's Daily* (Rangoon), the official news organ of the government.
11. In late 1992, the Thai press carried stories of Mon attacks on Burma army positions near the strategic Three Pagodas Pass. The present author was informed of the impending offensive by Nai Shwe Kyin, the leader of the New Mon State Party (NMSP), just prior to its launch. For further background, see Smith, *Ethnic Groups*, pp. 49–53.
12. Martin Smith, *Burma: Insurgency and the Politics of Ethnicity* (London: Zed Books, 1991), pp. 336–9; and *The Constitution of the TRC* (mimeo) (1 April 1984).
13. On the May 1989 'Border Areas Development Programme', for which Kt70 m. had supposedly been set aside for the building of roads, bridges, schools and hospitals, see Smith, *Ethnic Groups*, pp. 125–9; and Bertil Lintner, 'Ethnic Insurgents and Narcotics', *Burma Debate* (Washington), 2.1 (February/March 1995), p. 20. Since the BADP's establishment in 1989, the SLORC claims to have invested over $US400 m. (Kt 2.8 bn) in development initiatives in ethnic minority regions. While opposition groups claim that most of this expenditure has been on buildings and roads, with precious little being spent on projects where there is local participation: see Smith, *Fatal Silence? Freedom of Expression and the Right of Health in Burma* (London: Article 19, July 1996), p. 59.
14. Lintner, *Rise and Fall*, pp. 52–3; FEER, *Asia 1991 Yearbook* (Hong Kong, 1990), p. 87.
15. The author was at Manerplaw when, during a discussion with the late Kachin leader, Maran Brang Seng (1931–94), he was shown a cable the leader received informing him of the Wa and Kokang decision.

16. For a discussion of the 1963 peace negotiations, see Josef Silverstein, *Burma: Military Rule and the Politics of Stagnation* (Ithaca: Cornell University Press, 1977), pp. 115–16; and Revolutionary Council of the Union of Burma, *Peace Parley* (Rangoon: Historical Document no. 1, mimeo, 1963) (for the Rangoon Government's account). On the 1981 talks, which also included abortive discussions in Rangoon between Ne Win and members of the Revolutionary Council, with the KIO leader, Maran Brang Seng, see Josef Silverstein, 'Burma in 1981: The Changing of the Guardians Begins', *Asian Survey*, 22.2 (1982), pp. 183–5.

17. Human rights violations against the minorities who live in or near the war zone have been extensively documented by a variety of non-governmental agencies as well as governments; see, for example, Smith, *Ethnic Groups in Burma*, *passim*; and Amnesty International, *Burma: Extrajudicial Execution and Torture of Members of Ethnic Minorities* (London: AI, 1988). Subsequently AI open-dated this report, adding several others on the same subject. On the resolutions of the UN Commission on Human Rights (UNCHR), see United Nations Economic and Social Council on Human Rights, 47th Session, Item 10, *Question of Human Rights of All Persons Subjected to Any Cruel Form of Detention and Imprisonment, Torture and Other Cruel, Inhuman or Degrading Treatment or Punishment*, E/CN.4/1991/17 (10 January 1991). A follow-up session on Burma took place in February–March 1992 and a strong resolution again adopted against the SLORC. This followed a resolution on Burma in the UN General Assembly of 10 December 1991, which called attention to its failure to establish democracy and its continued detention (house arrest) without charge or trial of Daw Aung San Suu Kyi. As of March 1996, there have been similar resolutions in both the UNCHR and the General Assembly every year since. See Smith, *Fatal Silence?*, p. 76, on prison visits.

18. For an examination of the ideas of Burma's founding father, U Aung San (1915–47), see Josef Silverstein (ed.), *The Political Legacy of Aung San* (Ithaca: Cornell University Press Southeast Asia Program Monograph, no. 11, rev. edn, 1993).

19. Josef Silverstein, 'National Unity in Burma: Is It Possible?', in Kusuma Snitwongse and Sukhumband Paribatra (eds), *Durable Stability in Southeast Asia* (Singapore: Institute of Southeast Asian Studies [ISEAS], 1987), pp. 80–1.

20. *The Nation* (Bangkok), 25 May 1989.

21. *Working People's Daily* (Rangoon), 26 May 1989.

22. Ibid., 29 July 1990.

23. This description of the formation of the NCGUB was given to the writer by members of the original body. For a different description, see NCGUB, *Democracy and Politics in Burma* (Manerplaw: mimeo, 1993), pp. 236–8. On the 28–9 July declaration, see 'The Gandhi Hall Declaration, July 28–29, 1990', *Burma Review* (New York), 28 (July 1990), pp. 8–9.

24. *Statement of the Agreement between the Democratic Alliance of Burma and the National League for Democracy* (Manerplaw: mimeo, 14 December 1990 [original in Burmese]).

25. *Statement of Dr Sein Win, Prime Minister, the National Coalition Government of the Union of Burma, 18 October 1991, before the US House*

156 The Civil War and the Minorities

of Representatives Sub-Committee on Foreign Affairs (henceforth: Sein Win, 'Statement') Washington: mimeo, 1991), p. 5.

26. Democratic Alliance of Burma, *Statement on the Formation of the National Coalition Government of the Union of Burma* (Manerplaw: mimeo, 18 December 1990).

27. National Coalition Government of the Union of Burma, *Prime Minister's Speech, December 18, 1990* (Manerplaw: mimeo, 1990).

28. Sein Win, 'Statement', 18 October 1991, p. 28.

29. *New York Times*, 20 November 1991. At the time the resolution was reported out of committee (that is, the UNCHR), it was discussed extensively and in detail in the foreign media.

30. Kyodo News Agency (Tokyo), 5 November 1991.

31. DAB Central Drafting Committee, *Burma Constitution* (Third Draft, November 1991), ch. 2.

32. Ibid., ch. 3.

33. SLORC, *Declaration 1/90* (Rangoon: 27 July 1990), art. 10.

34. *Working People's Daily* (Rangoon), 25 April 1992.

35. See EIU, 'Country Report: Myanmar', 1st Quarter 1996 (London: EIU, 1996), p. 14.

36. Josef Silverstein, 'Some Thoughts About the Political Changes in Burma', *Bangkok Post* (Bangkok), 9 February 1994.

37. As of the time of writing (March 1996), the KNU continues to hold its positions on the southern Burma–Thai border in the Tenasserim area and has launched several assaults against Burma army units. In December 1995, a six-member KNU delegation travelled to Moulmein for talks with SLORC representatives, even though doubts had been expressed by the KNU about the usefulness of such ceasefire negotiations without 'any real dialogue about the political future'. As expected, the talks brought agreement no nearer, but both sides pledged themselves to further meetings. In an interview with a Thai newspaper, *Phuchatkan*, shortly before the second round of talks in February 1996, General Bo Mya explained the SLORC had ruled out discussions on the KNU demand that the Karens and other groups have their own governments as part of a federal state. In an interview in the same paper after the talks had taken place, the KNU's Secretary-General, Saw Ba Thin, explained that they had foundered on the military junta's refusal to entertain the Karen request for tripartite talks involving the SLORC, the NLD and all the ethnic groups which were part of the NCGUB. See further EIU, 'Country Report: Myanmar', 1st Quarter 1996, p. 14. The small ABSDF army continues its war against the SLORC because the military rulers do not recognise it as a minority group in view of the fact that its members are overwhelmingly Burman.

38. EIU, 'Country Report: Myanmar', 1st Quarter 1996, p. 14.

39. On the inauguration of the Democratic Voice of Burma, see Larry Jagan, 'Spies and Whispers in Burma', *Guardian* (London), 20 July 1992.

40. UNGA Res, A/C 3/49/L43, 2 December 1994 (adopted by unanimous consent by the General Assembly on 13 December 1994, para. 19); and UNGA Res., A/C 3/50/L52, 5 December 1995.

Part IV
The Challenge of
Development

6 Priorities for Burma's Development: the Role of International Aid

David I. Steinberg

INTRODUCTION

In July 1988, in the waning hours of the Burma Socialist Programme Party (BSPP), the ruling elite made two important decisions that were both implemented following the military *coup* of 18 September 1988. Both profoundly affected the economic structure of the state.

On 23 July 1988, at the extraordinary meeting of the BSPP during which General Ne Win announced his resignation as Chairman, the party determined that economic liberalisation was necessary, and that the private sector should be encouraged. That decision was probably prompted both by the economic chaos that an ill-conceived and badly implemented state-directed socialist structure produced (a problem that U Ne Win himself recognised a year earlier), and by the Japanese donors. Japan at that time was dispensing about half of the US$400 m. that Burma received annually and had provided some US$2.2 bn in foreign aid since 1954. That government had warned the Burmese in March 1988 that unless substantive, but unspecified, economic reforms were undertaken, it would have to reconsider Japan's economic relations with Burma.

The second decision, announced in early July, was to legalise and tax the border trade between China and Burma beginning on 1 October 1988 through formal opening of the land trade routes. They had been cleared in military campaigns ostensibly against the insurgents, and had previously serviced widespread smuggling. The government's intent was not the stoppage of the trade, which could not be denied, but who would reap its considerable profits.

Following the military *coup* of 18 September 1988, which, in effect, continued the regime by other means, both policies were implemented with important socio-economic effects. There is no question that there was widespread support for the resuscitation of the indigenous private sector and the introduction of foreign investment. Many, if not most, of the approximately 234 political parties that registered with the State Law and Order Restoration Council (SLORC) in anticipation of the 27 May 1990 elections (over ninety actually ran candidates) explicitly advocated encouragement of the private sector.

The regularisation of the China trade, and following that by acknowledging the informal but recognised, decades-old trade routes to Thailand, and a barter agreement with Bangladesh, both reflected and stimulated consumer spending on commodities. This was prompted and exacerbated by public fear of further national demonetisations such as occurred on 5 September 1987 (the third since the *coup* of 1962). The spurt in imports made even less effective the already marginally productive role of the State Economic Enterprises (SEE), the public sector that was already badly equipped, obsolescent, politically run, and inefficient in production and distribution but on which the state had formally relied for such goods.

In other circumstances, economic liberalisation would have been greeted by the multilateral and bilateral international donor community as a salutary change in economic policy that would both encourage growth and, consequently, prompt additional assistance. This change, however, was overshadowed by the coup, the repression that followed, and the dire situation regarding human rights. The resultant virtual cut-off in foreign economic aid since 1988 affected Burmese policies, and helped create a new set of economic issues in addition to those already exercising such a profound influence on society.

As donor organisations consider their potentially positive or negative roles in Myanmar in the late 1990s, such decisions will be affected and circumscribed by Burmese traditions, productive and trade cycles, current policies, regime attitudes, and past aid patterns. They should also profit from the lessons from previous foreign assistance to Burma. This chapter will examine some of these aspects before discussing future assistance programming in the light of history.

THE POLITICAL CONTEXT OF ECONOMIC REFORM

Burma: a *Dirigiste* State

It has been a cardinal characteristic of Burmese public affairs since independence that political considerations have influenced and guided economic policies. This is probably an accurate description of most societies. In Burma, the argument continues, this factor has been more pervasive and profound than in many other states, and has effectively vitiated many of the professed economic reforms that the ruling regimes have sought to initiate.

The origins of state intervention go back to and beyond the colonial period, on which we need not dwell here except to note that the socialist ethic, which was in apparent conformity to Buddhist principles and was an intellectual bulwark against European imperialism and foreign (especially Indian and Chinese) control over much of the economy, was very broadly accepted in Burmese circles in the 1930s.

Under the Anti-Fascist People's Freedom League (AFPFL) government until 1962, moderate socialism prevailed, and the state engaged in economic intervention in the economy as a whole. After about a year following the military *coup* of 1962, a rigid and doctrinaire socialist economy was dictated that virtually forced the economic collapse of the state, which had little of the technical and bureaucratic competence to run such a complex endeavour. The state was held together by centralised force, and – ironically – by a fragmented economy based on village-level self-sufficiency.

The result was the BSPP *mea culpa* of 1971 at the First Party Congress, at which a catalogue of national economic ills was presented.[1] The reforms that were approved in the early 1970s were modest, retaining socialist goals within a context of a new Twenty-Year Plan (and five four-year plans to achieve those targets of increasing incomes and reducing private sector influence) that was to stress the natural endowments of the country – agriculture, forestry, fisheries, and mining (in particular, oil and gas) – rather than trying to create an industrial proletariat. Foreign economic relations were once again encouraged. The BSPP did institute some modest economic and fiscal reforms, prompted by the World Bank. They were successful in generating some additional state income and effecting some modest improvements in the State Economic Enterprises.

Foreign assistance was sought: the World Bank was invited back into Burma, the state joined the Asian Development Bank (ADB), and bilateral support was advocated. Until that time, the Japanese had been the major supporter of the state, with the United Nations Development Programme and China playing a more modest role. In fact, it could be argued that without Japanese assistance during those difficult years of the 1960s, the regime might have collapsed.[2]

The underlying problems of the economy continued, however, masked and only ameliorated by two factors: the introduction of the newly imported high-yielding varieties of rice, coupled with an extensive party campaign that enforced their production in the seventy-two most important rice-growing townships, and the vast increase in foreign aid. Reported figures on growth in the economy (when they were accurate – Burmese statistics are noted for often being whimsical and shaped by the need to show continued progress to the top of the hierarchy) could essentially be attributed to agriculture, and more specifically, rice. Foreign assistance grew by approximately twenty times in the 1970s. These were not, however, structural reforms, which do not seem to have been considered or seriously debated at policy levels. Burma was affected by two factors that impeded its progress. The first was the role of the political process and a hierarchical structure of authority that instilled fear throughout the society, including in the sphere of economic activities. The second, unintentional on the part of donors, was the plethora of foreign assistance that took pressure off the Burmese for internal reforms, even as the donors pressed for them. Burma seemed ripe for foreign aid and attractive to donors; it was neutralist, poor, had relatively equitable income distribution,[3] seemed to stress social services, and was exotic. The Burmese government, on the other hand, believed that assistance was their due, and if it were appropriately proffered, they would take it on their terms.[4]

Elements of the government understood that the state did not have the capacity to micro-manage the economy, and some also admitted that they could not coordinate foreign aid between or among various ministries. Thus, as part of the reforms, the state theoretically, but only partly, freed state industries to hire and fire and set prices. In fact, there was no real administrative freedom, because there was no freedom from political fear. Prices could not easily be changed to reflect costs, in spite of a newly introduced system intended to allow it. The party (thus, in effect, the military) dictated hiring and firing. For example, even when the state ended its monopoly of the grain trade in 1987, the party pressured the agricultural corporations to retain the 6000 or so employees who had earlier performed that function but who were no longer needed.

The whole state apparatus, including and perhaps most especially the cabinet, looked to U Ne Win, and if it was felt that he was not sympathetic to any particular issue, it was not raised. Even the most mundane of decisions (such as the sending of a single individual abroad for study) had to have cabinet, thus U Ne Win's, approval. Bureaucratic and economic constipation in decision-making set in. But, at the same time, imports increased to fuel the SEE's needs in raw materials, intermediate goods, and spare parts; and debt rose. The crisis came to a head in the early 1980s, when world prices for Burmese exports fell, inflation raised the costs of Burmese imports necessary for the operation of public sector industries, and the Japanese yen appreciated in value, thus raising the burden of debt.

The longer-term result of foreign assistance was more infrastructure, but also more economic activities dependent in part on imported components. At the same time, although the state was able to raise more revenue through better taxation systems (based on World Bank suggestions), it continued to spend a major proportion of its current budget on the military, an amount estimated to be today (March 1996) at least 60 per cent over the published budgetary figures of 25–30 per cent.

The *dirigiste* concept of the state in Burma probably originates in early Indian concepts of statecraft with the leader and his capital as the magical centres of authority. These need not concern us here, but more germane are the current highly personalised concepts of power and the role of central authority, perhaps stemming from the same source. There has never been, in the Western sense, a separation of powers. There have also been few autonomous institutions, partly due to the legacy of British colonial rule. Those that did exist in the pre-1962 period, such as the *sangha* (Buddhist monkhood), were controlled by the state in the military period. Under the BSPP there were no autonomous institutions, and this centripetal force has continued to the present. It is evident that at every stage of Burmese life – the period of the traditional monarchy (pre-1886), the colonial era (1886–1942), the Japanese Occupation (1942–5) and since independence (1948 to the present) – the state has intruded, managed, controlled, and cajoled the whole economy, and, indeed, intervened in most aspects of Burmese society.

The opening to the private sector in 1988 was without question an important advance. Foreign investment was allowed, not only as in the past with the public sector (this was largely theoretical, as there had been only one such investment – a West German firm, Fritz Werner, close to U Ne Win and engaged in armaments among other enterprises), but with the co-operatives – that parastatal element of state control over distribution and some more modest elements of production, and with the indigenous private sector as well. The state reserved to itself a major portion of the economy, from oil and teak to banking and communications. (Since that early SLORC announcement, domestic private banks have been allowed under the Financial Institutions Law of 1990, and there are now fifteen in existence, but how independent they may be is still open to question [see further n. 7 below]). The media continued to be under state ownership.

The issue of *dirigisme* does not imply in itself a negative normative judgement. Some societies, such as that of South Korea, have a highly interventionist record, with major state control over perhaps one-third of

GNP during the period of quick economic expansion, complete control of institutional credit at critical periods, and a private sector subservient at that time to the regime in power. Yet few states have equalled the Korean economic miracle. The issue, therefore, is not essentially that of the *dirigiste* state, but rather whether there is an administration determined to use the ability of economists to make rational decisions that are, in turn, supported and encouraged by the political leadership, and implemented by an effective bureaucracy recruited on merit. Burma lacks all of the above.

The Effects of Economic Liberalisation under the SLORC (1988–96)

The SLORC has articulated its role as transitory, even if it may wish to have a profound, long-term impact on the society. It evidently intends to have veto power over any government that will replace it. Thus, although it may view its economic role as temporary, it regards its influence as permanent. The Minister of Planning and Finance, responding to a question by the present author in 1989 on why foreign firms might wish to invest in Burma before an election, the results of which were unpredictable, replied that the process of economic liberalisation was irreversible.

From a SLORC vantage-point, one that is both skewed and short-sighted, the economic liberalisation to date may be viewed as quite successful. Myanmar has edged onto the world economic map, where previously it had fallen off. Foreign businessmen are now prevalent in Yangon. Joint ventures have been formed. Consumer products are in supply, even if many are only obtainable on the black market. Indigenous entrepreneurs are appearing for the first time since March 1962. Significant foreign exchange has built up with reserves reaching an all-time high of US$674.7 m. in May 1995 although these declined dramatically to less than a half that figure by mid-1996. Attempts have been made to hold rice prices in check and thus limit public disaffection occasioned by the rising cost of basic commodities. The society is rigorously controlled by a rapidly growing and better equipped military with a more powerful intelligence arm. Foreign ambassadors (there are now more than fifty delegations in Yangon) pay appropriate courtesy calls on SLORC leaders, all of which are dutifully reported in the controlled press and provide the regime with added legitimacy. The previous Chairman of the SLORC, Senior General Saw Maung (in office 1988–92), went to China with a 52-person entourage and considerable fanfare in August 1991, and Burma has recently (27 July 1995) acceded to the ASEAN Treaty of Amity and Co-operation with the expectation of full membership perhaps as early as July 1997. Foreign debt (of just under US$6 bn) is pressing but can be manipulated. From a longer-range and professional perspective, however, the problems are acute, and likely to grow. The money supply is booming – increasing officially some three times over the period following demonetisation, and twice that before it. The government can engage in an extensive local reconstruction and resettlement campaign with these funds, and the bills will only come due later. Inflation is officially some 30 per cent, but even Lieutenant-General Khin Nyunt, SLORC Secretary-1, admitted it could be higher. The black market exchange rate is about twenty times the official rate of Kt6: US$1. The State Economic Enterprises, which have had their debt written off, are still a drain on the public budget, and, despite the SLORC's moves (since August 1994) to privatise some of the 12 000 small-scale enterprises nationalised in 1962–3, there is still no sign that the government is seriously considering change for the larger public companies. Their level of production is around a quarter of capacity. The major portion of the economy is in the informal sector. Most foreign donors have stopped assistance. The environment has been systematically raped through lucrative, but disastrous, contracts for teak logging and shrimp fishing, which have seriously depleted the state's natural reserves (see further Chapter 4 above).

Most foreign investment (with the exception of oil and gas exploration) was generally of a short-term nature, involving trade and labour-intensive industries that could easily be moved should greater profits in less precarious economic environments be found elsewhere. The costs of the increased military are shielded from public scrutiny, but prevent needed allocation of funds for development projects. There is still no separation of powers, so that there is no institutional means to mitigate inappropriate or ill-informed opinion. Under the BSPP, feedback into the *Pyithu Hluttaw* (People's Assembly) was an articulated element of the 'report back' system in which legislators visited their constituencies and heard complaints. It became formalistic and did not work well because of the hierarchical structure of power, but even that element has been lost under martial law between 1988 and the present (March 1996). At the same time, the SLORC was engaged in a continuing diatribe against most foreigners (especially those from the West), who were said to intend subversion of the state.

Because power is highly centralised and personalised, criticism from below is inappropriate and even dangerous. Although the proverbial messenger bearing bad tidings may not be shot, he is certainly suspect, and such news unwelcome. Because the 21-man SLORC is generally insular and poorly educated (ten have only secondary school education or less [Saw Maung, for example, left school at thirteen], and only four have university degrees or their equivalent), it may have only a minimal understanding of the external image that Myanmar, in its continuing and repressive military incarnation, is creating.

The effects of economic liberalisation, even in an economically incompetent *dirigiste* state, have not all been negative. There is little question that foreign capital is sorely needed (since the November 1988 Foreign Investment Law, some US$3.24 bn has been approved for investment, over half of it in the post-1993 development of the oil and gas fields in the Andaman Sea). Equally important, foreign technology is required. Despite the disappointing results of onshore oil exploration in 1992–3, the potential of the Andaman Sea gas fields is thought to be substantial, with reserves of some six trillion cubic feet estimated for the Yadana field alone (see further Chapter 4, n. 46 above). Burma, prior to the Second World War, had been both a major exporter of energy (for example, oil from the Burmah Oil Company [BOC] fields at Chauk and Yenangyaung) and food, in particular rice, of which Burma was the world's largest exporter (3.123 million tons in 1940). Some thought that the SLORC was essentially mortgaging its future by using the foreign exchange it gained from signing payments on these contracts to support the military, and banking on future oil and gas revenues to provide the wherewithal to support the life-style to which it had become accustomed.

Perhaps the clearest, most explicit, indication of military intentions to continue its *dirigiste* role was the formation in 1990 of the Union of Myanmar Holding Company, a firm held completely by the military (40 per cent by the Directorate of Procurement, Ministry of Defence; the remaining 60 per cent by military units, together with active duty and retired individuals). It was capitalised at up to Kt10 bn (US$207 bn at the official exchange rate) or about 22 per cent of the official GNP at that time. It had already formed a joint venture with the Daewoo Corporation of Korea to produce textiles for export.

At the same time, because of signing payments on oil exploration contracts, government agreements with the Thai for logging concessions along their frontier, and fishing rights in Burmese waters (as well as through sale of part of the Burmese embassy in Tokyo, which officially brought in some US$236 million out of a total estimated profit of some US$600 million), foreign exchange reserves rose. Although the Burmese have not officially published debt figures after the end of 1992, it seems evident that disbursed debt is just under US$6 bn (in 1992, US$5.32 bn), perhaps 55–60 per cent of an ill-calculated and highly dubious GNP.

Burma has serviced its multilateral debt, but is in arrears in its Japanese and German debt. The French have forgiven the regime some of its debt, and the Japanese have offered some debt relief. To get these benefits, Burma lobbied hard in the United Nations to achieve (in December 1987) Least Developed Country (LDC) status, a designation for which it did not actually qualify as its literacy rate of 70 per cent was thought to be far higher than the maximum specified level (but see further Chapter 8 below, under 'Education').

Burma seems to have been expending and mortgaging its foreign exchange reserves and potential foreign income from oil and gas, timber, rice, gemstones and fisheries for the purchase of arms, especially from China, with which it consummated deals with US$1.2 bn in August 1990 and US$400 m. in November 1994 (see further Chapter 3 above). The expansion of the military, from its 1988 level of 180 000 to its present 320 000 (with an anticipated 500 000 by the end of the decade), can only come from its continued printing of currency and use of its recently acquired foreign exchange: in December 1987 (following which the political deluge took place and the economy further faltered) Burma's total reserves amounted to about US$28 m. (enough for under one week's imports). It was thus virtually bankrupt. Military expansion of this magnitude, even in a *Tatmadaw* that is essentially labour rather than capital intensive, such as the Thai, can only undercut economic investment and progress.

The economic openings have been significant, but inadequate to achieve the goals that the regime seems to have set for itself.[5]

The Need for Reform

To catalogue the need for specific reforms in Burma is to catalogue the needs of the society as a whole.[6] If, as seems apparent to the present writer, the primacy of politics has prevailed, then single economic reforms, however important, are unlikely to be generally effective. Even more sweeping economic changes may not produce the desired results. What may have to come first are political changes.

Spain may offer an instructive lesson. In making the transition from a militarised dictatorship under Franco to a democracy and a more open economic system after 1975, Spain consciously made the decision to make political reforms before economic restructuring, although both were needed.

If, as this author maintains, politics are in command in Burma, then any economic reforms, however important and necessary, will be held hostage to political interests, which (if the past is any indication) will vitiate their effectiveness. Furthermore, economic restructuring will have serious negative effects in the short term on large segments of the society, such as those with vested interests, those on fixed incomes, employees of the State Economic Enterprises, civil servants, military personnel and others. It is unlikely that an unpopular regime could survive the considerable political, social, and economic tensions, such structural reform would inevitably generate, without the use of stark military power, which, in turn, would further undercut market restructuring. In spite of the ubiquitous slogans appearing in the press exhorting the public to love and respect the military, it is highly unlikely that the regime enjoys widespread popularity in its present administrative role, however positively some sectors of the Burman populace may feel for the military as an institution (and even this is debatable).

The first requirement, then, is for political reform in a manner that is acceptable to a wide range of the populace. This may also mean the creation of various social and economic safety nets to ease the economic transition (from a monopolistic public sector to a more competitive system). Spain accomplished this through increasing short-term debt, which it could afford to do given its healthy balance of payments position. Burma would be in a more difficult position should it attempt this route: the US veto means it is very unlikely to qualify for IMF structural adjustment loans of the size required (US$2–3 bn) to provide support for the free-float of the *kyat*, for example. Important here is the need for economic restructuring coupled with a social conscience.

Whatever the methodology adopted, there will have to be some transition to a more effective economic system. One is tempted here to reproduce an index to any standard economic textbook as the catalogue of necessary reforms, but it may be more productive to mention selective and priority needs. They would include:

1. creation of a politically independent central bank that would manage the money supply, set or monitor exchange rates, and set surveillance of performance of the banking system as a whole;
2. formation of a banking system autonomous from political interference (even if under distanced government ownership);[7]
3. provision of credit, based on objective criteria, for the indigenous private sector;
4. encouragement of indigenous entrepreneurship and production;
5. training and deployment of a professional, merit-recruited, apolitical civil service;

6. development of laws and regulations, backed by some form of guarantee, of predictable actions related to internal and foreign businesses and investment;
7. limitations on corruption; and
8. re-establishment of an educational system based on effectively administered standards.[8]

The reader will note that all of these requirements are, in fact, based upon the need for the effective divorce of politics from economics. In no state is such a separation complete, and the economic resources of any state are likely to determine how much separation is necessary or possible. Their continued interaction in Burma, however, without political change will mean an ineffectual economic structure not capable of meeting the needs that the future leaders of Burma will set for themselves.

There have been indications that these problems are becoming more acute, and if not ameliorated will undercut whatever progress may be made. In October 1991, for example, Major-General (now Lieutenant-General) Khin Nyunt[9] admitted that 'most' public service personnel in 1988 had followed the 'wrong path' and that recently 4545 personnel had been dismissed or disciplined for opposition to government policies, and an additional 10 516 for corruption. This purge, together with that of 1988 (when 15 000 were dismissed), means administrative competence has diminished even as loyalty to the military is stressed, and competence ever more acutely in demand.

The needs, then, are myriad.

The Role of Donors in Myanmar

What, then, might the role of foreign economic assistance in Burma be in the late 1990s? That potential role is influenced by factors both external and internal to Burma.

The first such factor is a major international trend which has direct implications for Burma. There is now almost universal agreement among major bilateral donors of the Development Assistance Committee (DAC) in Paris, including the European Union, Japan, and the United States, that human rights and political issues, as well as limitations on military expenditures, should and will play a role in the allocation of foreign aid. There is some discussion that within the context of sound banking policies, the World Bank and the Asian Development Bank are considering such actions, although such factors are not within their original charters. In any case, the bilateral donors have a pervasive influence in those multilateral institutions, and could effectively block loans to any country in violation of these principles, should the major economic powers so agree. China and South Korea are two donor exceptions to the list of those states currently expressing concern about Burmese human rights.

Conversely, it is also apparent that, if the record of bilateral assistance is examined for the United States during the period when human rights were said to be a major concern (that is, the Carter administration, 1977–81), then it is clear that there was considerable slackness in the execution of that policy, both because of political or security considerations, and when assistance was said to be designated to go to the poor. Yet, as those in foreign assistance know, money is fungible, and foreign aid for one project might free local government funds for some less 'desirable' endeavour. Although the human rights effort may have created an admittedly important impression of concern, reality lagged far behind rhetoric. But, because no major donor (except perhaps China) has strategic interests in Burma, the human rights considerations are likely to carry considerable weight unless there are important changes within Burma. As Chinese economic influence grows, greater concern on the part of both Thailand and India is evident, both to limit China's potential role in the region and to feed from the same trough.

There is no question that Japan is under pressure from Japanese business interests to lend to Burma once again, but as a member of OECD, the diplomatic influence of other donors, the USA in particular, may act as a deterrent. Yet a senior Japanese official told this writer in 1992 that Japanese human rights policies (the so-called 'Kaifu Doctrine') would not affect the US$1 bn lending programme to Indonesia, a state whose questionable political and human rights record had recently been thrown into sharp relief by the 12 November 1991 Santa Cruz massacre in East Timor. Japan is the critical bilateral donor, one whose policies toward Burma will be most important. Its new aid policies may thus be ineffective where its political or economic interests are seen as transcendent. Burma also holds a strong emotional attachment for Japan, an attachment which can be traced back to the Second World War, and, for Japan's own articulated policies to be effective in Burma, it may take the co-ordinated influence of other donor states.

Internally, there are several lessons to be learned from previous foreign aid efforts in Burma. The first is that foreign policy advice is anathema to the military, at least if publicly voiced. The second is that the military as in the past will continue its strong interventions in the economy and society as a whole. *Dirigisme* will thus remain the order of the day. The third is that too much assistance (as in the 1970s) will effectively cut Burmese interest in substantive economic reforms. A fourth is that co-ordinated economic planning involving intersectoral considerations (as opposed to individual projects) is presently beyond the capacity of the state both because of the lack of trained staff, and because such planning normally involves complex political decisions. These factors should provide a backdrop to, and cautions about, thinking on foreign assistance.

The late 1990s may provide, *mirabile dictu*, clear and distinct alternatives, although at the present time of writing (March 1996) this seems remote. On the one end of such a theoretical spectrum, political stasis continues indefinitely, first under martial law or rule by decree. (The military did this from 1962 to 1974.) At the other extreme, power is turned over to the elected representatives, the SLORC is dissolved, and the military return to the barracks, not to intervene in politics again. The former alternative seems far more likely than the latter, although the odds on both are long.

If the SLORC continues its present political policies and stasis is maintained, major donor assistance will be unlikely to be forthcoming for new activities during the coming period. The government, together with Japanese business firms, will likely put pressure on Japan to restart a new programme. China and perhaps South Korea would remain donors of some significance. Other foreign assistance would probably be denied, even though the multilateral donors, not now bound by political or human rights concerns, would feel under pressure to resume lending. A liberal and civilian regime would no doubt attract relatively massive assistance. There are dangers in this latter, if remote, eventuality as well.

More likely are less Cartesian situations, ones mixed both politically and economically. This writer believes the SLORC when it says that a multi-party political system will evolve. The timing of that system, if it does come, however, is unclear and will probably be longer rather than shorter. A multi-party system also does not necessarily mean a democratic system, nor one not subject to military veto. It also may not mean one in which basic human rights are honoured. Ethnic autonomy may not mean ethnic power.[10]

OPTIONS FOR THE FUTURE

The Political Context

To prognosticate on the next half-decade from the vantage point of March 1996 requires that we assess the events of the past five or so years to determine what trends are discernable, and then see what options foreign assistance might have under these circumstances. It is important, in this situation, to articulate the assumptions on which this analysis takes place. While some of these are verifiable, others must remain a matter of conjecture.

The first issue is the perception of the SLORC itself. Since it came to power in September 1988, the composition of the ruling junta has changed somewhat, especially following the replacement in April 1992 of General Saw Maung by the less mercurial, if not more liberal, General Than Shwe. The SLORC's growing exposure to the outside world is another facet of this change: following the 18 September 1988 *coup*, members of the SLORC could boast little foreign training or experience, and even short-term travel abroad was minimal. Furthermore, the general educational level of the military leadership was quite low. They were thus insular in their physical exposure to the external world as well as to its intellectual trends. This has now begun to change, with constant delegations of SLORC officials travelling around the world and attending international meetings, and many foreign delegations and dignitaries beating a path to the junta's door. How much of this exposure is meaningful in terms of policy formation is questionable, but there seems to be little doubt that exposure to the economic development of Burma's neighbours cannot but have an effect on the SLORC's assessment of what Burma has missed. This, in turn, may help push the realisation of the need for fundamental change to allow Burma to close the gap.

On the political front, exposure to the 'stability' (that is, long-term military authoritarian rule) of Indonesia, to quote SLORC Secretary-1, Khin Nyunt's, comments during his December 1993 visit to Jakarta,[11] and the politics of other Asian states, have all undoubtedly broadened the still modest international horizons of the regime. At the same time, Burma's involvement with ASEAN as an invitee to its annual foreign ministers' meetings in Bangkok (July 1994) and Brunei (July 1995) have expanded its range of outside contacts. Although foreign exposure may help accelerate a measure of economic liberalisation, the SLORC's experience with its ASEAN neighbours, especially Indonesia, Malaysia, Singapore and Vietnam, as well as China, may convince them that it is possible to combine a more open economy with authoritarian political rule. This is clearly not the kind of message which potential international donors want the Burmese authorities to get.

Although it may be quite incomprehensible to outsiders who look objectively at Burma's foreign relations, the present author is convinced that the SLORC continues to believe its own propaganda that foreign elements – of every hue – are out to accomplish both the break-up of the Burmese state and the secession of the minority areas. The junta thus hold fast to their view of themselves as guardians of the geographical integrity of their country, and the unity and sovereignty of their nation, the SLORC's three 'sacred causes'.[12] The world may have changed, but the SLORC's historical views remain fixed. Fears of potential foreign encroachments run deep and not without reason. Historic attempts to break up the state have been multiple: not so long ago ethnic rebellions, such as the Karen and Karenni, had independence as their goal, and elements in Thailand, India, Bangladesh, China, the US and Britain, have, at various times, and with varying degrees of official sanction, supported dissident rebel forces operating along Burma's borders.[13] That these historical precedents weigh heavily on the SLORC is understandable. Even if they do not recognise the changed circumstances of the times, it is hard for them to accept that neither the interests of their neighbours nor of the major powers will be served by seeing Burma's disintegration into a plethora of economically and politically unstable micro-states along the lines of present-day Yugoslavia.

One of the SLORC's major preoccupations has been the protection, some would say ossification, of Burmese culture against the threat of absorption and destruction by malign outside influences. Rigid standards are thus enforced in terms of dress, popular entertainment and other manifestations of egregiously harmful foreign tides.[14] This approach is, of course, in direct conflict with the need for foreign investment and attempts to entice hundreds of thousands of tourists to Burma in what is now 'Visit Myanmar Year'. It represents, in the present writer's view, an unwarranted fear. Far from being eroded by contact with the outside world, Burmese culture is today alive and well and living in Rangoon.

The SLORC, and the military in general, have exhibited little sensitivity to the other ethnic groups in Burma. Despite the fact that many of these self-same minority groups were once loyal members of the *Tatmadaw* and much public rhetoric is devoted to the intrinsic 'unity' of the nation, army-minority relations are vitiated by the military's arrogance, an arrogance born of a sense of belonging to a superior culture – and in some cases (for example, *vis-à-vis* the largely Muslim Rakhine [Arakan] population) to a superior religion. This usually prevents soldiers dealing with members of other ethnicities in the sort of peer relationships the latter so desperately desire. Worse, it also has an unconscious effect on the way in which the proposed constitution is currently being formulated by the government-appointed Burman members of the National Convention (see Chapter 1 above).

For the SLORC, politics is still in command. Although progress in the economic sphere is apparent, economics is essentially viewed as a means towards a political end – the maintenance of internal military supremacy – rather than as an avenue for raising the general living standards of the people as, for example, was the case with the post-1965 'New Order' regime of General Suharto in Indonesia, which the SLORC now wishes to emulate.

Whatever the SLORC's views, however deeply they may be felt, and however inaccurate a representation of reality, one thing is crystal clear: the SLORC is now (March 1996) more secure and powerful than it has been at any time since the September 1988 *coup*. This is true politically, economically, militarily and diplomatically. However much one might deplore the means whereby the SLORC has strengthened itself internally or enhanced its international credentials, few would deny its present position. Some might question its capacity to retain that degree of control over the long term, and the SLORC's sense of its own strength may well be shown to be ephemeral, but it has enabled it to deal with internal and external issues from a position of power.

This position is closely linked to the rebellions in the minority areas, rebellions which, although not completely vanquished, are now largely in a state of disarray. 'Standfast' (that is, ceasefire) agreements have been signed with sixteen of the ethnic insurgencies. Some may well prove no more than temporary truces, as has been the case with the Karenni (Kayah) – see Chapter 5 (p. 151) – and SLORC promises of assistance (for example, the Border Areas Development Programme) may remain undelivered (see Chapter 3, n. 15 and Chapter 5, n. 13 above), but they have enabled the military to expand its control over the peripheral areas while allowing the rebels to retain their arms and continue to engage in cross-border trade and other economic pursuits. While these ceasefires solve an immediate problem for the military, they do not address the basic causes of the insurgencies, in particular the issue of ethnicity and power sharing, nor do they effectively limit the amount of gain from the cross-border drug trade and other illicit activities. Massive arms deals with China (see Chapter 3 above) may have enhanced the *Tatmadaw's* capacity to perform its military tasks, but the security which comes from the peaceful settlement of political grievances continues to elude it.

Foreign investment has deepened, infrastructure improved and construction projects multiplied, but at a high cost in terms of the environment and human lives: under the euphemism of 'voluntary labour', perhaps as many as 2 million people have been forced into a modern form of corvée with whole villages being displaced from the path of gas pipelines or forced to hack out jungle areas to clear new rail-beds (for example, for the extension of the Ye–Tavoy line in Tenasserim province). Official figures approved by the Board of Investment, figures which do not include massive Chinese (mostly Yunnanese) investments, may have outstripped the reality of actual projects. But there have been real economic changes as well. Under more appropriate human rights circumstances, these might have been applauded by the international community as the first – though not sufficient – steps towards substantive economic reform.

On the diplomatic front, the SLORC has brought Burma into the ASEAN orbit and the state now sanctions the attendance of its representatives at various international meetings. Politically too, the release of Aung San Suu Kyi in July 1995 has afforded the SLORC a breathing space. But hopes that this might mark the dawn of a more liberal direction have been dashed by the continuing restrictions imposed on her freedom of movement and the SLORC's unwillingness to engage her in meaningful dialogue, despite the evident strength of her domestic and international support.

The interminable constitution-drafting National Convention, carefully scripted by the military, is likely to result in a constitution in which military power will remain unfettered and entrenched for the foreseeable future. Although there have been some internal protests from Convention delegates – most notably the 28 November 1995 walk-out (and subsequent SLORC expulsion) of the eighty-six NLD delegates over the SLORC's summary denial of a review of the Convention's working procedures – it is evident that the military remains in command of both the process and the product (see further Chapter 1 above).

Whether one sees the emergence of a 'civilianised' military regime, such as the SLORC seems to be currently planning, or an effective and representative multi-party system, or even the coming to power of a resurgent NLD, at the very minimum the military will continue to play a key role in Burmese affairs for at least the next decade. Not only will they retain an effective veto over major policy decisions, they will also remain in authoritative positions of power just as they did before the March 1962 coup. Thus their influence will be impossible to ignore even if democracy one day flowers in Burma.

Options for Donors

Burmese military authorities have indicated, as did those in the previous BSPP regime, that they view externally derived policy suggestions as unwarranted interference in Burma's internal affairs. Indeed, the SLORC's inherent xenophobia can be seen in the way they have responded to foreign influences of every stripe by vitriolic anti-foreign campaigns orchestrated through the state-controlled media. Thus, public exhortations by foreigners for change, human rights and the redistribution of power are likely to create an internal backlash. This does not mean that external pressures for change are not necessary, rather that necessity and short-term effectiveness rarely go hand-in-hand in present-day Burma.

The present author suggested in 1990 that the SLORC's neighbours should reaffirm Burma's territorial integrity by recognising its borders both to provide a measure of political reassurance and eliminate any misconceptions still harboured by the military regime. In effect, the subsequent trade agreements with Burma's bordering states (India, China, Laos, Thailand) have accomplished this – without any significant impact on the process of political liberalisation. The diminished importance of the minority insurgencies has also made the need for such reaffirmation unnecessary.

The existence today of a much more powerful authoritarian state in Burma, one which sees its future in terms of entrenched military rule and is continuously strengthening its internal control over a society reluctant to risk a repeat of the 1988 massacres, makes the task of foreign aid donors exceedingly difficult. Although the human rights situation in Burma is deplorable, there is still a lack of consistency in the way potential donors regard aid and trade links with Rangoon. The major industrial powers and most other countries (with the exception of China and Burma's ASEAN neighbours) have only peripheral political interests in the country. So the pursuit of economic gain *tout court* is likely to become the paramount consideration.

Whatever potential donors decide to do, realism dictates that it will be done in the context of ever increasing private foreign trade and investment. International sanctions will not be approved since China will exercise its veto power in the Security Council (should such proposals get that far, which is unlikely), and even individual national sanctions (such as those proposed in the US Congress) will not be effective alone. Indeed, US businesses will continue to explore opportunities in Burma despite the boycott of individual products or companies by Burmese expatriates and their supporters, and despite individual State, city and county buying embargoes (such as those imposed in Alameda County [Northern California], Ann Arbor, Berkeley, San Francisco, Madison, Massachusetts, Oakland, and Santa Monica, and currently being mooted in New York City). Daw Aung San Suu Kyi has stated that this is not the correct time to invest in Burma, and, although her arguments are moving, the international business community is unlikely to heed her advice to any appreciable degree. Burma is not pre-1990 South Africa. The level of international concern and willingness to make a boycott effective are simply not there at present.

Given this situation, foreign assistance will probably be provided on a piecemeal basis, donor by donor, as business pressures build up and ASEAN links become ever more substantial. Under these circumstances what should donors do? The SLORC no doubt wants foreign assistance. The isolation of the regime, whatever expatriate Burmese and their supporters may say, is unlikely to result either in the fall of the junta or evolution towards a more democratic form of government. Only internal pressures, in particular economic mismanagement on the scale of the pre-1988 Ne Win regime and military infighting, will bring this about. Yet those that argue that exposure to the outside world will effect political change may only be right if they think in terms of generations. It took Korea from 1961 to 1987, and Taiwan from 1949 (some might say from 1929) to 1992 for political liberalisation to be effective, to cite only two cases of far more internationally open and sophisticated societies.

Although human rights and good governance are now the standard guidelines of all the major donors, exceptions have been made when the national interests of donor countries take precedence over rights issues. The urge, which is usually very strong among donors, to lend or proffer assistance, need to be tempered by present-day realities. Experience has shown time and again that the Burmese military have taken assistance as a right, and have made little effort to conduct reforms. When aid is pouring in, as was demonstrated in the late 1970s and early 1980s, concerns for human rights and good governance fly out of the window.

Such assistance, if proffered, should be conditional and sequential on economic reforms. Modest, phased and carefully monitored by residential representatives of the multilateral and bilateral donors rather than through fleeting missions from headquarters, these reforms should be the *sine qua non* for further aid. Burma should be treated no differently here from any other aid-receiving regime. Discussions on political liberalisation and related issues should take place in an atmosphere of quiet diplomacy. (The UNDP's current 'Human Development Initiative' for Burma, which aims 'to improve the people's welfare through participatory development involving communities and grass-roots initiatives' is very much a step in the right direction here). Public posturing may be desirable for the donor's internal political purposes, but is much less likely to be efficacious in terms of changing regime policies.

While these questions are being debated and before major assistance is contemplated, there is an intermediate issue which needs to be addressed.

This has already proven to be highly controversial: namely, whether donors should now provide planning, such as sectoral studies, for any future lending, and/or training (but not funds) for Burmese civil servants charged with implementing aid budgets.[15]

The arguments run along the following lines: on the negative side, pressures on the SLORC to reform are diminished, the regime gains added legitimacy by being offered such assistance even if it brings no short-term economic effects, and foreign donors could experience difficulty in ensuring the selection of the most appropriate people for training, or checking that data for the sectoral studies is accurate. On the positive side, it would ensure that there was less of a hiatus between planning and execution of development projects, if and when conditions again become ripe for foreign assistance, and overall economic recovery would be speeded.

The debate is legitimate. In its extreme form, it is often couched as a dispute between those who are for dialogue with the SLORC and those who insist that no discussions on any issue should take place with the regime for fear that such contacts might be used to enhance its legitimacy. Many would say that if there are to be discussions, they should be held with the National Coalition Government of the Union of Burma (NCGUB) located in the rebel areas along the Thai border and in the United States, and composed of the winners of the 27 May 1990 election.

The prudent course for foreign donors, however, is to attempt to provide the external conditions for the internal resolution of Burma's problems, as outlined above, while, at the same time, continuing the dialogue with the SLORC and other authorities in Rangoon. This approach would inevitably entail trade-offs. The timing of the two efforts might be dovetailed: studies and training might be offered simultaneously as the process of negotiations is accepted or started. The immediate gains from such discussions might seem less initially than the legitimacy a clever government could extract from them, but, over the longer term, such dialogue could assist positive change. Donors should also be in contact with opposition elements as well.

At the same time, in order to build the potential human resources needed to manage some future Burmese state, support should be given to those promising Burmese outside the country who, under different political conditions, might be prepared to return to Burma. This dual approach would no doubt fail to completely satisfy all groups, but it may well be the most effective approach under current conditions, conditions that offer no real solution to the present political dilemma.

Official multilateral and bilateral assistance is one element of aid; another is that from non-governmental groups that normally supply small amounts of aid, often of a humanitarian kind, and prefer to work with elements of civil society in any given country. Humanitarian and relief assistance may be immediately desirable in particular areas, especially where local insurgencies have retarded growth and increased deprivation. It is necessary to remember that, as of the time of writing (March 1996), civil society effectively does not exist in Burma: private, non-governmental, organisations, except at the local temple level, are under state control and are not autonomous. The operational requirements, governmental clearances and co-ordination, and even the actual provision of goods or services for private foreign organisations working in Burma, are so very restrictive that the autonomy of the foreign organisation is bound to be seriously compromised. Unless the government liberalises its approach to private aid, there are serious questions whether many such organisations would be prepared to offer assistance. To date, the SLORC has preferred to deal with non-governmental organisations on an individual basis, and has been reluctant to establish dialogue with them as a group.[16] In fact, it could be argued, the SLORC is trying to create its own version of civil society, one completely under its own control, witness its establishment of USDA in September 1993.

Conclusions

One cannot be sanguine about the results of any foreign approach, be it public or private, multilateral or bilateral. Burma is likely to have major unresolved problems that defy foreign intervention and complicate internal resolution. Foreign assistance has not been, nor will ever be, a panacea for Burma's deep-seated political and economic ills. Mao Zedong once said that politics were in command. They certainly seem to be in present-day Burma, where the relentless attrition of the economic well-being of all the country's different ethnic groups, Burman as well as minority, continues apace. All seem caught in the web of internal power politics. If foreign assistance is forthcoming without at least some partial resolution of economic and political issues, inextricably linked as they are, the results will be less than efficacious. Over past decades, the roles played by foreign powers have not been as constructive as they might have been. Now the world has changed: the Cold War is over, and tensions are more regional than global. The powers, through appropriate organisations such as the United Nations and its agencies, could begin anew the process of reconciliation by making positive gestures. There is clearly a need to move ahead, even if the process is slow, tedious and halting. The process of real change and liberalisation must come from within, informed by a broader understanding of societal needs and national opportunities. There will no doubt be many blind alleys in the maze that is modern Myanmar, but we can be assured that minotaurs, even Burmese ones, are not for ever.

Notes

1. This is discussed in David I. Steinberg, *Burma's Road Toward Development: Growth and Ideology under Military Rule* (Boulder: Westview Press, 1981), ch. 3.

2. See David I. Steinberg, 'Japanese Economic Assistance to Burma: Aid in the "Tarenagashi" Manner?', *Crossroads* (Northern Illinois University), 5.2 (1990) (republished in Bruce M. Koppel and Robert M. Orr, Jr [eds], *Japan's Foreign Aid. Power and Policy in a New Era*. Boulder: Westview Press, 1993).

3. For disagreement on the issue of income distribution, see Mya Maung, *The Burma Road to Poverty* (New York: Praeger, 1991), pp. 188–91, 193–4.

4. Elaborate circumlocutions were sometimes made so that the Burmese would not appear to be asking for help from donors.

5. See David I. Steinberg, 'The United States and Burma: The Ephemeral Promise of the Private Sector', *Solidarity* (Manila), 121 (January–March 1989), pp. 42–7.

6. This has been done in John Badgley's chapter, 'Remodelling Myanmar', in Mya Than and Joseph L. H. Tan (eds), *Myanmar Dilemmas and Options* (Singapore: Institute of Southeast Asian Studies, 1990), ch. 10.

7. Starting with the Commercial and Development Bank (associated with the Chamber of Commerce), and the Myanmar Citizens Bank, an entity created by a number of Joint Ventures, a total of some fifteen domestic private banks have opened (thirteen in Yangon, one each in Mandalay and Taunggyi [Shan State]) since the 1990 Financial Institutions Law which allowed domestically-owned banks to operate again after a gap of twenty-eight years. At the same time, thirty-one foreign banks have been licensed to set up representative offices and twenty-two have actually done so. In order to comply with IMF recommendations – an IMF technical monitoring programme has been set up in Yangon in November 1995 with the aim of making Burma eligible for new IMF funds, the US veto permitting – the SLORC further liberalised the banking sector in December 1995, allowing foreign banks with representative offices to enter into joint partnerships with domestic private banks, provided the Burmese partner subscribes at least 35 per cent of the venture's equity. It also permitted private companies and individuals to exchange *kyat* at the free market rate of Kt125:US$1, see EIU, 'Myanmar: Country Report', 1st Quarter 1996, p. 25. Despite these reforms, it is still uncertain whether the private banking sector will be allowed to operate free of political influence.

8. Universities only reopened in May 1991 after being closed for three years. They were closed again in December 1991, and reopened in September 1992, see further Chapter 8, n. 7 below.

9. Speech delivered on 4 October 1991 in Rangoon and reported on Rangoon Home Service, see, FBIS, 7 October 1991. See also Martin Smith, *Fatal*

Silence? Freedom of Expression and the Right to Health in Burma (London: Article 19, July 1996), p. 46, p. 55 n. 3, quoting Lt-Gen Khin Nyunt as saying that 15 000 civil servants had been dismissed since the SLORC took power in September 1988.

10. For a discussion of this issue, see David I. Steinberg, 'Myanmar 1991: Military Intransigence', in *Southeast Asian Affairs 1992* (Singapore: Institute of Southeast Asian Studies, 1992), pp. 221–37. See also Chapter 5 above.

11. See Michael Vatikiotis and Bertil Lintner, 'Pariah No More: Asean Edges towards Closer Ties with Rangoon', *FEER*, 3 March 1994, p. 27; and John McBeth and Bertil Lintner, 'Model State: Burma's Generals Want Indonesian-style Politics', *FEER*, 17 August 1995, p. 27.

12. See Steinberg, 'Myanmar 1991', *loc. cit.* The three 'causes' of the SLORC – and, indeed, the previous Ne Win regime since 1962 – are (1) the integrity of the Union; (2) national unity; (3) the preservation of Burma's sovereignty.

13. To take as examples, the Japanese provision of two of the Shan States to Thailand in the Second World War, informal British involvement with the Karens in the later 1940s, US involvement with the Kuomintang in the Shan State in the 1950s, foreign Muslim support to the rebels in the Arakan, Thai tacit support to U Nu and his Bangkok-based Parliamentary Democracy Party (PDP) in the late 1960s and 1970s, as well as the minorites' own earlier statements, some of which included independence, some UN trusteeship.

14. See, for example, the article in *The Nation* (Bangkok), 17 November 1992, 'Rangoon's Fledgling Nightlife is Too Racy for Staid Generals'.

15. Multilateral donors are bound to continue projects already started or approved, if internal aspects of such projects allow. The UNDP programme is a right of all member states. Bilateral donors have different approaches, ranging from that of the United States, which stopped all projects already approved, to that of the Japanese, which continued approved projects but which did not start new ones. On the IMF technical monitoring programme, which is already in place in Rangoon to assist the domestic banking sector and prepare for the free float of the *kyat*, see above n. 7.

16. See Martin Smith, *Fatal Silence?*, esp. ch. 9.

7 Economic Reform and Political Conditionality in Myanmar

Paul Cook and Martin Minogue

INTRODUCTION

This chapter looks at economic policy changes in Myanmar,[1] analysing the reasons for the decision to move from a state-led socialist planning system to a more market-orientated system, and attempting to evaluate both the direction and sustainability of these economic reforms. As such it continues an earlier study (Cook and Minogue, 1993) in which we examined the contention that economic reform has become a hostage to political reform. The argument, both explicit and implicit in the approach of major aid donors, has two main strands. The first is that effective economic reform and growth require substantial external inflows of capital in the form of official aid and lending, principally through the International Monetary Fund and the World Bank. Official aid flows (up to the late 1980s, mainly bilateral aid) have been suspended as a result of government failure to carry through the political changes it began in 1988, and cease human rights abuses associated with the suppression of political opposition. Only substantive political reforms would reverse the aid embargo, and make possible genuine economic progress.[2] The second strand of the argument is that a higher level of economic development is more likely to be associated with democratisation.

This argument was challenged in our 1993 article on the grounds that it represents an overly simplistic analysis of political and economic development in Myanmar; does not correspond to models of successful development in neighbouring countries; and rests on misleading assumptions about causal relationships between economic and political factors. It was argued that the hostage model had a number of significant weaknesses. First, it assumed that economic performance would deteriorate further because the government lacked the will to implement reforms of a predominantly economic type. Second, it relied on all parties to the embargo to cease external support. Third, and more importantly, it assumed that all participants to the embargo on aid were in agreement concerning the degree of political reform that would be necessary to ensure a resumption of aid flows.

We argued, therefore, that a more sophisticated account must embrace an understanding of the historical roots of Burmese political and economic development, the history and nature of the Burmese state, and the character of Burmese military and political elites. We concluded that a more convincing explanation and realistic appraisal of contemporary development might be achieved by the construction of an historically-rooted 'political economy' of Burma/Myanmar, than by the defence of a flawed strategy of political conditionality.

In order to explore these issues fully we begin by examining the content of the recent spate of market-orientated economic reforms and attempt to explain why they were introduced. In the next section the hostage model is developed as a mixture of bilateral and multilateral negotiation positions. We then examine the weaknesses of the hostage model from the economic and administrative viewpoints. There follows an outline of the survival strategy that underlines the policy pursued in the late 1980s and early 1990s, and an examination of possible scenarios, with the suggestion that the future path of political and economic development is likely to be influenced by Asian, rather than Western, examples. The final section presents evidence that reinforces the central propositions of the counterview to the hostage argument.

THE MOVE TOWARDS ECONOMIC REFORMS

The first major step toward liberalisation in the 1980s came in September 1987 when the government removed restrictions on trade in major crops. These changes signalled the end of thirty years of central planning in which almost all activities, including large-scale manufacturing, mining, communications, services and banking were in the state sector. Later that year (December 1987), Myanmar was classified as a Least Developed Country (LDC) by the United Nations in a move designed to alleviate the debt situation. More substantial reforms were announced when the military State Law and Order Restoration Council (SLORC) took over in September 1988 as a self-declared caretaker government following substantial civil unrest.

In 1988 the government declared that it would depart from central planning and move toward a more 'open-door' policy. In November, the government enacted the Foreign Investment Law which legalised border trade with its neighbouring countries, although some exports were excluded from these arrangements. The Foreign Investment Law permitted foreign investors to form wholly owned enterprises or joint ventures, especially those engaged in exporting activities. Foreign investment was also to be induced by a number of incentives, including tax holidays and exemptions, particularly for businesses that reinvest their profits. In March 1989, the SLORC introduced the State-Owned Economic Enterprise Law which essentially opened the door for the private sector to compete in activities previously the exclusive domain of the public sector. The Private Investment Law was passed a year later, which, while recognising the part the private sector might play in the economy, nevertheless maintained an operating framework of strict regulation and licensing. Further measures that might eventually increase the competitiveness among financial institutions and strengthen their capacity to facilitate investment finance were enacted in 1990 through the Central Bank of Myanmar Law, the Finance Institutions of Myanmar Law and the Myanmar Agricultural and Rural Development Bank Law. These, at least, provided the framework for a more conventional role for the central bank in the use of monetary instruments and opened further channels for investment finance for the private sector.

Present policy can be interpreted as a survival strategy in response to deteriorating economic conditions (Cook and Minogue 1992). In part attributable to unfavourable movements in the terms of trade, particularly in the 1980s for major exports of teak and rice (Catling and Dunning 1989), deterioration was also due to mismanagement under the centrally planned system. This was not the first time the government had acted in this way. In the mid-1970s, new policy measures had been introduced in response to the deteriorating conditions and pressure from international lending agencies (Fenichel and Khan 1981; Hill 1984).

THE HOSTAGE MODEL

The hostage argument has been adopted by most of the bilateral donors and the international agencies through their aid embargo. A weaker variety has been exercised by the main UN agencies, such as the UNDP, UNESCO and the FAO, who continue to provide limited forms of technical assistance. Although the International Monetary Fund (IMF) also provides a small amount of technical assistance (for example, its technical monitoring programme established in November 1995), through twinning arrangements with the UNDP, their overall stance typifies the hostage approach.

The present deadlock in negotiations for standby and debt-relief arrangements between the government and the IMF, largely due to the stringency of US conditions (which demand progress on democracy, human rights and the fight against narcotics),[3] embody the characteristics of this model. On the one hand improved economic conditions are thought to depend on an externally assisted structural adjustment programme and on the other hand, it will not be forthcoming unless there is genuine democratisation and responsible government.

The IMF negotiated with the government in the context of several critical factors (IMF 1989). First, although the earlier attempts in the mid-1970s to reform met with some success in strengthening import substitution and were extensively financed by foreign loans, those policies eventually had a detrimental effect as the government extended its sphere of intervention in the economy. Intervention took the form of more direct controls and regulations over the publicly owned enterprises and the large number of small-scale operators that remained in the private sector (Hill 1984). Second, the reforms were not sufficiently comprehensive. Third, recent indications are that government expenditure overruns, resulting from pay awards (to avoid social unrest) and other non-wage outflows (defence and beautification measures prior to 'Visit Myanmar Year', which starts in November 1996) will have an adverse impact on inflation and the balance of payments.[4] Fourth, no exchange rate reform has taken place. The official rate has appreciated while the parallel rate, which determines a large share of domestic unofficial prices, has depreciated rapidly since 1989.

In the negotiations process the IMF advocates, through stabilisation policy, a reduction in demand pressures and second, via structural adjustment measures, a realignment of domestic prices from their distorted position. Initially, the government would be required to cut current expenditure as a prerequisite for further reform. The IMF would in time make further assistance conditional on a radical reform of the civil service.

Several stages are envisaged for the short to medium term: (1) the establishment of financial stability; (2) a reduction of inflationary pressures by lowering the domestic rate of monetary growth via cuts in government (current) expenditure; (3) an increase of revenue via improved public enterprise efficiency; and (4) a reform of the exchange rate with trade liberalisation. The IMF's recent mission rationalises the above approach by claiming:

> The experience of several countries (both middle income and developing ones) with liberalisation and progressive reliance on market

mechanisms shows that the payoffs in terms of growth and development of the economy can be substantial, as the elimination of distortions in goods markets, foreign trade, and financial markets promotes the disappearance of parallel markets, the widening of the tax base, the strengthening of confidence of domestic and foreign investors and the eventual emergence of new productive activities and employment opportunities. (unpublished IMF Mission Report, 1990)

The IMF's analysis is conducted on the basis of two scenarios. One portrays an unchanged policy situation in which the government continues along its present path. Of course, the interpretation of this path involves assessing the strength of commitment to undertake and carry through existing policies. Under this scenario growth is expected to be constrained by a shortage of foreign exchange as traditional exports decline. Present policy aims are not pointed toward debt rescheduling. Debt service arrears will increase. Such a scenario implies that imports will decline further and with low public investment, capital formation will decline. Under present policy, GDP growth is expected to be less than 2 per cent with price increases, balance-of-payments deficits, debt, and budget deficits.

The other scenario, which represents the crux of the hostage model, assumes the adoption of a comprehensive structural adjustment programme, which is supported by international aid and debt relief. Under this scenario the GDP growth target is 5 per cent with inflation reduced to 6 per cent over five years. The balance-of-payments deficit as a ratio to GDP will also be reduced. Delivering support of this kind has conditions which include reforms to the tax, money and exchange rate regimes.

The type of structural adjustment indicated has both interim and longer-term costs to consider. Imports are likely to rise with foreign investment in the transition period, although the current account deficit is expected to improve later. The gap in the interim period, however, is to be filled by external assistance (that is, bilateral and multilateral loans). This approach, therefore, has a political connotation by assuming a favourable outcome for the resumption of aid. Inconsistently, the IMF currently provides technical assistance to Myanmar without requiring any political change.

The external resources embodied in the IMF proposals for the future are not insignificant, exceeding in size total World Bank lending to Myanmar during the 1970s and 1980s. The IMF estimates that external assistance of US$600 m. is required for the first year, to take care of debt arrears, and a further US$360 m. for each subsequent year of the structural adjustment programme.

ECONOMIC WEAKNESSES OF THE HOSTAGE MODEL

In this section we argue that implementing economic change is not entirely dependent on political reform. Such a view assumes that capital inflows and technical assistance are required to achieve sustainable development and these in turn will not emerge from external sources until there is evidence of political change in the direction of a greater degree of democratisation, and a reduction of human rights abuses.

Undoubtedly, the present situation is characterised by a relatively low degree of economic efficiency and utilisation of human resource capability, and the question remains to what extent these deficiencies can be overcome without substantial external assistance.

The hostage model relies on a number of tentative assumptions. First, it assumes that economic conditions will continue to deteriorate because the government will fail or lacks the will to implement economic reforms. Second, like all sanctions systems, it relies on no external party breaking ranks. Finally, it assumes that all participants to the aid embargo are in agreement concerning the degree of political reform that would be necessary to ensure that aid flows are resumed. All three assumptions are open to debate. The 'hostage to political reform' view may, therefore, be too simplistic because it fails to interpret correctly the direction of domestic policy being pursued by the Myanmar government.

The government's policy stance on the political front appears to be based on defusing the opposition. On the economic front it is conceivably focused on reviving exports from a very low level and exploiting the economy's considerable mineral resources. For example, the major forms of foreign investment under the 'open-door' policy (a term subsequently [1990] dropped from official documentation) introduced after 1988 have been in risk-taking oil and gas exploration, first (1992–3) in onshore blocs, and, more latterly (and much more profitably) in the offshore gas fields in the Andaman Sea. Substantial rents were extracted from the foreign investors, which assisted with immediate balance-of-payments deficits.

Despite limited improvements in economic performance the government maintains firm control over economic agents in the economy. With the passing of new economic laws, the government continues to control the prices for goods produced by the state-owned enterprises. Instead of devolving financial responsibility to these enterprises, all financial matters have been placed in the hands of central government (Cook 1994). The private sector continues to operate under a system of strict registration and licensing and suffers from restricted access to credit from the state-owned banking system. The Foreign Investment Law provides an array of incentives to foreign investors, although most have benefited from joint ventures with domestic partners. Foreign companies have established themselves where natural resource rents can be exploited, such as fishing, timber, mining, and oil and gas or where they can benefit from the underutilised export quotas, particularly for textiles and footwear.

The 'hostage' scenario does assume that some form of structural adjustment, externally supported, is required for medium-term development. The theoretical justification for this strategy, however, has been shown to be inappropriate when applied to economies in decline (for example, in the case of Guyana, see Mosley, Harrigan and Toye 1991). Moreover, it takes insufficient account of the comparative advantage, especially in labour costs, enjoyed by Myanmar in the ASEAN and Pacific regions (Vokes 1990). It also presupposes that employment displaced through the recommended cuts in government expenditure will be absorbed by private sector growth.

Views about the required degree of political compromise vary among donors. Some (for example, Japan) may be willing to resume activities with smaller degrees of democratisation; still others (for example, South Korea and China) are imposing no conditions at all. This will inevitably weaken the bilateral coalition, but may also obviate the need for a comprehensive adjustment package if one significant donor, such as Japan, resumed lending activities. There are indications that some donors, for example, Japan, Germany, France and Switzerland, which were recently (November 1995) singled out by the SLORC's National Planning and Economic Development Minister, Brigadier-General David Abel, might be willing to extend their lending activities through the IMF, although the US veto is a heavy constraint here.

BUREAUCRACY AND THE HOSTAGE MODEL

The hostage model, then, seriously oversimplifies the government's position and role regarding economic reform. It assumes a coherent body half-heartedly pursuing reforms primarily for self-interested reasons. The policy-formulating process and capacity to implement policy, however, are clearly more complex than is portrayed in this model.

First, the history of the political and administrative system shows that it has neither always been monolithic, nor inefficient. While it is clear that, since the 1962 *coup*, small military-led oligarchies have dominated decision-making, various changes in personnel have indicated tensions and disagreements over economic policy (Steinberg 1981). While Silverstein suggests that 'Burma's problem was not making decisions, but implementing them' (Silverstein 1977, p. 74), Steinberg points to the 'not inconsiderable accomplishments' of the civilian bureaucracy in the late 1970s (Steinberg 1981, p. 189). The governmental system has in the past decade been weakened and made more subservient to the ruling group, yet both decision making and processes of implementation operate in different ways at various levels, especially in less politically sensitive areas such as health and school level education.

Second, decision making is highly unpredictable: before his retirement as Chairman of the BSPP in July 1988, General Ne Win would make decisions with theoretically obscure rationale. For example, unannounced decisions to demonetise in an attempt to break up parallel money markets took place twice in the 1980s (most damagingly in September 1987, when 80 per cent of the currency in circulation was wiped out), but were not made by either the Central Bank or the Ministry of Planning and Finance.

Third, there is no systematic co-ordination of policy analysis and implementation. A picture emerges of *ad hoc* arrangements which, below the Cabinet level, do not appear to be widely perceived and understood. Under the former planned economy there was an Economic Co-ordination Committee which disappeared with the reversion to annual budgeting. The annual budgeting process has been supplemented by the introduction of a three-year planning cycle. Policy co-ordination takes place in several interministerial committees, some of which correspond to Cabinet subcommittees. Given the small number of ministers responsible for around twenty ministries before January 1992, when the number of ministries was increased to twenty-six (with twenty-seven ministers and twelve deputy ministers) and the eighteen-man SLORC governing cabinet was expanded to twenty-one, it is difficult to ensure co-ordination by these means. Therefore, in the absence of a systematic set of co-ordinating mechanisms, and given the burdens on ministers, it is unlikely that there can be effective consideration of the full range of intersectoral implications of specific policy options.

Similarly, the policy orientation of individual ministries shows considerable variation. Some ministries adopt a static 'minimum reaction' position, seeing their role primarily in terms of administering particular laws. Other ministries adopt a more innovative 'directive' approach, in which they use the scope provided by the various laws in the economic domain for creative interpretation, and also act to identify problems which require further action and possibly legislation. Which of these stances is adopted seems to depend partly on the personalities of specific officials and ministers, and partly on the character of their policy responsibilities.

Fourth, the current wave of reforms, despite the centrality of decision making, emanates from different levels of government and stems from different agenda. Overall reform can be described as piecemeal and the significance of each reform measure varies in economic and political terms. Reform measures with significant political connotations are initiated and sanctioned by the SLORC while reforms which may be less politically sensitive, yet have widespread economic consequences, can be initiated through the bureaucracy and only require the SLORC's subsequent endorsement. In some cases (for example, energy, health), special interdepartmental committees (akin to British Cabinet committees) act as a link between the SLORC and the bureaucracy.

There can be little doubt, however, that administrative inefficiency and the lack of management skills, are major constraints on the implementation of any type of economic reform. To counter this, the UNDP, through its Management Development Programme, initiated a two-year technical assistance programme in 1990 to strengthen policy formulation and management development.[5] This programme rejected the comprehensive reform of the administrative structure and opted, instead, for a series of discrete measures, including analytical studies, consultancy support and institutional development, which would have small dispersed impacts throughout the large bureaucracy (Cook, Kennedy and Raitt 1989). This politically more acceptable approach, it was envisaged, would have a multiplier effect over time. Although the outcome is difficult to judge, most components of the project were completed with UNDP reports indicating that some key objectives, for example, those relating to skill enhancement and efficiency, had been broadly met.

The principal elements of technical assistance support consisted of reforms to the Central Institute for Public Services (the civil service training school), which has a substantial military emphasis for new entrants; the establishment of a general management services unit, which would review systems and procedures in various ministries and assist with implementing changes; the establishment of a policy advisory unit in the Ministry of Planning and Finance, which would provide a wider range of policy alternatives to the Cabinet; and a number of efficiency reviews of key ministries, which would spearhead future changes in administrative practices and procedures and support for financial administration through a series of training programmes. However, the combined effects of political and bureaucratic inertia have frustrated these intended reforms.

The argument about democratisation is germane to the economic reform process in the sense that a reforming government which lacks legitimacy and authority will find it difficult to secure the co-operation and energies required to ensure the success of innovative policies. Since 1987, the Burmese/Myanmar government has faced considerable and widespread opposition, given dramatic prominence in the May 1990 elections, which produced an overwhelming victory for political groups antagonistic to the military government. Since then, however, opposition has been substantially weakened, partly through legal and political attacks upon opposition representatives, and partly through increased military pressure on ethnic rebels in the regions, resulting in sixteen 'standfast' (ceasefire) agreements.

Clearly, at the same time, economic reforms are working slowly so that the government's 'carrot-and-stick' strategy is somewhat one-sided, with rather more stick than carrot. In terms of investment, particularly in the private sector, domestic investors and foreign entrepreneurs have, to some extent, opted for a cautious approach, preferring to act only when the administrative machinery of government has absorbed and enacted implementable policy as outlined in the already agreed legislative changes, and when greater political stability is ensured. Although investment, principally in the form of joint ventures with state-owned enterprises, has taken place, it has not yet occurred on a large scale. Domestic investors have been reluctant to take over large overstaffed public enterprises, though the extent to which there are real opportunities to do so remains unclear.

FROM SOCIALIST PLANNING TO SURVIVAL STRATEGY?

The decision to revert from centrally planned socialism to a more market-orientated system can be explained at one level by arguing that the pre-1988 Burmese state was never socialist but only centrally planned. Certainly, the Burma Socialist Programme Party (BSPP) was the only authorised political party in Burma after 1962 but as the *Asian Survey* in that year pointed out:

A more plausible explanation for the Council's 'Marxist' sympathies [in the 1960s] is ... to win over the rank and file of the Communists and fellow-travellers, thus terminating the fifteen-year insurrection. Once [this was done] the Council would proceed with a non-ideological development programme. (cited in Nyun 1989)

This has not prevented others including it in the category of socialist developing countries (see Morawetz 1980; UNIDO 1989). The economy was also well placed to change, because, as a result of the relative isolation, it was no longer in danger of being dominated by foreign interests. The paradox then was that although socialism was central to the anti-colonial struggle and independence, it was never embraced by the population as a whole. Indeed, ideologically committed groups were believed by the government to be destabilising elements in the 1970s. It has even been suggested that Burmese socialism should be seen 'as a middle path between the social democracy of the bourgeois right and the communism of the bourgeois left' (Taylor 1987, p. 297). It could be claimed, therefore, that moves to liberalise did not entail the relinquishment of Burma's distinctive version of socialism, with its amalgam of Marxist and traditional elements. Moreover, while liberalisation has, of necessity, involved some relaxation of formalised central planning, this is unlikely to involve a genuine decentralisation of central political control or central economic direction.

We suggested earlier that present policy can be viewed as a survival strategy in response to deteriorating economic conditions. In part, these conditions are attributable to mismanagement, but they are also due to unfavourable movements in the terms of trade, particularly in the 1980s. The survival strategy is based on the notion that benefits can be achieved in the relative short term. These benefits will accrue to the small middle-income urban business class (much of it non-Burman) that is emerging on the basis of trade and business activities stimulated by modest liberalisation measures and partly explains why there has been an emphasis on joint venture arrangements. Considerable economic power is also being transferred to the private sector through the establishment of joint ventures such as Myanmar Economic Holdings Limited, which is jointly owned by the Ministry of Defence and military personnel. This company has formed a number of subsidiaries which have entered into further joint venture arrangements with a number of foreign companies. In the longer term substantial investment in oil and gas exploration are key elements which the government hopes will both assist the economic transformation and minimise external dependency. Measures to reallocate resources and widen the export base, however, have been side-stepped. The exchange rate realignment, in particular, has represented a sticking point in the negotiations with the IMF.

The survival strategy is also more likely to work in view of the fact that although the economy was in relative isolation for thirty years, it never became completely outdated. Under the military regime intellectual exchange and innovation was to a large extent discouraged and there was an exodus of some of the country's best talent, but contact with other countries did remain. Aid-assisted programmes were quite significant in the 1970s and the early 1980s. The present government is now committed in principle to take opportunities to break its relative isolation although, as we have seen, without much international support, at least from Western countries. This is not to deny that present policy is short-sighted in terms of the loss of investment in human capital as a result of the closure of schools (1988–9) and universities (1988–92) in an attempt to eliminate sources of political opposition.[6] Policy-makers at the highest level in Myanmar still seem uncertain about the best economic strategies to pursue. Although privatisation is a stated policy objective, it is only being implemented through the joint venture arrangements, and the desire to hold on to the power and resources vested in large state corporations perhaps accounts for the lack of enthusiasm. In contrast to Vietnam, Mongolia, Angola and Mozambique, for example, political reform is lagging behind economic reform in Myanmar (Lenschow 1991). The strategy may be tenable from the government's point of view provided the following: technology can be acquired through joint venture arrangements; there is no significant external interference; ownership of public assets is retained (although selling some to pay off immediate debts and acquire funding for military defence); and the government can halt and stabilise the short-term economic decline.

POLITICAL–ECONOMIC LINKAGES: A BROADER PERSPECTIVE

The discussion of the linkage between economic change and political reform suffers from drastic oversimplification of the complexities of political–economic relations in Myanmar, producing incomplete academic analysis, and flawed political strategies, both based on misleading assumptions about present realities and future possibilities.

Scenarios for Myanmar's future must rest on a convincing account of the development of the Burmese polity and the Burmese state, with appropriate weight given to the political factors in the colonial and post-independence periods which conditioned and shaped this development. This is not the place for a full account, but it may be useful to sketch an outline. An examination of the history of Burma as presented by leading authorities (Silverstein 1977; Steinberg 1981; Taylor 1987 and Chapter 2 in this volume; Smith 1991) produces a strong sense of consistently recurring elements. One such element is a tradition of authoritarian rule, clearly present in the precolonial and colonial periods, and given harsher and more persistent form by military governments. Silverstein (1977) has suggested that military rule reflected elements of the precolonial past (elimination of rivals, separation of government from people); the colonial period (law and order, centralism, efficiency); and the nationalist movement (socialist ideology, elitist single party).

A second element in the Burmese political tradition is the resistance to authoritarianism through political dissent and oppositional politics, rooted initially in the anti-colonial struggle against the British (1824–1942) and the Japanese (1942–5) (Silverstein 1977; Taylor 1987 and Chapter 2 in this volume). While political opposition, particularly in the late 1980s, has often gained widespread support and the Burmese people have participated in at least four free elections since independence, five if one includes that of 27 May 1990 (with five others having been held, on a more restricted – 'Ministerial Burma' – franchise, by the British between 1935 and 1942), there has rarely been much enthusiasm for democratically elected governments. Indeed, the failures and divisions of the civilian political elite in the post-independence period led directly to the first '*coup*-by-consent' leading to General Ne Win's Caretaker Government (1958–60), itself the precursor of permanent military rule in 1962. This failure of civilian politics is more than a question of 'the faults in Burmese democracy' (Steinberg 1981, p. 20), or the vacillations of particular leaders. As Silverstein has pointed out, 'popular sovereignty and democracy had no counterpart in the [pre-colonial] political heritage of the Burmese' (Silverstein 1977, p. 22) and this is a significant reason for 'the inability of the party system to become a deep and meaningful part of the society' (Silverstein 1977, p. 30). Silverstein's considered judgement is that more than a decade of democracy had provided no evidence that it was a system that could govern. This history of the weakness of the democratic tradition in Burma cannot be ignored in considering future scenarios of democratisation.

Yet this weakness can be more readily understood in the context of Burmese social and political history. Burma as a nation has constantly been at war with itself. Its nationalism was inspired by opposition to British imperialism, but was actually achieved through the trauma of Japanese occupation (1942–5), and resistance to both Japanese and British control. Yet independent Burma was a place of endemic civil war, with central governments, whether civilian or military, struggling to contain armed rebellion both by political dissidents (for example, the Burmese Communist Party [1948–89]) and by ethnic insurgents (for example, the Shan, Karen and Kachin). Under these conditions, the military was an indispensable prop to the central (and increasingly ethnic Burman) government in Rangoon. Even more significant for the Burmese political tradition, the army was, from the very beginning, deeply immersed in politics and government. Indeed, there is an underlying continuity which links General Aung Sang (1915–47), General Ne Win (born 1911), and the present SLORC regime. Suppression of political dissent and repression of political opposition have a long history from the colonial period onward. So too has the tactic of gradual constitutional reform from above which concedes little real political change but which wards off internal and external criticism.

A final element, perhaps, is the weakness of the Burmese administrative system in the country's post-independence history. According to Silverstein (1977, p. 53), 'Burma's political leaders, whether civil or military, have not enjoyed the support of a well-trained and efficient administration'. Under military governments, the central bureaucracy has been weakened by defections and by political purges, while regional administration has effectively operated as a decentralised arm of the military oligarchy. While the bureaucracy in Burma/Myanmar is both more complex and more competent than is often supposed, it remains ill-equipped as a mechanism for economic reform, and incapable of acting as a political counter-weight.

An account of Burmese political history incorporating the elements sketched out above would usefully remind us that the present political and economic situation has to be analysed as a process that is adapting to a long-standing tradition in politics. War, violence, social and economic dislocation, and national crises have been endemic in twentieth-century Burmese history, and 'its political record incorporates the experiences of both democratic and authoritarian governments, neither of which has been able to solve the nation's problems' (Silverstein 1977, p. 197). Only on the basis of an historically rooted account can there be a convincing discussion of the possible trade-offs between economic and political reform in contemporary Myanmar.

More generally, the link between democratic systems and successful economies is not at all clearly established in the Third World. Howell (1991) refers to the assumption of a connection between multiparty democracy and successful economic development, arguing that such a focus serves to distract analysis from the specificities of political processes in the Third World. Indeed, it might well be claimed that, historically, democratisation has always followed, not preceded, economic change (see further Chapter 6 above, 'Options for the Future'). Most of the Asian success stories – South Korea, Taiwan, Singapore, Thailand – have been notable for their political authoritarianism rather than any democratising tendencies. India, a relatively stable democracy for most of its post-independence history, has been substantially less successful than either the newly industrialising countries in the Asia–Pacific region, or its great

Asian rival, China (Sen 1983), which has recently achieved remarkable double digit economic growth during one of its least democratic periods. An examination of democracy and economic reform in China suggests instructive comparisons for analysis of Myanmar. White (1991, pp. 4–5) argues that, in analysing the possibilities for political and economic reform in China, it is necessary to consider four characteristic features:

1. Political leadership faces a double task, both of basic economic development and of economic and political 'deinstitutionalisation', itself a destabilising process.
2. The major developmental tasks – accumulation, modernisation, democratisation, and social welfare – require a firm hand, and central direction, especially when resistance is encountered.
3. One of the chief structural obstacles to economic transformation is the vested interest of political-bureaucratic groups charged with economic policy and administration; the result may be 'an unsatisfactory hybrid economic system which combines the drawbacks ... of both central planning and markets'.
4. There are clear 'political limits to reform which stem from the basic structure and behaviour of an authoritarian regime'.

Noting that, in these conditions, relationships between political and economic reform are 'tangled and ambiguous', White (1991, p. 3) comments:

> While in the long term the introduction of market relations may be a plausible basis for democratisation, in the short and medium term the imposition of the market would seem to involve some degree of strong, authoritarian control.

He goes on to suggest that, up to the Tiananmen repression in early June 1989, China was developing a 'new authoritarianism' combining limited political change – 'deinstitutionalisation' – with the introduction of some market-based reforms. This concept of 'new authoritarianism', if applied to Myanmar, would suggest the following: a separation of the military from the administration; a reduction of military power in relation to state enterprises; limited economic liberalisation; and strictly controlled political liberalisation. The task of this new system would require, in a second phase, the organisation of the transition to democratisation and to full marketisation. White emphasises that vested interests would produce resistance, even in the first phase, and that threats to internal or national stability would strengthen the hand of these conservative groups.

A rather different model is offered by Indonesia which – like Myanmar – has experienced a thirty-year period (1966 to the present) of military government after an unhappy experiment with multi-party politics in the 1950s, when communal tensions were exacerbated by political pluralism. Military rule developed from the collapse of Sukarno's 'Guided Democracy' (1959–65) in the 30 September 1965 'Communist' *coup*, and the institution of General Suharto's post-1965 'New Order'. Economic transformation under a stable authoritarian political system, controlled by military and business groups, then replaced Sukarnoist autocracy. Considerable economic successes were achieved under this carefully regulated set of economic and political relationships, with a virtual doubling of GDP in the 1970s, and continued high growth rates in the 1980s, based initially on oil and gas exports, and subsequently (after economic liberalisation from the mid-1980s) on agriculture and manufacturing (Schwarz 1994, pp. 49–70). While pressures for a matching political reform are now emerging, the military-based governing class is likely to maintain close control of any reform process (Feith 1991).

Experience elsewhere in Asia emphasises the significance of political stability. Whatever the character of the regime, the importance of state-led and state-directed strategies is clear, even if these ultimately lead toward a reduction of direct state involvement in the economy. It is possible, then, to sketch out a scenario in which an economic reform process, resting essentially on authoritarian and directive political foundations, produces effective economic growth, which, in turn, leads to a greater or lesser degree of political democratisation. This is a reasonable summary of current developments in China, and, is by extension, a possible route for Myanmar.

ALTERNATIVE SCENARIOS FOR POLITICAL AND ECONOMIC CHANGE

Some limited economic reforms have been under way in Myanmar since 1988, and most commentators now agree that political reform must come too, if there is to be sustained progress in the future. What remains open, and subject to dispute, however, is the shape and speed of these reforms. As Smith admits in his recent monumental study of Burma's ethnic insurgencies, 'it is virtually impossible to make any accurate judgements about the country's future' (1991, p. 419).

What follows is a speculative attempt to outline two different political–economic paths down which the Myanmar political leadership may choose to go. The first would involve a new 'closing down' after what might be judged by the Myanmar military leadership to have been a misconceived attempt at 'opening up'. The military machine, bolstered by recent expenditure on modernisation, would tighten its grip on the already quiescent urban areas, and would systematically marginalise nationalist-dissident movements. Economic stagnation would produce recurring economic, social and political crises, which would be met with continued political repression. This might lead to an Eastern European-style political collapse, whose outcome would be highly unpredictable. It would certainly not open the way for a more democratic or a more unified Myanmar, and the human cost might well be considerable. A more flexible version of this scenario is already in place: a condition of political stasis in which a 'confused battle still exists between the army, the supporters of the democracy movement, and the ethnic nationalists' (Smith 1991, p. 424), and in which none of these elements is able to secure a lasting advantage.

This is by no means a novel situation. Taylor, writing about the colonial state in Burma, suggested that 'its great weakness ... was its inability to sustain support ... from the indigenous population' (Taylor 1987, 115) and noted 'an absence of serious and effective institutions to ensure that the colonial state developed some semblance of legitimacy.' We could substitute 'contemporary' for 'colonial' and these statements would retain their force.

An alternative scenario to collapse or stasis would be a state-led process of gradual economic and political change. The existing leadership's strategy of 'talking up' constitutional reform, while systematically reducing organised political opposition, would continue. Once the leadership felt safely in control of the political process of constitutional change, it would negotiate a constitutional settlement which could produce what, until recently (that is, May 1992, when popular protests forced the resignation of the Suchinda Government), could be called a 'Thai solution', namely, the introduction of a system of two-tier government with the military exercising an effective veto over a multi-party democracy, while always retaining the option of resuming formal control (Egedy 1988). However undemocratic, this 'settlement' might achieve a sufficiently stable political platform from which to launch liberalising economic reforms. It might also produce the renewal of bilateral and multilateral aid and investment resources needed to underpin effective reforms. This version of the 'political change first' model is less optimistic than the accepted version, but is more realistic, since it is based on assumptions about what the powerful military leaders of Myanmar are *likely* to do, rather than on moralistic assertions of what they *should* do.

The market-orientated economic strategy of Western nations rests on no reasoned argument about the linkages between political and economic reform. It, therefore, has little relevance for the analysis of the political obstacles to democratic change in Myanmar. For some countries, it is a stance of no little hypocrisy: both the United States and Britain, for example, who are so adamant in their insistence that aid and trade concessions must depend on a cessation of human rights abuses and moves to 'good governance', have signally failed to enforce such conditions on China, whose political record and approach are very similar to Myanmar's.

Britain has signalled its intention to maintain good relations with China, with recent visits to Hong Kong and Beijing by the Foreign Secretary, Malcolm Rifkind, and the Prime Minister, John Major. Earlier, at an international summit meeting in 1992, the latter was quoted as saying that 'if one wants to improve China's human rights record, it is best not to hold them at a distance' (*Guardian*, 1 February 1992). This effectively consigns post-Tiananmen positions on human rights abuses in China to the 'dustbin of history'. Indeed, it is difficult to avoid the conclusion that the 'political reform first' policy for Myanmar is driven by expediency rather than morality. The 'new political conditionality' also seems to rest on a somewhat unfocused and ethnocentric view of what constitutes appropriate and democratic systems of government: for example, the main British policy statement places great emphasis upon pluralistic systems, which, by implication, characterises a majority of Third World governments as undemocratic (ODA 1991). The link between 'good government' and economic and social progress is assumed, although various studies have produced no clear evidence for this, suggesting that political influences on economic policy are poorly understood (Grindle 1980; Sandbrook 1986). Moreover, while political factors have been significant in the implementation of economic reforms, there has been no clear relationship to particular types of political regime (Nelson 1990). Nelson further suggests that 'the complex and evolving processes of restructuring economies and political systems cannot be directed by outsiders' (Nelson 1992).

In view of these uncertainties, there is little firm evidence for, or analytical weight in, the argument that economic reform is hostage to political reform. The most realistic approach is to place Myanmar within its regional context rather than a wider international framework. In terms of the aid embargo and economic relationships Japan, Thailand, South Korea and China are substantially more significant than any Western country, other than Germany and (to a lesser extent) the USA. They are also more likely, in their different ways, to be role models for Myanmar's development than any Western country, especially, in the case of Japan, if gradual political reform permits the resumption of bilateral aid.

The recent shift in the Western stance on China may yet be a straw in the wind. With the Chinese leadership's embrace of economic liberalisation, Western governments appear to take the view that this will lead – in the long run – to political reform.[7] This stand reverses their political conditionality policy, and could perhaps lead to a reassessment of policy on Myamar if the military leadership were to follow China's recent economic initiatives. White (1991) suggests that changes in China have produced a 'new authoritarianism' which is compatible with a reformed, market-orientated economy. But it is a model dependent upon the absence of a credible alternative to the Chinese Communist Party. Given Burma/Myanmar's turbulent political history, it remains to be seen whether there is indeed a credible political alternative to military government.

RECENT ECONOMIC AND POLITICAL DEVELOPMENTS IN BURMA

Developments since 1991 do much to confirm our central contention for the need for a realistic analysis of Myanmar government strategies, and the limited expectations of political and economic reform such an analysis must produce. The argument is therefore considered further in the context of current economic and political developments.

Economic Issues

On the economic front a wide range of reforms has been implemented over the period 1991–6 that parallel those introduced in other Asian transitional economies (for example, China, Vietnam and Cambodia) since the 1980s. These economic reforms have been influenced by a variety of sources including technical assistance from both multilateral and bilateral aid agencies, most notably Japan; by governmental reviews of models established in neighbouring countries; and, in particular, through continued informal contacts with political leaders in those countries (notably Singapore, Malaysia and Indonesia). To some extent this has been an *ad hoc* process involving the piecemeal introduction of economic changes without externally supported structural adjustment programmes and their accompanying conditionality. In our earlier discussion (Cook and Minogue 1993), this was presented as a characteristic element of the government's survival strategy.

The poor and deteriorating economic performance throughout the 1980s prior to the turnabout in economic policy was largely due to the weak system of economic management and the consequences of the changing international economic environments that had earlier prevailed. The results of centralised economic planning and adverse movements in the external terms of trade had left the economy with two fundamental constraints to future economic prosperity. The first was the fall in export earnings as a result of an ill-planned drive for self-sufficiency, and the subsequent cessation of aid, both of which impeded the ability to pay for imports as an essential part of the growth process. The second was the pre-1988 emphasis on industrialisation. In particular, government support for large and poorly-run public enterprises foreclosed other types of public investment which could have induced private sector development. The result was a neglect of essential infrastructure in transportation and communication networks.

The current spate of reforms attempted to remove these constraints, and through a series of relatively *ad hoc* economic changes and political manoeuvres, tried to circumvent the consequences of the embargo. The economic reforms reflected three principal changes in policy to those pursued in the 1970s and earlier part of the 1980s. First, the reduced emphasis on public investment in directly productive activity permitted a relative increase in investment in transport, infrastructure, communication, power generation and social services and a scaling down of state owned enterprise investment in heavy industry. As a result, the sizeable private sector (Burma had over 12 000 private enterprises before the military government's 1962–3 nationalisations), dormant for so long during the era of state planning (1962–87), has shown signs of revival in recent years. This sector currently accounts for around 70 per cent of industrial output and 80 per cent of industrial employment.

Private sector growth, particularly in larger scale activities, has been aided by the second policy initiative towards encouraging foreign investment. This has led to the successful establishment of access to foreign capital and technology, through joint venture arrangements. Such agreements have extended beyond the contracts for exploration and exploitation of oil and gas resources in the Andaman Sea and have involved foreign investment in both the public and domestic private sectors (Cook 1994).

The third objective of becoming less self-reliant and more export-orientated, has been achieved principally though the re-establishment of rice exports (which topped one million tons in 1994/5 and are set to rise to 1.5 million in 1995/6, about half of Burma's pre-war total; see above, Chapter 6) and on a smaller scale, trade in a wide range of agricultural commodities, timber and minerals.

Information on economic performance continues to be partial and must be treated cautiously. Nevertheless, official statistics, used by the major international agencies, show that economic growth has been relatively high since 1991. The average rate of growth between 1989 and 1993 was 4.6 per cent per annum (by 1994/5, it had apparently reached 7.5 per cent), a figure which compares favourably with neighbouring countries, as shown in Table 7.1. Manufacturing activity expanded by 13.7 per cent between 1992 and 1993 from a negative growth rate in the fiscal year 1991/2.

Export performance has also been relatively buoyant. Overall, exports have grown by over 40 per cent per year between 1989 and 1993, which is higher than in most South Asian economies. Although the base from which exports have grown has been low, exports in absolute terms, measured by value, have exceeded those of Nepal, Bhutan, Laos, Cambodia and Mongolia, and represented about a quarter of those of Sri Lanka and Bangladesh in 1992.

Growth of foreign direct investment stimulated by favourable, but selective, investment packages has been steady and increasing. This has to some extent compensated for the relatively low levels of domestic saving and investment in relation to GDP when compared with other Asian developing countries. In 1993, gross domestic investment was 13.3 per cent of GDP, while gross domestic saving declined to around 12 per cent of GDP. Private sector investment increased relative to public sector investment mainly as a result of the easing of credit restrictions to the private sector, and the imposed restrictions on public enterprise capital spending (ADB 1994). In 1993, three years after the enactment of the Financial Institutions Law, private banks were permitted to operate as part of a committed move by the government to facilitate private business.

Table 7.1   Average Rate of Growth 1989–93 (per cent per annum)

Myanmar	4.6
Bangladesh	4.3
Nepal	4.4
Laos	6.4
Philippines	2.0
Vietnam	7.0
Mongolia	–2.7
Sri Lanka	4.7

Source: Asian Development Bank (Manila), *Asian Development Outlook*, 1989–93

Of course, significant economic problems remain, not least the inability to control inflation, the inability to match job opportunities with the growing labour force, and the misalignment of the official exchange rate. The embargo on aid has undoubtedly hampered public sector capital expenditure, which is predominantly financed by borrowing from the Central Bank, and, therefore, has inflationary consequences. Internally, the slowness to develop the financial system has also compounded the constraints on investment growth, and has reduced the possibilities for an effective stabilisation policy.

Political Issues

On the political front, the Myanmar leadership has pursued a carrot-and-stick approach. The stick has involved a successful military drive against ethnic rebel forces, the most notable results being the capture of the Karen military and political base, Manerplaw, in January 1995, and the signing of 'standfast' (that is, ceasefire) agreements with 16 ethnic armed groups. According to Lintner, 'only a handful of groups are still in armed opposition to Rangoon' (1995, p. 21). Even the powerful private army of the drug baron, Khun Sa, has recently (January 1996) been brought into submission.

These military successes have strengthened the government's hand politically, enabling them to make a series of concessions: 2000 political prisoners were released in 1992–3 alone (Amnesty International 1994); and, in early 1995, this amnesty process extended to senior opposition figures in the National League for Democracy (NLD) such as the Chairman, U Tin U, and the Deputy Chairman, U Kyi Maung. Most significant of all, discussions took place on two occasions in September and October 1994 between the military leadership and their principal political opponent, Daw Aung San Suu Kyi, resulting in her release from six years of house arrest on 10 July 1995.

The critical issue now is the pace and character of constitutional reform. The SLORC have kept tight control of the membership and procedures of the National Convention which opened on 9 January 1993. The NLD, despite winning 82 per cent of the legislative seats in the 1990 election, was only allocated 86 out of 698 delegates, and has recently (28 November 1995) withdrawn from the Convention citing its lack of influence over the constitution-making process. The SLORC has also insisted on entrenching the political and governmental role of the military in draft constitutional arrangements and has met attempts to express constitutional dissent with arrests and intimidation. The February 1994 report to the UN General Assembly by the special rapporteur of the UN Commission on Human

Rights, Professor Yozo Yokota, judged that the National Convention 'does not appear to constitute the necessary steps towards the restoration to democracy fully respecting the will of the people as expressed in the democratic election held in 1990' (GA Res. 47/144, para. 4, quoted in Diller 1994, p. 7). At the same time, a US State Department report was quoted as describing the Convention as a 'constitutional blueprint effectively guaranteeing the military's continued hold on power' (Diller 1994, p. 7). The SLORC's long-term political strategy is revealed by the formation (in September 1993) of the Union Solidarity Development Association (USDA), almost certain to be the basis for a new political party intended to act as an artificial front for military power in a new post-constitution political system. Daw Aung San Suu Kyi has effectively been written out of a presidential role through a clause which stipulates that any head of state must have been resident in Myanmar for twenty years (she only returned to Yangon in March 1988) and must not be married to a foreigner, but may still be crucial to the negotiation of an internationally acceptable constitutional settlement. What is likely to constitute 'acceptability' remains uncertain.

Critics of the regime would maintain that, at minimum, there should be genuine transfer to civil institutions, ratified through a referendum or electoral process; and a measure of accountability for past human rights abuses. Daw Aung San Suu Kyi argues that 'foreign investors should realise there can be no sustained economic growth and opportunities in Burma until there is agreement on the country's political future' (*Burma Alert*, October 1995, p. 18). But the military retains firm control of the processes both of political settlement and economic reform; gradualism, in both respects, is the predictable strategy and the most realistic prospect. In turn, a gradual softening of external hostility is already in evidence, with clear moves by both Thailand and Singapore to pave the way for Myanmar's eventual entry into ASEAN by the end of the decade. Under the regional grouping's so-called 'constructive engagement' policy, Myanmar has already been permitted to sign the ASEAN Treaty of Amity and Co-operation (27 July 1995) and is set to be granted full membership by July 1997, the thirtieth anniversary of the regime grouping, when the ASEAN heads of state meet in Kuala Lumpur. Economic recovery is likely to be reinforced by the negotiation of new economic agreements on trade, transportation, and infrastructure with China (ADB 1994). Crucial, too, is Japan's interest in resuming bilateral aid (it has already provided Yangon a US$50 million debt-relief grant in early 1996) not least because in 1988, Japan accounted for 78 per cent of all bilateral aid to Myanmar. Without Japan, an aid embargo is effectively dead (Nemoto 1995). For the present, however, Tokyo has indicated that it will not break ranks with the USA.[8] Meanwhile, more generally, there has been a noticeably reduced emphasis by major aid donors on the political conditionality strategy, especially in relation to China, a key point here being the American government's decision in 1994 to separate human rights issues from trade relations.[9] The politics of gradualism appear to be in the ascendant both inside and outside Myanmar.

Notes

1. In accord with official usage since June 1989, the name 'Myanmar' will be used in this chapter to refer to post-1988 events and conditions, and 'Burma' will be used in references to prior events, organisations, and so on.
2. Bilateral donors (with the exception of China and South Korea) have largely withdrawn support on the basis that it will not be resumed until the military government introduces substantial political changes (for example, multi-party rule). The election held in May 1990 to provide a constituent assembly which would draw up a constitution gave victory and an overwhelming majority to the National League for Democracy (NLD) led by Daw Aung San Suu Kyi (born 1945), daughter of Burma's first independence leader, General Aung San (1915–47). The military government effectively refused to recognise this outcome, and their resistance involved serious human rights abuses (confirmed by the UN Commission for Human Rights) which, in turn, led to a hardening of both international and multilateral donor attitudes.
3. See EIU, 'Myanmar: Country Report', 1st Quarter 1996, p. 11.
4. On the method of payment for the August 1990 US$1.2 billion arms deal with China, see Chapter 3 above.
5. The initial assessment mission took place in 1989 and the project commenced implementation in 1990 (Cook 1993). Even though the UNDP Governing Council decided in May 1992 to scale down the budgets of all projects, implementation of this programme continued, as did other forms of assistance, under the Governing Council Decision 93/21 of June 1993.
6. Primary schools were closed from September 1988 to May 1989, secondary schools from September 1988 to September 1989. Technical colleges and universities, also shut down in September 1988, were only reopened in May 1991, but were closed again in December after student demonstrations celebrating the award of the 1991 Nobel Peace Prize to Daw Aung San Suu Kyi. They did not reopen until September 1992, see further Chapter 8 n. 7.
7. Comment by Dharam Ghai during an address to the UK Development Studies Association, Swansea, 12 September 1991.
8. See EIU, 'Country Profile: Myanmar', 1st Quarter 1996, p. 26.
9. In addition, leading NGOs are moving towards the view that they should be fully active in Myanmar to ensure the delivery of humanitarian and development aid, even though this inevitably means involvement with the military government: see the report of an NGO seminar organised and published by World Vision (1995) and below, Chapter 8.

References

ADB (1994) *Asian Development Outlook, 1994* (Manila: Asian Development Bank).

Amnesty International (1992) *Myanmar: 'No Law At All': Human Rights Violations under Military Rule* (London: Amnesty International, November).

Amnesty International (1994) *Myanmar: Human Rights Developments, July to December 1995* (London: Amnesty International).

Catling, J. and A. Dunning (1989) *Myanmar ITC Sectoral Review Mission* (Geneva: International Trade Centre, UNCTAD/GATT, August–September).

Cook, P. (1993) 'Myanmar: Experience with Aid and Management Development during Transition', *Public Administration and Development*, 13.4, pp. 421–34.

—— 1994. 'Policy Reform, Privatisation and Private Sector Developments in Myanmar', *South East Asia Research* (New York), 2.2, pp. 117–40.

—— (1995) 'Privatisation in Myanmar', in P. Cook and F. Nixson (eds), *The Move to the Market* (London: Macmillan).

—— J. Kennedy and R. Raitt (1989) 'Initial Assessment Mission into Rehabilitating and Modernizing the Public and Private Sectors in Myanmar', unpublished report (New York: UNDP, August).

—— and M. Minogue (1992) 'Economic Reform in Myanmar', in R. Adhikari, J. Weiss and C. Kirkpatrick (eds), *Industry and Trade Policy Reform in Developing Countries* (Manchester University Press).

—— and —— (1993) 'Economic and Political Change in Burma (Myanmar)', *World Development* (New York), 21.7, pp. 1151–62.

Diller, J. (1994) 'The National Convention: Lessons from the Past and Steps to the Future', *Burma Debate* (Washington), 1.2 (October–November), pp. 4–10.

Egedy, G. (1988) 'Thailand: Stability and Change in a Bureaucratic Polity', *IDS Discussion Paper* (Institute of Development Studies, University of Sussex), 248 (August).

Feith, H. (1991) 'Democratisation in Indonesia: Misleading Rhetoric or Real Possibility?', in D. Goldsworthy (ed.) *Development and Social Change in Asia: Introductory Essays* (Clayton: Monash Development Studies Centre, Monash University), pp. 63–82.

Fenichel, A. and A. Khan (1981) 'The Burmese Way to Socialism', *World Development* (New York), 9.9 (October), pp. 813–24.

Grindle, M.S. (ed.) (1980) *Politics and Policy Implementation in the Third World* (Princeton University Press).

Hill, H. (1984) 'Industrialisation in Burma in Historical Perspective', *Journal of Southeast Asian Studies* (Singapore), 15.1 (March), pp. 134–149.

Howell, J. (1991) 'Multiparty Democracy and Sustainable Development: A False Trail?', unpublished paper delivered at the Development Studies Association Conference, Swansea (September).

IMF (1989) *Myanmar: Staff Report* (Washington DC: IMF, December).

Lenschow, A. (1991) 'Political and Economic Liberalisation in Socialist Developing Countries', unpublished report for the UNDP Management Development Programme (New York: UNDP, January).

Lintner, Bertil (1995) 'Ethnic Insurgents and Narcotics', *Burma Debate* (Washington), 2.1 (March–April), pp. 19–21.

Morawetz, D. (1980) 'Economic Lessons from Some Small Socialist Developing Countries', *World Development* (Oxford), 8, 337–69.

Mosley, P., J. Harrigan and J. Toye (1991) *Aid and Power* (London: Routledge).

Nemoto, K. (1995) 'The Japanese Perspective on Burma', *Burma Debate* (Washington), 2.4, pp. 20–5.

Nelson, J. M. (1990) *Economic Crisis and Policy Choice: the Politics of Adjustment in the Third World* (Princeton University Press).

Nelson, J.M. (1992) 'Good Governance, Democracy and Conditional Economic Aid' in P. Mosley (ed.), *Development Finance and Policy Reform* (Basingstoke: Macmillan).

Nyun, T. (1989) 'Country In-Depth Study: Myanmar' (Yangon: Institute of Economics, September).

ODA (1991) 'Good Government and the Aid Programme', speech by the Baroness Chalker of Wallasey, Minister for Overseas Development (London: Overseas Development Administration).

Sandbrook, R. (1986) 'The State and Economic Stagnation in Tropical Africa', *World Development* (New York), 14.3, pp. 319–2.

Schwarz, A. (1994) *A Nation in Waiting: Indonesia in the 1990s* (St Leonard's, NSW: Allen & Unwin).

Sen, A. K. (1983) 'Development: Which Way Now?', *The Economic Journal* (Cambridge), 93 (December), pp. 745–72.

Silverstein, J. (1977) *Burma: Military Rule and the Politics of Stagnation* (Ithaca: Cornell University Press).

Smith, M. (1991) *Burma: Insurgency and the Politics of Ethnicity* (London: Zed Books).

Steinberg, D. I. (1981) *Burma's Road Towards Development: Growth and Ideology Under Military Rule* (Boulder: Westview Press).

Taylor, R. (1987) *The State in Burma* (London: Charles Hurst).

UNCTAD (1992) *The Least Developed Countries 1991 Report* (New York: United Nations).

UNIDO (1989) *Industry Sector Review Mission to Myanmar*. Vienna: UNIDO, June.

Vokes, R. (1990) 'Burma and Asia – Pacific Dynamism: Problems and Prospects of Export-Oriented Growth in the 1990s', in M. Than and J. Than (eds), *Myanmar Dilemmas and Options: The Challenge of Economic Transition in the 1990s* (Singapore: Asian Economic Research Unit, Institute of Southeast Asian Studies), pp. 219–47.

White, G. (1991) 'Democracy and Economic Reform in China', *IDS Discussion Paper* (Institute of Development Studies, University of Sussex), 286 (April).

World Vision (1995) *The Role of NGOs in Burma. Report by the Policy and Research Department of World Vision* (Milton Keynes: World Vision, 6 June), pp. 1–39.

8 Responding to Myanmar's Silent Emergency: the Urgent Case for International Humanitarian Relief and Development Assistance[1]

Rolf C. Carriere

His Name is 'Today'

We are guilty of many errors and many faults,
but our worst crime is abandoning the children,
neglecting the fountain of life.
Many of the things we need can wait.

The Child cannot.

Right now is the time his bones are being formed,
his blood is being made
and his senses are being developed.
To him we cannot answer 'Tomorrow',
His name is 'Today'.

Gabriel Mistral,
Nobel Prize-winning poet from Chile

INTRODUCTION: THE SILENT EMERGENCY

Though richly endowed with natural, human and cultural resources, Myanmar has experienced political instability and economic decline over the past decade. After many years of inefficient central planning and widespread controls, it was designated a 'Least Developed Country' (LDC) by the United Nations in December 1987. The next year, following the political disturbances of August 1988 and the military coup which brought the SLORC to power (18 September), it forfeited all bilateral aid from its traditional OECD donors. Per caput income and essential imports have fallen while inflation has accelerated, with devastating consequences for the nation's women and children. At the same time, population growth threatens to outstrip the government's ability and willingness to cope with the basic needs of the annual additions to the population, let alone to begin reducing existing disparities. With a current growth rate of around 2 per cent, among the highest in the region, the population of around 47 million (35 per cent of whom are under fifteen) is set to double in the next thirty years, reaching somewhere between 75 and 95 million by the year 2025, depending upon current policies and the pattern of demographic transition. Already Myanmar belongs to the top twenty-five most populous countries in the world.

These circumstances and their effect on women and children can be described as a 'silent emergency', which, while not as visible as a flood, fire or famine, constitutes an equally compelling claim on the humanitarian sympathies and overseas aid of high-income countries. The fact that Myanmar has not won such attention and support must be attributed in part to a lack of information about its plight. At the same time, the government has been reluctant to open its doors fully to the outside world, tending to ignore or deny the crisis, and resorting to inflated or fabricated statistics in order to enhance its public image. Yet, indisputable evidence of the silent emergency exits. It can be clearly documented through a variety of indicators that are the stock in trade of UNICEF and other development organisations, namely:

1. An infant mortality rate (IMR) of 94 per 1000 live births. In other words, some 320 infants die each day or 117 000 die each year before their first birthdays. Myanmar's IMR is the seventh highest in Asia, exceeded only by Afghanistan, Bangladesh, Bhutan, Cambodia, Laos and Pakistan and significantly higher than those of India and Indonesia.

2. Of those children who survive to their first birthday, another 58 000 will die before reaching the age of five. The official under-5 mortality rate of 147 per 1000 live births makes it the fourth-highest among fourteen countries in the UN's *E. Asia Pacific Region*.

3. An appallingly high rate of severe malnutrition, ranging between nine and twelve per cent of children under three, comparable in severity with the malnutrition rates in Burundi, Mali, Pakistan and Sudan.

Sixty per cent of all pregnant women have iron deficiency anaemia. (Iodine and other nutritional deficiencies are present in other areas of the country.)

4. A maternal mortality ratio of at least 250 per 100 000 live births (the government only admits to 140 per 100 000). That is, eight women die each day from pregnancy-related causes, almost half of which are complications attending illegal abortions, which, in turn, are the result of unwanted pregnancies and a lack of affordable contraceptives. Myanmar's maternal death rate from abortions is among the highest in the world, fifty-eight dying every week, according to UNICEF figures.

5. Myanmar is already facing a severe AIDS epidemic with an estimated 400–500 000 HIV-positive cases reported, one-third of them women (see further Chapter 4, n. 41 above). The World Health Organization has put the severity of HIV infection in Myanmar at a level comparable to that of Thailand and India. See further Martin Smith, *Fatal Silence? Freedom of Expression and the Right to Health in Burma* (London: Article 19, July 1996), ch. 7.

6. A rural water supply coverage of only 31 per cent, compared with an average of 47 per cent for the group of forty-two LDCs and 58 per cent for *all* developing countries. The number of unserved people increases each year, since the rate of programme expansion (reaching 500 000 new beneficiaries per year) cannot keep pace with the annual population increase of just under a million.

7. Even in the capital, urban water supplies remain untreated for lack of chemicals, which must be imported. Moreover, urban water supply coverage is only 38 per cent, compared with an average of 54 per cent for all LDCs and 83 per cent for all developing countries.

8. A staggering 80 per cent of all children of primary school age either do not enrol or drop out, placing Myanmar on a par with such countries as Bangladesh or Nepal in terms of its educational record. Most of these children remain illiterate as there are no non-formal education programmes in place.

9. Many children are orphans, while others are abandoned, disabled, trafficked (there is a huge trade in teenage prostitutes, of both sexes, over the border to Thailand, see further Chapter 4 above), in the labour force, the army or militia, or in other especially difficult circumstances.

These are just a few measures of Myanmar's human distress and deprivation. They project a new image, an image that contrasts sharply with the lingering colonial-era memories of Burma as a land of golden pagodas,

Buddhist meditation, vast teak forests and paddy fields, and rich deposits of precious stones.

While a comprehensive picture of Myanmar's silent emergency must await the results of more intensive research, the following are some of the major problems faced by children and their parents in their daily struggle for survival and development.

Health and Nutrition

Although children under five make up only 15 per cent of the total population, they account for almost half the total number of deaths in the country each year. Of the roughly 500 000 deaths occurring annually, some 200 000 are young children. Clearly, very young children die at a rate that is disproportionate to their numbers. Once they have reached the age of five, the risk of dying remains consistently low until the age of about fifty-five, when it begins to rise again.

At least half of these deaths are caused by a few ordinary diseases that are easily preventable or treatable: pneumonia, diarrhoea, vaccine-preventable diseases (especially measles, whooping cough and tetanus), and malaria. Though not all affected children die, these illnesses can easily become fatal under one or more of the following circumstances: (1) essential drugs, which must be imported, are not available in the marketplace or in the public health system; (2) a child is already weakened by malnutrition or low birthweight; or (3) a child is born to a mother who is too old or too young to support a healthy pregnancy; or (4) whose body is depleted by conceiving too many children in rapid succession. In addition to the availability of medical care and supplies, these four principal risk factors – malnutrition, low birthweight, birth timing, and birth spacing and number – largely determine a child's chances of survival in Myanmar.

As a result of shortages of essential medical supplies and a lack of public awareness, Myanmar's widespread basic health care infrastructure remains underutilised. Although the private sector has, since the early 1990s, begun to import modest amounts of medicines, demand and need continue to exceed supply by a factor of five. Moreover, even when supplies are available, they may fail to reach beneficiaries as a result of petrol rationing and price increases.

As a rule of thumb, the risk of premature death doubles with each grade of deterioration in a child's nutritional status: from normal, to mild, to moderate, to severe malnutrition. Ten per cent of children under the age of three suffer from severe protein-energy malnutrition in Myanmar, while an additional 20 per cent, at least, are moderately malnourished.[2] A number of factors are at work in these statistics. Runaway inflation, estimated at 150–200 per cent in 1992–3 at unofficial prices,[3] has undoubtedly impaired the ability of many parents to feed their children, especially in the urban and semi-urban areas. The average unofficial daily wage in the capital, Kt45, is barely adequate to feed a family for a day, let alone meet other basic needs. The least-cost diet for a family of five in Yangon is Kt41, up from Kt34 in 1990.[4] Although the system of subsidised food rations provides some relief, access and rations are still limited. But the most common cause of malnutrition is probably repeated attacks of common childhood infections and worm infestations rather than insufficient food intake. Sadly, essential medicines required to treat these conditions are either not available or not affordable. The extent and severity of malnutrition in Myanmar must also be attributed to a lack of parental knowledge about nutrition or the prevention and treatment of diseases. In summary, while the underlying causes of malnutrition are known, the relative importance of each varies from region to region, and their interaction is not always understood.

Regarded as another form of malnutrition, low birthweight also compromises a child's health in the first few years of life. One out of five newborns in Myanmar will have a birthweight of less than 2500 grams. This statistic can be attributed to a number of causes: (1) childbearing by women who are under 140 centimetres tall; (2) inadequate weight gain during pregnancy, due less to a lack of food than to the belief that an ideal weight gain of 10 to 12 kilos will complicate labour and delivery; (3) smoking or smoke inhalation resulting from traditional household cooking practices, which can reduce a new-born's birthweight by 300 or 400 grams; and (4) the widespread practice of working up to the moment of delivery, which increases the risk of prematurity and low birthweight.

Unregulated fertility poses another threat to a child's chances of survival, as well as the mother's. Until recently, the government's pronatalist policy made ready access to affordable contraceptives difficult: only 5 per cent of couples have easy access to condoms, 6 per cent to female sterilisation, and 13 per cent to pills or injectables. Contraceptive prevalence stands at less than 15 per cent, with only some 480 000 couples practicing family planning in 1991. In an important policy shift in the same year, the government has now legalised contraceptives for purposes of birth-spacing and maternal and child health. However, since all contraceptive supplies have to be imported, the implementation of this new policy awaits allocations of foreign exchange. Meanwhile, maternal deaths due to pregnancy or delivery are estimated to occur to at least 250 women per 100 000 births, or 58 women per week. Almost half of these deaths are due to illegal abortions: 44 per cent of couples have ready access to the procedure, and the high abortion rate, estimated at 80 per 1000 live births, continues despite legal prohibitions and the injunctions of the Buddhist teachings. Other direct causes of maternal deaths include bleeding (20 per cent) and pregnancy-related complications requiring surgical or obstetric hospital facilities and services, which are often inadequate or unavailable. An important underlying cause of maternal deaths is anaemia, which is present in 40 per cent to 60 per cent of women of child-bearing age.

Many other health problems plague children and adults in Myanmar, including malaria, tuberculosis, hepatitis, leprosy, dengue, and a variety of disorders resulting from micronutrient (for example, iron and iodine) deficiencies. In addition, there is now an increasing incidence of HIV infection. The latter deserves special attention in this discussion because of its sudden sharp rise among intravenous drug users and other high-risk populations. A recent World Health Organization (WHO) report forecasts that Myanmar, like India and Thailand before it, is now on the brink of a serious AIDS epidemic unless the government takes immediate and aggressive action to contain it. Apart from a mounting death toll, the country faces an impending social disaster in the form of orphans, overcrowded hospital wards, unmanageable health care expenses, and other associated problems.

While the number of AIDS cases officially reported remained small until the early 1990s – a government survey published in September 1992 indicated that, since 1988, when the first HIV-positive case was discovered, nine people had contracted AIDS, of whom four had subsequently died[5] – the number of HIV-infected patients has risen dramatically, with many dying of tuberculosis and other wasting diseases before developing full-blown AIDS. Since screening for HIV infection and AIDS was first introduced in the late 1980s, 2700 out of more than 100 000 at-risk individuals who were studied through mid-1991 tested positive, including 161 women between the ages of fifteen and forty-nine, three children under five, and five children between the ages of five and fourteen. By mid-1992, that number had nearly doubled to 4330, according to government sources. In the same year, however, a UNDP report estimated the number of HIV-infected people at well over 100 000 – a figure which might be just 'the tip of the iceberg' in the words of the UNDP representative in Rangoon.[6] Indeed, by 1995, agencies were reporting estimates of 400 000 HIV-carriers in Myanmar and tested rates of 90 per cent HIV-infection amongst intravenous drug users in towns such as Myitkyina in the far northeast, estimates which, if confirmed, already bore out the WHO's warnings about the impending scale of Myanmar's AIDS epidemic (see Chapter 4,

n. 41 above). Besides drug use, the other major route of transmission was the sex trade with Thailand: many young women and girls in the border areas of Myanmar travel or are trafficked to Thailand to work in its girlie bars and brothels. Once found HIV-positive, they are reportedly sent back home, a practice that will only hasten the spread of AIDS throughout the population.

Water and Sanitation

While important gains have been made in extending rural water supply and sanitation facilities, more families do without these services than a decade ago because programme extension is unable to keep pace with population growth. Even now, the annual increase in rural water coverage is less than 500 000 people (as compared to 600 000 a decade ago), whereas Myanmar's population increases by just under a million annually. Thus far, some 13 million people, or about 28 per cent of Myanmar's current (1996) population, have access to water and sanitation facilities. With an estimated population of 54 million by the year 2000, another 41 million people will require these facilities. Universal coverage for rural water supply can be achieved at an estimated cost of over US$900 million. Universal sanitation coverage, including urban sewerage systems, can be achieved at an estimated cost of US$1.5 billion. The lack of water and sanitation facilities must be counted as factors in Myanmar's silent emergency because they pose serious public health risks. A high incidence of typhoid, diarrhoea, hepatitis, and other diseases calls for large investments in this area. In addition, limited coverage reduces economic productivity. In hilly areas of the country, villagers spend as much as four hours per day fetching water.

Education

Despite Myanmar's long tradition of public and vernacular education (the latter organised through the Buddhist *sangha* and its extensive school infrastructure), the system has now entered a crisis that can be traced to lack of equity, quality and internal efficiency. Following the disturbances of 1988, all schools remained closed for the best part of a year, and universities and colleges were only reopened briefly in May 1991 before being shut down for another nine months the following December because of pro-democracy protests inspired by Daw Aung San Suu Kyi's Nobel Prize.[7] This created an acute shortage of facilities and personnel that have prevented the educational system from meeting the needs of a triple cohort of school-age children. For every 100 children of primary school age, between twenty-seven and thirty-eight never enrol. Worse still, of those who do enroll, less than 30 per cent complete primary school. Only one in ten children completes primary school in the allotted five years.

While limited surveys among parents suggest that the high (opportunity) cost of education is the principal determinant of non-enrolment and dropping out, such studies neglect other significant factors such as dissatisfaction with teaching methods (for example, rote learning), curriculum relevance, and the rigid annual pass-or-fail examination system, which results in high repetition rates and labels a child a failure early in his or her school career. Ethnic minority children face yet another handicap: with few exceptions, instruction is not conducted in their native languages; thus, the majority must learn all subjects in a 'foreign' language (Burmese) starting from their first day in school.

While Myanmar's non-enrolment and drop-out rates are alarming, the situation is in fact more grave than these statistics indicate. For, unlike many other developing countries, Myanmar has at present no non-formal education programme to give children and young adults a second chance to become functionally literate or to retain literacy and numeracy. It is true that, in July 1992, the government did announce that a 'University of Distance Learning' would be developed, but this was focused on the privileged few in tertiary education rather than the much larger numbers who have never completed primary school. Besides, it seems, this measure was brought in for primarily political reasons: namely, in order to depoliticise the universities by keeping more students at home doing correspondence courses, thus minimising campus politics and the free association of students and teachers.[8]

In view of these circumstances, Myanmar's official adult literacy rate of 81 per cent (89 per cent for males, 72 per cent for females) must be recognised as a fiction. It is now estimated to be around 55 per cent, well below the 65 per cent average for all developing countries for which data are available. Clearly, the educational system cannot at present do the job of supporting and fostering national development.

Children in Especially Difficult Circumstances

The silent emergency is also manifested in Myanmar's growing population of Children in Especially Difficult Circumstances (CEDC): those who are exploited labourers, homeless, abused or neglected, institutionalised, trafficked, or the victims of armed conflict or ethnic discrimination. A systematic profile of these groups is not possible here, both because space does not permit it and because precise statistics are not yet available. However, it is worth noting that plans are underway to conduct a thorough survey in the near future and, building on the opportunity afforded by Myanmar's recent (1991) accession to the 1989 United Nations Convention on the Rights of the Child, to assist in the development of a national programme. For reasons that will become clear, the following discussion will focus on two categories of CEDC: child labourers and institutionalised children.

On the basis of preliminary investigations, it seems safe to conclude that child labourers are numerically the most significant CEDC population in the country. Perhaps 4 million of the nation's 11.8 million children between the ages of six and sixteen work, if only part-time. Rural children are generally employed by their parents in an agrarian or peasant mode of production. Though chores such as caring for younger siblings, fetching water and firewood, feeding and herding livestock, or washing clothes and cooking keep them away from school, they help socialise children and provide them with essential life skills. In contrast, a growing number of urban child labourers are exploited, working long hours for little or no pay in occupations that do not provide life skills or the possibility of an economically secure future and may well jeopardise their health or safety. These occupations include domestic service, construction, mining, heavy industry, and prostitution. Children are also used in duty labour, especially for porterage and road construction.

In the Shan State, proximity to the Thai border exposes many girls in their early teens to sexual trafficking. Parents are persuaded to part with their daughters with advance payments and promises that they will be given good jobs in the city. Reportedly, some 10 000 adult and child prostitutes from the Shan State work in Chieng Mai alone, where 40 per cent of prostitutes tested HIV positive in 1992.[9] Perhaps as many as 40 000 of Myanmar's hill tribe women are employed in brothels throughout Thailand in a state of virtual slavery. The spread of information about AIDS there has had the unfortunate effect of involving an ever-increasing number of Myanmar girls in prostitution. Though intended to reduce the health risk to customers, a compulsory six-month turnover of prostitutes trafficked into Thailand accelerates the spread of the infection. AIDS awareness has also increased the demand for younger girls, who, it is thought, are less likely to be infected. Both developments force traffickers to search further afield for novices to the trade. At the same time, there have been reports of local *Tatmadaw* officers in the border areas 'marrying' child brides and then sending them over the border to 'work' in Thailand.[10]

Precisely because it is a relatively small and accessible group, institutionalised children may also come to figure high among the priorities of a national CEDC programme. Approximately 8000 children inhabit state custodial institutions in Myanmar, with an additional, but unknown, number living in adult prisons with their parents and in voluntary institutions. While institutionalisation was introduced into Myanmar during the colonial period as a solution to the problem of distressed or disturbed children, it has, in fact, aggravated their plight and proven inappropriate to local circumstances and conditions. Whether they are orphaned, abandoned, runaways, disabled, or guilty of criminal infractions, institutionalised children fall into the category of CEDC because state and private facilities alike are ill-equipped to care for them. Even where such facilities manage to provide a nutritious diet, for example, they fail to meet the emotional, developmental, schooling or rehabilitative needs of their charges. In many orphanages, routine, order, discipline and tidiness are emphasised to the detriment of other aspects of child care such as love, compassion, trust, friendship and stimulation. Manifested in compulsive rocking, severe emotional disturbance is often the result.

The humanitarian and pragmatic consequences of failing to address the needs of Myanmar's children in especially difficult circumstances are grave. Because children are more vulnerable physically and emotionally than adults, their normal development is jeopardised in exploitative or abusive circumstances. A child physically or mentally disabled in this way grows up to be a disabled adult, whose economic productivity and social integration are impaired. In summary, CEDC, like malnourished, chronically ill or uneducated members of the coming generation, threaten the nation's future.

Of course, the situation of Myanmar's children is no different from that in most other LDCs. As we have seen, Myanmar's children generally find themselves near the bottom end of the human development indicators. But there is at least *one* important difference: while other LDCs have access to official development assistance, Myanmar has done without it since 1988. Deprived of marginal but vital imports for social sector development, it now faces an acute crisis.

Though the silent emergency is grim and daunting, proven solutions to most problems besetting Myanmar's women and children are ready to hand. Human development indicators from other countries demonstrate that even at lower levels of per caput income, it is possible to achieve dramatically better results both for children and in the social sector than Myanmar has done despite its deep-seated economic and political problems. The first step in achieving such results is to acknowledge the silent emergency, and, in the manner of the present enquiry, to identify its immediate and underlying causes. The next step should be to deepen the analysis, to bring to light the root causes of the silent emergency. Complex and interrelated, they include persistent poverty and economic decline, which, in turn, are the results of serious policy shortcomings, decades of widespread political and economic controls, and highly centralised planning. The root causes of the silent emergency are also intricately linked to the long drawn-out civil war, the lack of civilian mobilisation, and the absence of organisational capacity and pluralism.

The development of effective and sustainable programmes in the social sector is possible only if the government responds to the silent emergency, both independently and in partnership with donors, in ways that are commensurate with its nature, extent and severity. For a number of years and for a variety of reasons, such responses have not been forthcoming.

GOVERNMENT AND DONOR RESPONSES TO MYANMAR'S SILENT EMERGENCY

A government in charge of a country with a natural resource base as rich as Myanmar's, dominating as it does nearly all political and economic activity with pervasive controls over virtually all aspects of its people's lives, cannot deny responsibility for the silent emergency described above. Distorted priorities and inadequate political will are evident in:

1. the government's low allocations for human development;
2. its reportedly high military spending (currently [1996] amounting to 60 per cent of government expenditure);
3. its inadequate efforts on behalf of children;
4. its curtailment of the activities of non-governmental organisations, both domestic and international; and
5. its refusal to allocate foreign exchange from its export revenues for social sector development.

Human Development Expenditures

Details of the national budget are not readily accessible, and in any case do not reflect all government intentions and transactions. But even a cursory comparison of Myanmar's human expenditure ratio[11] to that of other countries highlights its paucity. This statistic can be attributed in large part to the low percentage of national income used for public expenditures (see Table 8.1).

Table 8.1

Country	Human expenditure ratio[a]	Public expenditure ratio	Social allocation ratio	Social priority ratio
Zimbabwe	12.7	52	49	50
Malaysia	6.3	32	29	68
Singapore	4.3	35	35	35
Korea	3.7	16	30	77
Thailand	2.5	16	37	42
Sri Lanka	2.5	31	43	18
Bangladesh	1.2	12	24	42
Myanmar	1.2	10	28	43

[a] Human development ratios above 5 per cent are classified as high; between 3 and 5 per cent as medium; and below 3 per cent as low.

Military Expenditures

Viewed from a different angle, the silent emergency is also the outcome of a high level of defence spending over many years. Statistics are naturally hard to come by, but military expenditures have generally been regarded as high for a country that faces no external threat, yet maintains an army of over 320 000 men (with plans to reach 500 000 by the end of the decade). How does such spending affect children? Commissioned by UNICEF, a 1991 Stockholm International Peace Research Institute (SIPRI) study, *Arms and the Child*, documents the adverse impact of military expenditure on the survival, protection and development of children in sub-Saharan Africa. These problems are not unique to the region; in fact, the negative effects of militarisation can be observed in many countries. According to the study, they operate through many pathways:

> By distorting national and governmental priorities; by reducing governmental resources available for programmes benefiting children; by increasing debt burdens, which preclude essential importation; by creat-

ing distortions in the economic system; by reducing economic growth; by producing conflicts and wars, which destroy children and infrastructure; and by creating a vicious circle of increasing militarization leading to developmental failures, which in turn create more conflicts.

These mechanisms are intensifed during periods of general economic crisis, as the report makes clear:

> Of course, all states and governments have legitimate security interests. But something is surely amiss when the very survival and socio-economic security of children – and therefore of the future generation – are threatened by defence spending.

Social Programmes for Children

To be fair, *some* government programmes have met with success in relieving the silent emergency. For example, the Universal Child Immunization programme achieved over 80 per cent coverage in 1990 in operational areas, and is estimated to have saved the lives of 60 000 young children, prevented 5300 cases of polio, and averted 2.4 million episodes of vaccine-preventable diseases between 1987 and 1990. Myanmar's nutrition programme was also scaled up to provide 17 000 (or one-third of the country's) villages with monthly services of growth monitoring and nutrition counselling services benefiting 150 000 pregnant women at any time, and around 860 000 children under three annually. A recent impact evaluation found a 50 per cent reduction in malnutrition among infants under six months, but no significant improvement in older age groups. In view of the economic decline, however, this outcome should be regarded as a success since non-programme villages recorded an increase in malnutrition rates during the same period.

It should also be noted that the government has recently made a series of pragmatic and needs-oriented political gestures by acceding to the 1989 United Nations Convention on the Rights of the Child, signing the World Summit for Children Declaration, and preparing a ten-year National Programme of Action for children to achieve the ambitious objectives of the Declaration. Furthermore, in signing the Master Plan of Operations with UNICEF, it has committed itself to the attainment of equally ambitious mid-decade sectoral goals. However, the fact that the SLORC Foreign Minister, U Ohn Gyaw, felt it necessary to enter two chilling reservations to Myanmar's accession to the UN Convention with regard to articles 15 (on freedom of association) and 37 (on torture and the deprivation of liberty) underscores the nature of the government's political agenda, even in an area as seemingly unambiguous as the physical protection of children (see further Chapter 1, n. 124 above).

On balance, then, the government's response to the silent emergency has been inadequate, partial and *ad hoc*. It is only because of the country's cultural resources – in particular, the extended family system, the high status of women and teachers, the extensive network of social service facilities and personnel supported by the ethic of private charity and voluntarism – that the quality of life of its women and children has not deteriorated more rapidly.

Role of Non-Governmental Organisations

Though much of the world now recognises that governments have exceeded the limits of their bureaucratic capabilities, that no single organisation – including massive state apparatuses – can solve the major social, economic and environmental problems all nations face today, the state of Myanmar continues to spurn the private not-for-profit organisations that are urgently needed to supplement its own efforts in the social sector.

While non-governmental organisations across the world have proven their effectiveness in enabling people to help themselves – and are even increasing in countries such as Vietnam, Laos and Cambodia – they have not taken hold in Myanmar. A few operate in the social sector, but almost all are either directly or indirectly under state control and dependent on government funding and technical direction. The country is, therefore, deprived of a critical resource. Elsewhere, NGOs effectively complement government programmes in many areas: child labour, family planning, prison reform, juvenile delinquency, disability, child survival, not to speak of women's emancipation, non-formal education and the environment. These issues are at the heart of the silent emergency.

Foreign Exchange Constraints

Like the situation with the NGOs, the issue of foreign exchange illustrates the way in which Myanmar's political failings and impoverished economy interact with and reinforce each other. Conveniently for the present discussion, government and donor responses to the nation's silent emergency converge on this issue. We have already seen that the root causes of the silent emergency are known, even if their interactions and relative importance are not always so transparent. On further analysis, it is clear that most of the persistent social sector problems (including the problems of children) have one crucial feature in common, namely a chronic shortage of foreign exchange.

In the interest of building and maintaining a large military apparatus, the government has chosen not to allocate any of its scarce foreign exchange revenues for use in (non-military) social sector development programmes over the past twenty-five years. In other words, the foreign exchange component of programmes and projects in health, nutrition, education, water supply, sanitation and social welfare was financed entirely by contributions from bilateral donors, multilateral organisations and a few large international non-governmental organisations (INGOs). At the same time, the government's halting efforts to achieve long overdue economic reforms has ensured that it has very little foreign currency to apply toward such expenditures, even if it were willing to do so.

Initiated originally by the Burma Socialist Programme Party (BSPP), this policy has been continued by the present SLORC government since September 1988. Throughout the 1980s, Myanmar's poor export performance, mounting debt service obligations, stagnating levels of official development assistance (ODA), and negligible imports of private investment capital, have crippled its ability to import essential capital and consumer goods.

The value of its reported export revenues declined from US\$409 m. in 1983 to US\$257 m. in 1987 and US\$229 m. in 1988. The decline in economic growth rates, extensive bureaucratic controls, and the overvalued *kyat* exchange rate caused this low export performance.[12] Meanwhile, though Myanmar's external debt as a percentage of GDP stood at 43 in 1987 – considerably lower than the average of 71 per cent for all forty-two LDCs combined – its total debt service payments of US\$295 m. in the same year amounted to a very high 95 per cent of export value, as compared to 27 per cent for the LDCs as a group.[13] At this critical pass, commitments of ODA from OECD donors began to falter. Between 1980 and 1987, they ranged between US\$129 m. and US\$402 m. a year; but by 1988 and 1989 they had fallen to US\$117 m. and US\$17 m., respectively.

Unfortunately, no breakdown of ODA by sector or purpose is available for the period.[14] According to estimates, however, approximately 5–10 per cent was allocated to social sector programmes for the crucial importable inputs required to sustain them. With the suspension of new lending from the World Bank and all ODA from Myanmar's traditional donors after 1988, this marginal but vital source of foreign exchange fell away altogether, preventing such programmes from importing supplies and equipment, including essential, life-saving drugs and medical supplies; soap and nutrient supplements; paper for schoolbooks, notebooks and posters; pipes, fittings and handpumps for rural water systems; chemicals for urban water treatment; latrine pans for sanitation programmes; and many other supplies normally taken for granted. To make matters worse, two prominent international non-governmental organisations (ICRC and Oxfam [UK]) in the human development field have recently suspended their activities in Myanmar.

Prompted by the desire to encourage political and economic reforms, the suspension of ODA in 1988 has done considerable harm to Myanmar's people. Instead of providing more assistance, the donor community provided less at a time when the people needed it most. In other words, this policy decision has aggravated the silent emergency. While it is almost certainly the case that some donors neither foresaw nor intended this outcome, others may have regarded it as a necessary evil in the service of a higher good: using economic leverage to persuade the SLORC to move toward democracy, respect for human rights, and a free market system. At present, the suspension of aid shows no signs of having this effect on the government. On the contrary, Myanmar appears to have entered a stalemate, both in its internal political affairs and in its relationship with the rest of the world. In view of these circumstances, the final part of this chapter argues that there are compelling reasons – pragmatic, political, and moral – for resuming bilateral assistance.

HUMANITARIAN ASSISTANCE REVISITED

The recent history of bilateral assistance to Myanmar can be characterised as 'all or nothing' – all prior to August–September 1988, nothing thereafter. This section charts a middle and more discriminating course that will further the goal of economic and political reform and relieve the silent emergency there, while meeting the demands of conscience and enlightened self-interest on the part of the donor community. If this prospect sounds too good to be true, it is perhaps because we have failed to synthesise and marshal the experience or wisdom and opportunities at our disposal, to broaden our conception of humanitarian assistance.

Relief versus Development?

The world is usually generous in providing humanitarian relief aid for natural and man-made disasters. Governments, inter-governmental organisations and INGOs respond compassionately and quickly, but briefly, to 'loud' emergencies: disasters with a sudden onset, such as floods, fires, earthquakes or typhoons. In 1991, for example, twelve bilateral donors, five UN agencies and two INGOs gave US$2 m. to Myanmar in response to the Meiktila fire and the Irrawaddy floods. For the reasons mentioned above, however, the silent emergency has gone largely unnoticed by the international community.

The time has come to extend the concept of humanitarian assistance, to help victims of the silent emergency that *each day* affects many times more children than all casualties and victims of the Meiktila and Irrawaddy disasters combined. Ours is not a plea for mere relief and welfare, but for long-term humanitarian and social development.

David Korten, in his book, *Getting to the 21st Century: Voluntary Action and the Global Agenda* (1992), draws a sharp distinction between humanitarian and development assistance, depending on whether funding addresses the consequences or the causes of poverty:

> Humanitarian assistance should be accurately labelled. If used to finance services that meet basic needs of a chronic or predictably recurring nature, funds should be appropriated with a clear understanding that a commitment to long-term assistance is involved. ... Under no circumstances, however, should commitment to an international welfare system be confused with efforts to eliminate the conditions that have created the need for such a system.[15]

While the need for a long-term commitment to humanitarian relief assistance in settings of chronic and persistent distress such as Myanmar is a point well-taken, Korten's distinction between humanitarian and development assistance is perhaps too rigid, too academic. For good reason, no donor organisation will be satisfied merely with treating symptoms, with providing relief and welfare to alleviate only the immediate suffering. Effective use of assistance entails addressing causes, reducing systemic vulnerabilities and strengthening local capacities. It also requires advocacy of policy and institutional changes that will promote equitable and sustainable development. If such assistance is ultimately to promote stable and enduring democratic reforms, it must build or strengthen such capacities at the grass roots level, empowering the common people.

In so far as assistance to Myanmar can simultaneously serve long-term social development purposes and address the deeper causes of the silent emergency, it affords an opportunity that should not be missed. Such humanitarian relief-and-development assistance might assume the following forms:

1. introducing a preventive thrust in the malnutrition control programmes;
2. empowering people with life-saving health messages;
3. assisting in the wider application of local languages of ethnic minorities in non-formal education;
4. advocating for policy change and new programmes at the highest levels, based on sound analyses of the local situation and opportunities;
5. reviewing legislation in light of the 1989 Convention on the Rights of the Child;
6. revising social statistics and generating new social indicators;
7. professionalising social communications (including prior behavioural research, use of advertisement agency methods, and so on);
8. mobilising all sectors (for example, artists, atheletes, professionals) around global issues; and
9. substituting essential imports by establishing local manufacturing capacity.

Given the political realities in Myanmar, some argue that outside aid will not be able to influence government policy and cannot truly lead to empowerment of the 'vast majority'. Others, such as David Korten, have urged that direct (that is, government-to-government) humanitarian assistance should only be given when countries have democratically-elected regimes capable of exercising budgetary discipline, in particular the ability to hold military spending to a minimum. Since none of these conditions have been met in Myanmar, assistance should be made solely through NGOs, close monitoring of expenditure being a *sine qua non* for all grant-aid.[16]

But the political realities in Myanmar are fluid and often contradictory. The government has grown increasingly receptive to the kind of social development initiatives advocated above. Examples of tangible results in this direction include widespread distribution of the Burmese version of the UNICEF/WHO/UNESCO, publication, *Facts for Life* (1989);[17] policy dialogues and shifts regarding birth spacing and child survival; surveys to establish new baselines and correct obsolete statistics on IMR, school drop-outs, and so on; depth analysis of the situation of children in exceptionally difficult circumstances and excercises aimed at making laws more child-friendly. Moreover, the national immunisation and nutrition programmes have recently created an infrastructure through which a whole range of essential primary health care services can be delivered. Work is also currently under way to design non-formal education programmes for young drop-outs and out-of-school youths. Clearly, humanitarian relief and development assistance can improve the lives of Myanmar's people, but it requires a resident presence, pragmatism, persistent advocacy, social vision and, above all, patience.

Potential donors also fear that even humanitarian aid will not reach the people and that it, in fact, fuels corruption. This was not the experience of UNICEF Yangon in the years in which the present author was head of mission there (1989–92). To be sure, misuse and pilferage of aid supplies occurred from time to time, but such abuses are infrequent. This may have something to do with the fact that UNICEF is now virtually the *only* donor of goods, that its supplies are clearly marked, that intermediary beneficiaries are notified of their impending arrival, and that a sizeable monitoring field staff goes around the country to check on the use of these inputs. Ironically, the government's authoritarian controls may also be responsible. Moreover, UNICEF lodges formal complaints with the government when cases of misuse and pilfering of supplies are discovered.

The New Conditionality: Helping or Hurting?

Of course, humanitarian relief-and-development assistance must impose certain conditions on the government. No donors write blank cheques, even in cases of straightforward humanitarian relief. UN agencies, for example, hold the government to what are termed 'Basic Agreements'. More importantly, all UN development operations require free, unencumbered access of staff and consultants to project beneficiaries and areas (without continuous military escorts); partnership with civilian government authorities and counterparts; community participation in project design and execution, *not* top-down development by decree; access to basic data and project reports; opening of the books for external audits; procurement through competitive bidding, and so on. In addition, project-specific conditions are negotiated including use of local languages, NGOs and volunteers, media for development communications, and so on. These are long-standing elements of what may be termed the 'old' conditionality.

But what of the 'new' political and economic conditions set by the major donors? The current insistence on 'good governance', democratic reforms, economic restructuring and respect for human rights as preconditions for aid seems to be gaining support among developed countries. These are worthy, indeed, essential objectives. Used as preconditions for continued aid entitlement, however, they are a blunt foreign policy instrument bound to victimise the innocent majority, at least in the short run.

As demonstrated above, this has been the case in Myanmar. In an effort to avoid legitimising the regime or delaying the final political solution, bilateral donors have suspended all aid. Despite the silent emergency, there is now talk of extending this punishing and apparently fruitless approach. Frustrated by the lack of progress toward democratisation, continuing human rights violations, and the ongoing economic and environmental decline over the past four years, some observers and policy-makers are calling for more stringent measures: economic sanctions and a trade embargo.

A ban on the sale of arms to Myanmar would be desirable, though almost impossible to implement. But blanket embargos are antithetical to the concept of humanitarian intervention currently under debate in the UN and other related fora, for example the G-7 group of developed countries and the Organisation of African Unity (OAU). Those who argue that the infliction of suffering on the Myanmar people is justified when a general embargo offers only the hope of promoting democratisation would do well to scrutinise this expanded concept of humanitarian intervention. In extreme circumstances, as when the Iraqi government blocked foreign aid to a portion of its people (for example, the Kurds and Marsh Arabs) following the Gulf War of early 1991, it would temporarily suspend national sovereignty to permit the delivery of supplies.

The moral justification for such humanitarianism is compelling, as the rhetoric of the UN Secretary-General's Executive Delegate on Humanitarian Affairs demonstrates. Of the sanctions imposed on Iraq, Prince Sadruddin Aga Khan had this to say: 'it seems an absolute aberration that this population, which has already suffered so much and is not responsible for what happened, [has to] pay an additional price'. The moral claims of this appeal seem all the more urgent where the lives of children are at stake. In its organisational policy, UNICEF advocates a new ethic on behalf of children, according them first call on our concerns and resources in good times and in bad:

> The growing mind and body of the child cannot wait until the 'right' government comes to power, interest rates fall, commodity prices recover, the economy returns to growth, or warfare ends. That a child survives, is well nourished, has health care, is immunized, or attends school should not depend on the vagaries of adult affairs. The protection of our children and, thus, of our future should not be a priority; it should be an absolute.[18]

In sum, an ethical or humane conditionality calls for the following measures with respect to Myanmar: though suspension of economic development aid benefiting the elite and powerful may send an important message to the present government, foreign exchange to finance specific humanitarian relief and development packages for the population at large (and its most vulnerable segments in particular) should be resumed, and exempted from any embargo that may be imposed in the future. It should be added that this ethical approach to policy making is not incompatible with political considerations. In fact, it will serve the very ends that motivated donors to suspend aid. A stable and enduring democracy can only be achieved when basic needs are met, and when citizens are literate and informed. Furthermore, as they empower the people of Myanmar, programmes in health, nutrition, water and sanitation and education will address a host of problems whose effects cannot be contained within the nation's borders. All countries have a stake in the fate of political refugees, the narcotics trade, deforestation and AIDS – in Myanmar and elsewhere. Of course, those who implement such programmes must probe the government's intentions and commitment vigilantly to ensure that aid is not put to the wrong ends.

Humanitarian Ceasefires

If humanitarian assistance of the kind advocated here is resumed, children affected by the various armed conflicts in the border areas of Myanmar should be accorded priority. They have suffered death, disability, psychological trauma, the death of their parents and families, dislocation, and forced labour either on civil works or as porters for the military. Such human rights violations have not yet been fully documented, but recent ceasefires may allow access to this population of children in especially difficult circumstances and the development of a programme on their behalf.

In the Shan State, for example, local ceasefires have been holding since the surrender of Khun Sa and his Mong Tai Army (MTA) in January 1996, and the government has invited international assistance to complement its own efforts (although the USA has shown its displeasure with Yangon for not allowing Khun Sa to be extradited to the USA to be tried for international drug trafficking offences by continuing to veto multilateral assistance for Myanmar from the IMF and the World Bank). Yet, apart from some pledges of limited funding by UN agencies, little response has been forthcoming from the donor community (only South Korea and Japan have shown any willingness to provide bilateral assistance to the SLORC, and the latter, in particular, is constrained by the tough line taken by the USA). Despite the risks and uncertainties, humanitarian initiatives (with appropriate conditions attached) should not go untried in the face of all that the local populations have suffered over the last forty years.

At a conference held in November 1991, 'Humanitarian Ceasefires: Peacebuilding for Children', the Executive Director of UNICEF, James P. Grant, envisioned the forms that such aid to child victims of armed conflict might take. Noting the special appeal of children, Grant called for 'days of tranquillity' and 'corridors of peace' in combat zones for the delivery of immunisations and other health services to the young. Applied to the border areas of Myanmar, such temporary ceasefires would not only benefit children, but may also help bring peace to the region.

Current Assistance and Unfunded Projects

Modest humanitarian and social development assistance for the silent emergency is at present available only from the UN system, especially UNICEF, UNDP and WHO, and to some extent from UNFPA (UN Fund for Population Activities), UNDCP (UN International Drug Control Programme) and UNESCO. Each specialised agency or fund works in Myanmar on the basis of its specific mandate from the UN.

US$25 m. is available from the General Resources of UNICEF for the five-year period 1991–5. Combined with Government funding of recurrent costs, this amount is expected to achieve significant objectives and reach large numbers of beneficiaries. Yet more assistance is urgently needed to allow expansion and extension of projects and programmes. Several of these projects (amounting to US$15 m. for a four-year period) have already been approved by the UNICEF Executive Board at its April 1991 session, but no donors have stepped forward. Not yet approved, other projects have been prepared with considerable variation in scope, scale, duration and field of human development.

For present purposes, estimates were prepared of the foreign exchange component of the supplies and equipment required for the silent emergency. The total comes to roughly US$65 m. per year, and includes items such as K-Mix-2 (for treatment of malnutrition), vaccines, the thirty most essential drugs (to treat 90 per cent of morbidity and mortality, including resistant malaria), contraceptives, impregnated nylon bednets, AIDS test-kits, water treatment plants for Yangon and Mandalay, water purification chemicals for existing urban drinking water systems, soap, potassium iodate for salt iodation programmes, nutrient supplements, pipes for gravity flow systems, chimneys for smokeless fuel-efficient stoves, solar refrigeration for the vaccine cold chain, solar cookers, and school notebooks and textbooks. Such humanitarian assistance for relief and development could be provided bilaterally (that is, government-to-government), multilaterally (government-to-inter-governmental-organisation-to-government), or through INGOs.

The UN Development System stands ready to act as a channel for any such assistance, and to help negotiate with the government for favourable terms, including the issue of the foreign exchange rate. For donor governments not yet prepared to resume humanitarian assistance bilaterally, the UN Development System offers a delivery apparatus that institutionalises the world's social and humanitarian concern. Likewise, for INGOs not yet prepared to set up their own offices in Myanmar, the UN Development System is available to act as a broker to help them get established, or to serve as a conduit for and administrator of their assistance. UNICEF has already performed this function on behalf of several INGOs.

FIVE PROPOSALS AND A CONCLUSION

Let me end by advocating five key proposals which I believe are essential to breaking the present humanitarian relief-and-development assistance impasse. Indeed, unless the international community is willing to muster the kind of energy and foresight it has demonstrated in Cambodia since the early 1990s, the problems of Myanmar, and their domestic and international consequences, are likely to persist. Only bold and tenacious efforts stand a chance of success. Based on the concept of humanitarian relief and development advocated here, the following points are proposed for a new international diplomatic initiative in Myanmar.

1. Review the humanitarian consequences of recent donor policies that link ODA (including humanitarian relief and development aid) to the requirement of democratic reforms in recipient countries.
2. Resume and expand bilateral and multilateral humanitarian assistance to finance the foreign exchange component of a specific package of relief and development services (approximately US$65 million annually as stated above).
3. Form an international consortium or consultative group of INGOs for Myanmar interested in donor government co-financing and committed to implementing the package. The International Council of Voluntary Agencies or another international apex organisation may be helpful in initiating this process, and the UN system would of course be prepared to act as an intermediary with the government.

4.   Reconvene the Burma Aid Group to discuss the conditional resump-
     tion of humanitarian assistance, and to consider proposals for convert-
     ing Myanmar's external debt into a local currency debt. This fund
     would be used to finance the local cost component of the package
     of relief and development services required for the silent emergency
     (as well as other initiatives, including environmental rehabilitation).
     Debt conversion could perhaps be more easily agreed upon with
     donor governments at this stage than complete cancellation of bilat-
     eral official debt (as foreseen under the LDC Paris Conference of
     1990).

5.   Open diplomatic initiatives in the context of the UN enabling UNDP,
     UNHCR, UNDCP, UNICEF and ICRC to offer a series of services
     aimed at reducing tension, confidence building, and ending conflict,
     including:

     (a)   periodic, UN-supervised humanitarian ceasefires in the war-torn
           border areas.
     (b)   massive educational efforts in the languages of the ethnic
           minorities on AIDS awareness.
     (c)   crop and income substitution programmes for poppy growers to
           promote a durable and pragmatic transition to an economy no
           longer based on narcotics.
     (d)   refugee assistance.

This initiative would protect the most vulnerable segments of society and
meet their immediate needs, while engaging the government in a dialogue
regarding long-term reforms. With the collapse of a bipolar world, such
initiatives should become the hallmark of a civilised and sophisticated
global community.

Notes

1.   The author gratefully acknowledges the helped received from Dr Jo Boyden
     (Oxford University) and Dr Catherine Quoyeser in the preparation of this
     chapter. Sources of most of the statistics cited can be found in UNICEF's
     report, *A Situation Analysis of Myanmar's Children and Women* (Yangon:
     UNICEF, 1991). Since this chapter was updated and edited in March 1996,
     an important study of health conditions in contemporary Burma since 1988
     has been published by Article 19, see Martin Smith, *Fatal Silence? Freedom
     of Expression and the Right to Health in Burma* (London: Article 19, July
     1996).
2.   Severe malnutrition is defined as less than 60 per cent of standard weight for
     age, while moderate malnutrition is defined as 60–75 per cent of standard
     weight for age.

3. See EIU, 'Country Profile: Thailand/Myanmar, 1994–95' (London: EIU, 1995), p. 55. The official consumer price index for Yangon (Rangoon) in 1993 was 31.8 per cent, a figure which had risen to 33 per cent in June 1995, see EIU, 'Country Report: Myanmar', 4th Quarter 1995, p. 40, the highest in the Southeast Asian region.

4. See EIU, 'Country Profile: Thailand/Myanmar, 1994–95' (London: EIU, 1995), p. 55, reports that the daily wage rate for workers in the public sector was Kt20 in April 1993, up from Kt15, after a rise in March 1993.

5. *Bangkok Post*, 10 October 1992.

6. Ibid.; and see further David Winters, 'Facing the Challenges of AIDS', *Burma Debate*, 1.1 (July–August 1994), pp. 22–7.

7. See Martin Smith, *'Our Heads are Bloody but Unbowed': Suppression of Educational Freedoms in Burma* (London: Article 19, 10 December 1992), pp. 10–11. All schools, colleges and universities were closed following the military *coup* in September 1988; primary schools were only reopened in May 1989, secondary schools in September 1989; and universities and other institutes of higher education in May 1991, after thousands of students had gone missing or been expelled. These last were shut down again in December 1991, following the pro-democracy protests which broke out at Rangoon and Mandalay universities during celebrations at the award of the 1991 Nobel Peace Prize to Aung San Suu Kyi. They were not reopened again until September 1992. On the issue of academic and educational freedom in Myanmar more generally, see further Martin Smith, 'Burma (Myanmar)', in World University Service, *Academic Freedom 3: Education and Human Rights* (London: Zed Books, 1995), pp. 92–107.

8. Smith, *Suppression of Educational Freedoms*, p. 11.

9. *The Nation*, 2 October 1992.

10. See Asia Watch, *A Modern Form of Slavery: Trafficking of Burmese Women and Girls to Brothels in Thailand* (New York: Asia Watch, 1993).

11. The human expenditure ratio is the product of three other ratios, namely the public expenditure ratio, the social allocation ratio, and the social priority ratio. The public expenditure ratio is the percentage of national income that goes into public expenditure (but excludes the budget for the State Economic Enterprises). The social allocation ratio is the percentage of public expenditure earmarked for social services (including education, health, welfare, social security, water, sanitation, housing and amenities). The social priority ratio is the percentage of social expenditure devoted to human priority concerns (namely primary education and primary health care). The UNDP's 1991 Human Development Report calls for the human development ratio to become one of the principal guides to public spending policy.

12. Since 1989, reported exports have risen, in part as a result of recognition of the border trade with China and Thailand in official statistics. See further Chapters 3 (Tables 3.1 and 3.2) and 4, pp. 117–9.

13. The percentage of Myanmar's export revenues that goes for external debt servicing during the 1980s ranged from 24 to 95 per cent, reflecting not only a poor, but also an uneven, performance in recorded exports. See further Mya Maung, *The Burma Road to Poverty* (New York: Praeger, 1991), Chapter 9 (esp. pp. 206–15).

14. As proposed by the 1991 UNDP Human Development Report, aid budgets, like government expenditures, can be analysed through four ratios: the aid: expenditure ratio, the aid: social allocation ratio, the aid: social priority ratio, and the aid: human expenditure ratio. An attempt to reconstruct the latter three, from the recipient's point of view, is currently underway.

15. David Korten, *Getting to the 21st Century: Voluntary Action and the Global Agenda* (West Hartford, Conn.: Kumarian Press, 1990), p. 230.

16. *Ibid.*, pp. 230–1.

17. UNICEF/WHO/UNESCO, *Facts for Life: A Communication Challenge* (Benson, Oxon.: P & LA [International Planned Parenthood Association] for UNICEF, WHO and UNESCO, 1989).

18. UNICEF, unpublished Organisational Policy Document (New York: UNICEF, 1991).

Glossary

baht	Thai currency
Bamar	term now used to denote the majority Burman ethnic group
Bo	military commander
Bogyoke	senior commander/general
Daw	form of address to adult Burman female
Khun	Shan royal rank
Ko	'elder brother' – form of address used among persons of same age and status when addressing each other
Kuomintang	Chinese Nationalist Party, led by Chiang Kai-shek
kyat	Burmese currency
Maung	'younger brother' – form of address used to persons who are younger or of inferior status
Mujahid	Muslim fighter in Islamic holy war
Myanmar	Burman literary term for Burma used by the SLORC since 18 June 1989 as the official name for the country
myo	town, city or administrative area
pongyi	Buddhist monk
Pyithu Hluttaw	People's Assembly
renminbi	Chinese currency
Rohingya	Muslims living in the northern part of Rakhine (Arakan) State
sangha	Buddhist order of monks
Saw	Karen form of address for an adult male
Sawbwa	hereditary prince or regent in in the Shan/Karenni states
Thakin	master (term used by young Burmese nationalists in the 1930s to indicate that the Burmese were the real masters of their country)
Tat	army, militia
Tatmadaw	Burmese army/armed forces
U	form of address to adult Burman male

Wa   Mon-Khmer ethnolinguistic group living mainly in the
              Thanlwin–Mekong watershed along the Burma-China
              border

yuan   Chinese currency

Suggestions for Further Reading

Asia Watch, *A Modern Form of Slavery: Trafficking of Burmese Women and Girls into Brothels in Thailand* (New York: Asia Watch, 1993).

Asian Development Bank, *Issues of Asian Economic Outlook* (Manila: ADB, 1996).

Aung San Suu Kyi, *Freedom from Fear and Other Writings* (Harmondsworth: Penguin, 2nd edn, 1995).

——, *Letters from Burma* (Harmondsworth: Penguin, 1997).

——, *The Voice of Hope: Conversations with Alan Clements* (Harmondsworth: Penguin, 1997).

Bray, John, *Burma. The Politics of Constructive Engagement* (London: Royal Institute for International Affairs, Discussion Paper no. 58, 1995).

Chao Tzang Yawnghwe, *The Shan of Burma: Memoirs of an Exile* (Singapore: Institute of Southeast Asian Studies, 1987).

Clements, Alan and Leslie Kean, *Burma's Revolution of the Spirit: The Struggle for Democratic Freedom and Dignity* (Bangkok: White Orchid Press, 1995).

Diller, Janelle, 'Constitutional Reform in a Repressive State: The Case of Burma', *Asian Survey*, 33.4 (April 1993), pp. 393–407.

Furnivall, J.S., *The Governance of Modern Burma* (New York: Institute of Pacific Relations, 2nd edn 1960).

Herbert, Patricia M. (comp.), *Burma* (Oxford: Clio [World Bibliographical Series, vol. 32], 1991).

Human Rights Watch/Asia, 'Burma: Entrenchment or Reform? Human Rights Developments and the Need for Continued Pressure', *Human Rights Watch/Asia Report*, 7.10 (July 1995), pp. 1–43.

Lintner, Bertil, *Outrage: Burma's Struggle for Democracy* (London: White Lotus, 1990).

——, *Land of Jade: A Journey Through Insurgent Burma* (Edinburgh: Kiscadale, 1990).

——, *Burma in Revolt. Opium and Insurgency since 1948* (Boulder: Westview Press, 1994).

Maung Maung, *Burma's Constitution* (The Hague: Martinus Nijhoff, 1961).

Maung Maung Gyi, *Burmese Political Values: The Socio-Political Roots of Authoritarianism* (New York: Praeger, 1983).

Mya Maung, *The Burma Road to Poverty* (New York: Praeger, 1991).

——, *Totalitarianism in Burma: Prospects for Economic Development* (New York: Paragon House, 1992).

Mya Than, *Myanmar's External Trade. An Overview in the Southeast Asian Context* (Singapore: Institute of Southeast Asian Studies, 1992).

—— and Joseph L.H. Tan (eds), *Myanmar Dilemmas and Options: The Challenge of Economic Transition in the 1990s* (Singapore: Institute of Southeast Asian Studies, 1990).

National Coalition Government of the Union of Burma, *Democracy and Politics in Burma. A Collection of Documents* (ed. Marc Weller) (Washington DC: NCGUB Printing Office, 1993).

Pilger, John, 'Burma: A Cry for Freedom', *New Internationalist*, 280 (June 1996), pp. 7–30.

Selth, Andrew, 'The Myanmar Army since 1988. Acquisitions and Adjustments', *Contemporary Southeast Asia*, 17.3 (December 1995), pp. 237–64.

Silverstein, Josef, *Burmese Politics: The Dilemma of National Unity* (Rutgers (NJ): Rutgers University Press, 1980).

—— *The Political Legacy of Aung San* (Ithaca: Cornell Southeast Asia Program, rev. edn 1993).

Smith, Martin, *Burma: Insurgency and the Politics of Ethnicity* (London and New Jersey: Zed Books, 1991).

——, *Ethnic Groups in Burma: Development, Democracy and Human Rights* (London: Anti-Slavery International, 1994).

Smith, Martin, *Fatal Silence? Freedom of Expression and the Right to Health in Burma* (London: Article 19, July 1996).

Steinberg, David, *The Future of Burma. Crisis and Choice in Myanmar* (Lanham: University Press of America, 1990).

——, 'Liberalisation in Myanmar: How Real are the Changes?', *Contemporary Southeast Asia*, 15.2 (1993), pp. 161–78.

Taylor, Robert H., *The State in Burma* (London: Charles Hurst, 1987).

Index

Index